Praise for Cherry Adair

White Heat

"A gripping and passionate story by up-and-coming Seattle based author Cherry Adair. This book grabs your attention on Page 1 and doesn't let go until the heroine welcomes her hero home with the final words."

—*The Seattle Times*

"Humor, sizzling sex and pulse-pounding danger add up to high-octane reading."

—*Romantic Times*

"A steamy fusion of romance and heart-stopping suspense."

—*Publishers Weekly*

Hot Ice

"[A] fast-paced and intricately plotted tale of danger, deception, and desire that is perfect for readers who like their romantic suspense adrenaline-rich and sizzlingly sexy."

—*Booklist*

"A very sexy adventure that offers nonstop, continent-hopping action from start to finish."

—*Library Journal*

Edge of Darkness

"Here's a trilogy that goes out with a very satisfactory bang. Themes of love, duty and sacrifice are expertly combined with a hefty dose of magic."

—*Romantic Times*

Edge of Fear

"Written with a pulse-quickening attention to sensual detail and a playful sense of humor, Adair expertly combines a tight plot and graphic romance with magical flourishes and exotic locales."

—*Publishers Weekly*

Also by Cherry Adair

Night Fall

THE EDGE BROTHERS TRILOGY

Edge of Danger
Edge of Darkness
Edge of Fear

OTHER TITLES

White Heat
Hot Ice
On Thin Ice
Out of Sight
In Too Deep
Hide and Seek
Kiss and Tell

A Novel

CHERRY ADAIR

BALLANTINE BOOKS • NEW YORK

A Ballantine Books Mass Market Original

Published in the United States by Ballantine Books, an imprint of The Random House Publishing Group, a division of Random House, Inc., New York.

BALLANTINE and colophon are registered trademarks of Random House, Inc.

This book contains an excerpt from the forthcoming book *Night Shadow* by Cherry Adair. This excerpt has been set for this edition only and may not reflect the final content of the forthcoming edition.

ISBN 978-0-345-49991-2

Cover design: Jae Song
Cover photograph: Age Fotostock

Printed in the United States of America

www.ballantinebooks.com

OPM 9 8 7 6 5 4 3 2 1

This one is for Lisa Marie McKay, with love.
In memory of the bright light that was Lily.

One

Novos Começos Medi-Spa
Rio de Janeiro
Brazil
0100

He was screwed.

Face pressed to the gritty sand, Lucas Fox attempted to unscramble his brain.

Think, dammit.

Unfortunately he'd fallen forty feet to land on his head. It wasn't nearly as hard as his friends claimed it to be. And speaking of friends—he could use a little help right about now.

The night sky was bright with the light cones of five military choppers illuminating a crosshatch pattern over both the choppy ocean and the narrow strip of beachfront where he lay. They *whop-whop-whopped* back and forth, stirring up sand and causing palm fronds to dance wildly. Down the entire sugary length of the beach, the rows of pastel-colored beach houses were strung like gaudy beads and the violently swaying palms were lit up as if it were high noon.

If he were visible, he'd be . . . fucking *visible.* He was a sitting duck out in the open. A ruffled wave lapped up to dance playfully against his foot. A futile attempt to move out of the surf made his head swim.

Acknowledging concussion—been there, done that—

Lucas focused on cataloging his injuries while his lungs automatically fought for air. Everything hurt like hell. By some miracle he hadn't broken his neck, a definite plus. He'd been shot, but only once, and in the fleshy part of his shoulder. Been there, done that, too. He'd live.

Maybe. Right now he was hanging onto invisibility by willpower alone. He'd been at the tail end of a Trace Teleport, following Mica Escar, a Half wizard, when his powers had fizzled out midair. He'd dropped like a rock. The sand wasn't nearly as goddamned soft as it looked.

Obviously he'd been unconscious long enough to hear the distant echo of his window of opportunity slam shut. A chopper flew directly overhead, making the inside of his eyelids burn red.

Lucas managed to stay out of sight until it passed. Sustaining invisibility was like holding your breath underwater for too long. Eventually one had to come up for air.

He *had* to teleport off the beach.

He gave it his best shot. Visualizing the hidden end of the long white beach, the sheltered, grassy section of land, he thought himself there.

Sand still pressed into his cheek. Damn it to hell. Nothing.

He faded in and out of consciousness. A bad thing. Apparently, it was impossible for him to use two powers at once.

He could maintain invisibility for only minutes at a time, but he couldn't maintain invisibility and attempt teleportation. One or the other apparently. Fuckit.

He needed cover, and he needed it fast.

Move.

Too dizzy to think, let alone stand, he fought to hold onto iffy invisibility, his only protection against the searchers. The vibrating ground, thanks to the heavy rotors on the low-flying Hueys, made his brain hurt, and swirling sand stuck like fire ants to his abraded skin. The shouts of the soldiers gathered south of his position let him know they were forming a grid to search the beach and surrounding area. His shoulder ached like a bitch. The bullet had gone through and through, and sand adhered to the bloody wound.

Well and truly screwed. Shit.

It took everything in him to remain cognizant. His stomach pitched again and his vision blurred. Great. Just frigging great.

Sucking in a hard-won breath, he considered his options before he passed out again.

Wearing a bikini and carrying a glass of chilled wine in defense against the lingering heat of the day, Sydney McBride stood to one side of the picture window and widened the gap between the slats of the wood shutters with her fingers to get a better look outside.

She'd been typing up the day's notes and contemplating a swim by moonlight when she'd heard the incredibly loud noise of helicopters overhead. She'd raced to switch off the lights in the bungalow so she could watch the action on the beach unobserved.

The night sky was artificially bright as searchlights strafed the white-capped surface of the water. The illumination also showed at least twenty gun-wielding, uniformed men searching the beach and surrounding area. "Who or what are you guys looking for?" she murmured, intrigued. Clearly someone, or many someones, dangerous.

Sydney's heart did a little tap dance. Woohoo! *Excitement.*

Thank God.

After five weeks of doing nothing more thrilling than

compensating for her surgically enhanced boobs, interviewing fellow plastic surgery patients, writing and walking the beach, she was ready to scream with boredom. This was the longest she'd stayed in one place in *years*.

Why all the guns? Was someone stealing penile implants? The thought amused her. A chapter in her new book *Skin Deep* on *that* subject would be entertaining to write if nothing else.

There was much yelling and talking as the soldiers moved with purpose toward her middle-of-the-row bungalow. Whoever they were looking for didn't stand a snowball's chance in hell. She felt a twinge of sympathy for their hapless prey. A *mouse* couldn't escape detection faced with such determination and manpower.

She observed several men knocking on doors far down the line of bungalows to her right. It wouldn't take them long to get to hers. The bungalows were all but empty. At least she thought they were. Sometimes when she'd been walking the beach late at night, she'd seen lights go on or off, and thought she heard voices. But she'd never seen anyone coming or going. As far as she knew, only nine of the twenty-five small, luxury beach houses still housed patients. Sydney knew them all.

Polly Straus, nose and boobs; Stan Simpson, chin. There was Karen with her enhanced butt and higher cheekbones, and Denise with her face bandaged after her skin resurfacing and full lift. There was flirty, movie megastar Tony Maxim who'd looked better *before* he was "done." And Kandy Kane, a porn star whose new double Fs made her look as though she were a Macy's hot-air balloon ready for liftoff. The soldiers might linger at Kandy's door awhile, but they'd be knocking at *her* door soon enough.

Sydney lifted her glass, taking a sip of cold, crisp Casa

de Amaro chardonnay and letting the fruity flavor roll on her tongue as the soldiers got closer.

Setting down her glass on the coffee table, she went to find a wrap before they got there. She had a few questions of her own to ask and her new, larger breasts distracted even herself. Crossing back to the window as she tied the belt of a short white robe, Sydney listened to the crunch of gravel as two men approached her front door. Her heart lurched in anticipation. God, she loved drama.

Reaching for the doorknob she froze in her tracks as a primitive chill of awareness raced up the back of her neck. Exactly the same chill as when she'd been a kid, and frightened to put her feet on the floor because of the monster under her bed. She'd always had a terrific imagination.

The hair on the back of her neck and arms stood up. This was not her imagination.

Someone was in her room.

She started to spin around just as a large hand curved over her mouth. The second he touched her, Sydney's eyes went wide and her teeth snapped together mid-scream as terror rendered her immobile.

Static electricity shot through her body, making her hair crackle and her heart skip several beats before picking up speed and knocking hard against her ribs. Ow! Had the son of a bitch used a Taser on her?

"What the hell—" her assailant muttered at the same time. He recovered from the shock faster than she did, and tugged her against him so that her back was flush to his front. He was a big man, yet he'd moved close enough to grab her without making a sound. Shifting slightly, with her against him, he leaned against the wall next to the door. Her body couldn't have *been* in any closer contact with his.

Holy Mother of God. He was naked.

Like an animal sensing the hunter was ready for the kill, Sydney's body went still, but her mind zigged and zagged as she tried to find a center of calm so she could decide what to do next. Whatever it was better be fast. And *soon.* But it was hard to think with the heat of his body surrounding her. The hot male smell of his skin overwhelmed her, making her thought process muddy and unwieldy. Her breath came in short, shallow gasps as mind-boggling carnal images—things she'd never done, let alone imagined—flooded her brain in a kaleidoscope of graphic pictures. She went hot, then cold, then hot again.

Bam. Bam. Bam. The soldiers were impatient.

The intruder's breath brushed her neck. "Take off the robe."

"N—" He stripped her of the garment before she'd finished the word. Left in just a few scraps of cloth that made up her bikini, Sydney felt the shocking, intimate touch of the man's powerfully muscled body from shoulder to thigh. He was tall, at least six three. His body the kind of hard that came from strenuous physical activity, not the gym. His skin felt hot. Wet. Gritty.

She sucked in a breath—

His left hand went back over her mouth and smothered her scream. "Tell them I'm your boyfriend." His hot breath as he whispered against her ear was a disconcertingly intimate assault of its own.

No way, buster. She tried to bite his palm. No go. Wiggling in his tight hold, Sydney kicked back with her bare foot. He didn't even twitch as her heel struck his shin.

The knocking got louder.

"Open it." His free hand snaked around her waist sliding down to rest securely, *possessively,* on her hipbone. Heat came off his large body in waves. He seemed to surround her. His hands were huge, cool, and implacable. The water on his skin formed a glue between them, sticking them skin to skin. She went absolutely still as the scent of him—heat, ocean, man—curled inside her like smoke. The sensual images flashed in her head. Something dangerous and crazy was happening to her.

Terrifying and thrilling.

She reached out to turn the doorknob.

He uncapped his fingers from over her mouth and controlled the door opening with his foot—just wide enough to reveal the two of them, but not wide enough for someone outside to notice that the man standing behind her was buck naked. She felt rough toweling against her left shoulder blade. He hadn't used her robe to cover himself, instead he'd slung it toga style over his shoulder. Boy, did he have self-confidence or what? Arrogant came to mind.

You picked the wrong woman, asshole.

"*Senhorita—*" the man looked at the piece of paper in his hand. "McBride?" His line of sight rose a few inches to land on her breasts. Clearly he was distracted. As was the man next to him. Pressured by her publisher, Sydney had caved and had plastic surgery in order to get a first-person perspective for the book she was writing. Reluctantly she'd gone from a perfectly decent B to a full C. And men not making eye contact was one more reason she was going to have the implants removed as soon as possible.

After a few, too long seconds the soldier's eyes shifted from her chest, bypassed her face, and focused over her head. Suddenly she was looking down the barrel of a very large black gun.

Talk about being between a rock and a hard place.

"Who is this?" the soldier's eyes narrowed. "You know this man?"

"Of course." The word "not" had been on the very

tip of Sydney's tongue. She frowned and tried again. "I don't—" *know who the hell he is, but I bet he's the guy you're looking for!* Even as she wasn't saying what she wanted to say, her mind raced. Here was the big story she'd been starving for. Dare she offer to help the guy in exchange for the scoop of the year?

It was a decision she didn't have time to debate. It was now or never. Uncharacteristically, she hesitated. Impulse and loving spontaneity was one thing, but using her good judgment served her better. Most of the time. In this case she had absolutely nothing to base an opinion *on.* For all she knew, the guy behind her was a serial killer.

As much as she wanted, needed, to play out the scene as he wanted, she wasn't stupid enough to invite a serial killer to hang around while armed soldiers searched for him. Hard to write a best-selling book on the experience if she died before she wrote word one.

Damn. It would've been so interesting . . .

"He's my *namorado.*" *What?* Sydney's eyes went wide with shock as the words came out of her mouth. *Where did* that *come from?* While she understood some Portuguese, she'd been here for over a month after all, she didn't *speak* it. How had *boyfriend* come out of her mouth with such ease when she didn't even know the word?

Frowning, the soldier pulled out his notebook, the gun weaving in his hand as he flipped pages. "He is not on guest list."

That's because he's the bad guy. Sydney's heart pounded hard enough for them to hear it. *Grab him. Haul him away in chains.* "He arrived this morning," she heard herself say smoothly. What the—had this guy *hypnotized* her?

The soldier hesitated, then slid the gun back into a

shiny new-looking hip holster. *"Como é seu nome, senhor?"*

What's your name?

Good question.

The intruder lifted his hand from her hip, extending it to the guy on the doorstep. His strongly muscled arm was tanned and forested with dark hair, the hand engulfing the uniformed man's. Chills ran up and down Sydney's spine. He could snap a person's neck in a heartbeat with those ginormous hands. Or melt her with the burning heat radiating off his body.

"Lucas Fox." As the two men shook hands, Sydney between them, the intruder's arm brushed against her already sensitized skin. The small hairs on her arms stood up, giving her goose bumps.

"You are two alone, *senhor*?"

"Bungalow's one room. Nobody here but us. Would you like to come in and search the place?"

Cocky. Really cocky, Sydney was astonished at the man's utter audacity. Especially since he was naked while the two men were armed.

With a feeling of dread she watched as suspicion died from the soldier's eyes.

"Não vai ser necessário."

Of course it was necessary. Jeez Louise, don't take this guy's word for it. Sydney wanted the two soldiers to come in. To see that the guy holding her so tightly was naked, and then . . . they'd believe his story that they were lovers. Even she was practically convinced.

Fox's big hand slid around her waist and he drew her impossibly harder against him. As casually relaxed as he sounded, Sydney felt the tension in his large body. It shocked her anew that he was pressed against her so intimately. Who the hell did this guy think he was? And where the hell were his clothes? Surely he hadn't just strolled off the beach bare-assed naked?

"Who are you guys looking for?" he asked easily, his thumb stroking the sensitive skin of her midriff just under her left breast.

The bikini had fit perfectly well a few weeks ago. Now her Cs were running over. The caress of his thumb made her nipple pebble, and her insides contract. Her heart was pounding hard enough for her to feel the rapid beat through her entire body, every pulse-point was on full alert.

"Is escape patient from—" the soldier thought a moment, probably translating from Portuguese into English. "*Como você diz isso?* Mental hospital?" He twirled a finger at his temple. "Have you seen such a man in the last hour?"

How about right behind me? Sydney opened her mouth, only to be cut off by Mr. Naked before she could speak.

"We were too busy with our . . . *reunion* to notice anyone," Fox's voice was smooth and smoky and conjured up all sorts of illicit activities.

Both soldiers' gazes were redirected to her new and improved breasts. Sydney was going to blacken both Lucas Fox's eyes for stealing her robe. And that was just for starters.

"Stay inside, and if you see anyone suspicious, *por favor* dial seven on the house phone."

"Shouldn't we go somewhere safe?" she asked hopefully and in her most even voice. She gave the soldier a speaking look that he didn't pick up on. "Up to the main hotel perhaps?" He clearly wasn't reading her signals, dammit.

"Not for the present, *senhorita*. It is only one man. I can assure you, he will be apprehended within minutes."

"I'm sure he will." Behind her Fox's tone was Sahara dry.

The soldier who'd done all the talking gave a half

bow as if to royalty. The deferential gesture was spoiled by the lascivious gleam in his eyes. *"Boa noite. Senhorita. Senhor,"* he said to her chest. He motioned to his partner to precede him down the stairs. Sydney and her uninvited intruder stood in the half-open doorway and watched them cross the small porch, go down the stairs, and turn onto the gravel path.

"They might get a little suspicious if we stand here like this all night," Sydney pointed out when he didn't move to close the door. Every muscle in her body was ready to make a break for it the second he released her.

She figured she could make it down to the path if she ran really fast, screaming all the way. The two soldiers hadn't even reached the empty bungalow to the left, and more men walked a few hundred feet away on the beach. This guy wasn't going to chase her outside. Not naked. Not with all eyes on him.

She knew *he* wasn't armed.

"Don't." His voice, lethally soft, was right in her ear.

Squinting against the bright lights, waiting for her chance. The searching soldiers were now right in front of her bungalow. "Don't what?" she asked innocently.

"Make a run for it."

"Why's that?" She tried to read his intent by the feel of him, waiting for the sensation of his muscles flexing against her. But there was no movement at all. He was dead still. Was he going to pull her back inside? She pictured the room behind her, mentally searching for weapons in case he was faster than she was and did manage to pull her in with him. If she could, she'd knee him in the balls, or head slam him, or use her palm to break his nose. Her brothers had taught her to fight dirty if it ever became necessary.

This was as necessary as it got.

The bungalow consisted of a small bathroom and one large living space. Bed. Kitchenette. Small sitting area.

The bathroom was off to the side, with no window. But she didn't *plan* on running *in*. She wanted *out*. Out where the helicopters' bright lights and the soldiers with their nice big guns waited.

"I'm a desperate man. Anything can happen."

"I'm a desperate woman. And you're damn right. Anything *can* happen."

He huffed out a breath. Amusement or irritation? He still wasn't moving. Why not? The door was half open, the light behind them, the helicopter spotlights turning night to day. Anyone passing the bungalow, and there were dozens of men doing so, had a clear view of the two of them just standing there.

"Did you really escape from the loon—mental hospital?"

"You think I'd tell you the truth?" His voice sounded tight, strained. Good. She hoped he was scared to death. No. Wait. Scared to death meant he'd take dangerous risks to stay safe.

"Why not?" The half-round table in front of the window a few feet from the door held her open laptop and half-empty wineglass. "I'm a captive audience."

"No."

She could lunge to the side and grab her computer and conk him on the head with it, but she seriously doubted a desperate man would let her get that far. "No what? I'm not a captive audience?" The fact that he wasn't *doing* anything unnerved her. What was he waiting for?

"I'm not an escapee from the local asylum."

"Good to know." Which meant she'd been right the first time—he was a killer. Her heart was going into overdrive, beating fast enough now to make her dizzy. Get a grip, she told herself fiercely. Just damn well get a grip. Because if she didn't start thinking, and thinking fast, he was going to have control of the situation. And she couldn't allow that to happen.

He could stand there as long as he liked, but she was going to make a run for it. As if he could read her mind his arm tightened around her middle. He was going to drag her back inside, slam the door, and do his worst.

There was the floor lamp—

The desk chair—

Or his penis.

She spun around in his arms, lifting her knee at the same time as she shoved at his chest, pushing him off balance. His bare chest, tanned and hairy, was higher than she'd estimated, and she found her hands on his rock-hard, sandy six-pack. Despite his height, he moved with animal grace, light on his feet. Fast and deadly.

"Watch that knee." He blocked it with his thigh and reached over her head to slam the door closed behind her. Her body was still blocking it. Ha! Take that. Sydney punched him in the solar plexus. He grunted, then grabbed her by her upper arms and pulled her up on her toes.

Suddenly she found herself staring into eyes a brilliant, glittering moss green. His strong jaw was shadowed by several days' growth. Dark hair, wet and crusted with sand, brushed his broad shoulders. She stared at his mouth. God . . . Panic at her inappropriate response welled up inside her and she struggled to get free.

His fingers tightened on her arms. "We have an audience."

"Put me down and I'll give them a show," Sydney said through her teeth. Her struggles were clearly useless. He was much stronger than she was, and she would just hurt herself unnecessarily. Still, her brothers were all a lot stronger than she was, and she'd bested them countless times.

"What's the plan, Stan? Gonna keep me up here until morn—" She saw the blood, wetly scarlet against the white of the robe he'd slung over his shoulder. Blood wicked into the fabric at an alarming rate. "You're bleeding. You need a doctor. A *hospital*—" She glanced back up at his face; he was watching her in the most peculiar way, his green eyes glassy.

Now that she was this close she could see that he was also pale under his tan, and his lips were white with strain. "Put me down, you moron, you're going to bleed to death right in front of everyone."

"You say that like you care."

"I don't," she told him with asperity. "But you're holding me six feet off the floor." It was probably only a foot, but she was getting altitude sickness. "If you drop me I'll likely break my neck. Put me down."

"What's your name, tiger?"

Sydney rolled her eyes. "Oh, please, don't get cute. I have eight brothers. Put me down before I emasculate you."

His teeth looked very white in his swarthy face as he grinned. Then the smile disappeared as he brought her closer, and bent his head.

Sydney froze as his mouth touched hers. The door was open—everyone out there would see them. The guy was insane.

Crazy like a fox.

Her chin jerked up and her eyes narrowed in warning. "Don't even think about it, pal." Hard to make a strong point while hanging between the man's ridiculously large hands, bare feet swinging. Sydney gave him the evil eye.

"Right. No second-guessing."

"*That's* not what I—" She braced herself for hard and fast.

What she got was slow and sneaky. His lips were smooth and cool. Despite being unhurried, there was nothing tentative about the way he angled his mouth over hers, then slid his tongue inside before she could clamp her teeth shut.

There was a second, just a second, when Sydney thought he would stop if she insisted. But the unbelievable sensuality of his kiss made her want to see what was on the dark side and she gave tacit permission by wrapping her arms, suddenly free, around his neck. His fingers plunged into her hair, bracketing her head, drawing her harder against him.

She heard the muted thud of the door closing behind her, but his fingers were in her hair, his tongue was in her mouth, and her insides felt like melting chocolate.

After several heart-racing moments he broke the liplock, leaving Sydney limp and dizzy. She blinked him back into focus as her feet touched the floor. Had he been holding her up that entire time?

"Blood bother you?" he asked, removing the bunched-up robe from his shoulder. There was a gory-looking patch between his clavicle and shoulder. Dark blood seeped, but was already clotting.

One or more of her brothers were bleeding at any given time. Blood didn't bother her at all. The fact that he was naked and oblivious bothered her a great deal. "As long as it isn't mine—" Sydney focused on the wound and tried not to run her gaze over his impressive physique. There wasn't an ounce of fat on him. The dark hair on his chest narrowed to a dark line that widened at his groin—

Apparently, it was true what they said about men with big hands. She dragged her gaze back up his body and forced herself to keep her attention on his face. She had to moisten her lips because her mouth was dry just looking at him.

"That is from a bullet, right?" She strolled casually to the small closet and removed a short turquoise cotton dress. He might find his nudity mundane, but she was overly conscious of being practically naked herself in the small bikini that barely fit anymore.

She did not want to be this naked with a strange man who was *completely* naked in the same room. Pulling a halter dress over her head, Sydney tied the straps behind her neck.

"Yeah." He was trying to look at the injury, but it was at an awkward angle. He went over to look at it in the mirror. His shoulders were broad, tanned, and corded with muscle, sloping down to a narrow waist and a tight behind that made her long to run her fingers down the smooth curve of each globe. She shook her head to get rid of the unwelcome, inappropriate sensual brain fog.

"Why are they looking for you? Did you kill someone?"

"Not today."

"Not *today*? How about this week?"

"Not this week."

"Just as a matter of interest, and in the naive belief that you might actually tell me the truth; are you the good guy or the bad guy?"

His eyes met hers in the mirror. "You won't believe me."

Sydney shrugged. Overhead the helicopters swooped and soared like noisy dragonflies, and their bright lights made stripes on the painted white floor between her and the naked guy.

"I'm a counterterrorist operative. I followed a suspect here to *Novos Começos*. Things went . . . wrong."

She flopped down into the easy chair, keeping the large bed between them. "*Wrong's* a pretty mild word for all those helicopters and gun-toting soldiers out there." Tilting her head, she tried to read his expression in the mirror.

There was a story here. A *big* story if terrorists were involved. In for a penny, in for a pound. She got that he was dangerous in spades. But he didn't appear to want to hurt her. It was crazy. Impulsive. Sure as hell was going to get her into more trouble than she could possibly handle. But—"I can be your cover."

He turned slowly. "My . . . cover?" His mouth relaxed into a slight smile. "You watch too many spy movies, Miss . . . McBride, wasn't it?"

"Sydney."

"Sydney." He rolled her name around his mouth like he was tasting it, like he'd just tasted her. She took a deep breath and dragged her gaze from what she imagined, *he* imagined was a smile. His lips barely moved but the brackets on either side deepened slightly with the lip twitch.

"You have no idea. My brothers took turns babysitting me. Spy movies, detective movies, and football was all they watched. It was an early night for me, or staying up and watching what they watched." She had a million and eight questions to ask him, but she could see he was hanging on by a thread. He'd lost a lot of blood. He should probably lie down, and she should call a doctor. There were plenty of them around.

The spa *had* given her carte blanche and access to whatever she needed as material for the book. And of course the free publicity it would generate off her notoriety from the *last* book. But she didn't think getting a doctor to treat a spy counted.

Time for questions in the morning. "I'm guessing you can feel there's another hole in your back?" She raised her eyebrows. The sight of the second wound, a little smaller that the one in front, but no less bloody, made her stomach lurch in empathy. Pain didn't describe how it looked. Agony might be close.

"Through and through." He lightly touched the bruised and bleeding skin around the wound. "This needs to be cleaned and stitched."

"Dial zero on the house phone. Someone can take you to the hospital." She tried to sound unsympathetic. The wound looked like it hurt like hell, and he was getting paler by the second. She didn't want to sound too eager. But she wasn't letting this guy out of her sight for a second.

Writing a book about a counterterrorist operative was going to be considerably more interesting than writing a book about vanity plastic surgery. She suddenly felt as though the rain clouds had parted and she was once again bathed in the hot glow of fame.

Time for a reality check, Sydney Marisa. Take this slowly, she warned herself. *Very, very slowly. Check your facts. Double-check. Quadruple-check.* She wanted to laugh and spin around in dizzy circles.

This guy, spy or not, had the story that was going to give her her life back. Woohoo and hallelujah. She could have kissed him. Again.

Instead she watched him go through the drawers in the small dresser beside the bed while she formulated the questions she wanted to ask him about his job and about the terrorists he was after. Looking at him was no hardship. His body was tan all over, sleek and well muscled. There was strength and power under skin that gleamed like polished copper. "What are you looking for?" In the drawer was the Gideon Bible and BOB. Her battery-operated boyfriend.

"Sewing kit." He went into the bathroom, seemingly oblivious to her flushed face. The fact that she was embarrassed that he'd been rude enough to open a drawer and see something so personal annoyed her.

"Put a towel around you before you come back," she called. Really, the man was as unself-conscious as a child about his nudity. And while she'd accidentally seen every one of her brothers naked at some stage of her life, this guy was not her brother. Seeing *his* penis didn't make her giggle, seeing *his* penis made her hot and bothered.

He came back wearing a towel slung around his waist and brandishing the resort's tiny sewing kit.

Sydney frowned. He couldn't mean—"You're going to use a *sewing kit* on yourself?"

"You'll have to do it. I can't reach back there."

Just the thought of jabbing a needle through his skin made all the blood drain from her head. "You're crazy. I flunked home ec three years in a row. I can barely *thread* a needle, let alone *sew*."

He glanced around the room. "Where do you want me? There?" he indicated the mosquito net–covered king-sized, four-poster bed between them.

Yes. But no. "I'm not playing around. You need a doctor. A *real* doctor. This is a plastic surgery spa. There are doctors up in the main building 24/7. There's a golf cart parked outside. I can have you there in less than ten minutes."

"It'll be hard to explain your dead 'boyfriend' to the housekeeping staff in the morning."

"For God's sake. Why do you have to be so stubborn? You can't expect me to sew you up. If nothing else you're a total stranger, a total stranger standing here naked as the day you were born—"

He patted his flat, towel-wrapped stomach. "Covered."

"I don't owe you anything. *You're* the one who showed up here and—" Sydney blinked at the space where he'd stood half a second before. "That's one way to win an argume—"

He was gone.

Poof.

Vanished.

Two

A pair of lightly tanned bare feet with bright red nail polish swam into focus. Lucas blinked. His gaze traveled up a pair of legs that seemed to go on forever. His hostess.

"Oh, good," she said cheerfully. "You're alive."

Could've fooled him. His head throbbed, his shoulder ached . . . and for fuck's sake, he smelled like a damn still. The stink of brandy, gin, wine, and who knew what else made his nose burn and his lungs catch.

Something soft tethered his left ankle beneath the sheet. He thought it gone. Sunlight streamed through the open blinds, turning the all-white room into a stealth missile directly targeting his brain. He closed his eyes against the harsh light, checking to make sure his cloaking power was activated. That power was still operational from the Teleport.

No wizard should be aware of his presence.

"Don't go back to sleep," Sydney—*Sydney?*—told him firmly. "You need to drink something, and I'm supposed to check your pupils again."

Lucas flung an arm over his throbbing eyes. "From the way it smells in here, I don't need anything else to drink. What the hell happened?" He didn't mind the occasional beer, or shot of tequila, but he didn't indulge in alcoholic free-for-alls. He didn't like anything that clouded his perception, or took away any of his control.

Didn't need a shrink to tell him it was because of the way he'd grown up.

"The soldiers came around asking questions earlier." Jesus, was she always this cheerful? And focused? "I told them you were passed out. Which they believed because I'd emptied out the minibar and left a bunch of glasses around before they arrived."

He removed his arm and stared up at her face.

Exotic girl-next-door with a mouth that would distract most men. He wasn't most men. That didn't lessen his appreciation, but distraction wasn't part of the game plan. Long, golden brown hair hung halfway down her back in a glossy, wavy fall that looked eminently touchable. Her eyes were large, long-lashed, and a deep almost golden chocolate, shining with intelligence and warmth. There was some Hispanic or Mediterranean in her gene pool, but her accent was all American melting pot.

A strapless bright yellow sundress showed off her lightly tanned olive skin. Unfortunately she showed no cleavage this morning, which Lucas found both a relief and a disappointment.

His memory hadn't suffered from falling on his head. She was a knockout, if he had the inclination to consider such things. He didn't, not when he was working. And hell, when wasn't he?

"Last time I checked, you were supposed to drink your way to a hangover, not take a bath in it."

"I just poured a little on the sheet. And hey, they fell for it, which saved your unconscious self."

She waited for praise for her cleverness. When it wasn't forthcoming, she forged on. "The place is *crawling* with soldiers, by the way. And since I suspect you're not the kind of guy to lie around in bed all day, I'll caution you to be *very* careful. They're looking for anyone and anything suspicious. You're not on the hotel's guest list, which seems to have already raised a red flag. They were here *twice* asking questions."

She flipped her hair over her shoulder. "Pay attention, because I have your bases covered. *When* you arrived? Two days ago—we've stayed inside since you got here, making love around the clock. *How* you arrived—a friend's yacht. *How long have we known each other*—six months. A whirlwind relationship. Your answers need to be the same as mine, got it? I wore my bikini and they didn't look at my pupils once to see if I was lying." She grinned, quite pleased with herself.

"I have a particular fondness for that red bikini myself." And he'd be more than happy to remove it and go directly to the "making love around the clock" part of the program.

She waved a hand dismissively. "Clearly you can't just wander around the grounds or go into the buildings unnoticed for a while. Besides, you've lost a lot of blood and you probably have a concussion considering that big bump on your head. Luckily that's covered by your hair, but I bet you have a whopper of a headache. You should hang around here for a couple of days. Rest up. Let the heat die down."

She'd apparently had plenty of time to think things through. Although she clearly didn't want his input since she talked so fast he couldn't get a word in. "Was I out long enough for you to get your medical degree?"

"Premed." She didn't miss a beat.

He closed his eyes again. "Wake me when you finish your residency."

He winced as the bed jarred when she removed her feet from their resting place on the mattress beside his hip. "No, really. Stop thanking me," she said acerbically. "Your awe and admiration for my quick thinking and lifesaving techniques is too much. Really. It was nothing. I do stuff like that for strangers every day back home."

"You did good." *Other than dousing me with alcohol and tying me up.*

"Damned by faint praise. Fortunately for me I did it out of pure human kindness, not *expecting* your thanks. No good deed goes unpunished."

His lips twitched. "There is that."

She narrowed her eyes. "The least you could do is thank me for covering your a—behind. I saved your life, you know. I went on the Internet and got instructions on how to sew you up with that puny, inadequate sewing kit. It was kinda cool, I must admit. Gross in an intriguing way, but really interesting. Not that I think I'll ever have the opportunity to sew human flesh anytime again. But, hey. You never know."

"Thank you. I'm humbled by my ability to contribute tools to your already considerable skill set," he said dryly, trying to piece the last few hours together.

"You slept—off and on—for seven hours. I had to keep waking you up because of the concussion. I looked that up too, so I've been checking you all morning. You fainted, then disappeared—Why don't you take a few minutes to figure out how to explain *that* nifty trick to me? I'll get you that glass of orange juice."

She padded over to a small area with a microwave and mini-fridge. She was as sexy from the back as she was from the front. His gut tightened as he noticed her truly spectacular legs, magnificently exposed by the short dress.

Business, Fox. *Business.*

The show of "military" force at the spa intrigued him. There was a shitload of money behind the Hueys and the uniformed men. Their weapons were top-of-the-line AKS–47s. So the Half had told them—whoever the hell they were—that he'd been followed. More Halfs? Or had he come across a nest of full wizards? He didn't sense them, but that didn't mean they weren't there. He wasn't sure if that power was on the fritz, or there just weren't any wizards to pick up on. Possibly cloaked. But he didn't think so.

Where the hell had Escar gone if not here? *Novos Começos* Medi-Spa was the Half's point of entry. *Why* here? A resort spa destination for the rich and famous. The very rich. The place cost a mint before one even partook of its laundry list of plastic surgery services.

Escar was a low-level bad guy. He ran with a group of tango Halfs called Splinter. Splinter was run by a Greek by the name of Karras. Well-organized, they were into a bit of this and a bit of that. Everything from money laundering for the mob to doing errands for more powerful wizards, many of whom were terrorists. Halfs weren't thinkers. They were followers.

What was Escar up to? His latest behavior was more puzzling than alarming. He'd come to Brazil two dozen times in the last year. Why? Lucas would find out. Anything a Half, and Splinter, did was of interest to T-FLAC/psi.

"Did you faint again?" she asked when he didn't respond fast enough to suit her.

Fainted? "Passed out," Lucas corrected, keeping the conversational ball rolling.

"Same as fainted," her amused voice came from the other side of the room. Clearly her moods were mercurial, because she no longer sounded pithy. Glasses clinked and liquid rushed.

He counted six quiet, barefooted strides back to the bed. The glass was placed on the table near his head with a click. The crisp smell of something floral—gardenias?—pushed aside the stink of stale liquor as she leaned over him. Long strands of her hair swept his bare shoulder, the silky stroke shot straight to his groin, thankfully covered by the boozy sheet.

He frowned. He couldn't fathom why she'd helped him in any way. He'd been unconscious. She could have—hell, *should* have—run. "Why did you cover for me? For all you know I'm one of the 'bad guys.' "

"I haven't discounted it, which is why I removed all possible weapons from the kitchenette and tied your ankle to the bed," she said calmly, golden brown eyes steady. "Don't do anything stupid. I can see five soldiers from right here. A good scream—and I can scream loud enough to wake the dead—and they'll be in here so fast you won't know what hit you. Sip this. It's delicious. Fresh-squeezed."

She'd gone from threat to nurture without skipping a beat. Forget fresh-squeezed OJ. The smell of her skin made his mouth water, and made him remember the kiss. He'd wanted to cement the picture of the two of them as a unit into the soldiers' heads; he hadn't realized how deeply he'd been sucked into his own game of make-believe.

A little frown of concentration appeared between her dark brows as she leaned closer to look at his pupils. Lucas could see himself reflected in her eyes. He smoothed out a scowl and tried to appear affable and benign. He was neither.

He resisted reaching out to feel her skin. He already knew it was as smooth as it looked. "Will I live?" Where was the Half wizard he'd followed? Lucas sensed no other psi powers within a ten-mile radius. He'd widen the search and do some poking around shortly. The Half's signal had been suspiciously strong when Lucas had Trace Teleported right behind him. A Half that strong was unusual, and dangerous. Halfs were the scourge of the wizard community. Pit bulls for hire.

"You're safe with me," Sydney assured him, unaware

that he was only partially listening. She sat back down in the nearby wicker chair. She was gorgeous and sexy in a freshly scrubbed way, but he wasn't buying flowers today. He had things to do and places to go that didn't involve a woman he was pretty sure had been Homecoming Queen and voted most popular by her BFFs in high school.

"Are you really a counterterrorist agent?"

"I really am. I'm with a privately funded U.S. counterterrorist organization called T-FLAC." He didn't mind telling her. Hell, let her ask anything she liked. One of his powers was the ability to make people remember what he *wanted* them to remember. And forget what he wanted them to forget. Empathic Perception also allowed him to make adjustments to exactly what a person remembered. A handy tool.

"You'd better tell me who's trying to kill you and some of the why." She was all big eyes and earnest concern.

"Some?"

She shrugged. "Well, I'd love hearing every gory detail, but I suspect you'd have to kill me if I knew too much. So just give it to me in broad strokes and we'll go from there."

Jesus. Was she for real?

He reached up to touch his bandaged shoulder. Fortunately, he had amazing recuperative power, and her quick treatment would speed things up even more. She must've used an entire box of Band-Aids on him.

"You're not my first," she inserted into the silence.

Lucas raised a brow.

"My first *now you see me, now you don't.*" She took a sip of her own drink, then licked her upper lip.

He remembered the feel of her tongue in his mouth, of her plump breasts flattened against his chest, and had to bend his knee to tent the sheet.

"I've seen that disappearing trick before," she told him blithely. "I have no idea how it's done—some special government spy secret that civilians shouldn't know about, I'm sure."

It had nothing to do with being an operative, and everything to do with wizards. "You've seen people disappear around here?" Plural. Clearly there was more than just the Half wizard he'd been tracking. A low-level Half with some very nasty connections. Lucas felt a little zip of electricity spark his attention. So the Half he'd followed had come here to join more of his kind. All he had to do was figure out who, where, and why.

"A couple of guys." Sydney drew her very pretty feet up onto the chair, wrapping her arms around her knees. "About a week ago. It was dusk and I was swimming. Obviously they weren't aware that anyone could see them. As if that wasn't spooky enough, and even more impressive than two guys going poof—a *yacht* suddenly appeared out of the blue right at the pier out there." She jerked her chin in the general direction of the window and the bay beyond. "A big yacht. *Huge*."

She took a sip of her juice, then balanced the glass on her knee. "And on *another* night a plane suddenly materialized out of thin air on the landing strip behind the hotel—" She cut off, clearly waiting for his response.

"Maybe you were hallucinating," Lucas offered mildly, biting back a smile when she looked quite put out. He really needed to sit up to get the full effect of her.

"Maybe I *wasn't*—" she said emphatically, then jumped out of the chair as if spring-loaded, somehow not spilling a drop of her drink in the process. She put her glass on the table. "Here, let me help you to sit up, tell me if you get dizzy." She gathered pillows and stacked them against the headboard.

Her slender arms were quite strong, but her strength wasn't his most immediate observation when she touched him. Lucas was suddenly aware of the heightening of his powers. His ability to block increased, his awareness of the absence of other wizards amped up, and his physical strength intensified. He didn't need help, but he wasn't going to refuse to have her arms around him and her hair brushing his face while he tried to figure out the alchemy of their touch.

"Okay?"

He nodded, breathing in the fresh, floral fragrance of her skin before she straightened. He accepted the chilled glass she handed him when he was settled against a pile of pillows. He drank, suddenly aware of how thirsty he was.

So vehicles and people were teleporting in and out? Interesting. Proof enough that more than one Half wizard was ankle-deep in whatever was happening at the medi-spa.

"How do you suppose they did it?" he asked idly as she went back to the chair and resumed her position, resting her chin on her knees.

"I haven't a clue. But then civilians—regular people—wouldn't, right?"

"Right. Spy stuff."

Her eyes gleamed with excitement. "Pretty *cool* spy stuff."

"Yeah, it is that." He took another sip of the tart drink. "And what are you doing here?"

She shrugged slender shoulders. "Vacation, a little boob job." She grimaced. "Which my family will kill me for if they ever find out."

It was hard to keep his gaze on her face. Her magnificent breasts were well covered, but he'd glimpsed them last night, framed deliciously by a skimpy red bikini top. "It's your body, why should they have an opinion about what you do to it?"

"You're kidding, right? If I get a hangnail my family is

interested, and determined to find the cure. Nine guys with a combo Irish/Cuban heritage? I'm the only girl. You think they wouldn't have an opinion on *why* I wanted bigger breasts?" She laughed, genuinely amused. "You must come from a very small family."

"Very." He was the only one in his family. "Do you really have eight brothers?"

"I do. *And* I'm the youngest."

As sexy as she was, as innocuous as it was to lie here talking about her family, he had things to do, and places to go. It was too bad he couldn't linger. She was refreshingly guileless, smart, and funny. In a different place and time, he might've pursued her. Then, in keeping with his normal pattern, he'd lose interest. There was something challenging and exciting about the chase, but he'd never yet met a woman who held his attention for more than a few months.

The fact had never bothered him; hell, it had never crossed his mind that there was more than a night or two of hot sex. Part of it was the demands of his job—not exactly conducive to a relationship, and part of it was the whole being a wizard thing. The few women he'd trusted with that information had run for the hills. Lucas had wiped their memories so they wouldn't go share his unique talents with the world, but he'd long ago learned that it was best to keep his own counsel. Of course, that didn't preclude the occasional physical relationship.

Still, a few more minutes while he mentally cataloged his injuries and mustered the strength to get out of her bed, wasn't going to hurt.

"Sergio is the oldest, then there's Carlos, Tomás, Hugh and José are twins, Ramon and Rián are also twins, then Seán, who's ten minutes older than me."

"Your poor mother had three sets of twins?"

"She was very happy to have us in batches." Sydney's

smile lit up her face. "Said it saved time." She glanced at the empty glass he'd returned to the table. "More?"

He shook his head. "I have to go."

"Go where?"

"I followed a suspect here. I have to find him, or at least find out why he came to a place famous for plastic surgery."

"Because he wanted to change his appearance?"

"Possible."

"I can help you with that."

He raised a brow. "Is that so?"

"I've been here for more than a month. First of all, I know my way around pretty well. Second, I can go where spa guests *can't* go. Into the medical building. In fact I have a follow-up appointment there today after lunch. We could go up to the main hotel, have lunch, and wander around to your heart's content. What do you say?"

"I don't take civilians with me when I'm working."

"Fine. Go by yourself." Sydney rose. "You're just like Tomás. Too stubborn for your own good. FYI, you can't get into the medical facility without a pass. And you sure as heck can't stroll around anywhere other than the main floors of the hotel, without proving you're a guest."

His lips twitched. "You think I need a key card to get in anywhere?"

"You can take the hard way if you like. I just don't see the point when you can do it the easy way and have a nice lunch to boot. It's crazy to go anywhere for a couple of days anyway. You should at least wait until that hole in your shoulder heals a little, but taking a wild guess, you'll leave anyway."

"Right." He didn't wince as he sat up a little more, but every damned Band-Aid she'd used pulled with the movement.

"Ah—news flash, Mr. Bond. You don't have any clothes, remember?"

He hadn't been able to Trace Teleport with anything on him. No clothes. No weapons. Never happened that way when he'd Trace Teleported before. But this wasn't the first time his powers had malfunctioned. Pissed him off, and if he was honest with himself, freaked him out just a little. If it happened again he'd call Mason Knight, his friend and mentor, and see if Mace could figure out what the hell was going on. Keeping in close contact was a little harder since Knight had moved to live in London a couple of years ago. But he was pretty good about getting back to Lucas when he called.

"You could go and *get* me some clothes."

She looked down at him. "I suppose I could. Spy or no spy, you can't go around naked without drawing attention to yourself. You'll need shorts, and a T-shirt to cover the bandage. I can get the basics at the gift shop, but we'll go into town later today or tomorrow and buy you a few more things. Town's within easy walking distance, but I have the golf cart if you'd rather—"

She was nuts if she thought he'd take a civilian anywhere near the kind of tangos he dealt with on a daily basis. But she was damn cute while she choreographed his actions to catch them.

"Thought this all through, have you? Do you boss your brothers around like this?"

"Of course. I love them." She nibbled on her full lower lip. An action Lucas was contemplating doing to her himself. "You could use this as a base of operations if you like. Since the soldiers have already met you they'll accept that you're my boyfriend, so you can come and go freely in the public areas without anyone asking questions."

Sydney tried to sound merely casually helpful; she couldn't let this opportunity pass, but she wanted him to think her suggestion had merit. Pushing her hair over one shoulder, she leaned back. Relaxed. Unconcerned if he took her offer or not. Mentally she had her fingers crossed. In for a penny, in for a pound.

She should get on the Internet and research guns. She presumed he used one when he was armed. Could she write both books at the same time? *Skin Deep* was almost finished. She'd take plenty of notes. She was already thinking of a title for the new book as she said, "You have to take me with you while you look for your man. I know. I know. Crazy idea. But it makes all kinds of sense. Taking me with you will allay suspicion. Just two lovebirds strolling around. I'll let you do your thing without interference, don't worry. You'll hardly know I'm there."

There, Sydney thought. Logical, and not too enthusiastic. Helpful without sounding excited by the prospect.

Without countering her offer, Lucas swung his legs over the side of the bed. How had he managed to untie the robe's belt she'd used to secure his ankle?

He held up the corner of the sheet, ready to fling it aside. "Up to you. Close your eyes, or look your fill. I'm up and outta here."

Sydney's breath caught, but she managed a quick save. "Have at it. I've seen more penises than a urologist. Much as I hate to dash your ego, seen one, seen 'em all. Including yours. I put you to bed, didn't I?"

She hadn't seen that many penises actually, but she bet his was one of the most impressive.

"I want a shower, then I think I will take you up on that offer of the clothes. How long will it take?"

"I have the golf cart outside. I can go up to the resort gift shop and pick you up enough to cover you until we can do some serious shopping. Twenty minutes tops."

"In that case—" He stood beside the bed totally unselfconscious in his nudity. And why not? He was a magnificent specimen. Not an ounce of fat on him. His hard body was ripped and toned, and her fingers curled into her palms because she knew what his skin felt like. Hot satin. Since her tongue was stuck to the roof of her mouth with lust, she didn't respond as he padded across the room and shut the bathroom door with what sounded to her like a triumphant snap.

She stared at the door. "Well, hell."

She might go to hell for manipulating him like this. But she wasn't letting this man out of her sight for a second once he was decently covered. Not until she got the whole story.

And if she had to act like some Florence Flipping Nightingale-slash-Pussycat Doll to get him to cooperate, then so be it.

Hell, she might have to bring back the red bikini.

Whatever it took to get the story.

He'd almost agreed to take her with him. A few more subtle and not-so-subtle hints and she'd have him eating out of her hand. Sydney almost did a happy dance right there on the beach. Deciding that walking would be faster than the cart she took off her sandals, carrying them in one hand as she started toward the main building.

Whatever Fox was doing here *had* to be considerably more interesting than a book exposing the trials and tribulations of plastic surgery. Sydney already had dozens of questions formulated, but was one hundred percent sure he wouldn't answer *any* of them. Not if she asked flat out. Eight brothers meant that she'd had to become a tactician to get anything out of them.

She could do subtle. It didn't come naturally, she thought, lips twitching, but she'd had plenty of practice. The fact that her wounded warrior was a spy-type guaranteed he'd be even more of a clam than her twin Seán, who personified closemouthed. And as tough a nut as her brother was, eventually she could wear him down, making him putty in her hands.

A dozen armed soldiers in brown camouflage patrolled the exquisite swath of sugary white sand, spoiling the idyllic picture-perfect scene as Sydney veered off toward the hotel along a winding, shrub-lined shell path.

The beautifully manicured gardens were a riot of brilliant color, the freshly mown grass the same Irish green as Lucas's eyes.

Forget his eyes, Sydney warned herself. As bootylicious as he was, he had something far more important to give her than his admittedly fabulous body. He had a story.

She wanted that story more than she wanted her next breath of fresh ocean-scented air. And she was going to get it. With a feeling of excitement and anticipation she refrained again from twirling in a circle right there outside the hotel.

A row of luxury shops lined a wide, tiled courtyard, but before going inside Sydney paused. Heart pounding, she took her iPhone out of her pocket and tapped the number for her agent in New York. Her agent Kiki was in a meeting. Of course she was. Lately, she was always in a meeting when Sydney called.

She left a message, determined not to let this get her down. Once Kiki heard what she had to say, things would get back to the way it had been. Before.

Dying to share the good news she hesitated, trying to decide who she could call who'd support her unconditionally. Someone who'd be as excited as she was. Calling her brothers—*any* of them—was out of the question. They'd insist she come home immediately, and/or one or more of them would be on the next flight to Brazil to make sure she was okay.

And while they had all, in varying degrees, forgiven her for what she'd done, telling them she was involved with a *spy* would stretch her credibility to breaking point. Her heart squeezed as it always did knowing how much her first book had adversely affected her family. While that hadn't been her goal, she'd realized far too late that taking poetic license with Tomás's life—turning her mentally ill brother's story into a first-person account—was wrong on many fronts.

It took her father and brothers *months* to talk to her after the shit had hit the fan. Their loving support meant everything to her. She'd deserved their anger. But it had been brutal to take.

God. Did she never learn? The fiasco of *Being Michaela* had only happened nine months ago. Now she was considering calling her brothers to tell them she was involved with a spy. Not only a spy, a spy who could disappear. She let out a mirthless laugh. Yeah. They were sure to buy that one with her track record.

She had a small group of close friends she was tempted to tell. Bethany would be all agog but she wasn't known for keeping her mouth closed, and besides, her husband worked for a local newspaper. The temptation to spill her guts would override any secrets Sydney might tell her in confidence. Suz would take the practical approach and tell her to stay clear of Lucas. Michelle would tell her to sleep with him, but not get involved. Which left Deb.

Sydney tapped her friend's number. "Before you say anything—I'm sending pictures. Hang on." She quickly e-mailed the five pictures she'd taken while Lucas slept.

"Oh. My. God," Deborah said breathlessly. "Is he my birthday present?"

"No. He's mine." Sydney moved into the shade as she filled Deb in on Lucas's arrival, and who and what he claimed to be. She was glad to have Deb with her, even if she was thousands of miles away.

"What was the name of the organization he said he worked for?" Deb asked, typically practical.

"T-FLAC."

Sydney heard her friend's fingernails on her keyboard.

"Nothing comes up. He's bullshitting you, Syd. He told you he's a spy just to have sex with you."

Sydney laughed. "Trust me. This guy is so hot he wouldn't have to lie about anything to get a woman to go to bed with him. Take another look at that second picture. Of course T-FLAC wouldn't be on the Internet. I seriously doubt spies have Web sites. Let's say he *isn't* a spy. Then he's hiding *something*. And whatever that something is must be pretty darn important for all those soldiers and helicopters to be searching for him so diligently."

"Good point. Maybe what he's hiding is that he's a serial killer! And if he *is* a spy he could use you as a shield and get you shot." There was a pregnant pause. "Or worse."

"He doesn't have a gun," Sydney pointed out dryly. "What if he's telling the truth? What if he *is* a counterterrorist operative and he's here to find terrorists." She sucked in a deep, excited breath. "Wouldn't that be an *amazing* story? It's a win-win situation."

"I doubt he'll take your rabid interest lightly. Does he know you're there to write a book?"

"Not relevant."

"It's relevant if you plan on exposing a secret agent, for God's sake, Syd. Think about it."

"I won't use his name." But she'd *have* to. If she didn't it would be history repeating itself.

"No," Deb said, half amused and half appalled. "Just pictures of him naked on your bed."

"I was going to delete those."

"Well, *do* it."

Sydney held the phone away and deleted the pictures. Reluctantly. The lighting wasn't good anyway. "There. Done. I'll be careful. Maybe I'll find out how they make things disappear. That alone will make a mind-boggling story. Throw in a spy, a pinch of espionage, a dash of an exotic foreign locale, and mix with close proximity, and—woohoo! I'll have a freaking bestseller."

"I'd be a lot more worried about you if I truly believed he *was* a spy. I'm not sure what he is, or how he's doing whatever you think he's doing. Just be careful, for God's sake! What did your agent say about all this when you called her?"

"She was in a meeting."

"That sucks. She's been in that fricking meeting for six months! But maybe it'll give you some time to decide if this is really something you want to get involved in. Just because you're all psyched about this doesn't mean your agent or publisher will be," Deb cautioned. "What about the book you're there to write? Almost finished, isn't it?"

Sydney's heart sped up a little as she saw four soldiers strolling along the path toward her. "Almost. And of course they'll be interested, are you kidding me? This has bestseller written all over it."

"You already wrote one of those, remember?"

Sydney's stomach gave a familiar cramp. "Hard to forget."

"Look, Syd. Be careful, okay? I know this sounds like the big break you need, and I hope it is. You deserve it. But don't let your guard down and don't trust this guy to play straight with you. You have a charming tendency to see the glass half full when it's really almost empty. Promise me. Be careful and be cool."

Before saying good-bye, Sydney agreed to call. In fact, it made her feel safer knowing that someone knew who she was with. If anything happened to her, her friend would be on T-FLAC's doorstep demanding answers. If such a thing as T-FLAC even existed. A sobering thought that again reminded her to be careful.

Glancing at the elaborate clock over the gift shop she saw she'd already been gone almost ten minutes. Sydney speed-shopped, then, shopping bag in hand, started back. Shading her eyes against the bright sun reflecting off the water, she walked down the path toward her bungalow. She smiled as she stepped down onto the soft sand, heading toward the water to walk the last few hundred yards.

Lucas wasn't going anywhere naked. He had to wait for her. To her right was the small marina where she'd seen a yacht appear late one night. Another huge yacht was anchored there now, gleaming white against the crystal clear turquoise water of the inlet. A single gull soared overhead and waves lapped around her ankles. She wondered if the owner of the fancy boat was a movie star or politician. She'd glimpsed a few of both over the last few weeks.

She'd been given the go-ahead by the spa to request interviews with any of the patients. Many had agreed to talk to her, some had not. She respected their privacy, and if they didn't want their names mentioned, she honored those wishes. Surprisingly, dozens of patients had even permitted her to take before-and-after photos of them.

She was doing her best to make the book both interesting and informative. And she knew it would be somewhat of a success as the publisher was cashing in on *Being Michaela*'s notoriety and getting *Skin Deep* fast-tracked to be on shelves in thirty days, exactly one year after her dizzying fall from grace.

Several colorful small one- or two-man boats for the use of guests were tied up at the pier in the distance. A single-story rental building painted pale teal with crisp white trim offered Jet Skis and other water toys.

She'd availed herself of several of them before she'd reluctantly agreed to have the stupid damn surgery she hadn't wanted at the insistence of her publisher.

As far as they were concerned, the public knew she'd lied once. They wanted verisimilitude for her second book. There couldn't be much more believability than going under the knife herself.

She'd liked her average-sized breasts just fine. But she was damned if she'd have a nose job so no one back home would recognize her. She didn't need a brow lift, or lip plumping. She liked having all her ribs exactly where they were, and she didn't *want* J.Lo's behind.

She still couldn't get used to her larger cup size. Walking around with bigger breasts reminded her of when she'd first learned to drive. All she could see from behind the steering wheel was the hood ornament. All she could see when she looked down were her boobs.

It was hard to change her mind when she'd already spent the advance, not to mention they were the only publishers willing to give her a second chance on her nose-diving career. She hadn't fooled herself into believing they thought she was the best writer on the planet. They'd wanted to cash in on her notoriety.

The breast implants could and would be removed, but the embarrassment was going to stay with her for a good long while.

She rubbed the goose bumps of humiliation from her arms with both hands. Just thinking about the call she'd made to New York while she'd been shopping for clothes for Lucas earlier made her heart pound so hard she felt dizzy.

She shook her head. Crazy business—elective plastic surgery. When her publisher suggested the book idea, she asked if she couldn't write a book about life-changing facial reconstruction surgery. But that wasn't what they wanted. They wanted light. Upbeat. Salacious.

Without a topic choice, she'd been determined to make the book the best book ever written on the pitfalls and advantages of destination medi-spas around the world. In the last five months her publisher had sent her to India, Italy, Germany, and South Africa to interview and observe plastic surgery patients. Brazil was the zenith resort destination for plastic surgery.

Her last stop.

Her last chance.

She veered away from the water to cross the sand, not wanting Lucas to sneak out wrapped in a sheet while she was too busy congratulating herself to notice. Crossing her fingers, she muttered under her breath, "Please make this everything I need. Please."

As prayers went it wasn't much. But oh, God, it was heartfelt. She needed a big break. Something to restore her reputation. Something to make everyone sit up and take notice again. Something to show everyone she took her job seriously. Something she could sink her teeth into while proving her writing chops. Again.

Novos Começos. New Beginnings.

Please God . . .

Three

The front door opened just as Lucas emerged from the bathroom, drying his hair with a towel. He knew it wasn't his nubile hostess. Despite their stealth as they approached the bungalow, he'd heard the two men even before they'd quietly shoved open the front door. He dropped the towel over his injured shoulder.

Before she'd left, Sydney had closed the blinds, and the room had been cool and dim when he'd gone in to shower. Now the gloom was sharply cut by the triangle of blinding white behind the two soldiers just before they closed the front door behind them.

"Afternoon, gentlemen," Lucas said easily, padding to meet them halfway. He plucked a bright blue-and-yellow striped beach towel off the back of a chair, and wrapped it around his waist. "I know we're all guys here, but you coulda knocked."

Weapon drawn, the man in front, shorter than his partner by at least a foot, demanded aggressively, "Identification, *senhor.*"

"As you can see, I didn't think to take my ID into the shower. Besides, you're in *my* bungalow." Lucas said in English, holding his hands out to the side, clearly unarmed. Despite his civility the guards kept their weapons trained on his chest as they advanced. There was no caution in their movements. They were loaded for bear, and he was pretty much buck naked.

Didn't bother Lucas any. Even without his powers he was a formidable fighting machine.

Still, this type of situation was when he'd normally use his Empathic Perception power, making the men perceive him as harmless so they'd leave, satisfied he wasn't their man. He didn't want to kill them merely because they were zealously doing their jobs. He gave EP his best shot.

Nothing. By the suspicious expressions still on their faces, the power hadn't worked worth spit. "Is this how you treat guests at *Novos Começos*?" he asked coolly. "Just bust in, guns drawn? You guys watch too much television."

"Last night, the *senhorita,* she say you join her yesterday. But have no record of you at the check-in desk as is required."

Yeah. And Lucas's EP hadn't worked a hundred percent then, but it had worked enough to move them on to the next bungalow without too much suspicion. Clearly it hadn't lasted. "I'll check in today." He smiled at the taller soldier. "If Miss McBride was your girlfriend and you hadn't seen her and her new . . . *enhancements,* would you waste time checking in?"

The soldier in back flicked on the ceiling light, then looked around. "Where is your luggage?"

Lucas kept his tone cool. "I travel light."

The short guy's attention suddenly fixed on the bandage on his shoulder. His fingers flexed on the trigger, and he jerked up his chin. "Remove the coverings."

Lucas raised a brow. He gave EP another shot, then dropped both towels onto the floor at his feet.

The soldiers exchanged quick glances. Indicating the inept, multiple Band-Aid dressing on his shoulder, the front man demanded, "How did you sustain this injury, *senhor*?"

"Bee sting. Highly allergic. Swell up like a toad if I'm stung. My girlfriend loves to play doctor."

They didn't comprehend three words in ten, but what they understood they didn't believe. They stepped forward, parting to present two targets should he—*what*? Shoot bullets out of his dick?

"*Senhor* has the *passaporte*?"

"Of course. And I'd be happy to show it to your superior officer this afternoon, and once I'm dressed."

"We see identification immediately, *senhor*. These are our instructions."

"By?" Who else knew he was in bungalow twenty-three?

The soldiers exchanged uneasy glances. "*Como?*"

"By whose orders are you here?" Lucas acknowledged to himself that he was trying to buy these two some time. He was just fine with killing as his job required. But hell, if EP could take care of this, he was all for the bloodless way of doing things. Magic was cool. His powers were cool. If he couldn't use them then he was just a T-FLAC operative with limited choices in the "get rid of this guy" department.

"By my own order, *senhor*." Not so friendly now. "You will produce your papers. Your *passaporte*. *Um passagem aerea*. The airline ticket. Also the *carteira*—*senhor's* wallet."

"Okay. Okay. Chill. I'll get my wallet out of the dresser—" he indicated the chest of drawers across the room. He'd have to walk between the two men to reach it. This was not going to end well for the gung-ho soldiers. He tried his EP power again. Not even a flicker. Hell.

He didn't need special powers to move fast. In three strides he crossed the few feet necessary, yanked open a drawer, and pulled out a seven-inch carving knife hidden by Sydney under the jumble of her see-through underwear.

He spun, kicked out one foot, and knocked the submachine gun held by Tall flying. The soldier went down, and while Short fumbled to squeeze off a shot, Lucas kicked him in the head. The second guy lurched, but didn't fall, and rushed Lucas, head down like a charging bull. Tall staggered to his feet as Lucas circled them, keeping his body between them and their weapons as he sliced the air with the knife. It wasn't his Ka-Bar, but it would do the job.

He made it fast and efficient. He'd just cut the throat of Short when Sydney walked in.

"Why didn't you just open the shutters instead of turning on the li—" Color drained from her face as she stopped dead three steps into the room. "Holy Mother of God." Clearly horrified, she crossed herself.

"Shut the door."

"Shut th—Hell no." She backed up, dark eyes wide and bewildered as she took in the bloody scene. First the gore splattered on him. Then, with a frown, the twin pools of scarlet spreading on the whitewashed floor at his feet. Her head turned in his direction, but it took several more beats for her gaze to follow. She swallowed hard, then put a hand over her nose as the stench hit her.

"What happened? Why—"

"Shut the door, Sydney," he repeated. "Anyone walking by will see in. I need your help, come over here."

With a blink she reached behind her and shut the door, blocking out the strong sunlight. Blocking out help. Blocking her own escape. Closing herself inside with a killer. It was without a doubt the dumbest thing Sydney had ever done in her life.

Was she still under his hypnotic spell, or would she do anything for this story? Anything stupid. *God, I'm desperate.* That wasn't completely true. Though she was willing to do practically anything to redeem herself, she was usually a pretty decent judge of character. Relying on instinct and adrenaline, she crossed the floor.

God . . . There was so much blood. "Are they dead?" Of *course* they were dead. Lucas had slit their throats.

"Very. Here. Hold this."

Heart pounding, cold sweat breaking out on her skin, Sydney took what he held out without looking to see what he'd handed her. She had never seen a dead person up close and personal, and in movies one couldn't smell the sickly sweetness or get the full Technicolor impact. She swallowed the nausea rising in the back of her throat.

Her fingers had automatically closed around the hilt of the knife, but now she let go, dropping it to the painted floor with a clatter. "Are you *insane*? Why did you give me that thing?"

"Because other than two dead guys, you're the only one who knows I'm here. Your fingerprints on that knife will ensure your discretion."

Appalled, she stepped back. The shock of the situation was wearing off and reality crept in. She was going to be sick. She'd walked into a nightmare. It was like hitting a wall that looked as soft and innocuous as clouds, and finding it was, instead, made of steel. She moistened her lips. As her grandmother used to say, be careful what you wish for, you might get it.

"Why would you do that? I've already told you I'd help you. There was no reason to implicate me in a double murder." The anger turned to accusation. "And what did they do to you? You just killed two men in cold blood."

"Go wash your hands," Lucas instructed.

Sydney looked down. Her palm was smudged with fresh, bright red blood. She looked from her hand to Lucas, feeling oddly detached. She was back to shock. *Don't chat. Don't just stand here. Get the hell out of here. Now.* "What are you going to do with them?" she asked, throat tight, voice hoarse.

"*We.*"

"Oh, no. There's no 'we.' " Knees weak, heartbeat stuttering, she bent to pick up the shopping bag she'd dropped on the floor. As she straightened, she watched Lucas's muscles tighten in anticipation of her ripping open the door and making a mad dash outside.

She'd had plenty of evasion practice with her brothers. She threw the bag at him. "Clothes. Go put them on, for God's sake." Without looking at him, or the two bodies on the floor at his feet, she detoured to the small sink in the kitchenette, her mind in turmoil.

How the hell had he found the knife? She'd hidden anything she considered he could use as a weapon in her underwear drawer.

Sweat popped out on her skin as she convulsively swallowed bile, scrubbing her hands hard enough to turn them bright pink. How in God's name had she imagined that she could use this guy for her own interests? He'd flat out told her who and what he was. A counterterrorist operative.

No. A killer, the killer she'd imagined him to be. Had the increase in her bra size decreased her IQ, for God's sake?

"You told me you were a good guy." Sydney heard the accusation in her voice again, and hoped he didn't hear the tremor of nerves. She wondered vaguely when seeing a naked man covered in blood had ceased to shock her. She casually kicked off her sandals in preparation for running like hell the second his guard was down.

By the time she'd dried her hands and turned around he'd hidden the knife. He turned back to her. A trickle of blood ran down his chest in slow motion. Sick to her stomach, Sydney watched it, transfixed.

"You think good guys don't kill?" he asked derisively,

bending to pick up the bag she'd tossed him. "Lady, don't be naive. I do my job so you sleep nice and safe in your pink lace canopy bed at night."

"Leave. And take them with you," she told him tightly, without looking at the two men on the floor. The sight of them would forever be etched into her brain. And of course he couldn't carry two dead men out by himself. The only person leaving was her. ASAP.

"You're a bossy little thing, aren't you?"

"I'm neither little, nor a thing. I'm Irish/Cuban." Sydney used her heritage as a warning. One day, over a beer or two, she'd tell her brothers and father about her run-in with a killer spy. Maybe. No. If she made it out of here alive, she wouldn't tell a soul. If Fox didn't kill her, her brothers would. For her sheer stupidity.

She'd been dangerously mistaken in believing she could manipulate this man. She might yet pay for that mistake with her life. A fine sheen of perspiration made her skin itch, and her heart beat so fast she could feel the intense throb in every pulse point on her body.

"And I'm your loving boyfriend, remember?" He pulled on the black shorts she'd bought him. Oh, God. She'd bought them right after she'd called her agent in New York and left a message about the new book she was going to write about a sexy spy with mesmerizing green eyes. Oh, hell. What had she done?

Damn him for not being what she needed, *wanted* him to be. "I did that to help you, so no one would get hurt," Sydney told him furiously. "Consider the offer rescinded." She pointed at the door. "You can go wherever double-murdering spies go after a kill." Her rapid heartbeat threatened to make her black out and washed her in waves of sickening heat and icy cold.

He pulled the black-and-white T-shirt over his head. She wanted to scream at him to wash the blood off his skin first. She took a baby step backward. The door was maybe a yard behind her. Three steps to freedom. Then she'd scream her head off and the soldiers out there still looking for him would be in here, and have him under arrest in seconds. She took another step back.

"You know I can't let you go, Sydney." His voice was easy. Scary casual. His green eyes, so attractive an hour before, were now pantherish and predatory. A hunter focused on his prey. Her fear ratcheted higher. Pressure built behind her eyes, her palms felt slick with perspiration. Dear God. Was he going to kill her now?

Sydney fumbled for the door handle behind her, yanked it, and hurtled herself outside—

Straight onto the crowded platform of a train station.

Disoriented, she looked around wildly as the crowd jostled her to the very edge of the platform, and a piercing whistle heralded the enormous face of the oncoming train. This was crazy. Insane. Her hair whipped against her face and neck as she tried to find something familiar in the teeming mass of humanity. Where was the beach? The ocean? The frigging *sky*?

The air smelled like wet dog and coal steam. Voices were raised, a blur of voices. Speaking—French? A child cried, machinery huffed, and chugged, and the train *clack-clack-clacked*, louder and louder as it approached.

Sydney didn't recognize anything. Anyone.

Carrying umbrellas, the people around her were dressed in winter clothes, wet raincoats, hats, scarves. She shivered as an icy wind snuck through her short cotton sundress, and someone's long, wet raincoat dragged against her bare arm and leg taking the shiver to a full-blown shudder.

Her red-tipped toes protruded over the edge of the cement platform as it vibrated beneath her bare feet. Someone's elbow dug into her side as they pushed and shoved around her. The train clattered on the tracks, getting closer and closer, and the enormous engine bore down on her at a dizzying speed. Scared spitless, her heart beating a mile a minute, Sydney teetered six feet over the railway line below.

Hail Mary full of grace, the Lord is with thee. Blessed art thou among women an—

Suddenly she was yanked backward with dizzying speed.

The front door slammed behind her. Silence. The scent of the ocean. She was back inside the bungalow. She blinked up at Lucas, who had his fingers wrapped around her upper arm in a death grip. His hand felt hot against her icy skin.

Growing up with so many older brothers, she'd learned that a strong offense was the best defense. Except that she didn't have a clue what the hell had just happened. "What—? How—?" Her first impulse was to fling herself into his arms and burrow against his chest for comfort. That thought was swiftly followed by the urge to beat the living crap out of him for terrifying her like that. Though after seeing what he'd done to the two soldiers, she did neither.

She couldn't even shake his hold on her arm, because, much to her chagrin she realized she needed his support to remain upright. Which made her even angrier. Fury beat fear hands down. Locking her knees for support, she peeled his hand off her arm with icy fingers, then stepped away from him. "What did you do to me, you homicidal maniac? Hypnosis? Drugs?" Rage made her voice shake.

She was a sweaty, shaken mess. *He* looked implacable, unshaken, and infuriatingly smug. The son of a bitch. And when exactly had he had time to wash the blood off his arms and legs? *And* his clothes?

"I told you not to leave."

Which didn't explain the train. The station. Or the people wearing raincoats and carrying furled umbrellas when it was ninety degrees outside. "You told me," Sydney said through her teeth, "that you couldn't *let me go*. Which is bullshit of the first fricking order. *No one* tells me when and where I can do—*anything*."

"Calm down."

She stared at him. Was he out of his ever-loving mind? "Are you stupid enough to tell an angry woman to calm down? *Calm. Down?*" She advanced on him, blind to everything around her. She was going to make minced meat of his handsome face. She was going to pummel the crap out of his pecs, his glutes, and his whatever else that rippled muscle. She was going to twist his dick into a corkscrew. She was going to—

She blinked as she looked around the room, suddenly aware that something had changed. "Where are the bodies?" Not only were the two soldiers gone, there wasn't a mark on the whitewashed floor. The rumpled bed was now neatly made. Her sandals had been placed, side by side, in front of the shuttered closet doors.

Green eyes glittered. "What bodies?"

"The guys you—" She'd been called a lot of things, but crazy wasn't one of them. And having this man pretend to doubt her veracity made her blood boil. She'd had enough of that to last her a lifetime. *Twenty* lifetimes. She hadn't imagined two dead men on the floor. She hadn't imagined the knife, or the blood, or even that damned railway station.

Right now she wished with all her heart she was imagining Lucas Fox. She'd overestimated her own charm and cleverness. This man wasn't like any of her brothers. Not even close. In fact, he was unlike any man she'd ever met.

"Come on." He held out a large, strong hand. "Your blood sugar's low. Let's get that lunch and tour you promised me."

She hesitated a moment, then let him pull her to his

side. Her head barely cleared his shoulder and she had to tip her head a little to meet his eyes. He was looking at her with an expression she couldn't begin to comprehend. She stared back. She couldn't believe he was standing there pretending nothing had happened when what had happened had effectively turned her brain inside out.

"You're hungry." It was a statement, not a question, but he answered anyway.

"Yeah. Aren't you?" Leaving his fingers entwined with hers, he smiled.

For a moment large brown eyes scanned his features. Her features smoothed out and she gave him a sweet, innocent smile. Excellent. The EP had worked this time. Whatever had blocked it from working on the soldiers didn't seem to be stopping his effect on Sydney.

"Starving," she said briskly. "Let's do it. I'll get my shoes."

He opened the door, then waited while she slid her feet into her sandals. Jogging down the steps he stood at the bottom until she followed him out into the sunshine. The illusion of the Paris Métro station had done the trick. His powers were back to normal, and he was having lunch with a beautiful woman. Life was good.

He'd teleported the bodies to the garbage team in nearby Rio, and used a minor power to clean up the mess left behind. More important, his Empathic Perception power was fully back in operation, and Sydney wouldn't have nightmares about what she'd seen. If and when he needed to have her recall the incident, he could.

"We'll take the golf cart."

"Sure," he said easily, letting her get a bit ahead of him on the shell path so he could admire the scenery. And very nice scenery it was too. Long tanned legs flashed beneath the short yellow dress as she walked. She moved as if she were going somewhere important.

Things to do, Lucas's lips quirked, places to go. She had a temper, and she was probably used to sparring with her brothers. She intrigued him, which was interesting in and of itself. It had been awhile—more than awhile—since he'd felt any interest in a woman for anything other than sex.

Two years to be exact. Shit. No wonder he was intrigued. He caught up with her in two strides, and called his Trace ability power as they walked in silence. Nothing. Until he lightly touched the small of her back and an arc of electricity bonded them for a moment. She stiffened, but kept walking.

Escar was here at *Novos Começos*. Lucas felt it. Here but cloaked. If the Half were shrouded, then he was in collusion with other wizards. It was just a case of finding him. He'd have to track him the old-fashioned way.

There was no rule that said he couldn't enjoy lunch with a beautiful woman while his Trace powers continued scanning for Escar.

"Thanks for the clothes," he said to her slender back. Had anyone ever bought him clothing? He supposed someone must've when he was a child, but he didn't remember it. Ruthlessly he pushed aside the small tear in his equilibrium and shoved his hand into the back pocket of his shorts. He frowned. "What's this?" He held up two fingers showing her the folded cash she'd stuck in there.

Sydney's lips tightened. "It's only about fifty U.S. dollars. I thought you might need some money. For a gun or bullets or something."

"I'm covered, but thanks—I'll hold onto this in case I need to buy *anything* while I'm here." It was a toss-up if her generosity amused or made him more suspicious of her. She was *too* generous. *Too* considerate. Not traits he associated with women in general. "If you're an example of the work they do here, I take my hat off to the surgeons."

She turned to glance his way, her eyes shaded by large white-framed sunglasses. "You're a breast man, apparently."

"Leg man until now," he corrected dryly, trying to interpret her body language, which was a little stiff and disjointed. As though she were thinking about something hard enough not to be quite as graceful as she normally was. "And those are spectacular, too."

"This is mine," she told him, her voice just a little flat as she indicated the cart parked with several others in a cleared area between two bungalows. The thing was the color of Pepto-Bismol with jaunty toothpaste-green trim.

Sydney glanced at him as the vehicle started up with a low hum. "Why are you scowling like that? The color isn't going to affect your masculinity."

He angled his head to look at her. Her flirty yellow dress was nice and short and rode up her tanned legs, the sun beat down on his head, and he was alive. Things could be worse. "It only goes five miles per. We could've walked faster," he said lightly.

"Twenty on a real road. They encourage the patients to use them so we don't spend too much time in the sun. And taking the cart now is so you *didn't* have to walk and take the chance that you'd pass out. But hey, don't let me stop you. Feel free to hop off if you like. I'll see you at the restaurant. Order a Coke for me while you're waiti—"

She cut herself off as she caught sight of movement up ahead. "*Bom dia.*" She switched gears to cheerfully greet three soldiers walking on the shell path toward their slowly moving—he couldn't even call it a vehicle—cart.

The young men, all spit-and-polished, and wearing shiny new uniforms, carried state-of-the-art AKS-47s.

Lucas felt naked without a weapon. For fuck sake, he wasn't even wearing underwear.

The guys returned Sydney's good morning, smiling at her loveliness, and keeping a close eye on him. Lucas, sensing their distrust and suspicion, used a mild form of Empathic Perception on them, making them see him as harmless, and keeping their interest in Sydney rather than himself. It felt good to have his power back at full strength. He slung his arm across the back of the seat in a possessive gesture they couldn't mistake. Sydney's bare shoulders tensed as he cupped her shoulder and ran his thumb lightly across her satiny skin.

"Did you find the guy you were looking for last night?" she asked the soldiers innocently, leaning forward just enough to dislodge his hand.

The guy in the middle glanced at the men on either side of him, then volunteered himself as spokes-soldier. He shrugged. "*Náo compreendo.*"

The guy understood English just fine. Lucas could tell by their body language when Sydney had asked her question. He spoke fluent Portuguese, himself, but he shook his head when Sydney cast those big brown of hers in his direction. "Sorry. I don't speak the language either."

The men stepped aside to let them pass. "Relax," he told her softly as they turned a corner on the wide path and the shrubbery of the gardens hid the soldiers from view. He noticed her hands were shaking, and her skin glowed with nervous perspiration.

"Don't tell me to relax, tension is the only thing holding me together." The joke fell flat. She licked her lips before speaking again. "Do you think they really didn't understand me, or were they just being evasive?"

"Neither. I think they understood you just fine, but they're so far down the food chain they don't know who it is they're looking for or why. And if they did, they wouldn't give it up just because a pretty girl asked them."

Sydney pulled up under the portico and parked in an angled line of brightly colored golf carts. Lucas didn't play golf, but he couldn't imagine any self-respecting golfer wanting to tool around in a confection-colored cart. On the other hand, look at what golfers wore.

"Got a phone?"

Getting out of the cart Sydney handed him the iPhone from a side pocket of her dress. It was warm. He tapped in his code as they crossed the expansive entry to the resort. "Hi, Mom," he greeted his Control, a big bear of a man named Saul. "My suitcase got lost en route. Send me a bag of clothes and my shaving gear. ASAP." Clothes and ordnance.

"Sure, honey," Saul said using the voice synthesizer which made him sound like a sixty-year-old, chain-smoking woman. "Everything all right there?"

"A small landing snafu. Nothing a Band-Aid didn't fix. Hey, remember that kid I told you about on the flight over? Lost track of him."

"Would you like me to send some of your brothers over with your luggage?"

He wasn't sure at this point if this op needed a full team. He kept the option open. "Not right now. Thanks, Ma."

Lucas heard Saul on the computer tracking his coordinates. "Twenty-two degrees fifty-five seconds south, forty-three degrees twelve seconds west?"

"Yeah. *Novos Começos*. Bungalow twenty-three."

"That it?"

"For now."

Saul rang off. He'd teleport what Lucas needed directly to Sydney's cabin within minutes.

"How many brothers do you have?" Sydney asked as they walked into the restaurant. As he suspected, she'd heard some of the conversation. She had good hearing.

"One," he lied easily.

It was early for lunch, but quite a few people sat outside on the beachfront stone patio, shaded by large white umbrellas as they ate lunch. Brazil had over four thousand miles of coastline, and while the Atlantic Ocean wasn't that warm to swim in, the beach was littered with sun-baked bodies wearing *tangas,* Rio's minuscule version of a bikini.

Lying sack of shit, Sydney thought. His mother had said "Do you want me to send *some* of your brothers." *Plural.* She'd about used up every scrap of self-control to get him to this public place. She wanted to be somewhere safe and well populated before she let him have it with both barrels.

She hoped he was distracted enough by the nearly naked girls on the beach so she could jab a butter knife into his giant ego. Did he really think she'd just forget a double homicide because he *smiled* at her? He was very sure of himself. Was he delusional, thinking that if he denied everything that had happened she'd believe she'd *imagined* it? She hadn't been kidding when she'd told the lying, murderous swine beside her that her nerves were holding her together. They were.

"Oi, Paulo. Como vai?" Sydney greeted the middle-aged waiter who beamed at her as he always did when she came in. There were at least thirty people seated outside on the restaurant's patio, and more inside. Perfect.

Sun glinted off the marine blue of the water, and raised voices of vacationers and *Cariocas,* locals, alike mingled as they swam, played ball, or trolled the beach, all to the backdrop of pulsating samba music. The music was addictive, and very sexy. Just hearing the beat made Sydney's blood run faster. She did *not* want to feel sexy around Mr. Fox.

She'd underestimated him, but he had no freaking idea just how much he'd underestimated *her.*

"*Prazer em ve-la, Senhorita* McBride. It is my pleasure to seat you this fine day." Paulo started leading them to a table for two, but Sydney pointed down the other end of the patio.

"*Por favor—nos queriamos*—over there?" She indicated the far end where several tables filled with diners crowded close to the edge of the beach.

"There's a game of *futevolei* going on," she told Lucas. It was the most crowded section of the patio. There was safety in numbers, and Sydney wanted to be right in the middle of all those people while she tried to figure out what her next move was.

"Foot volleyball," she explained, waving at several people she knew as they passed. The more people seeing her with him, the more people who would be able to describe him to the police later. "It's really fast. Volleyball with soccer rules. No hands, no arms. I love watching them play.

"*Sim.* This is perfect." Right in front of everyone looking at the game, the half-naked girls, or the beach. "*Faz favor,* Paulo."

Sitting in the plush upholstered chair, she absently fingered the knife at her place setting. Lucas radiated controlled energy as he took the chair to her right, just a foot away. He wore the sunglasses she'd bought him, and she couldn't see his eyes. A pity. She felt them on her as she placed a crisp linen napkin across her lap.

Intentionally Sydney crossed her legs, letting the fabric of the dress slide to expose as much thigh as possible. She wasn't entering this fight without weapons. And a butter knife wasn't one of them.

four

The waiter handed over the menus, then went into a lengthy explanation of the specials in reasonably good English. Lucas tuned him out. Using his powers, he scanned the area for the Half. He immediately picked up on two women seated across the patio. One sported bandages around her face. The older woman with her, wearing enormous sunglasses that obliterated most of her features, was covered from head to toe in a toweling robe. Both were Halfs.

The good news was that his ability to recognize other wizards still worked . . . as long as Sydney was close by. The bad news was he still didn't sense the Half, Escar, he'd come here to find. With his own powers cloaked, Lucas systematically checked out the individuals seated around them for any tells. He discovered one full wizard, male, and two more female Halfs. He didn't recognize any of them—understandable given that they'd all had some sort of plastic surgery—but with his special ocular tetrabyte image capture implant he sent them to Montana for identification against T-FLAC's database.

The waiter lingered. Lucas wanted to tell him to take a hike, but he settled into the comfortable wicker armchair and watched Sydney charm the guy. She was trying to understand the finer points of the foot volleyball game, and the waiter was only too happy to explain the intricacies to her.

While Lucas found the waiter's interest in Sydney mildly annoying, *he* found her just as charming as the older man did. He tried to resist the compulsion to stare at her, but that was like telling the ocean not to rush to shore. Sunlight tangled in her honey-streaked brown hair and glanced off the smooth curve of her cheek, golden in the sun. Everything about her was gilded. Her hair, her skin, and her personality.

She sported a half-inch-long scar under her chin, another, almost faded, on her left knee, yet another behind her left elbow. She didn't seem the type of woman to be accident prone. Her small imperfections intrigued him almost more than her beauty.

Animated, she punctuated each sentence with a wave of graceful hands and an easy laugh. He couldn't take his eyes off her. She was light to his darkness, drawing him to her like a moth to a flame. An aberration, of course. She was nothing more than a means to an end.

Lucas didn't want to be intrigued by her. Keeping his expression impassive, he observed her discreetly as she flirted with the waiter. He was good at impassivity. He'd practiced it all his life. His heart might pick up speed looking at the line of her slender throat, or the curve of her breasts beneath the strapless yellow dress, but his self-control was complete, and while he wouldn't admit his attraction to her to anyone, he rarely lied to himself.

Blithely unself-conscious when she mangled the language, Sydney would repeat the correction, then forge on, willing to try again.

Lucas felt a pang of . . . hunger. And it wasn't for food. Aware there was a nude beach south of the resort, he wondered if Sydney had been there during her stay. His agile mind stumbled on the image of a naked Sydney, frolicking on a beach, and he forced himself back to his assessment of his surroundings. Everyone at the restaurant was required to wear at least a swimsuit, or what passed for one here. As far as Lucas could tell no one was armed beneath their flimsy clothing and gauze bandages.

This was an unlikely location for terrorists. Unless they were here for plastic surgery to change their appearances. But even that was improbable. The spa, while exclusive, was extremely public. Although the facility boasted top-of-the-line surgeons, and utmost privacy if so desired, this was not the place to come if one didn't want to chance being caught in the flash of a paparazzo's camera. *Novos Começos* wasn't *that* private.

Pleased that EP had worked on Sydney, Lucas considered his next plan of action to keep her with him. He suspected blackmail wouldn't work with her. Seduction would. Whatever worked.

He didn't know how or why, but close proximity to her amped up his waning powers. It'd been several weeks since his powers had started short-circuiting like a worn-out toaster. This latest malfunction had bothered him enough to put in a call to Mason Knight. Unfortunately, his mentor had so many irons in the fire that he was hard to pin down. Lucas had had to make do with leaving a detailed message. *If anybody could fix this shit, it'd be Mason.*

Sydney laughed at something the waiter said, and Lucas wondered how the hell long it took to rattle off a short list of specials and take a damned drink order?

He had the knife with her fingerprints on it but that incentive was lost because he'd wiped that memory from her mind. That evidence was useless. He'd have to come up with something else to bind her to him, or allow some of the memory to surface. Just a hint would keep her off kilter enough to do the job. If she was the catalyst for his powers, he wanted her next to him every second until Mason could figure out the glitch in his abilities.

He'd positioned himself to her right, with a decent view of the medical buildings. He'd figured out that it wasn't the waiter prolonging the conversation, it was Sydney. Lucas gave the waiter a mental shove and shifted his seat a little closer to hers as soon as the man left. *His power strengthened as his leg brushed against hers.* He had no idea what it meant, or why it should happen with this particular woman. From as far back as Lucas could remember, his powers had always been consistent. They'd neither short-circuited as they'd been doing lately, nor had they intensified as they did when he was with Sydney. God, he needed to talk to Knight about this.

The second her new best friend had gone to turn in their order, she'd turned her entire attention to the game being played on the beach. Without addressing him, she watched four buff young guys, wearing nothing but skimpy Speedos, kick around a ball. He'd rather look at her.

Slouched in her chair with her gaze fixed toward the game, she gave the appearance of casual comfort. Until Lucas noticed how she fiddled with the butter knife on the table, and compulsively smoothed the edge of the tablecloth. In fact, even though her head was turned to take in the game, her eyes weren't following it. She was looking beyond the kids and out across the beach and ocean.

Something was wrong.

He ran through what would be her last memory between them; Sydney going shopping for clothes for him. She'd been chatty and eager to help. Nothing there to get her in a snit.

He wished he was adept at reading women's minds. Unfortunately, or fortunately, that wasn't one of his powers to call. And like most men confronted with a silent woman who clearly had something on her mind, he wasn't sure whether to dive right in and tackle it head-on, or come at it from the side.

Because he couldn't seem to resist, he reached out and gently stroked her sun-warmed cheek, which felt like warm satin. She deliberately shifted out of his reach, but not before he experienced a burn of electricity up his arm.

"How long did you say you've been here?"

Her jaw tightened, but she didn't turn and make eye contact. "Almost a month." She winced as the ball smacked one guy hard on the nose as he tried to volley it over the net using his head. The crowds watching went wild. "I leave in a few days. Right after Carnival."

He'd be long gone by then, leaving her sexually satisfied and unaware that he'd used her. Not a hard job, all things considered. Lucas picked up her hand fiddling with the knife. A strong jolt of energy shot through him like he'd grabbed the live end of a high voltage cable. He felt an immediate surge in his powers like a satellite image coming crisply into view. Stronger than anything he'd felt before, including a few lightning bolts he'd had tossed at him by a particularly talented wizard whose claim to fame was harnessing electrical charges from out of thin air.

Her head jerked around and he noticed the rapid throb of her pulse in her throat. She tried to pull away. He held on, lightly but firmly. "Static electricity." He ran his thumb over the back of her hand as she went from startled to skeptical.

She looked at him with wide-eyed incredulity. "*Outside?*" She tried to tug her hand away from his again, but he exerted just enough pressure to hold her there, his fingers on her jumping pulse at her wrist. She was agitated. Scared, but maintaining a thin veneer of sang-froid. "On a tiled floor?" Her tone had a decided bite to it.

"Apparently so." She had small, graceful hands with long slender fingers. No rings. Her long nails were painted the same fire-engine red as the polish on her toes. Just looking at her hands turned him on.

While Lucas processed the phenomenon of having someone else amp up his powers, she turned in her chair, leaning in close enough for him to smell her citrusy shampoo and the musk of her skin. Hell, it wasn't going to be any kind of problem to present themselves as lovers. If the heat they generated translated into the bedroom he'd be hard-pressed to even give a shit about tangos or his quarry.

He leaned in to run his lips across the line of her jaw . . . and jerked back in his seat when he realized that far from caressing his hand, she had his thumb twisted in a lock that hurt like hell.

"You'd better have a *damn* good explanation for what's going on, Lucas Fox." Sydney kept a firm grip, applying just enough pressure to give her more leverage, and him some pain. Of course he could get out of the hold, but the fact that she'd put him in it without him even realizing what she was doing was mildly disconcerting.

"A *damn* good explanation," she snapped, her voice low and annoyed as her eyes narrowed, glittering between long, thick lashes. "Disappearing bodies." With each word she exerted a little more pressure, twisting his thumb down with just enough strength to keep his hand immobile and focus his attention.

"Trains, winter in the tropics. Dead guys. Dead guys disappearing—Start anywhere, Fox. But I want logical answers."

The high, angry color in her cheeks was very flattering, but he bet she didn't want to hear *that* right then. *Fuck*. "You *remember*?"

She blinked. "Remember? I don't have Alzheimer's. Of *course* I remember. It only happened half an hour ago. Why are the soldiers looking for you? Why did you kill those two guys, how in God's name did you make me believe I was in some French train station, and why are you embroiling me in whatever mess you're involved in? If you really are some hot-shit spy, then you shouldn't involve a civilian. And especially not *me*."

He gritted his teeth against the pain in his hand and decided some of the truth wouldn't hurt, for now. "I'm a wizard, Sydney. T-FLAC has a paranormal division, and the reason I'm here is because I Trace Teleported; I was following a Half wizard named Mica Escar. He kidnapped two people in Sicily last week."

Her pupils flared. "Did I give you the impression at any time in our short acquaintance that I'm two bricks shy of a load? Tell me the truth, damn you. You owe me that m—"

"Look at your left hand."

Sydney didn't trust him to take her eyes off him completely, but she took a quick glance at her left hand. A large, very shiny rock glittered on her ring finger. It hadn't been there half a second before. Sunlight refracted bursts of rainbow colored prisms onto the table.

"Nice parlor trick. Any two-bit amateur magician could do it." She hoped. Because if this wasn't a run-of-the-mill sleight of hand, she was venturing into some pretty weird territory.

Her heart hammered with a combination of excitement and fear. She didn't want to be fascinated, but she couldn't help herself. She'd never met a man like Lucas Fox in her life. The strong physical attraction didn't surprise her. He was a great-looking guy. But his physical attributes were nothing compared to the unleashed energy that radiated from him. He was complicated. Interesting. He was a force to be reckoned with, and she better not forget that for a moment.

Worse. He was tempting enough for her to take a risk on trusting her judgment again. The last time she'd done that it had almost destroyed her.

Lucas unlocked his thumb from her grip with an ease none of her brothers had ever achieved and, to his credit, with barely a wince. He flexed his fingers experimentally. "Hand me my wallet out of your purse."

She hadn't brought a purse. Her key and phone were tucked in the side pocket of her dress. And of course Naked Man didn't *have* a wallet. "Stop stalling and cut to the chase," she snapped, struggling to pull the ring from her finger. It didn't budge. It didn't hurt, but it was on her finger tightly enough that she'd need soap and water to remove it. How had he gotten it on her finger in the first place? She'd had his hand in a death grip between both of hers the entire time.

She tugged some more.

"That won't come off until I take it off." Lucas picked up a clutch from beside the table and handed it to her. "Here's your purse. Inside it, you'll find my wallet."

"I don't have a freaking pur . . ."

The small bag was the same bright yellow as her dress and cork-wedged sandals. She'd never seen it before in her life. After a moment's hesitation, she opened the bag. Inside was her iPhone, which she'd returned to her pocket after Lucas had used it outside a few moments before. A lipstick she'd never seen before. Her door key.

And a man's black snakeskin wallet.

Despite the bright sunshine flooding the patio, she shivered. "How are you doing all these tricks?" Part of her wanted to jump up and run like hell. He wouldn't shoot her in such a crowded place, would he? But, God, the part of her that found mysteries and puzzles so intriguing, found the how and why of Lucas *riveting*.

He put his fingers inside and withdrew the wallet, then flipped it open on the table. He looked grim in his driver's license picture. It listed his date of birth and an address in New York. He flipped to a clear plastic section crowded with photographs.

There was a photograph of—Mary Mother of God—the two of *them*. Laughing up at each other, dressed for hiking, their hair disheveled by an unseen wind, their arms around each other. She even recognized the place. It was the Alpine Pass Route, crossing over the Hohtürli down to Kandersteg. She and Deb had gone on a Swiss hiking tour two years ago. The next photograph was of her huddled with Lucas on top of a red London bus, the Houses of Parliament behind them and fat snowflakes dotting their hair and shoulders as they stared lovingly into each other's eyes. She'd gone to London alone last year right after the shit had hit the fan.

A chill raced across her skin as she raised her eyes slowly from the doctored photos to Lucas's face. "How—"

"I can call things when I need them."

Call things? "Really? Then why didn't you *call* yourself some *pants* when you showed up at my place *naked*?"

"My powers are—" he looked a little uncomfortable. Sydney was just fine with that. "Malfunctioning."

"Malfunctioning?"

"Yeah. Short-circuiting."

"Didn't feel like a short circuit to me." She rubbed the goose bumps on her arms and almost got blinded by the sun glinting off the ring. "That felt like a surge of—whatever."

"Happens."

"Happens?"

"Yeah." His response sounded decidedly testy.

Liar, liar, pants on fire. Honestly, having eight brothers was a blessing in disguise. Sydney could spot a male liar at a hundred paces. No matter how good he thought he was at it. So. The power surge thing hadn't happened before. Not only that, he didn't like it.

She wondered how she could use that information.

Paulo arrived just then with their lunch. *Piri-piri* grilled prawns for her, and *empanadas* for Lucas. Both dishes looked and smelled divine. She waited until the waiter left. "What does being a wizard entail exactly?" she asked, humoring him.

"It entails not telling the general population so that they don't ask a lot of questions about something that's supposed to remain secret."

She clucked her tongue. "I could say I'm a wizard, then. No collaboration, no checking facts, no having trustworthy sources." Just saying those words made her sick to her stomach. She'd had all that and more after *Being Michaela* hit the *New York Times* bestseller list last year. And fact had turned to fiction in a sickening heartbeat.

"You'd have been born a wizard."

"Like you?"

He picked up his fork and stabbed it into his *empanada*. "Yeah. Like me."

"Like . . ." Sydney glanced around. She used her chin to point at two women, clearly taking advantage of the mother-daughter two-for-one special weekend. "Like those two?"

He gave her a surprised look. He brought the fork to his mouth. "Halfs."

He had an answer for everything. Even if the answers didn't make a whole hell of a lot of sense. She bit into a shrimp, chewed and swallowed before asking, "Halves of what?"

"*Halfs*. A Half isn't a full wizard. Those two are Halfs."

Oh, for—"You're kidding, right?" She'd heard some bizarre things in her life, but wizards outside of Harry Potter took the cake. But, damn, he was good. He said it with so much conviction one could almost believe him. Almost. It was a supercool fantasy, though; Sydney almost wished it were true. Talk about a bestseller. Wizards would trump a book about spies and terrorists.

"Eat. You don't want to be late for your doctor's appointment."

Sydney ate. Very little put her off her food. As she chewed, she thought of spies, and wizards, and bestsellers. Fiction or nonfiction. He was a story just waiting to be written.

And she was just the woman to do it.

"Stop pulling at the ring. It's not coming off," Lucas told her as they walked out of the restaurant, passing between the small crowd waiting for tables.

"Then make it smaller," Sydney told him with asperity, surprising him with the request. "I don't want to be mugged for a faux rock."

"That's six carats of flawless diamond, and you want it smaller?"

"If it really *was* six carats of flawless diamond, I'd be scared of losing it, and if it's glass it's bulky and getting in my way."

He changed it to a three-carat. "There. Better?"

She glanced at her hand. "Oh yeah. Much better. Let's walk." She set off ahead of him, leaving the ridiculously cheerful golf cart in front of the restaurant. She had an incredible ass, Lucas noticed not for the first time as Sydney forged full steam ahead. The cotton knit dress cupped her butt and flipped saucily around her thighs as she walked. Her legs were long, tanned, and taut with lean, well-conditioned muscles. This was not a woman who sat around much.

Honey-brown hair flowed halfway down her bare back, bouncy and shiny with golden highlights. Lucas wanted to thread his fingers through the heavy mass and feel its silk trail down his body.

As he walked he scanned the area for Half wizards and other undesirables. The manicured grounds were spectacular, lush with tropical vegetation and flowering plants he didn't recognize. High, dense hedges gave a sense of seclusion, although dozens of people walked on the paths, or sat on shaded benches angled for ocean views.

For all that they were dressed just like the guests, there were bodyguards, all packing, strategically positioned around the property.

He came alongside Sydney. "What do you know about the layout of the building?"

"Not a thing."

"Sydney—"

"News flash, superspy. That tone doesn't work with me."

"I know several things that *would.*"

She shot him a fulminating glance and picked up speed. "What's to say I won't go blabbing to every Tom, Dick, and *Half,* that you're a wizard?"

"I have the power of Empathic Perception," he told her evenly. "I'd erase the information from your mind before you could tell anyone."

She hesitated. "Empathic Perception? Mind wiping? God. You have a rich imagination. I'd love to explore your brain for a few hours. Ever think of writing a book?"

"No."

"Probably a good thing. I presume you realize that everyone seated around us back there heard and saw everything?"

"Veil of silence."

"Oh, please—"

"I used an invisible veil to seclude us."

"Oh, for—" She shook her head. "Do you have a freaking answer for *everything*?"

"I am what I am."

"A spy? A wizard? A killer?"

His lips twitched. "To name a few."

"I'll start alphabetizing them," she told him dryly. "The medical facility is that three-story building over there."

A dozen similar buildings were tucked discreetly between the exotic landscaping on the grounds of the resort. Tiled paths, wide enough to accommodate six people walking abreast, were lined by brilliant pink flowers. They perfumed the air and reminded Lucas of something he couldn't quite pinpoint. Something from further back than he cared to remember. A woman. Warmth. Comfort.

His jaw hardened, as he shoved the memory aside. Probably a television commercial he'd seen or an abstract sense of familiarity because the fragrance was so clean and sweet.

"And . . . ?" he prodded, gritting his teeth to stay in the present.

Sydney stopped dead in her tracks to glare at him. "What do you think would happen if I screamed blue bloody murder right now?"

"This." The smell of her mingled with the evocative fragrance of his suppressed memory. Lucas tunneled his fingers through her hair, drawing her face up, bringing her flush against his body. Body stiff, she lifted her head, her eyes shadowed by her long lashes. "Breathe," he urged softly.

Her lips parted and her eyes fluttered closed.

Yes.

She breathed his name. An invitation or a curse.

Lucas closed the gap, kissing her as if they were alone in a dark room instead of standing in a fairly crowded path in the bright sunshine. Her mouth tasted of spicy mango. He found himself starving as he swept his tongue against hers in a slow dance of sensation. She felt perfect in his arms as she clung to him, her soft breasts pressed against his chest, her body molding against his as she dueled with his invasion and gave as good as she got.

His mouth moved over hers, and he caught her lower lip, tasting the delicate interior with the tip of his tongue. Sydney moved against him, her hands coming up to comb through his hair as she nipped his upper lip between her teeth, then laved the sting with her tongue.

The simple act of kissing Sydney was stunningly arousing. He didn't want to stop. He hadn't planned on anything more than showing her that he was in control, but he hadn't expected the intensity of his response to her. And instead of showing her he was the one in control, he found that she'd turned the tables on him, and was kissing him back and demanding more.

She made an aggressive sound in the back of her throat as she arched her soft body full against him and slanted her mouth against his, changing the tempo and the rhythm of the kiss. The round firmness of her breasts pressed against his chest, and the smooth, bare length of her legs stroked between his. He felt the warm caress of her palm against his face as she brushed his cheek with her hand. Her touch was strangely more intimate than the kiss.

Her hips pressed hard against his swollen dick, and he almost groaned out loud at the sweet torment of it. Pure, unadulterated primitive male triumph roared through him at the evidence that she wanted him as much as he wanted her. Holding her firmly against him, he tangled his fingers in her hair and captured her moan on his tongue.

Lucas gradually became aware of where they stood, of the sun beating down on his head and shoulders, of the sweet evocative fragrance of the flowers at his feet, and the arousing scent of Sydney's skin, which seemed to have permeated his synapses like a drug.

Struggling for control, the taste of her still lingering on his lips, he gently put her away from him. Her eyes were closed, and he could see the flush of desire on her skin. "Easy, sweetheart. We're in a public place, remember?" He steadied her with his hands on her bare shoulders as she swayed, her eyes unfocused, her lips swollen.

Blinking, she focused on him, then looked away and muttered "Bastard," without inflection, wiping her mouth with the back of her hand. She started walking, continuing to talk as though there'd been no interruption. "The exam room, doctors' offices, and, I think, the labs are on the ground floor."

She wasn't unaffected, he noted with savage satisfaction. The pulse at the base of her throat beat hard and fast, and her cheeks were flushed.

"Do you have to walk so close? The path's plenty wide enough for us to stay six damn feet apart." She walked faster. "I think the two top floors are the ORs and the patient rooms. I had my surgery on two, and my room for the few days I was in recovery was on the same floor."

"What else?"

"I came here for a vacation and surgery. I wasn't sent in by the CIA to steal blueprints of the facility. You want to know what's where? Find out for yourself." She spun on her heel and started back the way they'd come.

Lucas snagged her upper arm, pulling her to a halt. "I need you t—"

She socked him in the chest. She was slender, but there

was power behind the small fist. She grabbed the front of his T-shirt and stood on her toes to meet him eye to eye. "Don't you *ever* grab me and kiss me like that again, you hear me, Fox? I don't give a damn if you're King Kong and Harry Potter combined. Nobody, but *nobody* kisses me unless I say so."

She released the twisted front of his shirt and stepped back. "I leave in six days. Don't even *think* about ruining the rest of my stay here by—" she waved a vague hand. "By doing whatever."

Hands in his pockets, he shot her an amused glance. "I can do anything I want. Six days, six weeks. I can keep you right where I need you, Miss McBride."

"I doubt you've needed anyone in your life. You don't need me to show you around, and I'm not touching any more damn murder weapons." She spun around and grabbed him, reached up she pressed her mouth to his, taking him by surprise. Her tongue flicked over the seam of his lips, and she slid her hands up around his neck. Slender fingers grabbed hold of a hank of his hair in back, although it was unnecessary for her to hold him still.

She explored his mouth leisurely, deliberately, pressing her sexy body against his. Blood rushed to his groin. Jesus . . .

She pulled away.

"What was that about?"

She smiled enigmatically. "Just leveling the playing field."

Any more level and he'd have her flat on her back right there in the open. He wanted to take her in the sunshine, Lucas thought, startled by the deep hunger he felt for this woman. He wanted to taste her smooth olive skin, to touch her naked breasts, to sink his fingers into her wet heat. "You have eleven minutes to make that appointment."

"You're not wearing a watch. Are you clairvoyant too?"

"Clock on the tower over there." He jerked his head to the left.

She shook her head and headed toward the medical building. Lucas tagged along. Low, rain forest–covered mountains made a spectacular backdrop to the building painted the same soft rose color as the resort. Spanish Colonial architecture, with thick walls, high arches, and fancy tile work all set in the magnificent gardens brilliant with color. "This way."

In the lobby a three-story rock waterfall splashed into a wide, shallow pool surrounded by lush local greenery. Plush, expensive, and discreet. Half a dozen people milled about, waiting for appointments, or coming from them. Sydney knew most of them by name, and reluctantly introduced him to several people as her boyfriend who'd just arrived from the States.

None of them missed the rock on her ring finger, and she had to make up a fake engagement that everyone seemed delighted to hear about. Kisses were exchanged, Lucas's hand was shaken until Sydney grabbed him and dragged him away so she could make her appointment.

Sydney gave her name to the receptionist and was told the doctor was ready to see her immediately. Lucas almost asked if he could come along. But since that was the suggestion of a thirteen-year-old boy, he refrained. Still, the idea of seeing, touching her breasts, real or enhanced, made his mouth water.

"How long do you think you'll be?"

"I'll meet you back here at two-thirty." She walked away briskly, not looking back.

Focus, Fox. He opened his Trace ability wide. Nothing. Not a fucking wizard or Half in range. He caught up to her in two strides and put a hand on Sydney's arm. "Hang on a sec."

Yes. There. A faint trace of Escar. It was barely discernible, but definitely there. Good. He'd get his answers sooner than later. He released her, and the faint Trace disappeared. "See you here in half an hour."

She gave him a curious look. "What was that about?"

"I like touching you. See ya." He strolled off.

Too many people around to teleport without notice. He meandered down a deserted hallway until he'd left the patients back in the lobby. Trace Teleporting, he shimmered, following coordinates of the Half's faint signal to the third floor.

Too late. The signal cut off within seconds of Lucas materializing in the stairwell. He paused, trying to pinpoint which direction to take next. There was a staircase going up another flight. Presumably to the roof. The Half had been close. There was no indication that he'd teleported, thereby mixing the signal, and the chances of Lucas and the Half teleporting at the exact same instant were minuscule.

Either the Half was dead, or he'd somehow cloaked his signal. Thing was, Halfs weren't good at cloaking, it wasn't in their inferior DNA. So if Escar *was* cloaked he had help.

The door was locked, and he looked through the window onto the wide corridor beyond.

Unlike the lobby, with its soft music and lush decor, the third floor was utilitarian, more in keeping with a serious medical facility. Half a dozen soldiers paced the length of the wide corridor. While there'd been security on the ground floor and outside the building, it had been discreet. There was nothing discreet about the AKS-47s they carried.

Interesting.

Even without his own weapons, getting one wasn't a problem, he could easily relieve a guard of his. Or better yet, stroll around among them without being seen until he could ascertain where Escar was. Not a problem. Invisible, he could go anywhere he damn well pleased . . .

Except, Goddamn it, he couldn't seem to dematerialize back to invisible.

He needed a boost.

He needed, he thought savagely, *Sydney.*

Five

Arms folded, Lucas was leaning negligently against the wall across from Dr. Forster's office when Sydney walked out after her appointment. If anyone seeing this man imagined that he was relaxed, they weren't looking hard enough. Casual pose notwithstanding, his green eyes glittered, and tension hardened his jaw. Fox was a rebel without a pause, and so hot she needed to fan herself.

Two women walking past him practically tripped over their own feet as they openly admired his chiseled physique. Their silly behavior irritated Sydney for reasons she couldn't explain. As soon as he saw her, he lithely pushed away from the wall.

She'd seen that same quietly lethal remoteness on her brother Ramon's face a few times when he hadn't realized she was in the room. Ramon had been an Army Ranger, but he'd kept the horrors he'd witnessed a closed secret. Even from family. Yes, she'd seen that expression enough times to make her take note now. She knew nothing about this man other than what he'd told her—which was mostly bullshit. But his expression was real. Very real.

"What's wrong?" she mouthed. A chill went through her as she hurried to meet him halfway across the wide terra-cotta-tiled hallway. Vaguely she noticed that the women glanced over their shoulders for a final look.

Lucas cupped her cheek in what she knew looked like a loverlike gesture, his fingers cool against her skin.

"Let's give them something to watch." He closed the gap and leaned in to leisurely kiss her. Nothing about the kiss was hurried, although the heat was instant and passion spiked as their mouths moved in perfect synchronicity.

His kisses made her feel deliciously jumpy inside. Even as angry as she was at him, Sydney loved the way he kissed. The taste of him was shockingly familiar. Rich and robust and straight to the point. Full throttle even though they stood in the middle of a very public place and had at least two pairs of avid eyes watching them.

Yet as heated as his kiss was, she sensed he was holding something back. She doubted Lucas ever gave a woman more than a superficial part of himself; still, what he was giving her was mind-boggling enough. She suspected he'd left a trail of battered female hearts in his wake, and that if he gave her everything he had she might melt into a puddle at his feet.

Sydney's heart pounded, and she closed her eyes as the original question went completely out of her mind. She heard a feminine sigh and wasn't sure if it was her own, or that of one of the women watching their PDA.

She knew his kisses were a means to an end, but she didn't give a damn. They were so good, so sinfully intensely erotic, she just didn't care. If his banked kisses made her hot and steamy, Sydney wondered what would happen if this was more than just a farce.

He lifted his head, and she was delighted to see that his eyes were just a little glazed as he looked down at her for a meaningful moment. "You're going to have to trust me."

Ha! Not in twenty lifetimes. Hot kisses or no hot kisses.

He was so damned cool. And complicated. Controlled fit him, too. "Hi, Kandy." She half waved at another of Dr. Forster's patients as they passed. Another boob job. "Looking good." If you wanted to be a porn star, which the other woman was. Sydney took several running steps to keep up with Lucas's long strides.

"The doctor gave me a clean bill of health. Thanks for asking." Which he hadn't, and that was probably a good thing. The doctor had cleared her for sex and other activities she hadn't indulged in in years. Like horseback riding. Parasailing . . . Oh, hell, who was she kidding?

When the doctor had okayed her for sex she'd had a few salacious thoughts about Lucas. She'd never been so instantly, insanely attracted to a man before in her life. She could hear the nuns from grammar school clucking and scolding even as she glanced at him from the corner of her eye.

But it was understandable. He held in his spy/wizard hands what was possibly her salvation to restoring her good name in the publishing world. Fact or fiction. She didn't care. She'd write the truth either way.

She was fascinated by him. By the way his mind worked. Liar or not, she wanted him. So which of them was the crazy one? She wanted to laugh at her insanity as the self-proclaimed wizard dragged her along behind him like a tugboat in a stormy sea. Being conflicted was new. She usually made up her mind quickly, and rarely regretted doing so.

She'd never had sex with a man who claimed to be a spy. Nor with one who sincerely believed he was a wizard.

She'd always enjoyed living on the edge.

She'd stop at the gift shop and buy a few boxes of condoms. It was always good for a girl to be prepared.

Lucas maneuvered her down a hallway where a dozen people milled about waiting for various appointments.

"Where are we going in such a freaking hurry?" she demanded, tugging on his hand as he turned into another hallway. A couple of people Sydney didn't recognize walked past them. They did the polite smile thing and passed each other in the wide hallway.

"There's a men's room down this way."

"I'm sure you don't need me to go in there—*here* with you, I'm not your mommy—Jeez Louise, Lucas. Slow down." Letting go of her hand, he started shoving open stall doors. After checking the last empty stall, he came back. "Escar is somewhere on one of the upper floors."

The bathroom was as beautifully decorated as every other room at the spa, but there was no mistaking that she was standing in the middle of the men's room. "Okay. So?" Any second now some guy was going to stroll in unzipping his pants. Sydney would prefer not being inside waiting for him when that happened.

"I mentioned my powers are short-circuiting?"

"Peeing isn't a superpower, Lucas. I'm sure you can do it all on your own. Why don't I wait outside for you?"

On the other hand, if she *didn't* buy the condoms, she told herself, she wouldn't be quite stupid enough to let her hormones dictate her activities. There was no way she'd take a chance with that. It was like the whole leg shaving before a date thing. If a woman shaved her legs, it influenced how the date would end.

No condoms, she told herself firmly. No leg shaving. The decision would probably save her thousands in therapy dollars down the road. Smart decision.

"Promise me no matter what you see or hear, you won't say one word until I tell you it's safe to do so."

She wasn't promising any such thing. "N—"

"Close your eyes."

She pretended to close her eyes, watching him

through the thick fringe of her lashes. What an interesting guy. Weird, but interesting. "Don't do anything disgusti—"

A dizzying blur of white made her squeeze her eyes shut for real. She felt Lucas's hand clamp over her mouth just as she was about to scream with surprise.

"Shh." His voice in her ear was so soft it was almost a thought. "Not a sound."

Sydney nodded and his hand moved away from her face. She blinked. They were standing at the end of a long unfamiliar corridor flanked by closed doors. Two uniformed soldiers walked right past them. Each man cradled a large, black gun and both looked fierce and deadly serious. Neither glanced their way, and she wondered why the hell not. She and Lucas had no authority to be in a restricted part of the facility.

Where exactly *were* they?

No matter where they were, she was pretty sure claiming they were lost wasn't going to cut it. She didn't recognize the surroundings, nor understand how Lucas had moved her from one place to another without physically guiding her. She glanced over her shoulder to ask him, but he wasn't there.

"They can't see you," Lucas breathed in her ear. Surprised that he'd gotten that close to her without her seeing him do so, she jumped. God, the man moved as quietly and stealthily as a jungle cat. His chest pressed against her back and he slid his cool fingers down her warm arm until he found her hand.

Sydney felt him touching her. She was aware of her muscles and tendons cooperating as he lifted her arm out in front of her. His warm breath against her cheek raised goose bumps on her skin.

"Look."

There was nothing to see.

She blinked. Her vision was just fine. She clearly saw

the dark blue speckled carpet on the floor, the gray walls, the soldiers. She saw the three nurses chatting quietly at the nurse's station halfway down on her left, and the elevator doors on her right. But up close and personal there was nothing to see.

Impossible.

Improbable.

She was invisible.

Sydney squeezed her eyes shut, counted to ten, then opened them. She still wasn't *there*.

She considered that, somehow, Lucas had drugged her while they were in the men's room. But she felt fine. Shouldn't she feel weird if she were drugged? She touched her fingers tentatively to her arm. She *was* there. But—not.

"I'll explain later." He slid his fingers between hers. His palm was large and cool against her much smaller, quite sweaty hand. "Let's check this first room. The guards can't see you, but they'll hear you. And trust me, those guns shoot real bullets."

Was his voice in her head? Some form of telepathy?

Either this was an elaborate hoax, some form of hypnosis for reasons she couldn't fathom, or the government had come up with some amazing developments they'd kept secret from the public.

Either way, Sydney's heart slammed hard against her chest as she considered her options. She could let out the scream hovering just under her rib cage. She could run like hell. Or she could keep her mouth shut and see what else Lucas had up his sleeve.

She tightened her fingers in his.

The brilliant white light slammed into her again, and when she opened her eyes they were in a hospital room. Excitement rushed through her, making her dizzy. Please, God, let this be the real deal.

The first time Lucas Fox became invisible . . . Oh yeah. A great first line to the new book she was going to write. Hell, why not a movie . . . ?

She allowed herself to be tugged toward the bed where a man lay with his eyes closed. His skin was sunken and a pasty yellow. He could be fifty or eighty. His frail body barely made a bump under the smooth, light blue blanket. The side rails were up, and machinery around him regularly and rhythmically beeped and flashed.

Clearly he hadn't come in for plastic surgery. Vanity was one thing, but this guy was really sick. Why was he here? He looked vaguely familiar, though why he should, Sydney had no idea. She moved forward, bumping into Lucas in the process. "I know him," she whispered as quietly as she could. "I think." She tried to put the man's face in context, but couldn't connect him to anyone or anything.

"Who is he?"

Sydney shrugged, then realized Lucas couldn't see her. Or could he? She brushed a hand up his bare arm. As always, his skin felt cool and hard under her fingers as she brailled her way over his biceps, across the short sleeve of his T-shirt, across his broad shoulder, and up his throat to find his ear. She leaned in close. "Can you see me?"

"No. Who is he?"

She closed her eyes. Beneath her fingers she felt the pulse at Lucas's throat. It felt nice and steady. Calm. Fearless. She left her hand there while she thought about where she knew the guy from. Her brothers had a million friends, so did her dad . . . She got a picture of the guy in a cowboy hat. A horse—

"Oh, my God," she whispered excitedly. "Lucas, he's James Pritchard."

"The actor?"

Sydney nodded against his arm.

"Give me a minute to look around." The second he stepped away from her Sydney didn't feel nearly as brave and confident as she had with his solid presence beside her. Even not being able to see him, the feel of his large body had grounded her.

She didn't know what any of the machines were, but she vaguely remembered reading Pritchard had gone somewhere to dry out. The actor had played a drunken doctor on a long-running cowboy series on cable, and apparently his acting had blurred with his real life. Sydney tried to remember if she'd read anything else in the tabloids while standing in the grocery checkout line.

"Let's get out of here." Lucas took her hand. This time she wasn't surprised by his unexpected touch.

With a now-familiar flash of light, she found herself, a little unsteady on her feet, alone on the landing of a stairwell.

Wow. This mode of transportation was pretty damn cool. Could they travel to Paris for dinner and be back in Rio for a midnight snack? Could they zap to Cairo, see the pyramids, then zap to see the Great Wall of China in the same day?

"Sure it was the actor?" Lucas materialized beside her. He was carrying a gun, which he hadn't had before.

It was weird. She should have been scared by the gun, or at the very least concerned. Instead she felt safer, knowing he was armed and even sexier in that dangerous kind of way. She wanted to kiss him. Hard. She resisted. Barely.

"Well, I don't know the man personally. But yeah. I'm pretty sure that's him. Last I read he'd gone to rehab somewhere in Arizona. Where did you get that gun?"

He was checking it, but glanced up. "Lifted a soldier's

sidearm. He won't miss it for a while. Why would you remember some actor's drinking history?"

She shrugged, getting a kick out of Lucas's reaction to the level of the strapless dress as it slid down a bit on her new breasts. He liked them a lot. She hid her smile. Her new boobs were growing on her too. They did a nice job holding up the thin stretchy cotton fabric, and she enjoyed the heat in Lucas's pale green eyes when he looked at her.

"Tabloids are my guilty pleasure," Sydney confessed. He didn't seem concerned that the guys on the other side of the door might see them. And if he wasn't worried, she wasn't going to be either.

"The bonus is that my brother Sergio watched *Guns and Lace* every Thursday night for ten years. We had a bet about what was in that bottle Doc swigged from in every episode. I said whiskey, Serg swore ice tea. Apparently I was right. As far as I know Pritchard's only been in a handful of walk-on roles in the last five years. The tabloids claim he's an alcoholic." Sydney leaned against the opposite wall. "I'm guessing he's beyond rehab."

"I'd take a wild guess he's here for a liver transplant."

"Even though he's an alcoholic? Geez, money buys anything."

"I suspect this is a private donation. He'd have to have been on the donor list for some time. Looks like he's in end-stage renal failure."

The actor had looked close to death. "But why would he come to Brazil? I get that there are surgeons at *Novos Começos,* but they do face-lifts and tummy tucks. Different skills than transplant surgeons," she whispered.

"We have to go back inside, check the charts at the nurse's station, see who else is a patient. Are you having any side effects to teleporting? Nausea? Dizziness?"

God, that question sounded cool, almost rational. Sydney shook her head. "No. I feel great." And she did.

Exhilaration surged through her. Her blood pumped faster as her mind went a mile a minute. She couldn't wait to get to her computer to start Lucas's boo—

White light and *zap*! They were back inside, standing beside the nurse's station. A heads-up would've been nice. Three nurses stood talking behind the curved teak counter.

"—schedule for the first surgery tomorrow." The exotic-looking woman was in her thirties, had skin the color of bitter chocolate, gorgeously high cheekbones, and seemed to be in charge. She turned to the short blonde to her right. "See if Doctor Howard can do Mrs. Klugg's procedure. Dr. Fennermen wants to do the heart."

The third woman, local by the sound of her accent, was middle-aged, plump, and softly spoken. "I thought the lung donor wasn't due to arrive until Thursday?"

"She was brought in half an hour ago," the first woman told her. "She's in seventeen. They'll harvest just before surgery."

"How many did they get from—"

Lucas tugged at Sydney's hand and she missed the rest of the conversation. Organ transplants. Holy shit, what next?

For the following ten minutes she got used to the bright flashes of light every time Lucas moved them from room to room. Once she knew why the patients were there, she started to put names to some of the faces she saw.

There were several famous people whom Sydney immediately recognized. All the patients on the third floor were there for some sort of organ transplant, according to the charts hanging on the hooks at the ends of their beds. The rest of the patients she didn't recognize, but she bet they all had lots and lots of money.

Sydney hung back by the door as Lucas did whatever he was doing each time they entered a room. Seeing the sick and dying, recognizing some of the patients, was starting to wear on her. Lucas wanted to check everything out, but that didn't mean she had to get up close and personal. Besides, Lucas moved as soundlessly as a ghost. She wore backless sandals, and while slipping them off would be quieter, she was damned if she'd go barefoot in a germy hospital.

When her mother had fought her protracted battle with lupus, the numerous trips to visit her in intensive care had given Sydney a strong aversion to hospitals. She'd been eleven years old when her mom had died, and even now the strong scent of medicine and hospital smells made her slightly queasy.

Used to Lucas touching her when she couldn't see him, she curled her fingers between his when he suddenly tightened his grip. "What's wrong?" He did that whisper thing that sounded as though he were inside her head.

"Nothing," she lied. Despite the sick feeling in her stomach and heart, she wasn't going to miss this experience for all the tea in China. Knowing she couldn't embarrass herself, or worse, give their presence away, she'd tough out the nausea.

Bullshit. She was flagging, Lucas could feel it. He was fucking out of his mind for dragging her with him, he thought, irritated as he shimmered to the next room. The invisibility and teleporting were probably making her nauseated. That's what Knight had always told him could happen. Of course, he had no way of knowing since he'd never teleported anyone he didn't plan to kill soon after transporting them from one location to another.

The fact that he needed her with him now pissed him

off. He'd never needed anyone in his adult life, and he hated like hell dragging a woman into T-FLAC business. More, he hated not understanding the necessity of keeping her close to keep his powers at full capacity.

Lucas didn't relish the idea of placing a civilian—especially *this* civilian—in harm's way. He had to damn well get his powers back to being fully operational PDQ, Goddamn it. The insane notion that he'd have to drag Sydney with him to every op for the rest of his goddamned life was fucking lunacy. He made a mental note to give Mason another call. See if he could figure out what the hell was happening to drain his powers like this.

But for now he needed Sydney. The how and why she was able to amp his powers had to wait until he talked with Knight. Until then he'd do whatever he had to, to do his job.

He'd discovered five prospective heart transplant patients, two kidney recipients, the Mrs. Klugg the nurses had mentioned was there to get a lung, and three patients waiting on livers. That was a hell of a lot of desperate, end-stage patients hanging around a hospital in the slim hope of getting a compatible organ.

Lucas suspected that for various reasons none of these people would be eligible if placed on a regular waiting list. The thing they had in common was . . . what?

Wealth? A given.

They were all over fifty, some twenty to thirty years older. Hardly prime candidates for the limited number of organs available through legal channels, even including the black markets in India, Pakistan, and a few other developing nations willing to turn a blind eye to the practice of selling body parts.

The actor was an alcoholic. Hard living. Hard drinking. The Klugg woman, according to Miss I-Love-the-

Tabloids, was some sort of society maven in LA. She hadn't come to *Novos Começos* for the medi-spa's claim to fame, a face-lift. She'd come to receive a new lung.

As he and Sydney entered the last patient room, Lucas tried to connect the dots. What was the common denominator?

The elderly woman, whose eyes were bandaged, stirred. She was as tanned and wrinkled as a walnut. Her scrawny arms and fingers were weighed down with chunky, diamond-encrusted gold jewelry. "What do you people want now?" she snapped. "Can't a woman take a nap in this place, for Christ's sake?"

She couldn't see, but the woman had the hearing of a bat. Lucas snagged her chart. Cornea transplant. "Sorry to disturb you, Mrs. Cohen, I'm Mike Johansson from the lab. I thought this was Mrs. Klugg's room."

"Do I look like that fat old wheezing bitch? Get out, you idiot."

Charming.

"Yes, ma'am. Have a nice day."

"Hey. Wait a minute. Since you're here, scratch my left foot." She stuck the gnarly appendage out from under the covers. "Near my big toe. Hurry the hell up, I don't have all day." The overly tanned, veined foot wiggled impatiently. "The itch is making me craz—"

Lucas grabbed Sydney's hand and shimmered to the next room. The room was empty, and he materialized.

Sydney flopped down on the edge of the neatly made bed flushed, wired from nerves. She still smelled like gardenias, like summertime, and he wanted to tumble her back onto the mattress and kiss her breathless. He resisted.

Her eyes were bright with mirth as she sat on the side of the stripped bed. "Mike Johansson? Man, you're an accomplished liar. And *quick.*"

"I—" He strode over to her and said urgently, "Give

me your hand." She did so without question. If Lucas had any doubts that her touch amped his powers he was now completely convinced as a slide show of images zipped through his brain.

Her fingers tightened in his. "What's happening?" she whispered.

"Wizards. Three of them. Heading this way."

Six

"Harvesting one of our own is a mistake," Dr. Lewis Bergen told the other two wizards as they wheeled Mica Escar into the ER on the third floor. "Word gets out about this and we'll cut off our source of donors for good."

"*Word?*" Dr. Cummings repeated, amused. "Think there's a Half grapevine with current updates? Jesus, Bergen, who the hell's gonna know we used this guy for parts? Who the fuck would *care*? Halfs are a dime a dozen."

"Good point."

Escar was already unconscious and had no say in the matter. He'd claimed someone had Trace Teleported behind him when he'd arrived. No unknown wizard's trace had been picked up in the hours since his arrival.

Paranoia? Bergen wondered. Still, on the off chance that Escar had been right and someone *had* Trace Teleported after him, killing the young Half was expedient. Someone might have followed him to the medi-spa, but that was as far as that Trace would take them. It was the end of the road.

Fair warning that they had to keep an eye out for a rogue wizard. It would be impossible to cloak him- or herself indefinitely. The wizard would be found, cross-matched, and used for spare parts, just like Escar.

"He didn't give us a choice, did he, the stupid fuck? He was compromised. Shouldn't have allowed himself to be followed," Dr. Seth Cummings said offhandedly, standing aside as orderlies maneuvered the gurney into position beside the operating table in the center of the room. At sixty-something, Cummings had a Trump comb-over, was a good fifty pounds overweight, completely amoral, and the best transplant surgeon, other than himself, that Bergen had ever encountered.

The OR was state of the art. Bergen's baby. He was damn proud of all the bells and whistles that had been added at his say-so over the years by a boss he'd never met. Whatever he asked for was produced. And why not? Bergen's surgical team was the best in the world, bar none. He'd solicited and trained most of them. Bribed those reluctant to leave some Hollywood practice where they'd earned maybe ten percent of what they made now.

Black-market organ transplants was a lucrative business.

Mica Escar's body was worth eleven million dollars to them. Eleven million reasons to get over the faint niggle of conscience Bergen was experiencing. He shrugged off the thought like a snake shed its skin. Business was business.

"He's young, healthy, and type O positive. We fill a week's worth of orders from him. We don't have to waste time doing the cardiopulmonary bypass to preserve the organs, since all the patients are in residence now."

"Bone marrow is a decent match for that leukemia patient. We've hit a bonanza," Nia Ledgister said in her deceptively gentle, rolling Jamaican accent. She didn't have a spark of human kindness in her. No softness, no compassion, not a single damn feminine trait, despite her exotic beauty and *Playboy* centerfold body. She was a soulless killing machine.

Cummings and Ledgister transferred Escar's limp

body onto the table like a bag of laundry. He was unconscious, thanks to a skillfully wielded hypodermic by Nia three hours ago. Unconscious, but still alive. As Nia ran the central venous catheter into a vein in Escar's groin, he groaned but didn't wake up. Good.

Because what was to follow was the nightmare of all nightmares, at least for the donor. The donor was paralyzed, but fully aware, and capable of feeling pain. No matter how many times he'd participated in these procedures, Bergen felt a twinge of guilt as he wondered when the Hippocratic oath had stopped meaning anything to him.

There was no need as far as he was concerned *not* to anesthetize the donor. It was Nia's sick game to keep the patient aware and immobile. Nia's game, but they all played it. Which made them no better than she was.

His commitment to his oath had faded when he'd been offered a percentage of the multimillion-dollar organ transplant industry thriving behind closed doors at the medi-spa fifteen years ago. *Novos Começos* was a convenient cover, and lucrative in its own right.

They were doing the patients an invaluable service, Bergen thought, pushing aside the ever-increasing pang of conscience he'd been having lately. Normal transplant candidates were forced to endure longer waiting times for an organ, many of them dying or becoming too ill to be considered viable candidates under the legal guidelines.

Fuck legal guidelines. Here, for the right price, any organ could be purchased. No questions asked. Here, people with money—and lots of it—were raced to the front of the line. They didn't ask where their new heart/kidney/cornea came from, nor did they care.

Harvesting, itself, would take less than an hour with four teams working simultaneously. The last part of the harvest, untethering the heart from the pulmonary veins and aorta after all the other organs were removed could all be done fast. As each organ was removed it would be rushed to a nearby OR filled with other specialists in the field, to be given to patients needing lifesaving new organs. It was the transplant into the new host that would take up to twelve hours in surgery.

Ka-chiiiing.

Nurse Ledgister motioned for the young blond surgical nurse to position the half dozen instrument trays closer to the table where they'd be needed. "All set, doctors," she told the two men with brisk efficiency. "The other teams are on standby."

Anyone thinking Nia Ledgister was merely the head nurse was underestimating the woman's power at *Novos Começos*'s secret, exclusive, and multimillion-dollar enterprise on the third floor. First, she was a full and powerful wizard. Second, she had a finger on every pulse—literally—on the third floor.

Lewis Bergen wondered, not for the first time, if Ledgister had access to the building behind this one, the building that was so hush-hush, so secret that no one knew what the fuck went on in there. No one had ever been seen coming or going, yet his own curiosity had taken him over there dozens of times. The place was locked down with a wizard spell harder to crack than Fort Knox. Nia might know. Hell, she knew everything else around here. She knew who the donors were and where they'd been found, she knew how the Halfs picked up their victims, and she made sure they were well paid for the service. The Halfs, that was.

The organs were harvested from the victims, their carcasses immediately disposed of using alkaline hydrolysis. A lye bath, three-hundred-degree heat, and sixty pounds of pressure per square inch, much like a pressure cooker, destroyed what was left of the bodies. The process left not a scintilla of evidence that they'd ever been there. All that was left was a brown, syrupy liquid that was deposited in large stainless steel tanks in another building.

The Halfs whose job it was to produce the right blood type for harvesting chose their victims from colleges and high schools around the world. Young, healthy adults. No smokers or drug users. No STDs. Preferably little or no family to be concerned with their disappearance. Once their donor had been selected, it was a simple matter to teleport them from wherever they were in the world to here, Brazil. All in a matter of minutes.

It was, of course, getting a bit more difficult to find such clean-living young adults. But if one knew where to look—and the Half on the operating table had known—there were body parts available for every occasion. Bergen frowned.

Escar had been excellent at procuring donors and had been doing so for more than two years. Killing him like this, while not posing an ethical or moral dilemma for Bergen, smacked of cutting off their noses. He didn't like killing the goose that had brought in so many golden eggs. He liked the donors to be just that. Donors. An impersonal commodity. He'd once had a beer with Escar.

"Eleven hearts. Three kidneys, twelve livers, seventeen corneas, and eight pancreata for islets isolation," Ledgister read off a sheet. She didn't need a piece of paper to tell her. Everything was kept in that beautiful head of hers. She had a mind like a computer, and the heart of one, too.

She glanced up, frowning over her mask as doctors Howard and Fennermen, followed by their respective teams, came into the OR like a parade. "Take his left hand—I've arranged for that patient to be teleported in immediately. He's in India. He'll be ready when we are." She tapped the headset that was always on her ear, waited a few seconds, then said into the mic, "Still need a penis? Would I be calling if I didn't? Now. Five million. No, Doctor Haryana, it is not. How many guys do you think need a penis *today*? Take it or—fine. I'll have you and your patient picked up as soon as the fee is deposited—Then hurry and pay, Doctor. We're harvesting the organ now."

Ledgister's smile was sharklike. "Take the penis," she told the team, glancing up as the two surgical teams bustled about getting ready to proceed. "You're late, gentlemen, please take your positions."

She turned back to Cummings. "We have confirmation for two long bones for a Mr. O'Shea who'll be here later tonight. Also a larynx. All typed and cross-matched to Escar. Take everything."

She stepped back, talking into her mic. "Let me know when Haryana's five mil is deposited. Who? Oh, yes. Good. Arrange transportation for the lung, and for the penis when the money's cleared."

Bergen tuned Ledgister out. She was always wheeling and dealing. They'd done this hundreds of times. He tied his mask and approached the table. Time was money. They had a grocery list of organs needed immediately, and paying patients who could afford any organ they wanted. "Let's get to work, then." Bergen motioned his surgical team to gather at the foot of the table. He rotated his shoulders like a prizefighter getting ready to go into the ring. There was no need to ask if everything was in order to proceed. Nia ran things like a drill sergeant, leaving nothing to chance. And as was the case with Escar, she left no donor organ or body part unused. If they had it, she found a recipient willing to pay the steep price to have the transplant.

"Fifty people are ready, Doctor," she said briskly. She motioned to the technician to start hooking Escar up to cardiopulmonary bypass, a ventilator to keep him breathing and a bypass to maintain blood flow to his heart and other organs, which would keep his heart beating and his lungs inflated and viable while they cut into him for the next hour. They'd take the skin and corneas last since they had the longest post-death shelf life.

Another nurse gave the donor a shot of heparin to prevent his blood from clotting as they worked, and Ledgister ran a critical eye over each team as they fell to work in an almost choreographed dance around Escar's body. By the time they finished harvesting, there'd be little of the Half wizard left.

Fennermen performed a median sternotomy to expose the mediastinum. After he'd made the long incision in Escar's chest, his surgical nurse handed him the rib spreader and he cracked open the patient's rib cage to get to the lungs and heart. This was no civilized laparoscopic nephrectomy. The *donor* wasn't paying upward of a million for a fresh new organ. He was expendable. Just a product on the shelf at the grocery store where a commodity could be obtained for resale. Nothing more.

Dr. Fennermen was already prying the broken ribs away from the cavity, while his support team crowded in to assist him. While he worked, Dr. Howard positioned himself at the head of the table and removed hair follicles, after which he'd remove both corneas, which would go to an elderly and faded movie star whose face was already so tight one could bounce a penny off her cheekbones. Then he'd start the laborious and meticulous removal of the face for an autograft replant.

"Lungs are in excellent shape. Ditto the heart. Healthy guy. Too bad he had to die so young." Cummings laughed at his own joke. He said it over practically every donor. Bergen wondered why, this time, it pissed him off so much.

* * *

"Why didn't those guards or any of the wizards sense us?" Sydney asked, starting the sentence in a whisper and finishing in a normal tone when she realized they were back in her bungalow. God. She could get used to this mode of transportation. It was so darn cool.

Even though there wasn't any blood to be seen, Sydney walked around the spot where the two bodies had been only hours earlier. It felt like a lifetime ago.

Lucas was already across the room checking out several black bags piled in the corner that hadn't been there when they'd left. Although maybe they *had* been, Sydney thought, as he sank to his knees and removed a monstrous black gun from one of the packs. Hard to remember anything other than the two dead guys waiting for her when she'd returned from shopping.

"I had us cloaked," he told her absently, spreading a stained blue cloth from one of the bags on the floor in front of him. The material smelled strongly of gun oil, a smell familiar to Sydney because all her brothers had some sort of gun at one point or other in their lives. They'd taken turns teaching her to shoot so that she didn't end up accidentally shooting herself.

She sat on the foot of the bed to watch him, distractedly removing her left hoop earring, then reached for the right. It wasn't there. Her heart literally stopped, then immediately started racing. She moistened her lips. The earring must've fallen off somewhere. "Was it cloaked like the veil?" Maybe it was in the golf cart, which was still parked up near the main building. Or had it come off when Lucas had kissed her on the path?

Or it was on the third floor where she shouldn't have been and wasn't seen? She wiped her damp palms on the bedspread on either side of her. She'd been invisible. Did that mean the earring, if that's where it had fallen off, would still be invisible?

Lucas had by this time removed several other guns

and had them all lined up in front of him. He shot her a glance. "Something like."

"How did your mother get you all this stuff here so fa . . . That wasn't your mother, was it?"

He fieldstripped a handgun in seconds, checked all the parts, and reassembled it before going on to the next. "Teleported. I don't have one."

Sydney frowned, detoured for a moment by his flat statement. "Don't have one what? A mother?"

"Right."

"What about your father? Brothers? Sisters?" The woman on the phone had said something about sending his brothers . . .

"No."

"Wait a minute. You said—"

"I lied."

"How wonderfully honest of you to admit you lied," Sydney said dryly. "Anything else you've lied about?"

"Probably."

Hmm. "So, no brother? Uncles? Aunts? Nieces? Nephews?"

"No."

"That's terrible! Is that the case with all wizards? Or all spies? You don't have families?"

"Of course wizards have families, so do operatives. We're not hatched. But in my case I was raised in the foster care system. I had a—mentor rather than a parent. Good guy. I was lucky."

Having no family at all—and a foster father that wasn't a father but a "mentor"—sounded pretty damn sad to Sydney. "As much as my family drives me insane sometimes, I can't imagine life without them."

He shrugged and continued to work over his weapons. "Can't miss what I never had. They died when I was too young to remember them. Hit by lightning on a hiking trip."

"Struck by lightning? *Both* of them?" It sounded like something out of a Gothic novel. Sydney's heart squeezed in empathy. "Oh, Lucas."

He glanced up. "Jesus, you're not going to *cry*, are you?"

"Of course not," she said indignantly. "I rarely cry. But you might when I tell you I lost an earring somewhere."

"Let me guess. Third floor."

"Honestly, I don't know. I just noticed it was missing a few minutes ago. What if someone finds it where it shouldn't be? God, I'm so sorry, Lucas. What if—"

He held out his hand. "This it?" The gold hoop glittered on his palm.

Her jaw dropped. "Holy—how'd you *do* that?"

He lightly tossed it to her and Sydney caught it midair. "I told you, I have the power to call things."

"That's a handy talent." She put the earring beside her on the bed. "What kind of gun is that?" she asked, pointing, determined to get all her facts right.

She was fascinated by his hands, strong and sure as he checked each weapon, his attention focused. She suspected his hands were as much a weapon as the guns in front of him.

"This one here? 9mm Sig Sauer. This, a Glock, this baby goes on my ankle, I need to get some long pants. This big boy is a modified MP5A, submachine gun." He hefted the gun to his shoulder, testing—what? The balance? The feel of it? Apparently satisfied, he started fieldstripping it, checking all its parts before reassembling it and lowering it back into line on the floor. His movements were fluid and amazingly quick.

"You've done this before," she murmured.

One of the bags started to vibrate, sounding like a bee in the room. Lucas reached in, grabbed a phone of some sort, and brought it to his ear. "You psychic?" he asked the person on the other end, tucking the small phone between his ear and shoulder as he took out more clothes and several knives in holsters.

"Just walked in. Not yet, but I *did* run across three fulls where they shouldn't have be—What was that?" His lips tightened as he listened. "London the target or something out of the city limits? Shit—Yeah. Get back to me." He snapped the phone shut. "Let's see what the rest of the world is saying while we wait."

Sydney knew he wasn't talking to her. He didn't appear to be aware that there was anyone else in the room. Yanking off the towel she had thrown over the flat-screen TV, he picked up the remote beside the bed, turning on the set.

She had no idea what Lucas was alluding to, but she pulled her legs under her tailor-fashion on the foot of the bed as a commercial for room freshener came on. "CNN is channel twelve," she offered, noting absently that the clock on the top left-hand corner of the picture was now set to 00:00. She made a mental note to call maintenance again to have them look at it as Lucas switched the channel.

Crowds of screaming, crying people showed behind the reporter as he talked somberly into the camera. "—is now closed until authorities can ascertain what the substance was. What police believe to be a terrorist attack at the intercity Crystal Palace station southeast of London has proved deadly. Thirty-nine people are confirmed dead with the numbers expected to rise. Hundreds more, injured in the blast, have been taken to hospital. The cause of the blast is not yet known."

The camera panned the area around the reporter, bringing the destruction on-screen. Sydney made a soft sound.

"The London Development Agency has been hard at work bringing the park back to its former glory. This underground explosion will most certainly put paid to their plans for the foreseeable future."

The park was the least of their problems, Sydney thought as cameras tracked more of the massive damage, including a red double-decker bus that now looked as if it had been peeled by the jaws of life. Smoke still billowed off the wreckage. Crowds of people, some screaming in agony, others numbly silent, stared at the enormous hole in the ground. Debris and dark red blood littered the ground behind the area cordoned off by the police. A medevac tent had already been constructed off to one side and ambulances came and went in rainy red blurs of sound and light.

"Authorities ask that anyone with any information contact the Anti-Terrorist Hotline on 0800 789 321."

The screen filled completely with the activity at the scene for several sickening minutes before the reporter came back on-screen. "This is a coordinated terrorist attack. The deputy director of the Transnational Threats Initiative at the Center for Strategic and International Studies informed us just minutes ago. Mr. Herrol is also part of Multilateral Terrorism Intelligence Sharing Project and the Private Sector Advisory Group. His work focuses on information sharing as well as intelligence, operations, and terrorist groups. A world authority on the matter of terrorism, Herrol has authored two books on the psychology of terrorism and extreme viole—"

Lucas turned the TV off and punched a short number into the phone in his hand. "Get someone else to cover the situation in Rio. I want the London op."

Oh, no, no, no, Sydney thought, feeling a surge of panic as she saw the opportunity for her life to rise like the phoenix from the ashes of her demolished career slip between her fingers like water. She crossed the fingers of both hands in her lap, and said a little prayer to St. Francis de Sales, the patron saint of writers. She'd save St.

Jude, the patron saint of lost causes, for the next emergency. With Lucas around there was sure to be one.

"Dammit, Saul . . . ." Lucas jerked open the wood blinds with a clatter. Brilliant late afternoon sunlight flooded the room, making Sydney squint.

"Yeah. Yeah. Got it. Just keep me apprised—What are they thinking? Anthrax? Or one of the new—Yeah. Yeah."

Anthrax? New—what? Sydney leaned forward. She couldn't hear what the person he was talking to was saying, but Lucas did not look happy. Oh God. Could the situation get any more complicated and filled with any more nail-biting suspense? The book was going to be a *mega*hit. Sydney couldn't wait to get started.

"What the fuck *kind* of bacteria?" Lucas demanded, then frowned as he listened for a minute. "Good. Appreciate it, thanks, Saul. Yeah, will do."

Lucas glanced over at Sydney. She was still sitting cross-legged on the foot of the bed, watching him wide-eyed. "Holy crap. You really are a spy."

He rose to go back to unpacking the shit Saul had teleported. Clothes, passport, cash, credit cards, ordnance and the standard first-aid kit. "Thought I was kidding?"

Was the explosion in the London Underground the point, he wondered, or was there something more involved? Saul's initial intel had authorities suspecting a chemical attack. They'd ruled out both anthrax and SARS. This was something worse. Damn. He wanted to be there in the thick of things.

To make matters worse, he'd lost track of Escar. No way could the Half mask his trail on his own. He'd had help. Full wizard help. For all Lucas knew, the guy had managed to split to parts unknown, leaving him in Brazil without an op. Shit.

"You can't leave in the middle of whatever's happening *here,* Lucas." Sydney threw her long legs over the end of the bed and stood. "What about the guy you followed? You haven't found him yet."

"He's probably long gone by now."

"You don't believe that, otherwise you wouldn't still be here. Not to mention that you should look into all those patients on the third floor. That whole situation looked highly suspicious to me."

Lucas bit back a smile as he walked toward her. "Is that so?"

"You know so." Her eyes fluttered shut as he curved his hand around the back of her neck and drew her closer. Touching her was like completing an electrical circuit. It shocked his heart into beating faster, and made his breath catch. As did Sydney's.

The skin on the back of her neck was delicate and warm, and the weight of her hair fell like a silk blanket across his forearm. "You wanna be my control, sweetheart?"

"What's a control?" she murmured, bending her head to give him better access. She shuddered as he skimmed his lips up her neck and tasted the shell of her ear.

"The person who tells the operative what to do and when to do it."

"Yes. I want to be your control."

Seven

Lucas smiled and did a quick push to test the protective spell he'd placed around the bungalow. Solid.

Good.

London was being monitored; Saul would fill him in when he had updates. The situation up at the medical building needed further investigation, but not necessarily right this second. He backed Sydney toward the bed. "You like to be the boss, do you?"

"I excel at it," she told him modestly. Sydney's lips parted and the heat between them flared. "Put yourself in my capable hands." Her eyes, bright with amusement and feverish with need, locked with his. "Trust me."

They toppled over onto the mattress with a light bounce. Somehow Sydney twisted, getting him on his back. Straddling him, she threaded her fingers through his, carrying his hands up over his head. Tiger's eyes searched his face. "I want you—*this*—more than I've ever wanted anything in my life. How can that be when I don't even know you?" She lowered her head to graze her lips over his.

Soft. Slow. Unbearably sweet.

"How can I feel this much in such a short time?"

Yeah. All that.

Soft skin, eager, delectable mouth.

His.

Every cell in Lucas's body was consumed with the need to flip her over and plunge inside her wet heat. He couldn't breathe, he wanted her so bad. He had to grit his teeth just to maintain. It wasn't as though he hadn't had plenty of opportunity. He just hadn't bothered there for a while.

Now the heat was on. Sydney wasn't just scratching the itch. He'd wanted women before. What made her different? Because *she* was different. *This* was different. Being touched by this woman was mind-blowing and electrifying. Literally. The hair on his body responded to her touch as if an electrical current ran from Sydney directly through him.

His chest felt tight, his dick painfully hard, and his blood pumped fast and furious. "Are you going to chat, or are you going to get to the good stuff anytime soon?"

Her lips twitched. Closing the gap, she kissed the corner of his mouth, his nose, his cheek, his jaw, then trailed her lips back to his. Nibbling his lower lip, Sydney stroked his cheek, then used both hands to bracket his face. This close he noticed that her brown eyes had a darker rim around the pupil, and her lashes were ridiculously long and thick, and that she had a small mole punctuating the end of her left eyebrow.

"I'm going to have my wicked way with you in my own sweet time, Double O Harry Potter. Just lie back and relax."

As much as her leisurely exploration felt like a slow form of water torture, Lucas let her—God, *let* her? He welcomed her controlling the kiss, even while his heart hammered when she licked his lip, then nipped it with her sharp white teeth.

He inhaled the musky scent of her arousal, and the enticing female perfume of her skin mingled with the balmy ocean breeze coming through the partially open window.

He lifted his leg between hers, and she rubbed against him as sensuously as a cat while nibbling and tasting his mouth and driving him to the edge. He wanted to touch her, he needed to feel the weight of her breasts, craved tasting the nipples pressed against the plane of his chest.

Her tongue, warm and wet, tangled with his, turning him inside out as she explored every inch of his body, apparently in no hurry. He closed his eyes, then had to open them again because being blind heightened the sweet torture. He wasn't ready to completely lose control. For now this was her show.

Lucas figured he was showing amazing fortitude by not taking over the lead and rolling her over to plunge into her, hard and fast. His pulse raced as slow kisses turned ravenous. Their syncopated heartbeats pounded between them. His hands fisted above his head as she shoved her hands up beneath his T-shirt, her fingers doing a slow, meticulous exploration with feather-light strokes, lifting the shirt up his body as she teased and played with the hair on his chest.

She lifted her mouth from his to pull his T-shirt over his head and he took the opportunity to bring his arms down so he could touch her. He observed the sharp little points of her nipples through the soft cotton of her strapless dress, and pulled the sunny fabric down to her waist.

The yellow material pooled between her spread knees and over his belly. She wore a scrap of a bra made out of lace and some silky fabric that matched the color of her skin. She looked, he thought a little frantically, good enough to eat. He let out a desperate breath.

"Too big, do you think?" She looked down critically.

Lucas ran his fingers across the swell of her breasts above the scallops of lace cupping her. "Perfect." He was a leg man, but there was plenty to admire here. Her breasts plumped enticingly, beckoning his exploration. Her skin, the rich, warm color of caramel, felt like warm satin. “What did the doctor tell you this morning? Anything we shouldn’t do?”

“I’m still a little tender, but I got the all clear this morning. Nothing you’d do will hurt me.”

He ran a finger between silk and skin, making her arch her back. “You’ll tell me?”

“Ye—That feels—amazing.” Her voice was smoky, thick with her own climbing need.

Observing the way her ragged breathing affected the rise and fall of her breasts made him hot. “Yeah, it does.” Touching her made him hotter. He ran his hands down her narrow rib cage to the sleek curve where her hips met her waist. “Lose the bra.”

Like a practiced stripper Sydney reached behind her arched back with both hands and unfastened the bra. Sliding it off, she tossed the scrap of silk and lace somewhere behind her and smiled a siren’s smile. “Let’s take them for a test drive.”

Hell, yeah. Lucas slid his hands around her bare waist and gently tugged her forward. She was all sleek, dewy curves. All female. All his. He nuzzled his face against her impossibly soft skin. The evocative fragrance of her, a complex mix of florals, earth, and ocean, was all Sydney. He rubbed his cheek on the swell of her breast, cupping the weight of it, running his thumb across the hardness of her nipple before bringing it back to his mouth. Grazing his teeth over the puckered areola, he reclaimed the nub, biting down lightly.

She exhaled a shaky breath, tangling her fingers in his hair as she pressed his head harder where she needed it. He sucked on her until she melted against him, grinding her hips against him, the heart of her right where he wanted it. But minus the several layers of fabric still between them.

“Lucas . . . .”

Raising his head he breathed her in as her mouth

roamed across his jaw while her hands explored his chest. The backs of their hands bumped as he explored her breasts, and she stroked his chest. Her mouth moved down his throat, making touching her breasts counterproductive.

While she kissed her way down his chest, Sydney's hand moved down, making his belly jump. He closed his eyes in reverent invocation as she paused to look up the length of his body. "Oh. I should probably ask—Wizards have all the required body parts, right?"

Lucas laughed. "Everything is where it's . . ." Her hand slipped beneath the waistband of his shorts and he sucked in a breath as her fingers grazed the hard length of him. "Supposed to be."

"Just bigger and better."

His laugh choked on his raging need. "You know what you're doing."

"Um . . ." He was surprised to see a blush heat her cheekbones. "Frankly, up until now this part of the program has been purely academic. But I'm a quick study." She peeled his shorts down with one hand, and he helped by kicking them free of his feet as her hot breath drifted south. Every muscle in his body clenched in anticipation.

"You can say that a—" His airway closed off as she tasted him.

Her eyes were huge and dark as she looked up at him. "You like that?"

Hands fisted above his head, Lucas groaned as she took him into her mouth. Holy hell . . . Sweat sheeted his skin, and he fought for control.

"I love the way you taste."

He could tell by her enthusiasm and attention to detail. He brought his arms down, tangling his fingers in her hair as he gritted his teeth. Jesus. He loved the feel of her cool slick tongue against his hot pulsing flesh. He loved the feel of her smooth hand cupping his balls, and the glide of her breast against his thigh as she moved over him. The silky slide of her hair against his belly made his nerves jump and tense in anticipation.

He was filled with acute pleasure. But this wasn't where he needed to be right now. No matter how damn good it felt. He needed to be inside her. *Now.* He materialized a box of condoms to the bedside table, then mentally removed one, placing it close at hand.

Sydney closed her eyes as Lucas's fingers tightened in her hair. The novelty of what she was doing captivated her. She hummed against his hard length and felt victorious as his entire body jerked in response. God. There was power in having a man in this position. Vulnerable. Needy. Desperate.

"Uncle," he breathed raggedly, gripping her shoulders to drag her up his body. "Not this time, sweetheart. Lift your arms." He gathered the fabric of her dress in handfuls, then pulled it over her head. "I need you naked when I come inside you." He stroked her breasts, using both thumbs to stroke across her sensitive nipples, then slid his hands low on her hips. "Now isn't this convenient?" He tugged at the small bows on each side of her bikini panties, then pulled the fabric slowly from between her legs. Sydney's skin jumped, and her heartbeat went into overdrive.

"Do you—" have protection? How could she not have thought of it? Oh God. She didn't have anything, and it had been years since she'd been on any form of birth control. "Please don't tell me we have to sto—Oh. You Boy Scout, you. Thank God. I just love a man who can magically produce the necessities of life." She ripped open the small foil package with her teeth, then rolled the condom down his length.

His fingers gripped her hips. "Top or bottom?" he asked, his eyes hot as he watched her.

"Bott—"

He flipped her on her back, his narrow hips coming to rest between her thighs. She felt the hard pulsing length of him right where she wanted him and curled her legs around his hips, crossing her ankles over the rock-hard muscles of his back to draw him deeper.

Her breath stopped as she felt his hard shaft against her wet heat. Sydney arched against him as he drove home.

"Lu-cas," she could barely breathe his name. The sensation of him inside her—full, heavy, and so snug, he made her entire body pulse and tighten.

"You are so damned beautiful." His voice was low and husky as he rocked against her. He bent his head to take her mouth in a kiss that ratcheted up her heart rate to an impossible driving beat. He consumed her inside and out, sucking on her tongue while his hips pounded against hers in a dance as old as time.

His hand came between them and he teased her with his fingers. She tightened her legs around him as she tilted her hips to better deepen his every thrust.

"God, you're soft, sleek." Like his touch, his whisper seemed to surround her. Sydney was dying of sensory overload and didn't care. "I love touching you."

And she loved being touched by him. Sydney had never experienced such aching, almost painful, pleasure. *Lucas. Lucas.* Consumed by her arousal she met his every thrust. "Lucas . . . I—"

He slid deeper, his verdant eyes going dark and opaque. A ragged breath escaped him as he moved inside her, touching every sensitive nerve ending until Sydney couldn't tell where she began and he ended. What he was doing felt so incredibly good she wondered at her body's capacity for this much pleasure.

She loved the feel of his steely muscles under her hands, the way his hair brushed her face as he moved.

His mouth pleasured her as much as his body until she was almost delirious, hanging onto the edge of a climax that threatened to leave her in pain.

He tightened his arms around her. Their bodies, slick with sweat, shifted and slid. She could feel his heart. And hers. The same rhythm. The same manic beat. She physically couldn't climb any higher. She'd reached her peak and then some. Her internal muscles tightened, and tightened, and—*"Lucas."*

"Come for me." His breath was hot against her throat.

Yes. Yes. Yes.

One soul-shattering climax after the other rolled through her in tidal waves as his body went rigid in her arms. She felt her own pleasure, and his, surge through her simultaneously, too sweet and sharp to endure.

Breathing harshly, she clung to him as the rolling climaxes ebbed. He held her so tightly she was amazed her bones hadn't shattered. Then she realized that she was holding on to him just as tightly. God. Oh God. This was insane. She couldn't possibly feel this much for a man she barely knew. Not this deeply. Not this fast. How could this have happened? Where had this deep well of emotion and connection come from?

"Okay?" He stroked one hand down her back and gently cupped her behind. Like hers, his heart still thumped and danced.

"I haven't sweated this much since I ran the Boston Marathon."

"Yeah?" His finger dipped and stroked. "When was that?"

"Two years ago."

"I ran it that year, too."

"You did?"

"Yeah." He rested his forehead on hers as she shifted. "Don't move yet."

Sydney closed her eyes as he nuzzled the hollow behind her ear. Limp and replete, and content never to move again, she wondered what would have happened if they'd met two years ago. "I could stay like this until I need to move into the senior center. Or until authorities come in here and have to hose us down to separate us," she said, a thread of amusement running through her voice. She felt ridiculously . . . *happy*.

They stayed that way until Sydney's stomach gurgled. "Sorry, I'm suddenly starving."

"Wanna stay here, or go up to one of the restaurants?"

"Here. But not for a while. I just want to lie right here and bask in my postcoital glow until starvation forces me to move."

"I'm good with that." Lucas rolled her over on top of him.

She was about to break into song, so before she humiliated herself, she focused on business. "What do you think the deal is with the patients on three?" Sydney rested her chin on the hand she had splayed on his hairy chest. She tried to concentrate on the conversation, but it wasn't easy. She couldn't get enough of touching him and stroked her knee up and down his thigh. She felt bonelessly limp and replete, utterly happy right where she was.

"Most, if not all of them, are on immunosuppressants. I checked and those meds are traditionally given to transplant recipients."

"Do you think they do transplants when plastic surgery goes bad?"

He combed his fingers through her hair, pushing it over her bare shoulder, then stroked her arm as he spoke. "Educated guess? I'd say they're waiting for new organs to be brought in. They couldn't stay in business if they depended on botched surgical patients for organs. They'd kill their reputation as the medi-spa. Black-market buys from poorer villages, or even from some third-world country makes more sense."

"God, I'd read somewhere that people sell their organs. But it's hard to believe that anyone would be, *could* be, desperate enough to sell an organ to a stranger."

"There are people who are desperate enough, believe me. And you can live a pretty healthy life with just one kidney, or half a liver."

"Then where are the donors? Somewhere in the medical building I presume? That would make sense."

"Yeah. That's logical. They must have lists of donors willing to give up a body part for a price. When they have someone willing to cough up the big bucks, they bring them in."

"Sounds immoral, if not illegal." It also sounded like another big breaking news story to Sydney. A wizard/spy *and* illegal transplants. She'd hit the mother lode!

"Oh, yeah. And big, big bucks."

"That would explain the planes taking off and landing—or disappearing and appearing—patients are being flown here. Are they ordering a body part from a menu, and then when the spa gets the part the patient needs, the kidney or whatever is flown in?"

Was that what the Half was doing? Bringing in the donors by teleporting them in? The more he thought about it, the more it fit the circumstances. Teleportation was expedient. Fast, reliable (except in his case), and usually untraceable. And, as Sydney had just pointed out, she had seen large modes of transportation arriving and departing by what could only be teleportation.

Unless the patients were wizards, they needed a conventional way to and from the spa.

Now, the whole Escar connection made sense.

"I suspect they're being teleported here. There's a

reasonably small window of opportunity to make the match and remove the organ from the donor and perform the transplant. If the donor is dead it makes that window smaller," Lucas mused, playing with her hair.

Sydney wanted to purr.

"I'll go back and reconnoiter in a couple of hours and see what I can discover."

"I'll go with you." And take as many mental notes as she could stuff into her head. Sydney was almost giddy with excitement. God. Where to even begin? Wizard? Spy? Illegal organ transplants? Three best-selling books, right there. She also wanted to jump up and find her computer to start making notes to keep all the stories straight.

"No." Lucas's fingers lingered on the small of her back. "It was pure, damn *luck* we didn't inconveniently materialize this afternoon. I'll go in alone this time."

"What if you're seen?" The thought chilled her, and it had nothing to do with books. Lucas wasn't a book, she thought, feeling a twinge of guilt. He was a man doing his job. He was now her lover.

He's a *story*, a small voice reminded her. A story that would take her career out of the toilet and give her back what she'd lost.

"I've been doing this awhile."

"Still . . ."

Lucas shut her up by kissing her. The kiss was hungry and consuming, effectively muting the little voice in her head.

They made love again, slowly.

"I'm starving." Sydney tossed back the sheet. "I'm going to take a shower, and then I want a thick, juicy steak—" She leaned over to give his fine behind a kiss on the cheek and a small smack before hopping off the bed. Her bare foot encountered something sharp on the floor.

"Ow!" She bent to pull the sticker out of the ball of

her foot. Her earring—She held it up to the light. It was a similar gold hoop, but this was not hers. "Uh-oh!"

"Mmm?" Lucas's voice was muffled by the pillow.

"You called or whatevered the wrong earring. This isn't mine."

"I'll buy you new earrings, sweetheart."

"The woman this belongs to is going to wonder about a strange earring suddenly appearing. We have to go and switch these before that happens."

Eight

It was late afternoon and only one nurse manned the nurse's station, yet there was an air of bustle, of things happening, on the brightly lit floor. They approached the central desk and he indicated by touch that Sydney should stand against the wall while he searched the area for her earring. It wasn't anywhere he could see and he went back for her. She started when he took her hand.

He remembered feeling the earrings as he'd kissed her earlier out in the stairwell. But they'd checked there first. No earring. Lucas didn't think it was that big a deal, he was here merely to humor her. Every now and then she'd tug on his hand, and he'd take her into a room they'd visited before, just to check.

As they retraced their footsteps from earlier in the day he noticed that many of the previously occupied rooms were now empty. In fact, most of the rooms were empty.

"I think they're all in surgery," Lucas told Sydney when she asked after they entered the fourth vacant room.

"All at the same time?" Sydney didn't look up as she scanned the floor for the missing gold hoop. "Hmm, I don't know. And don't hospitals usually try to perform surgery in the mornings?"

"Yeah. But organ availability can't tell time. Stay here, I'll check."

"No way. I'm going with you. Either I'll suddenly become visible just as they wheel the patient back in here, or you'll appear at an inopportune moment."

Right. Which didn't make Lucas happy. His waning powers were an inconvenience to say the least. He'd call Knight again when they got back to the bungalow. He couldn't do his job if he had to rely on a civilian to ensure his powers worked. Ridiculous. "Be prepared to be teleported back to the cabin without warning."

"Okay," Sydney, now invisible, whispered. "But be prepared not to be able to do magic without me. Let's go."

Point to the lady. Fuck.

Hand in hand, Lucas led Sydney into what was clearly a waiting room for family members. Curiosity got the better of him, and he figured that since he was there anyway, he might as well take a closer look at what was going on.

A dozen people paced, read, or stared out of the large windows in a stylishly decorated waiting room overlooking the grounds. Visitors had a spectacular, million-dollar panoramic view of both beach and ocean and the anticipation of another magnificent Brazilian sunset. Invisible, it was simple enough for Lucas and Sydney to walk between them.

Doing a mind probe, he confirmed that they all had family members in surgery. He lingered to see if anyone had pertinent information he could use, but worry overlaid most of their thoughts. Nobody was chatting.

As he and Sydney walked down to where the corridor doglegged at the end, he got a telepathic tickle; he wasn't the only wiz on the premises. With each step, the sense of wizards became stronger and stronger. They turned the corner. Lucas felt a flicker—just a faint Half flicker—before it was gone. But he knew.

Mica Escar *was* here.

Good. Lucas had questions. The son of a bitch had

answers. Lucas shimmered from room to room. Six ORs filled with people. The place was bustling at seven P.M. Illegal transplants were big business.

Sydney's hand in his was a little damp as they moved silently from a lung transplant to the OR where they were performing a bowel resection. The smell of blood and heavy-duty antiseptic permeated the cold air. Sydney's finger's tightened, and her hand became slippery with sweat as they paused to observe before moving on.

Heart.

Kidney.

Lungs.

Surgeons and surgical teams worked like well-oiled machines. Six operating rooms going full bore.

Six lucky recipients with shitloads of cash to bypass the transplant recipient line.

The next room had only three people in it.

Two orderlies and what was left of Escar.

Fucking hell. Lucas had never seen anything like the eviscerated body of the Half.

He'd literally given his all.

Lucas imagined for a moment his eyes had been filled with fear and the knowledge of what was to become of him just before he'd been carved up. They'd taken his organs in a bloody snatch-and-grab that left skin and bone and what remained of Escar's guts hanging out of the hollowed-out core of what had once been a man. The smell of entrails and chemicals was almost overpowering.

Mica Escar had run smack-bang into hell. And known it.

Jesus.

The two orderlies had apparently preceded Lucas and Sydney by mere seconds; they halted the gurney in the middle of the room beside a large, deep tub filled with colorless liquid.

"We are all going to go to hell for this." The taller of the two, speaking rapid Portuguese, engaged the foot brake on the gurney, then crossed himself. Tall and cadaverous, he had the bad teeth of a meth addict and looked to be in his late forties.

"Are you suddenly getting a conscience, Alvaro?" The other man, with similar bad teeth and skin, positioned himself at the head of the gurney. He grasped the corners of the sheet as his partner did the same at the other end. "You spend your pay without worrying what God thinks."

Alvaro gave a one-shoulder shrug as he adjusted his hands to bear the weight. "Ready?" At the other man's nod they expertly slipped Escar's remains into the tub of faintly camphorous-smelling liquid with barely a splash.

HCl. Hydrochloric acid.

That explained the bad teeth. Chronic occupational exposure to hydrochloric acid was known to cause gastritis, chronic bronchitis, dermatitis, and photosensitization in workers. *Not* meth. Prolonged exposure concentrations also caused dental discoloration and erosion.

They'd done this for some time. Without masks. Jesus.

The liquid bubbled and steamed, turning pink as the chemicals dissolved the Half's body. "He has *already* punished me for this sin. The good Lord gave me cancer."

"Yes. A blessing. He made it impossible for the doctors here to carve you up for parts like this man. That is a good thi—What was that?"

That was Sydney gagging. Lucas had attempted to block her view, but she must've just gotten a look at Escar's naked, mutilated body slowly liquefying.

White-faced with fear, the two men spun toward the sound, crossing themselves frantically when they didn't see anything. Lucas pressed Sydney's face against his chest and teleported her out of there before puke became mysteriously visible on the floor at their feet.

They materialized behind the medical building in a densely wooded area. Clearly not a location used by hotel guests. No paths, no mood lighting, no neatly manicured flower beds here.

He wrapped his arms around her as Sydney sagged against him, burying her clammy face against his chest. "Sorry. But that—What—Oh, my God. That poor—" she wrapped her arms around his waist, hanging on tightly as her entire body shuddered.

Lucas stroked her silky hair, understanding her revulsion. The sight of Escar's hollowed-out corpse would make anyone want to puke. In fact, *his* entire body felt weighted, and his normally cast-iron stomach curled in on itself sickeningly. "Shh. It's okay. Anyone would gag seeing that." His voice sounded as hollow as his belly felt. Heat suffused his body, then disappeared as suddenly as it had washed over him, leaving him cold, weak, and shaken.

What the fuck?

He'd seen more dead bodies than your run-of-the-mill coroner. What the *hell* was wrong with him?

Sydney lifted her head. Her face was dead white, soft skin drawn tightly over cheekbones made more prominent by the graying shadows around them. Huge dark eyes reflected the horror she'd seen. "I'm okay. Really." She swallowed, clearly forcing herself to be "okay" by sheer force of will. His estimation of her rose several notches.

Touching his cheek with icy fingers she scanned his features, then frowned slightly. "Freaked you out, too. Admit it. You're as white as a—"

Something—some force like a giant magnet—was sucking at his power. What th—? "Gotta get out of here." His voice was slurred, his vision compromised.

"Sure. Okay. I'm ready—" Her arms tightened around him. This time it was Sydney supporting his weight. "What's the matter? Lucas? Teleport us back to the cabin, you're scaring me."

Scaring myself, Goddamn it. Scaring the fucking hell out of myse . . .

Sydney took his weight as every ounce of strength leached out of his body. Legs, arms, torso . . . limp as an airless, deflated balloon. Unable to bear his dead weight, Sydney went down with him. They fell to the loamy ground, Lucas on top.

Get help. "Get . . ." *Who?*

Lips thick. Body paralyzed. Vision darkening. Brain shutting down. "G—" *Go. Run like hell.*

Sydney struggled from under his weight, her own nausea and revulsion forgotten as she realized that he'd passed out cold. "Lucas?" She tapped his cheek, then laid two fingers at the base of his throat as her own heart stuttered with fear. Mary Mother of God. Was he dead?

"Alive. Thank God." She looked around for help. They were between two buildings. The medical building was several hundred feet away. Another building, a little closer, was just visible through the trees.

She wasn't sure if the other building was part of the spa grounds. It was a low-key, greenish-gray cement color, blending very well with the tall shrubs and undergrowth around it. "Forget the scenery. Get help." She hated to leave Lucas lying on the ground unconscious. But she couldn't help him herself.

Getting to her feet she looked around, trying to orient herself. No flower-lined paths back here. No people. No help. They were behind a building filled with doctors.

Wizards, he'd said. It had to be the people Lucas took such care to cloak himself—and her—from. Hell's bells—

Crouching beside him she released the gun from the

harness in the small of his back. It was useless to Lucas while he was unconscious. And God help her, if she had to, she would shoot someone to protect him. If she had to.

"Open your eyes. Please?" How could she possibly move him by herself? The golf cart! "I'm going to get the cart and get you back to the bungalow, we'll go from there. Stay put." If nothing else, Lucas had had some sort of communication device that he'd used to talk to his control. She'd call—someone.

He didn't move. Casting him a quick, worried glance, Sydney took off through the bushes. Branches slashed at her bare legs as she ran, but she barely noticed. She'd changed into a white, stretchy, off-the-shoulder top and red capris before they left. Jogging wearing a demi bra to hold up her new size Cs was a new experience. At this rate she was going to give herself a black eye with the damn things. She ended up cupping her breasts as she ran flat out. From now on she'd wear a damn sports bra when she was out with Lucas.

Within minutes she was around the medical building and on the path leading to the hotel and restaurant. She had to let her boobs do their own thing, because the first couple that saw her gave her very odd looks. The diamond ring on her finger flashed as she smiled and waved. Just having a nice jog before dinner.

The coral-and-green cart was where they'd left it before lunch. There were ten or fifteen other little carts parked in the area. Their bright colors looked jaunty and festive. People gathered in the outside bar before going out on the ocean-view patio for dinner. The exotic sounds of steel drums blended with the tropical breeze rustling in the palm leaves. The faint scent of the ocean mixed with women's expensive perfumes, and the fragrance of flowers coupled with savory meals cooking on the outdoor grill.

Sydney swung into her cart and pressed the starter, then backed out between a lemon yellow and white number and one of blue and orange. Both had parked too close. A lot of people were there to enjoy drinks and dinner while watching the sunset.

It took only a few minutes to return to the medical building. No one was around outside, but the windows on all three floors blazed with the reflection of the setting sun, making it look as though the place were on fire.

The path dead-ended on the wide patio area outside the huge double doors to the building. Without a second thought, Sydney drove through a bed of pink flowers and across the lawn. Fortunately, it hadn't rained that day, and the grass was dry and springy and easy to maneuver across.

Heading toward the mountains and the row of shrubs separating her from Lucas, she coaxed more power and speed from the little cart. "Come on, come on, come on."

What was wrong with him? He'd been fine when they'd been walking around the third floor. Or at least she'd thought he was fine. She was the one whose stomach was doing somersaults looking at all that blood and gore.

Somehow she didn't think Lucas was the kind of guy who'd pass out at the sight of blood. And while the corpse in the last room had almost made her puke, Lucas had seemed pretty impervious to it.

It was harder going, forcing the golf cart through waist-high plants, but Sydney finally came to where Lucas lay. He hadn't moved in the time it had taken her, and that worried the hell out of her. Did wizards have the same physical ailments regular people had? She considered herself a reasonably good caregiver unless the person was throwing up, or bleeding, or—well—dead.

Her heart skipped several beats as she jumped off the

cart to kneel beside his prone body. Sydney felt his pulse. Thready, but still there.

"Lucas, I can't lift you, can you help me get you into the cart?" Of course he couldn't. He was unconscious. She considered her options.

She didn't have any.

That made matters simpler.

He outweighed her by at least sixty pounds. There was no way she could lift him, even though the cart was fairly low to the ground.

The fabulous sunset didn't reach behind the building, and it was getting dark pretty fast. She needed, *somehow,* to get Lucas into the cart and drive him—*where*? While the bungalow had appeal—Lucas had an arsenal of weapons there—the weapons weren't going to help her if something was seriously wrong with him.

And he wouldn't be unconscious if there wasn't something seriously wrong with him. Shit, shit. Shit.

"First things first, Ace." Get him up onto the seat. Wrapping her arms around his broad chest from behind, it took every ounce of strength Sydney had to haul Lucas about twelve inches. His head lolled to one side, and his features were slack. Even in the iffy light he looked terrible, the skin beneath his tan was dead white.

She dragged him another few inches, the muscles in her shoulders and arms screaming for mercy. She probably wasn't doing the incisions under her boobs much good either.

Her calves bumped the cart. Now for the hard part. "Anytime you want to pitch in, let me know."

By the time she had half his body on the floorboard of the cart, Sydney was huffing and puffing. "Don't you dare die on me when I'm going to all this damn trouble, Lucas Fox." She pulled and shoved another few inches, then leaned her head on his thigh while she gathered enough strength to stand. Unfortunately, Sydney felt as though some horrible under-the-bed monster was breathing down her neck, and a little panicked voice in her head told her to hurry.

She managed to stand upright, stretch her back and then grab his legs. Swinging the rest of his body inside the cart was a feat more of desperation than strength. He looked uncomfortable as hell, but he was in. Sydney slid in beside him and started the small engine.

Following the crude trail she'd forged through the shrubbery, she regained the path. Lights, and soon—people. How was she going to explain Lucas wedged into the floorboard and unconscious? She glanced at him worriedly.

What if the number he'd called wasn't in his phone? What if—She had no idea who to call to report that he was sick. Was T-FLAC even in the phone book? She had no idea where the company was located. It could be anywhere in the world. Or nowhere at all. She only had his word that such an organization really existed. She gripped the steering wheel tighter, holding the cart steady through the brush.

The cart gained speed once she was back on the tiled walkway. If she took the long way round it would add about ten minutes to the return trip, but it would also bypass the most populated areas. No contest. She knew he'd want her to avoid attracting attention. She turned left. Away from the dinner crowd, away from people strolling down the shortcut to the beach. The sound of samba wafted on the breeze above the sound of the little electric motor.

Lucas lifted his head. "What the fuck?" Shaking his head slightly, he uncoiled from the floor and pushed himself up onto the seat beside her. "Jesus. What was that?"

Relief flooded her and her voice quivered a little. "I'm presuming that's a rhetorical question?"

He ran both hands through his hair, his jaw tight. "Yeah."

"How do you feel?"

"Perfectly fine."

She wished she could say the same for herself. The rush of nausea seeing the poor eviscerated guy, followed by the flood of adrenaline taking care of Lucas had left *her* feeling shaky at best. She still might want to throw up now that she thought about it. A nervous laugh bubbled up. "Perfectly *fine*? You were unconscious for a good ten minutes, maybe more. As a tactic to stop me from falling apart and throwing up, it was masterful, but a little extreme, don't you think?"

"Got your phone?" He glanced over his shoulder, checking their surroundings.

"At the cabin."

"Turn around."

"Turn around? You mean go back to where I just hauled your dead weight into this cart? I don't think so. You need to see a doctor. Maybe your concussion kicked in again, and—"

"Go back. Stop the second I tell you to stop."

Sydney bristled, irritation quashing the fear that raced through her system at the idea of returning to that dark patch of parkland. "Hey, news flash, Mr. Wizard. I'm not your limo driver."

"Something, or someone, back there sucked out all my power. I want to see what or who."

"Are you insane? First of all . . ." She had no idea what first of all *was*. Sydney yanked on the wheel and started back against her better judgment. "You're out of your freaking mind, you know that? What do you mean something or someone sucked out your power? That's impossible . . . Isn't it?" But wasn't tooling along in a golf cart beside a *wizard* insane?

"An hour ago, I would have said yes."

"You should call someone," she said a little desperately.

"And tell them what, exactly? I have no idea what happened."

"And yet," Sydney turned to look at him, "you want to go right back there and see if it'll happen again?"

"Something like that. Yeah."

Nine

"Back up!" Lucas braced a hand on the front of the cart for support as strength leached out of his body and black dots obscured his vision. It felt as though his very muscles and bones were liquefying. Christ. As fast and debilitating the second go-round. Same physical location, same physical reaction.

"Ya *think?*" Sydney sounded as breathless as if she'd been running, but it was nerves, pure and simple. Hauling on the steering wheel she turned the cart—if the damn thing could've gone any faster it would have flipped over. Fortunately, it was slow, and all it did was a clumsy turn that flattened a three-foot-high shrub at less than fifteen miles per. Skinny branches and leaves slapped at the undercarriage of the low-to-the-ground vehicle, fanning out on either side of their legs before snapping upright behind them.

As they moved away, his vision slowly cleared, and strength trickled back into his body in small, nauseating waves. The total loss of both his physical and mental power shook him to the core. *Be honest.* Scared the living crap outta him.

"I hate to say I told you so, but dammit, Lucas, why would you do something so asinine as going *back?*"

"Because I had to know whether that was an aberration or not." He concentrated on his breathing for a moment.

"I'm guessing 'not,' then, huh?"

"Not," he agreed. "I also wanted to see if the power grid was *between* the buildings or emanating from the one in back. Which it is. Some powerful wizard or wizards have cast a protective spell over the damn thing. A magical Do Not Disturb." Still shaky, he tossed her a glance. "Didn't affect you, did it?"

"It affected my nausea."

"What?!" He swung around in his seat quickly enough to feel the remaining dizziness and looked her over closely.

"I was just about to throw up or pass out when you stole my thunder by collapsing. Took the thought of my own problems right out of my head." She shuddered but kept her shoulders straight and hands firm on the steering wheel.

Lucas hid a smile and his relief. She was really something. "Now I know what Superman felt like." What was in that building? Something they wanted no one to see. Something that necessitated one of the strongest, most powerful power grids Lucas had ever encountered.

She gave him a worried glance. "Superman? Do wizards have some form of kryptonite or something?"

"Not that I've heard." But he'd sure as hell find out. They rounded the corner of the medical building and cut across the lawn, following what he knew were the tracks she'd made coming to get him. Up ahead dozens of people strolled the paths, or sat on well-placed benches to watch the sun set. Sydney slowed a bit, then angled the golf cart across the already crushed pink flowers and bounced onto the tiled path. Several people turned to watch their progress, frowning disapprovingly as she flattened a second swath through the flower bed, narrowly missing them as she skidded onto the path.

She grimaced, yelling out, "Sorry!"

Lucas placed a hand on her arm. Not only to get her attention, but to boost his powers. They surged as if jump-started. Another anomaly he had no explanation for. "Slow down before you run over someone." Using Empathic Perception, he wiped the memory of everyone they passed, magically removing any trace of them or the golf cart's fast and erratic path through both the lawn and flower beds.

Jaw tight, Sydney eased off the gas a bit, but her fingers were still white-knuckled on the steering wheel. "How are you feeling? Faint? Sick? Any other symptoms? Would it be safe for me to take you to the doctor or do wizards have to see specialists?"

"I'm fine."

"You didn't see what you looked like lying on the ground. You were dead white, and ice cold. That's far from damn well *fine,* Ace. Don't die on me. It would really put a crimp on the rest of my vacation plans."

He barked out a laugh. "I'm touched by your sympathy. Rest assured, I'm not dying." Said with far more conviction than he felt. While he'd like to believe that whatever was back there had sucked out his powers, it was, quite frankly, *unlikely.* He'd dealt with some of the strongest wizards alive, on every level. The good, the bad, and the worse, none of which had this level of magic. None of which had been capable of knocking him flat on his ass in a matter of seconds without being present and in view.

Nor had any of those encounters—what? Absorbed? Depleted? Stolen? His powers.

Reality check, Fox. His powers had been on the blink for weeks. Long before he'd come to Brazil. Just because he'd experienced the same debilitating effect twice in the same physical location didn't mean the location had anything to do with what he'd felt. Coincidence?

Fuck. Not only didn't he believe in coincidence, his gut told him his physical reaction was directly related to whatever power grid was nearby.

He had not felt that way in the medical building despite knowing other wizards were in the vicinity. It wasn't until he was outside, between the buildings, that he'd experienced the draining effect.

He had to figure out a way to get inside the second building. See what the hell was in there. What was so secret, so powerful that the use of such strong magic was needed to keep wizards out? Sydney curled her hand where it lay on his thigh and gently stroked up and down. His heart gave an odd clutch. It was a very female, nurturing touch, not even sexual. Although God knew, even under the present circumstances, he wanted her.

He liked her hands on him. He needed the extra surge of power the contact generated. Yeah, right. It was all about the power. Although, hell, he needed all the power he could get right now. Just because she was a conduit didn't mean he planned on keeping her around.

She gently squeezed his leg. "Actually I'm *hugely* sympathetic. And a lot scared."

That was a start. He suspected she was normally fearless. Being fearless was dangerous. "Good. Scared will keep you on your toes. Whatever's going on here requires an intense power grid. Considerably stronger than necessary for masking an illegal transplant operation."

Sydney withdrew her hand to lean forward over the steering wheel, as if by doing so she could make the cart go faster. They could *walk* faster. And if he hadn't been worried about passing out again, he'd prefer walking to moving so fucking slowly.

"Like what?" She veered left before they reached the front courtyard outside the main hotel. "This way is quicker," she told him before he asked.

"Whatever it is, that building has been given powerful wizard Keep-the-Fuck-Out energy." He didn't know of any wizard *that* strong and powerful. "I don't know who or what, but I will."

Lucas felt his powers even out the farther they distanced themselves from the two buildings. The sun was almost down, giving its last hurrah in a blaze of fireball red and mango orange. "It would be a smart plan to leave here. Tonight."

Lucas materialized sunglasses for both of them. Sydney gave a little start as the dark glasses appeared on her nose. "Hey. Thanks." She turned her head briefly in his direction. "Leave? Both of us?"

"I have a job to do, remember?" He'd followed Escar here because he'd suspected the Half was involved more deeply with the Splinter terrorist group than intel reported. He'd been right. The Half was certainly integral in the organ-trafficking operation. Was this a Splinter operation, or had he stumbled onto yet another terrorist group run by Halfs?

Escar had been important, and yet, he'd been killed and used as a smorgasbord for parts himself. Were the recipients full wizards or Halfs? Lucas had no idea what the ramifications might be of using organs from a wizard inside a nonwizard. The patients he'd encountered up on the third floor had not been wizards. Or even Halfs.

He'd call Knight and find out. Since Mason Knight was not only Lucas's mentor, he was also a trusted friend, maybe he could help him with some answers to the questions Lucas was accumulating. Maybe he could answer the questions and Lucas could go back to his relatively normal life.

Sydney glanced at him with a small frown. "No one *knows* we saw anything, right? Besides, I'm paid up for another five days. I'd hate to miss Carnival, I've really been looking forward to it."

"Sydney—"

She held up a hand. "Look, I'm not stupid. If you tell me that in your professional opinion I'm in danger staying here, I'll leave. If you tell me that my presence is putting *you* in danger, I'll go." She pulled up beside several other carts in the little parking area near her bungalow and turned off the engine.

Beyond the beach the ocean appeared as a dimpled sheet of copper as the sun hung just over the horizon.

Curving her knee up on the seat between them, Sydney turned to face him, her expression serious. Lucas could see his own grim expression reflected in her glasses. He'd rather see her pretty eyes.

She shoved her hair over one shoulder, an unconsciously sensual and wholly feminine action. "I'll go if you tell me to go. But there's something else to consider. For some reason my presence does . . . *something* to magnify your powers. If I hadn't been with you, you wouldn't have been able to turn invisible today. *Twice.* If you hadn't been invisible, you couldn't have gone up to the third floor, unseen, could you? Not without arousing suspicion. And who knows what would have happened to you if I hadn't been with you when you passed out? What if, for whatever reason, you can't use your powers at all if you're not with me? Then what? Don't look at me like that. I'm just saying."

Yeah. She was just saying what he was just thinking, damn it to hell. "My job," Lucas said, jaw tight, "is to protect *you*. Not the other way around."

"Okay," Sydney agreed mildly, climbing off the cart and waiting for him to join her on the shell path. He was apparently over his near-death experience. She slipped her hand in his, enjoying the feel of his palm against hers, of having his fingers automatically clasp hers. "Fine. Go ahead and save me when it's my turn to have my powers fail. In the meantime—"

Lucas suddenly turned into her, pressing his palm across her mouth.

Sydney went from reasonable to annoyed. Unacceptable. Un-freaking-acceptable. The last guy who'd tried to muzzle her had needed eight stitches in his palm. She understood the rush of adrenaline, and the aftermath, but—*get your damn hand off my face, buster!*

Lucas dragged her back into the shelter of an empty bungalow two doors down from hers. "Shh," he said quietly, breath fanning her cheek.

Geez. She got it. Sydney peeled his fingers off her mouth just as she heard someone knocking on a door. She looked at him over her shoulder. "Soldiers?" she mouthed.

Lucas suddenly had a gun in his hand. He shrugged.

The man knocked again.

A woman called out, "Who is it?"

Sydney went hot, then cold, then hot again.

The voice was hers.

But she was hiding twenty feet away.

Lucas indicated he was going to teleport them inside. Sydney was good with that. She would have preferred whoever was knocking at the door to be teleported to another part of the estate, but hey. She shut her eyes.

When she opened them again she and Lucas were inside her bungalow. So freaking cool. The guy knocked again. She glanced at Lucas. He stood in the kitchenette area with a clear view of the front door, but where someone standing there couldn't see him. He used his gun hand to indicate that she open the door.

"Just a minute," she called, sounding eerily like the not-her voice a few seconds before. She opened the door. "Yes?"

The guy wasn't a soldier. He had on the uniform of a bellman. Sydney hadn't realized she'd been holding her breath until she let it out. The guy offered her the snakeskin wallet, a wallet that Lucas had materialized what felt like a hundred years ago. "Mr. Fox, he left the wallet at the restaurant."

Taking it, Sydney pulled the equivalent of five bucks out of Lucas's bogus wallet and handed it to him with a smile, then shut and locked the door. Tossing the wallet onto the table by the door, she cast a quick glance at her closed computer. How was she going to finish the book with Lucas around? She wasn't. But she still had a couple of weeks to meet her deadline. A week left here, then home for a week. It was doable. She leaned her hip on the table and gave Lucas a stern look. "What if that had been one of the bad guys?"

"I would have shot him."

"Every day with you around is an adventure, isn't it? I presume leaving the wallet to be found wasn't an accident?"

Putting the gun down on the table beside him, he stretched out on the bed, his hands stacked under his head, his ankles crossed. "They wanted to know who I am. Now they do."

"Is everything in there as real as those photographs?" The photographs that gave them a history that Sydney was starting to wish were true. Which was silly, and just asking for trouble. The broken-heart kind of trouble. This man was a warrior. A fighting machine. Did he even *have* a heart?

Back to the realist; the find-out-all-her-secrets kind of trouble. Fortunately, she was only going to be here for another few days. Not enough time to get into too much heartache, just enough time for a fabulous holiday fling. Nothing wrong with that. In fact, a fling with Lucas held enormous appeal.

Lucas's eyes flared as she stepped out of her bright red capris leaving her wearing a tiny red thong. The way he looked at her made Sydney feel slinky and sexy. Pulling the stretchy white top over her head, she tossed it over the chair, then flicked off the overhead light, plunging the room into the rosy glow of the dying sun.

He swallowed and when he spoke, his voice was rougher, grittier than usual. "It's usually best to stick as close to the truth as possible."

Since she had a few secrets of her own, she chose to drop the subject. The less said the better. "I'm starving. Let's call room service." Dressed only in a strapless bra and thong, she found the leather-bound menu in the desk drawer and went around the foot of the bed to sit beside him so they could look at it together.

Before room service answered the phone Lucas had her bra off. By the time he'd ordered an appetizer and a bottle of wine, she was on her back beside him. By the time he'd placed the order for their main course, he'd tossed aside the menu and was nibbling his way across her belly.

Throwing down the phone in the general direction of the bedside table, he tugged her closer. "Forty-five minutes. What would you like to do to pass the time while we wait?" The heat in his green eyes telegraphed exactly what she was going to be doing.

"Show me."

Leaning over her, Lucas stroked her hair away from her face. "You know what I see when I look at you?"

"Jessica Alba?"

He grinned. "Pales in comparison."

Sydney grinned back. "Do you even know who she is?"

"Not *you*." He stroked her cheek, then ran his thumb over her lower lip. "I've never met anyone like you."

Her heart did a little flip and she nipped his finger lightly. "Well, I've never met anyone like you, either."

And that had nothing to do with his being either a spy or a wizard, although both were pretty astounding.

She slid her hands down his arms, the corded muscles hard as steel and covered with satin-smooth tanned skin shades darker than her own. Cupping her face he kissed her deeply. Sydney slid her arms up around his neck.

Shifting to lie over her he nudged her thighs wide, and Sydney cradled him between her legs, feeling the heat and weight of him, welcoming him inside her. Their skin warmed, their breath mixed.

Hunger grew. Lust intensified. But unlike the first time, there was no hurry. They let the heat and energy build slowly. As if they had all the time in the world.

Their simultaneous climax rocked her world. It took several minutes for her hearing to return and her pulse to slow to a less manic beat. "I think we should pace ourselves," she told him, voice thick.

"That was paced. Believe me." There was a knock at the door. "I'll get it." He waited until she shifted her head from his shoulder, then rose, taking the Glock out of the bedside drawer before he went to the bathroom. He grabbed the other robe on the back of the door; coming out he tied the sash, slipping the gun into the pocket. As he passed the bed he picked up the sheet where they'd kicked it to the floor, pulling it over her naked body. Bracing both arms over her, he gave her a lingering kiss.

Sydney gave him a satiated smile as he straightened. "Good timing. I'm too weak to move. You might have to feed me."

Lucas opened the door for the waiter. "Put it on the desk." He did a double take. The kid was the spitting image of his friend Alex Stone. Christ, he didn't just *look* like Alex. He was an exact, younger doppelgänger. Did his friend have a son? The resemblance was uncanny and impossible to mistake. Lucas and Alex had grown up together. He, Alex Stone, and Simon Blackthorne had been Mason Knight's favorite "projects," as Knight had called them. The three boys had been inseparable and had maintained the close friendship as adults.

"Thanks." Lucas pulled a couple of bills out of his wallet and passed them over after the waiter set the table. "Worked here long?" He asked in English.

"About a year," the young man returned in almost flawless English as well. "Will that be all, *senhor*?" The kid's eye contact was steady and a little impatient.

"Where are you from originally?"

"I was born here, *senhor.*"

"In Rio or one of the outlying villages?"

"Rio," he said, lifting the domes off their food. Yellow orchids decorated the plates.

"Your family? Brothers, sisters?" Lucas pressed.

The younger man looked up at him with Alex's eyes. "I was raised by nuns. Why?"

"What about your parents?"

"Never met them, *senhor.*" The waiter began to back out of the bungalow. "Enjoy your meal."

Lucas tried to remember if Alex had ever mentioned spending time in Brazil. He couldn't recall, but he was going to find out when next they talked. And suggest he run down to Rio with a Q-tip and about eighteen years of back child support in his suitcase.

"Okay, that was weird." Sydney wagged a finger between Lucas and the door.

"He's a dead ringer for a friend of mine. I wonder if it's possible that Alex has a son. Crazy."

"Are you going to ask him?"

"Hell, yeah. We both grew up in the foster care system. If Alex has a son, damn straight he'd want to know." He'd also put in another call to see if he could catch Knight this time. He didn't really want to leave a message. His waxing and waning powers were nobody's business but his own.

Picking up a napkin, he reminded himself to ask Mason if he'd ever encountered a power grid similar to the one here, and while he was at it, he'd have Knight take a look at the London situation. As a world-renowned microbiologist, Knight was well respected by anyone having anything to do with biological warfare. "Do you want to eat there, or over here?" Lucas started picking off the flowers scattered all over the food, dropping them into the trash can. Food didn't need to look pretty.

"At the table. If we attempt eating in bed I'm afraid we'll never eat." Gloriously naked, Sydney tossed the sheet aside, and took a flimsy white dress from the small louvered closet on her side of the bed. Pulling the almost see-through material over her head she came to the table.

"God, this looks and smells fabulous." She sat in the chair he pulled out for her and took a healthy gulp of water. She smelled like flowers and sex. Not only could he see her skin glowing through the flimsy fabric of her dress, he could easily make out her nipples and aureoles. The wisp of material teased him even more than her nudity.

Damn. He wanted her again. Her hair looked as though they spent an hour making love; silky, disheveled and sexy as hell, it draped her shoulders and the upper swell of her breasts bared by the dress. Just looking at her made Lucas hungry. God. How could that be? He'd come twice in the last hour already, yet he couldn't seem to get enough of her.

She picked up her fork. "What would you do if you found out you had a son or daughter you didn't know about?"

Family. The one thing he tried *never* to think about. "I'm not careless." *And sure as hell not about something that important.*

"No. You materialized an entire *box* of condoms right when we needed them." She took a bite of *Bolinho de bacalhao.* "These are the salt cod fritters, right? Try one." She scooped up a mouthful, offering it to him on the tines of her fork even though he'd ordered the same appetizer, and it sat right in front of him. "Good, huh?"

"Yeah. Great." He didn't give a damn about the meal. Food was just fuel to him. But he found Sydney fascinating to watch. She seemed to do everything with fierce concentration, even eating. And she savored and clearly enjoyed every bite.

He reached for the wine and raised an inquiring brow.

She nodded and slid her glass toward him an inch or two. "But you think your friend was careless?" she asked as he poured the ruby wine into their glasses, picking up his own.

"Not as far as I know, but mistakes happen." He took a sip. A pretty decent 2002 Boscato Reserva Cabernet Sauvignon.

He drank, then put down the glass to eat. "What do you do when you're not having a destination vacation?" he asked, feeling relaxed and strangely peaceful. Another anomaly, not knowing something about someone he was in close proximity to. Under normal circumstances, by now he'd know her entire background from birth. Yet all he knew about this woman was that she was practically fearless, curious, fascinating, and spectacular in bed. And had eight brothers and lived in Miami. And had incredible breasts. Mind-blowing legs. And . . . it was time to stop thinking about her body.

The appetizer was followed by a roast top round of beef with *molho campanha* sauce. The meal was excellent, the company charming.

"What do I do?" She took another bite of beef and hummed a little. "Oh, a little of this, a little of that. I'm still trying to decide what I want to be when I grow up. I was a florist for a while, but I wasn't really creative enough. Then I tried being a personal trainer. Interesting for about three months, then I got bored. I dabbled in writing, but that didn't pan out either. I have a short attention span if I'm not totally engaged in whatever I'm doing."

"What kind of writing? Journalism?" Christ, was she a tabloid journalist? That would make this interlude interesting. He was perfectly comfortable having Sydney know just about anything about him. When their time together was over, he'd use Empathic Perception to wipe the memory of himself from her mind, and she'd only recall having a pleasant, uneventful vacation. Lucas wondered why the knowledge that she'd never remember him bothered him as much as it did.

"I wrote nonfiction. Nothing anyone ever heard of. Maybe I'll join T-FLAC." She shot him a sassy grin. "Do you have female operatives?"

"We do." Lucas didn't want Sydney working for T-FLAC. Most ops weren't this low-key. Real bullets were fired. People got seriously injured. People died. And just because none of that had happened yet, didn't mean the shit wasn't going to hit the fan soon. It usually did when tangos, Halfs, and fulls got involved.

He rolled the wineglass between his palms. "I don't think going from florist to firing handheld rocket launchers, or sneaking up behind someone to stab them in the kidneys is exactly a logical progression. You might want to give it a little more thought."

Sydney paused, fork midair, gaze horrified and arrested. "You stabbed someone in the kidneys?"

Many. And among other parts of their anatomy. "The

pain is so bad they can't scream. It's an effective way of killing."

Sydney grimaced. "Lovely dinner conversation. Remind me not to piss you off."

Which just showed he wasn't used to a meal with a woman without a T-FLAC agenda. Sydney wasn't a tango or an informant. She was just a beautiful woman on vacation. It had been so long since he'd enjoyed an uninterrupted meal with a female companion, Lucas felt completely relaxed.

"Tell me about your enormous family." He'd have been happy to listen to Sydney recite the phone book. She had a very sexy voice. He enjoyed the way her mind worked. He asked her about her brothers and their families while they sipped wine and finished a leisurely meal.

Replete, he pushed his plate aside. Leaning back in his chair he held his almost empty wineglass, sipping now and then. "How come some lucky guy hasn't snapped you up?"

"How do you know I'm not married with five kids, three dogs, and a house in Peoria?"

"You told me you live in Miami," he reminded her lazily, watching her finish off the last of a huge portion of food. Where she put it all, he had no idea. "And," he added, "you strike me as a woman who doesn't prevaricate. I suspect if you were married you'd either tell me," his lips twitched, "or tell me to get lost."

"I'm not married. Never even been close." She watched him over her glass. "Probably because my father and brothers vetted all the guys I dated from when I was thirteen. Hard to get past the first line of defense. You?"

Clearly the men of her acquaintance hadn't pushed through the defenses hard enough. "Married? Yeah. Eight years ago. Lasted two years. We parted amicably."

"How did she feel about you being a wizard?"

"Okay. It was my *job* she hated. Too much travel. She didn't like being alone in the house. Didn't like not being a couple socially."

"She married the wrong guy then," she said, not particularly sympathetic.

"Now she's remarried to a nice guy who sells insurance and comes home every day at five. House. Mortgage. Two kids. Girls. Cute. I hang out at their place for the Fourth of July or Thanksgiving if I'm in country."

"Very civilized."

"Yeah." And he always felt ridiculously like the poor kid standing outside in the snow, nose pressed against the candy store window. He didn't begrudge Natalie her life. She was a hell of a woman, she deserved good things. And God only knew, he couldn't handle being domesticated. Never could. T-FLAC was his family. He was good with that. He slugged down the last inch of wine in his glass.

"I can't eat another thing. How about a walk?" Shifting caused her dress to drop off her right shoulder, baring more of the swell of her breast.

A walk. Getting out of the small bungalow sounded good. He couldn't spend the entire op making lo—*screwing,* although the thought had merit. A walk would give him an opportunity to take a look at the boats along the pier, and walk off the excellent dinner, killing two birds with one stone.

"Let me make a call first." He materialized the sat phone into his free hand, and called Saul, filling him in on the power grid, the transplants. When he was done, Saul gave him an update on London.

The chemical used in the London subway was now confirmed as LZ17, a new and lethal coronavirus similar in effect and composition to SARS, but ten times more deadly. It was also impossible to detect until people presented with the horrific symptoms and it was too late to treat. The death toll in London had doubled in the past seven hours. This was molecular and cellular biology at its worst.

Lucas made a mental note to ask Knight if he knew any more about it when they spoke. His mentor would know more of the technical details than Lucas did, which was why Knight was frequently called in to T-FLAC as a civilian expert.

Saul told him he'd already left a message for Lucas's mentor. "Good man." Where the hell *was* Knight? It was unlike him not to return Lucas's call like this. Lucas was starting to get worried. "Saul, on a personal note, put in a call to both Stone and Blackthorne. Have them give me a buzz when they can. See if they've heard from Knight. Keep me up to date on the London situation. And get the rest of that intel back to me ASAP." Intel about Escar's connection to Splinter, and if there was any noise about Splinter being involved with black-market organs.

He shoved the sat phone into a front pocket and turned to see that Sydney had thrown a bright red and yellow fringed shawl over her shoulders. "As pretty as that looks on you, I prefer you without." He'd prefer her without the see-through dress as well.

"That's nice, but I want to go for a *walk*."

"Okay."

"No. I mean it, Lucas," she said sternly, backing up as he stalked her. "I want a brisk walk on the beach. I need fresh air, and ocean, and exercise—Oh."

They were outside. She looked around, eyes glowing with wonder and reflected moonlight. "Oh!"

He'd materialized a king-sized floating bed, with a filmy white fabric canopy that drifted softly in the warm salty breeze. "Ocean." He kissed her throat. He waved a hand to encompass the water lapping beneath the bed. They stood ankle-deep in the froth of a wavelet.

"Air." With a wave of his hand her colorful wrap billowed off her bare shoulders to float onto the bed behind her. He skimmed his hands up her hips, preferring to remove the almost see-through white dress personally.

"Exercise." Lucas toppled her backward onto the cloud-soft mattress.

Ten

0400

Lucas returned Sydney to the bungalow, then cast a protective spell over her as she slept. The balmy breeze blowing off the ocean had cooled some, and he drew the sheet up over her sleeping form, pausing to *really* look at her.

She wasn't just beautiful, or just funny, or just smart—she was a combination designed to take him by surprise. And she had.

He added "concern for her" to his growing list of firsts. Usually on an op he only worried, if he worried at all, about himself. If and when he worked as part of a team he knew the others would take care of themselves. He watched their backs, they watched his, but he didn't *worry* about them.

It would be best to send her away, but he was caught between a rock and a hard place. Safety and tradition said to get her out, but his flickering powers demanded she stay. Like a good luck charm, she provided the needed jolt to do his job and not get killed in the process. He hoped to hell keeping her close didn't come back to bite him in the ass.

He glanced at his watch; he didn't want to be gone long. He wasn't even sure if the protective spell would work if he and Sydney didn't have a physical connection. What if . . . Dammit. He couldn't what-if himself now. He had a job to do. Powers or no powers. And, Goddamn it, there was no reason to believe that she'd be in any kind of danger. He had to be satisfied with that.

The pier and marina were less than two miles away. He attempted to teleport. Couldn't even dredge up a small spark of power. Fuck.

Pissed, he took off running.

Leaves and palm fronds rustled, following his progress as he ran down the length of beach. It was quiet. No sound of steel drums at this hour, just the sibilant *shhh-shh-shh* of the surf ebbing and flowing on the beach in lacy curls, and the soft thud of his black running shoes on the sand.

Easily slipping into the shadows of lush vegetation on the edge of the beach, Lucas headed west, leaving the string of picturesque bungalows behind. Glancing to the right, he could see the top few floors of the hotel above the trees in the distance. A few squares of yellow light broke the darkness, and red helipad lights blinked on and off up on the roof.

What else was being hidden at *Novos Começos* Medi-Spa? What was inside that building with the force field around it? God. He was dying to get inside. But not without a backup plan. Dying would be the key word if he tried to force his way in.

Sydney had seen boats and people appear late at night from the marina. Wizard transpo for sure. Concentrate on one thing at a time. Picking up speed, he tried not to think about his inability to use his powers. What would it mean for his job with the paranormal division of T-FLAC? If he'd lost or was losing his powers, he still had the training and skill to be a T-FLAC operative. Yeah. He'd be that. But being a wizard was who he was. Who he'd been for thirty-four years.

How the fuck was he going to deal with it if this

wasn't some kind of aberration? A virus, like a bad cold or flu bug, that had temporarily stripped him of his powers? What if it became permanent?

His heart rate rose, nothing to do with running balls-out. Sweat-drenched hair slapped at his skin, stinging his eyes. Removing the sat phone from his pocket as he ran, Lucas checked to see if Knight had returned his call. He hadn't. He swore, going from concern for himself to deep worry about his old friend. Sydney *and* Mason. Fuck. He stuffed the small phone back into his pocket.

Worry was hell.

Mason Knight must be well into his seventies now. A heart attack or stroke was possible—Lucas put the thought from his mind as he ran. Saul was going to send someone to Knight's other house in Barcelona. Old coot was probably on some beach somewhere with a sexy blonde and drinking a mai tai with an umbrella in it. And even if something were wrong, there was nothing, *nothing* he could do about it right now.

Time to focus on what he could do.

A bright security light shone up ahead, illuminating part of the pier and the front of the marina building. He smelled cigarette smoke, and heard two men speaking Portuguese in low baritones, the voices carrying on the breeze. It always made his job so much easier when others did theirs badly. Lucas quietly stepped from the sand onto the wood decking of the pier, the Glock in one hand, and his D2 combat impact fixed-blade tactical knife in the other. What the six-inch blade didn't stop, a bullet would. He was itching for an old-fashioned brawl. A couple of lazy-ass guards weren't exactly up to his fighting weight, but they were the only game in town. There was a pretty good chance they wouldn't make him. The larger boats tied up along the dock cast long, deep shadows, and there were plenty of places to hide.

Problem was, Lucas wanted to go on a little fishing expedition of his own, look around without the risk of some minimum-wage soldier, toting a weapon that cost more than his annual income, taking him by surprise.

He didn't like surprises.

He crept silently toward the smoke rings.

Man, that smoke smelled good. It spiraled up in a series of almost perfect circles from the back of the building where the men were taking their break. Lucas had given up smoking five years, eleven days, and some hours ago, but the smell of Camels still made him want to light up. He'd figured a bullet would kill him long before he'd ever die of lung cancer, but jonesing for a smoke while he was on a stakeout for weeks on end in a jungle sucked. He'd given up smoking cold turkey while sweating in the rain forests of Venezuela right outside a tango's stronghold.

He was still a nonsmoker. Didn't mean he didn't crave a drag every time he smelled one.

Lucas removed a black metal cylinder from his back pocket. Fitting the silencer to the end of his pistol he spun it into place soundlessly.

Strolling around the corner with his favorite weapon, a custom Glock, in hand, Lucas smiled. "Morning, gentlemen, how's it hangin'?"

The one leaning against the wall pushed himself forward. The second guy tossed half a Camel into the water behind him. Both looked really surprised. Both carried locked and loaded Uzis. Lucas took in their firepower in a glance. A thirty-two-round magazine, times four—they each had second magazines welded to the first. Sixty-four times two, to his seventeen rounds.

Piece-a-cake.

Before they could react, Lucas punched the short guy right between the eyes. He was that close. The guy's head jerked back against the wall where he'd been lounging moments before, shooting the breeze and smoking the cigarette Lucas wanted. The impact of head against wall made a very satisfying thunk. The guy slid down the wooden siding to sprawl on the ground. Not unconscious, although he probably wished he were. A smear of blood had followed his descent.

Before Number Two got his shit together, Lucas squeezed off a shot. The guy looked surprised, the hole between his eyes small and neat. The force of the bullet propelled him over the side of the dock and into the water. The splash made more noise than the sound of the bullet.

Number One staggered up, his eyes wild. His pal was somewhere under the black water, his Uzi ten feet away, and Lucas, sighting down the blunt action of his Glock, stood between him and his weapon.

With a bellow of rage and stupidity, the guy charged. For a nanosecond, Lucas considered stepping aside, letting him join his pal in the water. But that wasn't smart. In combat you either did some hurt or you died. The secret was knowing you had to hurt the sons of bitches before they killed you. Before they called in their buddies to help.

Putting down the enemy before he could do it to you was the name of the game. Lucas had played the game many, many times.

A solid center-chest hit, and it was over. Unscrewing the silencer with the bottom of his shirt, holstering his weapon, he dragged the guy to the edge of the pier and slid him over into the water with a quiet splash.

"Could have told you smoking was bad for your health."

The entire confrontation had taken less than six seconds. And other than Lucas's greeting, not a word had passed between them.

Lucas went back around to the front of the single-story structure—a bait, tackle, and boat rental shop that had been designed to look weathered and old. But a quick inspection showed that it was solid and well built. He shimmered inside, going through a few file drawers and looking around. Nothing of interest. Other than the fact that he could shimmer without thought. Good news.

Teleporting outside, he tried to go invisible. Fuck. On. Off. On. Fucking off. What the hell was going on?

It was what it was. He wanted to check the registry of the boats. See if he could find any clues to . . . any-fucking-thing. Transplants and the mysterious, wizard-locked building. But for now the marina and boats were his objective.

He walked down the long wood pier to the accompanying sound of lapping water, the groan of wood, and the creak of ropes. Someone had left their bait slops strewn beside the steps down to the water. The fishy stink mingled with the scent of the water and the faint smell of fresh paint.

Lucas bypassed a cluster of day-tripping small sailboats, catamarans, and Jet Skis for rental. What interested him were the murderously expensive oceangoing vessels, white with miles of polished brass, bobbing gently on the black water on either side of the wide wooden pier. Some of the boats had lights twinkling on their rigging, but most were dark. Either the owners and crew slept, or they'd checked into the hotel. Or medical building.

Without thinking, he went invisible. Then realized that this time he *was* in fact, *invisible.* While he was relieved that his power worked, he wasn't banking on it *staying* that way. He proceeded as if he *were* visible.

Using his ocular camera, he captured boat names, shooting the images to HQ in Montana for ID. The first was *Frayheyt.* A hundred and seventy feet of white trideck Motoryacht, still smelling faintly of fresh paint.

The stairs were down. The wizard power shield up. Interesting.

Unlike his earlier encounter with a kick-ass power grid, this Keep-the-Fuck-Out wasn't hard to bypass. Half power. Lucas could counteract that on a bad day.

He passed through and then repaired the block in case anyone came or went. It was unlikely at this hour of the morning, but he took the precaution anyway. Invisible, his power back on board—*literally*—he grinned as he walked stealthily up the metal stairs. The sounds of the small marina accompanied his ascent. Creaks and the splash of the water against a dozen hulls. This baby probably cost upward of thirty mil and the thing only slept ten or twelve. Double that with crew. It flew the flag of, and was therefore registered in, the Grand Cayman Islands. Lucas started at the top, not needing the Maglite as the moon was plenty bright enough to illuminate his way.

On the sundeck he found a couple of white, furled sun umbrellas standing sentinel near an outside dining area, and a hot tub with turquoise-colored water, lazily steaming.

Two champagne flutes and several plates with the remnants of dinner littered the table. A mirrored tray held the residue of four faint lines of coke and a platinum razor blade. Lucas walked toward the hot tub, leaning down to feel one of the towels tossed on a couple of blue-and-white striped loungers. The towels were damp. Dinner and a dip. Cristal champagne. Coke.

Two romantic someones. Dollars to doughnuts still on board.

He hit the wheelhouse next, sucking in an appreciative whistle. Makore and mahogany wood paneling and columns, state-of-the-art Satcom: Nera Inmarsat

Mini M, Nera Inmarsat B, Nera Fleet 55, SEA Inmarsat C. It was all there. Everything a guy with money to spare could buy. And then some.

"Who owns you, baby?" Lucas whispered under his breath, going through the file drawers built into the captain's desk. Registry: Georgetown. Irrelevant . . . "What do we have here?" A bill of sale. Paid cash a week ago, did you, you son of a bitch? And you are? Lucas took out the Maglite and shone the narrow beam onto the last page of the contract.

Well, well, well. What the fuck do you know? Leonidas Karras, head of Splinter.

So Splinter *was* involved.

Karras was barely fifty years old. Was he here for an organ transplant? Couldn't be; the Half was a health fanatic. Hell, he looked like a man fifteen years his junior. Vegan, fit, nonsmoker, non—

Lucas stopped. Nondrinker.

Two champagne glasses upstairs. *Not* Karras? Had three people done those lines? Two drinking Cristal? Or two people, one of them *not* the owner?

Lucas would have Saul do some checking on Karras's health and whereabouts. Going through the rest of the file cabinet for anything else of interest, Lucas felt a surge of excitement. They'd been after Splinter for more than two years. And here Karras was. *This* close.

Maintaining invisibility, Lucas padded down the narrow, paneled hallway toward the master stateroom. Karras had done a protection spell over the stairs, but there was nothing to stop a determined full wizard from strolling right inside and tapping the guy on the shoulder.

Or tapping him in the head.

T-FLAC had an order to apprehend, not kill unless deemed necessary. Protected by his own magic, Lucas stepped inside. All the lights were on in the spacious stateroom. The room smelled of an excess of sex and booze.

Mathematical problem solved. Karras, a blonde, and a brunette. Snuggled up together like puppies on the wide, rumpled bed.

Very romantic.

But what was the head of a tango group doing on board a brand-new boat, docked in the marina of a black-market transplant hospital?

Sprawled on her stomach, Sydney was fast asleep when Lucas got back less than an hour later. He stroked his palm down the small of her back and she stirred but didn't wake up. Too bad. He already had his regular morning hard-on. A swim would cool him off. Sydney had had a busy night; let her sleep. Smiling like a fool, Lucas scrounged around and found shorts in one of the bags Saul had sent. It was barely light outside, but he pulled them on. A jog, followed by a swim, then back to the bungalow to wake Sydney by making love to her again. Christ. He was insatiable.

Throwing open the door, he stopped in his tracks at the top of the stairs. A couple took a step back as they were about to knock. Lucas pulled the door closed behind him, where Sydney lay naked on the bed.

"Can I help you?" It was barely dawn. Not exactly the time people usually paid a social call. Automatically he captured an image with his ocular implant and sent it to HQ for the analysts. Perhaps they were spa guests, although they weren't dressed for it. They had New York written all over them. He'd never seen them before.

"Lucas Fox?"

"Yeah?" He didn't recognize the perky blonde or the redheaded guy with her.

The blonde held out a well-manicured hand. "Kiki

Wyland, Sydney's agent? And this is Brian Reed. Photographer."

Lucas didn't take the woman's hand. "Agent?"

"Literary agent. For the book. Brian, get some shots here. We'll take more later."

"What book?"

"Sydney called and filled us in. Spy? Wizard? This has bestseller written all over it."

The door behind him opened. "Who on earth i—" Lucas didn't turn, but he heard Sydney's indrawn breath as she stepped up beside him so she could see who their visitors were. "Kiki."

"My God, Syd. When I got your message about the new book idea, I had to fly out here and see this amazing spy/wizard creature for myself." She turned blue eyes on Lucas. "Do . . ." She waved her hand. "Something magical."

"Something . . . *magical*?" He shot a puzzled glance between the two women. "Like what?"

Color high on her cheeks, Sydney shot him a pleading look. "Disappear?"

"Sure." He stepped around her, pointedly not touching her at all, and went through the open door and shut it behind him, leaving the three of them outside on the steps.

Sydney's cheeks flamed. "What are you *doing* here, Kiki? I've been leaving you messages for *months*. All of which you ignored. Now here you are in *Brazil*, out of the blue."

"When one of my clients calls to tell me she needs a photographer because she's stumbled across a man who is a cross between James Bond and Harry Potter, I come running. And I really had to bust my ass to catch that flight, let me tell you."

She glanced from Sydney, dressed in a black off-the-shoulder top and brightly colored tiered, cotton gauze gypsy skirt, to the empty bottle of wine and two glasses on the tray of dirty dishes Lucas had set outside the door the night before and looked up at her client with derision in her eyes as plain as the dawn.

"But you know what, Sydney?" she said with disgust, "I'm done with you. I'm the only person who stuck by you all this time. Who is he? Some *actor* you picked up here? Dammit, Sydney. I believed you when you told me you had the story of a lifetime right here under your nose. But you just can't stop bullshitting, can you? Despite my better judgment, I've believed in you all these months, more fool me.

"If it wasn't for me, Bainbridge Books would never have even taken a chance on you."

"*Chance*? Cashing in on my notoriety, you mean."

"Jesus, you're ungrateful! I got you five months' paid vacation *and* new tits, for Christ's sake."

"I am grateful, Kiki. But you have to admit writing the destination spa book was good for you, too."

"Fifteen percent of nothing is fucking nothing, Sydney. You know that. I like you, but business is business. Brian and I took a red-eye here because you sounded so pumped. Now I'm asking you. What's the *real* deal?" Kiki stepped closer to Sydney and folded her arms, pinning Sydney with a glare like a moth to a board.

"Is that hunk in there *anything* you told me in your voice mail? More important, can you verify and back up whatever you're going to tell me? Because I'm not going out on a limb for you again without having every fact checked and double-checked. At your expense."

The cool, early morning ocean breeze stung Sydney's fire-hot cheeks. Inside she felt ice cold and leaden. "Go back to New York, Kiki. Better yet, go to hell."

The hard-edged blonde snorted. "I thought so. Goddamn it, Sydney. Are you some kind of serial liar? Never mind. Is the book you were paid to write *finished*?"

Sydney's chest felt so tight, her face so hot, she thought she'd explode right there. Humiliated. Furious at herself. Guilty as charged. God. How could she have been so damned stupid? Hadn't she learned her lesson? Apparently not. "Almost."

"*Almost* better be by deadline. You have two weeks. No wiggle room." Kiki opened her Coach tote and pulled out a stiff envelope. "Here's the cover. Don't make me regret having a soft spot for you, Syd. Get the spa book in on time, and next time, stick to soft news. No more exposés in hardcover. You don't have the chops for it. Maybe freelance for magazines, or switch to fiction. If you can ever get anyone to read your stuff after this. I'll represent you through this book going to press, but don't call me again unless you have something more to offer than some good-looking guy you're screwing. Come on, Bri."

For several minutes Sydney stood frozen at the top of the steps, watching Kiki's blond ponytail bounce on her back as she walked away. Crushing the envelope in both hands she looked away from her future, and stared out at the still, gunmetal-gray water gently lapping at the beach. The color of her world right now was gray, gray, and gray. As if all the joy she'd experienced the night before in Lucas's arms had been leached out of the day.

Nobody had ever died of humiliation, but it sure as hell felt as though *she* might.

The door snicked behind her. She couldn't hear or feel him, but he was *there* right behind her. A solid, disapproving presence. "Come inside."

Her morning of horrors wasn't done yet. She shook her head. Cowardly, but she just couldn't face Lucas's scorn on top of the home truths she couldn't deny from Kiki. Her entire body felt brittle and as though just one more word would break her. This would all be a lot easier to take if she wasn't the one responsible for her own downfall.

Unfortunately, everything that had happened could be squarely laid at her own door. And while there'd been no need for Kiki to show up with the photographer, but for Sydney's excitement when she'd left the message, the two of them wouldn't have shown up here in the first place.

She drew in a ragged breath. She couldn't stand outside on the steps for the rest of her natural life. She might as well go in and face Lucas's music and get it over with. He stepped back to let her precede him inside.

One didn't need super hearing to have heard every word. "Sit." He pointed to the chair beside the table. "Give me your best shot. Let's hear it."

Eleven

Sydney's chin went up and her eyes narrowed. "First of all, I am not a *dog*. Second, my 'best shot' is the *truth*. And third—" She flopped down in the chair in a swirl of her brightly colored skirt and glared up at him. While the long, flouncy thing covered up two of her best attributes, her spectacular legs, the off-the-shoulder clingy black top did amazing things for her other two best assets.

Her cheeks went from pale to flushed, which had been Lucas's objective all along.

"Okay, I don't have a third," she said crossly, leaning back and folding her arms. "But give me a minute, I'm sure I'll come up with one."

He propped his shoulder against the doorjamb and materialized a carafe of coffee and a couple of oversized mugs onto the table. One was filled and steaming right in front of her. "Where do you want to start?"

He doubted she'd drink the coffee, but it would give her something to do while she tried to come up with some excuse for her actions. People were intrinsically liars. That was just fact. They lied to save face or to cover a criminal act. They lied to advance themselves financially, or politically, or whatever the hell they wanted that a lie would help them achieve with the least, or no, pain.

Lucas had heard them all. He waited patiently for Sydney's lie. She was smart and creative, a writer, for fuck's sake, she'd make it good. He looked forward to hearing just how good she was. Didn't matter. He'd already planned to use Empathic Perception to wipe the memory of him from not only her mind, but anyone she might have told about him.

The fact that his powers were FUBAR might blow that idea out of the water, but he chose not to go there until necessary. Out of the corner of his eye, he saw the white towel covering the TV slip off and fall to the floor, distracting him for a moment and exposing the digital clock that she'd asked him to fix. About to turn away, the movement of the numbers caught his eye. The clock went from 00:02:00 to 00:01:59—00:01:58-57-56. Not a time clock. A *countdown* clock. He frowned. Countdown to what? And by whom? Obviously the people running the illegal organ op—but what were they waiting for?

"I'm sorry, Lucas," Sydney said quietly, reclaiming his attention. Cradling the mug between her hands, her big brown eyes were dull as they met his. "Really, really, genuinely sorry."

He did a double take. Sorry? Not, it was your fault for dragging my ass into a black op? Not, what did you think, moron, that I'd keep something like that a secret? "For what?"

"Betraying who—*what* you are." Her gaze was steady and hard-won, belying the tension in her hands. "It was thoughtless. Dangerous. Selfish."

"Wow. That's some hair shirt, Sydney. You really think some New York literary agent and her boy photog could walk in here and get the drop on me?"

He didn't need experience or training dealing with liars both pathological and habitual—Sydney McBride was as clear as rainwater. She'd rather be anywhere but confronting him. He felt a returning swell of respect for her. She was embarrassed, and by the rapid and erratic pulse at the base if her throat, scared.

Shit. Of *him*?

"I called yesterday when you were sleeping, and left a message for Kiki to send a photographer. It was before . . ." She looked down into her coffee cup, darker color flooding her cheeks.

Before they'd slept together. Before they'd made love. Yeah. He got it. He supposed he could cut her a little slack—especially since he planned on doing a mind-wipe anyway. "Tell me about the book you're contracted to write."

"Kiki found a small-press publisher who agreed to let me write a book on destination surgery/spas. I've traveled to four other countries in the last five months, getting the inside story by interviewing doctors and patients. That's why I had to have—" she pointed to her chest and grimaced. "That was part of the deal. A first-hand experience. Or should I say a first boob experience?"

"And?" He tilted his head slightly and studied her.

A frown gathered between her brows. "What do you mean 'and'? And what?"

"So the book will be finished in a couple of weeks. Is it any good?"

The question clearly surprised her. "I'm a pretty decent writer. So yes. The answer is yes. *Skin Deep* will be unbiased, well written, and informative."

"Then why does your agent think she did you a big freaking favor?"

Sydney drew in a deep ragged breath and her fingers tightened again around the mug of coffee she clearly had no intention of drinking. She held on to the ceramic mug like a lifeline. "My first book came out last year. Shockingly, unexpectedly—it was—it was a huge hit. *USA Today*, number two on the *New York Times* best-seller list. And stayed there for fourteen weeks. It was . . . Amazing. I did all the big talk shows. God . . ."

Sydney's eyes rose to meet his. "My third oldest brother, Tomás, is bipolar. Manic-depressive, paranoid schizophrenic. He lives in a group home in Texas. He's an amazing man. So damn bright *and* brave and very much aware that he's different. Damaged. When he's on his meds he's articulate and present. When he's not on them, he believes the government is bugging his room. He hears voices. Always telling him to do *bad* things. Telling him *he's* bad. I wanted to tell his story. To let people see what living with that kind of challenge is like. To show how he deals with it. How his family deals with it."

"You love him. I can't see how this could've blown up in your face."

Her cheeks went pink. "You heard."

"Cryptic and tainted by your agent's point of view, yeah, I heard."

"Her point of view is the truth. And my truth was that I never thought that many people would even know about the book, let alone *read* it. I thought his story would be more compelling written in first person. And that's how I wrote it. From the point of view of 'Michaela,' weaving the facts of Tomás's life with anecdotal information I picked up from visiting him in Texas. Kiki shopped the manuscript around. Frankly, I could tell she wasn't that enthusiastic about it, but to give her props, she tried."

Sydney pulled her feet into her chair, sitting the way he'd seen her their first morning together, chin resting on her knees, holding the forgotten coffee.

"No one was interested, and I finally ended up paying a couple of thousand dollars to self-publish it. Somehow someone gave it to a talk-show host to read, and the rest is history. I went on his show and didn't tell him that there was no such person as Michaela. He was moved by her story. The producers of the show wanted me to convince Michaela to come and talk. I was caught between a rock and a hard place."

Looking at her hands, she bit her lip, then lifted her eyes to look at him. "No. No I wasn't. I was caught right where I *wanted* to be. In the spotlight. Feted. Photographed. Invited to exciting places and meeting cool people. And the more money I made, the more people who admired me for my courage, the less I remembered Tomás, the brother I'd set out to help, the brother I love. The brother I'd based my fictitious Michaela on. *Based* her on? No, I'd elaborated and fabricated some of the anecdotes, to make them more *entertaining*—"

She rose from her chair, set the full mug on the table, and with a flash of bare feet started pacing. The countdown clock on the television read 11:02:01.

"I was invited to Hollywood with Kiki." Sydney started pulling the covers up and making the bed. "We were in talks to make a movie based on Michaela's 'life story.' God . . . I sat there with a dozen men in suits, and I thought 'This is all a big fat lie. What am I going to do?' It was just snowballing, out of control, and I couldn't—didn't want to—do anything to stop it."

"You're putting the housekeeping staff out of work. Come and drink your coffee."

She tossed the pillow she held onto the head of the bed, but didn't come back to the table. "They wined me and dined me, and afterward I went back home to Miami. And I was terrified that this huge lie was going to come out, and what was I going to do if that happened? And months went by, and *nothing* happened. And I started to relax a little."

She walked to the kitchenette, then to the closet where she opened the double louvered door and stood there with her back to him, contemplating the clothes hanging there.

Taking out two garments, she tossed the colorful fabric on the bed, staring down at them as if they held the answers to the universe. "Then the TV show called and booked me again. And I thought—woohoo. Look at me. Nobody cares how I did it, people are hearing what I have to say about mental health. People are *aware*. I've done something *good*." She looked at him from across the room.

"I went back on his show. Sexy red suit, Jimmie Choo heels. I looked fabulous, and was filled with confidence, and God help me, my own self-importance."

Clearly this was not going to end well. Lucas wanted to go to her and take her in his arms. He stayed put, leaning against the doorjamb.

"The second the cameras turned on, the talk show's host accused me flat out of being a liar. Of making a fool of not only himself, but all of America. An online watch group had researched everything. Proving there was no such person as Michaela. None of my anecdotes were fact. The nonfiction book I'd been touting was, in fact, mostly fiction. The book was a hoax. I was a frau—"

The satellite phone buzzed on the table. Saul. Shit. Lucas debated letting it go to voice mail. He could call him right back . . . Christ. As much as he wanted to be in the now with Sydney, T-FLAC had priority. "Hold that thought, sweetheart—Can it wait?" he asked his Control.

"Explosion and bio attack," Saul said without greeting. "Hong Kong Stock Exchange. Same signature as the bombing in London."

"When?"

"Seven minutes ago."

Lucas's gaze swiveled to the television screen across the room. 11:57:00 The sat phone beeped in his ear and

Lucas pulled it away to check the caller ID. Mason. "Knight's on the line. Gotta take it. Hold."

Across the room another phone rang. Or rather played Corinne Bailey Rae. Sydney scrambled through her beach tote for her cell phone, then remembered it was in the yellow clutch Lucas had materialized yesterday.

The bag was on the top shelf of the closet. Grabbing it she pulled out her iPhone just as Lucas said into *his* phone, "Mason? Where've you been?"

The number was an unfamiliar upper Manhattan area code. "Hello?"

"Sydney? This is Paula Sager at Bainbridge Books. How's the book coming?"

I'm putting it in a damn bottle and floating it to New York right now. It should be there in about—Sydney caught herself. "Great, just polishing it. You'll have it by the end of the month."

". . . look into a couple of bombings and we suspect the use of LZ17," Lucas was saying, his back to her. "London and now Hong Kong just minutes ag . . ."

". . . ew boobs? Enjoying them?" Paula asked.

"Fabulous," Sydney told her with false cheer, trying to listen to two conversations at once.

"Okay, then. I hadn't heard from you for a while—"

Paula hadn't heard from her since she'd threatened to sue and get back all the money the publishing house had spent to send Sydney to all the spas. Unless she picked a surgery, *any* damned surgery. It had been in her contract. The part of the contract Sydney had skimmed because she was so damn happy that a publisher was willing to take a chance on her.

"Everything's fine, Paula. You'll have the manuscript by the thirtieth. Don't worry."

"Is there anything salacious I can hint at for the next sales meeting?"

Sydney blew out a sigh and felt a cynical smile twist her lips. "Oscar-winning movie stars, country western singer. Big, big names. Don't worry. You'll get your money's worth."

"Don't sound bitter, Sydney. Bainbridge gave you a chance when no one else would."

"You're absolutely—" Sydney punched the end-call command on her phone. One of the things she'd learned years ago when she'd been temping as a receptionist was if you wanted to cut someone off, always do it when *you* were the one talking. It was much more believable when you claimed later that it wasn't your fault. Turning the phone off she dropped it back into the magical yellow clutch and tossed it to the back of the closet.

"Thanks, Mason. You know T-FLAC appreciates the shit you help us with. Yeah, yeah. I know. I'll come in when I'm done here and you can check me out. You too, take care." Lucas paced back toward the center of the room and looked at the small screen on his phone, pressing one of the buttons on it.

"That was your foster father/mentor guy? Is he okay?"

"Yeah." He held up one finger and turned back toward the window. "Saul? Yeah. Mason will talk to our lab and see what he can help them with. Yeah. He sounded really inter—What did you find out about the—No shit? Karras's *mother-in-law*? Lungs? Well, I'll be damned. That might be the only reason he's here, but I bet he brought her here because he's ass-deep in the black-market business himself. Yeah. Yeah. Dig deeper.

"And while you're looking into all things *Novos Começos,* monitor a countdown clock here. Yeah. Right. It started a new countdown minutes after the Hong Kong incident." Lucas finished the call and stuck the small phone into his front pocket.

Fascinated hearing Lucas's end of the conversation,

Sydney's heart did a little two-step of excitement. "Mrs. Klugg, I remember her, she's the one that got the double lung transplant, right?"

"Mother-in-law to Leonidas Karras. A Half, he's head of a terrorist group called Splinter." Lucas picked up Sydney's mug and drank some of her untouched coffee. "It's a large group of mostly disgruntled Halfs. There're into shit like money laundering, or working for more powerful full wizards. Halfs aren't the brightest bulbs. It's a genetic thing."

Sydney reclaimed her mug. Now she was ready for her caffeine fix. She refilled the mug and drank deeply. "That's a highly prejudicial statement, isn't it? Surely not all Halfs are stupid. Like any other group there might be stupid Halfs. But there must also be Halfs that are smart, and entrepreneurial."

Lucas's lips twitched. *"Entrepreneurial?"*

She rolled her eyes at him. "You know what I mean. I don't think lumping an entire group of people under one sign is particularly smart. If you're convinced all of them are stupid and incapable of doing—" Sydney waved a vague hand. "Whatever. You could be dangerously underestimating them."

"True." His conciliatory tone said he was listening. His relaxed stance said he wasn't all that worried.

"You don't underestimate them, do you?"

Lucas shook his head.

Of course he didn't. Sydney gave a theatrical sigh. "Fine. You know what you're doing. What happened to Mr. Knight?"

"Doctor Knight. He was working on something in his lab. When he's in there the roof could fall in and he wouldn't even glance up." He indicated the closed closet. "Everything okay with you?"

So far. "Mm. That was the publisher. Checking to see if I'm going to deliver."

"You'll deliver," he said with casual confidence. "What's she going to do if you don't deliver? Take away your birthday? Demand that you hand over your implants by Friday?"

Sydney cupped her breasts as if Lucas were going to whip out the implants right then himself. "Now that I've stopped tripping over them all the time, I'm starting to enjoy these things."

"I'm learning to enjoy them, too. Change into that mind-boggling red bikini. We'll swim, clear our minds, and then make a plan."

She narrowed her eyes at him. He seemed to be pretty damned cavalier about what she'd done. "You took my . . . *betrayal,* for want of a better word, pretty damn well."

"Sydney—I've worked in this profession for most of my adult life. I've been a wizard all my life. Do you know how many people know about either of those things? Maybe thirty. And out of those thirty I'd trust three or four of them with my life. If I don't want a person to remember that I'm either of those things I have a power called Empathic Perception. I can either make a person forget completely, or only remember selective events. I wasn't worried that you knew."

Her heart, her irrational, already in *love* heart, gave a dull throb. "So all this time you *didn't* trust me. You knew when it was all over—when in fact, *you'd* used *me*—that you would conveniently wipe my damn mind. Nice, Lucas. Really, really freaking *nice.*"

Twelve

"Son of a bitch bastard, rat fink, dickhead. *Male!*" Sydney muttered under her breath as she strode down the beach. The long, brightly colored fabric of her gypsy skirt flapped wetly around her ankles as she kicked up water.

"*Wipe* my mind? Wipe *my* mind? Wipe my *mind*?"

She hiked the skirt up her thighs with both hands so she could walk a little farther into the waves. Didn't matter how the hell she said it, wiping a person's mind sounded ridiculous. Bizarre. And damned . . . *unfair.*

She couldn't believe he'd used her, then planned to make her *forget* everything. Shit. And once she got past the bullshit part of it, the fact remained that being able to clear someone's memory was really damn cool. The repercussions alone were endless.

The writer in her thought so, you bet, but the woman part of her thought it *sucked.* She could forgive his wizardly tendencies—he was what he was and God knew, she'd dated worse. No, her hot button, after the whole Michaela fiasco, was the trust issue. She thought she'd been offered that trust by Lucas, only to find out that he'd been planning a mind-sweep thing all along. He was going to steal her memories, every second she'd had with him, and it hit her where it hurt.

She was still a little raw from the past year with people calling her a liar to her face. A year of people telling her they no longer trusted her. Tears of embarrassment and hurt—yes, dammit, *hurt*—filled her eyes and made her chest feel tight.

Even though she knew it was ridiculous to feel this depth of pain, that a man she barely knew could inflict a wound so deeply, it ripped at her. Like having salt poured on a festering gash.

Even her usually one hundred percent supportive family had been devastated that she'd fabricated Tomás's story. They loved her, but they hadn't understood, still didn't really, what had made her take the family's pain and turn a spotlight on it. To them, she'd used something very private for her own profit. Which, to be fair, she had.

Unintentionally. None of it started out that way. She used both hands to wipe her wet cheeks as she splashed through the warm shallow water. A sob caught in her throat. She wanted to fling her arms out wide and spin in a circle, yelling out at the top of her lungs, "I screwed up, okay? I fucked up and I'm *sorry.*"

Sorry that she'd made up a better, more interesting story to bring attention to mental health issues. Sorry that she'd kept her mouth shut and not corrected everyone when they thought it was a true story. Sorry that she'd been caught. Sorry that she's been held up for public ridicule. Just damned well, freaking *sorry.*

Her embarrassment had been a constant for almost a year. She wanted to shed it like a lead-lined jacket. She wanted to step back into her great, challenging, *interesting* life without that dark cloud forever hanging over her. Instead, she'd invited it back in with a single phone call.

The sun beat down on her head and bare shoulders, and the water splashed playfully around her calves and knees. None of which made her feel better. If she cried for twenty-four hours straight, it wouldn't help. And she didn't give a damn that she was feeling sorry for herself, or that everything that had happened was her own fault. She felt like crap all over again, and her heart ached—*all over again*—for everything good blowing up in her face.

She kicked a wave. "The road to hell is paved with good intentions," she told the empty beach. "And God will never give me more than I can handle." Closing her eyes, Sydney stopped and dragged in a deep shaky breath. She let it out slowly. "Yeah, right. Pity party officially *over.*"

The heat stung her shoulders and back, and sand clung like cement shoes to her feet and ankles as she veered away from the lapping waves and back toward the bungalow and Lucas.

"Hey, gorgeous." Tony Maxim, star of stage and screen, and multiple marriages, yelled from outside his bungalow.

Sydney returned his wave, then changed direction slightly and angled across the beach toward him, her wet skirt slapping at her legs.

Deeply, faux-ly tanned, he wore crisp white linen shorts, and an unbuttoned red and yellow Hawaiian shirt as he lay on a lounger in the shade cast by the small bungalow behind him.

Bruises and all, he was a hunk. A hunk as shallow as an evaporating puddle, but a hunk nonetheless. Sydney had seen a couple of his action movies. They were fast-paced and exciting, but the action was a cover for the fact that he couldn't act his way out of a wet paper bag. But he sure *looked* terrific holding an Uzi in one arm and a pretty girl in the other.

Of course Lucas's whole life was an action movie. As much as she'd enjoy having him as a scapegoat, she wasn't mad at *him.* She was embarrassed that he'd seen her at her very worst, and he'd heard Kiki out her, reviving her dirty little secret that apparently was destined to follow her for the rest of her days.

She wanted to save her career, and he was out to save the world.

How could she compare with that? And despite the fact that his powers were fluctuating and must be incredibly frustrating for him, he didn't whine or complain about it, he just focused on his job. She admired that in him. Admired his dedication. Admired the way he focused. And, dammit, she wanted Lucas to admire things about *her.* Things unrelated to her new breasts.

She'd thought he was coming to care for her. Not falling in *love* with her of course, she doubted if men like Lucas *fell* in love. But maybe care. Just a little.

Again. This was *her* problem. Not his.

Own it, Sydney McBride. Suck it up and own it.

She'd go back in a few minutes and kiss and make up with him. Nothing too intense. Keep it light. Keep it casual. Move on. But *before* she did that, she needed to cool off and regain a little of her bravado. These were all *her* issues. Not Lucas's. She shot a quick glance a few doors down to see if he was looking for her. He wasn't. She dredged up a smile for Tony.

Folding the script he'd been reading, he tossed it on the lounger, rising to meet her, both hands extended. She let Tony clasp her hands in his, but took a step back to disengage after a few seconds, leaning against the nearby table, ankles crossed.

"You look like a million bucks," he said as he sat back down, his blue eyes filled with the kind of admiration her bruised and battered ego needed right now. Even from someone like three-times-divorced Tony Maxim.

"How about dinner tonight?"

She smiled and shook her head. "No thanks."

"You don't know what you're missing, babe."

"I know, I know. I just can't handle looking across the dinner table at a man who's prettier than I am. Totally puts me off my crab cakes. Not to mention—for the nine-hundredth-and-seventy-ninth time—you're too young for me."

"Aww." Tony pouted up at her for a moment, then amped up his trademark killer grin. "How about just making it a booty call, then?"

Sydney shook her head again, but smiled. "In your dreams."

"I do have dreams about you tipping over with your new boobs. And I'm always there to catch you. So—how are you coping with the girls?"

Interesting the way she'd stopped thinking about them as something alien. *Lucas* had done that.

"I'm still having the implants out when I go home."

"You'll get used to them, babe, and then you'll want to come back for the Ds. Everbody does." He had two black eyes, and the skin surrounding his new nose was a sickly greenish yellow. He'd had his nose reshaped a couple of weeks before and the bump that marred its perfection was gone. He'd also had lipo, resulting in a spectacular six-pack. Sydney tilted her head, checking out his features, now sans bandages. He was still ridiculously handsome, even with swelling and bruising. "Your nose looks great."

He touched it gingerly. "I feel like Big Bird. Wanna come in and make breakfast for me?"

"No."

"But . . . I'll starve. You know I can't cook."

"*You* don't even have to boil water. Dial three on the house phone."

"Man, you're cruel and heartless." He rubbed a hand across his bruised, waxed hairless chest. "You're killing me here, beautiful. Hey, did you hear all those helicopters the other night? The soldiers came and knocked at my door at like two in the morning, scared the crap outta me. Looking for some deranged killer who'd escaped a mental hospital." He gave a dramatic shudder.

"I heard. Hard to miss," she told him dryly.

"I wanted to come over and check on you, but, um . . . I figured with all the helicopters, and all those soldiers with guns, you'd be fine."

She didn't blame Tony for not wanting to go outside and get involved. Only a crazy, deranged spy-wizard would be out there in the middle of the damn night being shot at.

"Get out of the sun," she told him sternly, taking his arm. "The doctors told you to be careful in the heat, and besides, you still look like you did six rounds with Wladimir Klitschko."

"Wada who?"

She didn't bother to sigh. "Wladimir Klitschko. IBF, WBO, and IBO heavyweight boxing champion? Big Ukrainian guy? Defeated mandatory challenger Ray Austin in 2007?"

Tony shook his head. His trademark shaggy blond hair, highlighted and low-lighted and looking completely, expensively *natural,* flopped over his forehead in a perfect fall. "How do you know this shit?"

"Eight brothers—" Someone brushed her hair behind her ear, making Sydney shiver despite the heat of the sun.

"Come back to our place, we weren't finished talking." A familiar voice whispered against her ear.

She swatted at the Invisible Man. *Our* place?

"What's the matter?" Tony asked as she slapped Lucas's invisible arm.

"Bugs. Pesky, annoying *bugs*. Let's go inside. You *can* offer me a gallon of coffee and try charming me. Maybe this time, you'll get lucky."

"If he so much as touches you, he's a dead man."

Tony bowed as Sydney squeezed past him, Lucas right beside her. Either Tony leaned over to be courtly as she passed, or to get a look down her top. If she had to guess, it was probably the latter.

He grabbed his midriff when he straightened. "Ow, shit."

"God smote you for looking down my top, Tony." Or Lucas had done something. Sydney brushed past the actor and stepped on Lucas's foot as they walked up the stairs into Tony's bungalow. Lucas ran a hand across her bare shoulders above the black spandex top. She ignored him.

Tony's place looked pretty much like hers, except it smelled strongly of pot and burnt coffee. Sydney wrinkled her nose. She was not staying inside with Tony and Lucas. Her day had already been bad enough.

"Here." She handed Tony the stylish Outback-style hat from the table by the door. "Put this on. You can take me for brunch up at the hotel instead." She didn't want to be anywhere near that unmade bed. Not with Tony. Not with Lucas.

"I'm not hungry now," Tony said with his million-dollar pout that Sydney was sure made women melt. He flashed that megawattage smile again and ran a finger down her arm. Tony knew he was top box office, and wasn't shy about letting her know what a privileged life she could live if she'd just put out for the duration of their sojourn in Brazil. She'd politely declined when she'd met him on the surgery floor a month ago. And every day since.

He, Sydney, and Kandy had been the only tenants of the bungalows for the past couple of weeks. Tony had been flirting with both of them since they'd met, despite both women's clear lack of interest. Sydney had been too busy interviewing people for the book and trying to get into writing something that didn't hold her heart or her interest.

Kandy had a biker husband back home in Vegas who looked like a pit bull in his photographs.

Movie star, handsome, rich as Croesus, Tony Maxim had not been alone. He trolled the restaurants and bars every evening, and Sydney had seen him several different times going into his bungalow with one of the women he'd picked up.

On her left, Lucas slid his hand around her waist. Settling his big palm under her right breast. She tried prying his hand off her midriff one finger at a time. His chuckle vibrated against her side.

"Well, I'm *starving,*" she assured Tony, who was admiring his reflection in the television monitor. His stupid clock didn't work either. Lucas had said he'd fix hers, and he'd forgotten. Oh, well, back to the towel. What she didn't see couldn't annoy her.

Unless what she couldn't see was a *who,* and that who was Lucas. He seemed to be particularly gifted at annoying her.

"Me too," Lucas whispered in her ear, his invisible breath warm on her cheek. She tried again to dislodge his hand and push him away from her. But he was immovable.

"Admit it," she told Tony, trying to disengage from Lucas. She walked over and hooked her right arm through Tony's left, Lucas attached to her like a barnacle. "You're bored out of your mind. Let's go and eat something yummy. You can tell me all about yourself while the half-naked girls on the beach ogle you. You know how you love that."

He stuck the hat on his head at a rakish angle, pausing to admire himself critically. "You already know all about me."

"Tabloid stuff. You can tell me about the real you." She edged closer to the door.

"I can tell you about the real him in one word. Waste of air."

Sydney bit back a smile. "That's *three.*"

Tony glanced over his shoulder. "Three what?"

"Three rumbles of my stomach."

She got the fifty-million-dollar Tony Maxim grin. "Okay, let's go eat. Anything for a demanding woman."

Sydney laughed, not because Tony was anything special, but because Lucas had come to find her. Because Lucas was nibbling her bare shoulder, and because his presence warmed her heart and soul. "God, you're easy."

"I keep telling you that." Tony's smile went up in wattage. "But you won't say yes."

She looked at the man millions upon millions of women fell in love with every day, and her heart didn't even miss a beat. "Tony. Was yesterday your lucky day with me?"

"No." Lucas's whisper was silky and right in her ear. "Because it was me inside you yesterday. Me making you moan. Me making you wet."

Sydney jabbed her left elbow into his rock-hard abs. Abs he'd gotten honestly, not by plastic surgery. Tony pouted. "I didn't even see you yesterday . . . Did I?"

"No. But even if you did, like every other day you've offered, you won't get lucky today, either."

"Damn straight." Lucas's hand tightened under her breast.

"Aw, Sydney. Most women—"

She cut Tony off. Honest to God she felt as if she were hearing voices, just like Tomás did. "Most women fall at your feet 24/7," she told the movie star, trying to concentrate on just one conversation at a time. "I remember your mentioning it. Consider this a day of rest. We'll talk like normal humans and enjoy brunch. What do you say?"

"I'll do my level best to keep my hands off you, but you're hot, Sydney. Really, really hot. I'm only human."

"Guess the guy needs a script, huh?"

The three of them managed to walk abreast down the stairs and onto the shell path without anyone breaking their necks.

"I'll let you drive," Tony told her magnanimously as they approached the golf carts.

"Good of you, but we'll walk. You've got your hat and you haven't been out in days. You need the exercise."

He sighed, then slid his hand down her behind and gave her butt a little squeeze. She smacked his arm. "Hands to yourself, Romeo."

Suddenly Tony fell over into the shrubbery beside the path in a tangle of tanned arms and legs. He yelled as he got snared in a flowering bush and had to fight his way out.

Biting back a smile because it was such a ten-year-old-boy thing to do, Sydney spun toward Lucas. "That was childish, dammit."

"Hey!" Tony scrambled to his feet, one hand holding his faux abs, the other brushing at his clothes. "I tripped. Don't make it sound like I did it on purpose."

Sydney bent to pick up his hat, finally dislodging Lucas's arm from around her waist. "Here." She punched out the crown with a little more force than necessary, then handed Tony his hat. "Did you hurt yourself?"

"Why," Lucas whispered in her ear. "Will you kiss it better?"

"Maybe I will."

Tony blinked. "Will what?"

"Kiss it better," Sydney snapped.

"Dead man walking," Lucas said against her cheek. "Wanna see something cool?"

"No," Sydney snarled, doing everything in her power not to laugh. "I do *not*. Go away."

"Shit on a shingle, Sydney." Tony spun around to look at her, a frown on his bruised, handsome face. "You run hot and cold. You asked me to brunch. If you've changed your mind just say so."

"I—"

Lucas suddenly materialized beside her, making Tony jump and do a double take that wasn't acting. "What the f—" Tony's face went from startled to inquiring as he glanced from Lucas to Sydney.

With his arms back around her waist, Lucas stuck out his hand. "Fox. Lucas Fox. Sydney's boyfriend. How're you doing?"

"You didn't tell me you had a boyfriend," Tony accused, stuffing his hands into his grass-stained shorts pockets.

"I didn't?" She held out her left hand so he could see the sparkle of her diamond.

"Ah. Engaged? Congrats. Great meeting you," he said to Lucas. "Gotta run, I have a script I wanna read. See you, Sydney." And he turned and strolled back the way they'd just come.

Trying to keep a straight face because God only knew the whole thing was insanely ridiculous, Sydney turned to Lucas. "You just wiped that poor man's mind."

His eyes were forest green as he brushed her hair over her shoulders, and his hands lingered on her skin. "No, genetics did that. I just eliminated the last ten minutes from his memory."

Thirteen

Sydney punched his arm. "That was mean. He's a nice guy." God, she loved the delicious shiver running across her skin as he trailed cool fingers over her sun-warmed shoulders. She struggled to maintain a little self-control because they *were* in full view of anyone coming down the path.

"You have on too many clothes."

She bit back a smile. "A skirt and a top? Please." Thong. No bra. Not even shoes. "I'm practically naked." There. That was the lightness she'd wanted to achieve. She leaned against him, winding her arms around his neck. All thought of a studied, casual, kiss-and-make-up fled her mind when she was in his arms. He smelled of—Lucas. Hot sexy male.

She wanted to taste him, wanted to roll around on the grass and make love until she couldn't see straight, then do it again until she could. She couldn't get enough of him.

He breathed in her ear before sucking lightly on the lobe.

"How fast can you teleport us back to the bungalow?" Sliding her palm down his arm, Sydney stepped away from him, grabbed his hand, and tried to pull him in the direction she wanted him to go.

Her immovable sex object smiled as he snagged her around the waist and tugged her back. "I can't wait to get you inside. I want to taste you now. I want to feel the weight of your breasts, and taste your nipples. I want to hear that little noise you make when you come. Here. *Now.* No one will see us."

"They most certainly w—" Being invisible hadn't lost its fascination. "Okay. They won't. But what if your power . . ." She felt the slight tug accompanied by a metallic musical jingle as he removed the multiple chain belt from around her hips. "And we're out here in front of God and everyone . . ." There went her skirt. Pretty hard to hold a rational conversation when nothing about this moment was rational.

She felt the coolness of his hand as it lingered on her bare hip. He stroked her sensitive skin with his slightly callused fingers, making all her girl parts sit up and take notice. Sydney combed her fingers through his hair, loving the soft texture as she twined the strands between her fingers. How such a hard man could have anything soft about him intrigued her.

Although she couldn't see him, she could feel the solid muscles in his chest and belly, and the radiating heat from his body. She could smell that unique fragrance of his skin, and taste the familiar texture of his mouth.

Vaguely aware of the heat of the sun beating down on her, she was deaf to all but Lucas's murmurs as he nuzzled her throat.

". . . rather go rent a sailboat." The masculine voice, so *close,* made Sydney literally jump and freeze, clenching her fingers in Lucas's hair. Lucas chuckled soundlessly, a mere movement of his chest pressed to her, and dragged his teeth up the side of her throat as a middle-aged couple walked by, coming within two feet of where she and Lucas stood. Close enough for her to feel the brush of the woman's swimsuit cover-up across the back of her bare leg, and smell the man's spicy aftershave.

"We did that yesterday," the woman said firmly.

Lucas raked her skin with his teeth, pausing to suck

gently, then licked the small sting in a far from soothing caress. Rolling her head to the side to give him better access, Sydney squeezed her eyes shut and shuddered.

"Today I want to swim," the woman cajoled. "No one comes to this part of the beach. We'll have it all to ourselves. Come on, Frank, you agreed we . . ."

"Think they'd be shocked?" Lucas whispered wickedly against her ear. His hot breath sent cold shivers dancing down her spine. One arm firmly around her waist, he ran the other hand up Sydney's side, taking the stretchy spandex top up and up and up, until he bared her breasts. "Mmm. No bra. Thanks."

She'd almost forgotten that they were standing right there on the path, practically *naked*. In broad daylight. The couple moved away down the path to the beach. Pulling the top free over her head, Lucas tossed that aside too, leaving her in a tiny triangle of fuchsia lace and a bit of satin ribbon. Too bad he couldn't see what he'd unwrapped.

She shuddered again as he toyed with her nipples. "You're quite welcome. You're also insane."

"Yeah." He ran the back of his finger under the front edge of lace, and his touch, so close to where Sydney wanted it, was almost electrifying. "I think I am." He did something magical to make her thong vanish. Unfortunately the hand that had come so close disappeared as well.

God, she loved . . . She loved the satiny feel of his skin under her exploring hands, loved the roughness of his chest hair as it arrowed down to his erection and tickled her skin. "Can't we—"

He pulled her hard against him, making the air in her lungs whoosh out in a soft grunt. Hard mouth, hot naked Lucas. His mouth was avaricious on hers as he turned his head slightly, one large hand cupping the back of her head to angle her where he wanted her. Hell, where *she* wanted her. She wasn't going anywhere. Sydney felt as light as thistledown even as her blood pounded through her veins and heat pooled between her legs. Holding her loosely in the circle of his arms, Lucas slid his chest against hers; the hair tickled her sensitized breasts and made her nipples achingly hard as he kissed her.

God, the man could *kiss*.

He bit her lower lip, sucking it into the hot cavern of his mouth, then worried it with his teeth, spiking her heartbeats and making her dizzy with lust. With a small helpless moan, she opened her mouth wider to meet his tongue. She had to tighten her arms around his neck to keep her balance. Kissing him back with everything in her, she hooked a leg around his waist.

Gripping a handful of her hair, he tugged her head back to rest in his palm, then bent her over his arm, trailing his lips down her throat, across her chest until his mouth fastened on a nipple, sucking the hard peak into the wet heat of his mouth.

Sydney's back arched and her fingers tightened on his shoulders as he cupped her other breast, rubbing a callused thumb over that peak. The doctor had been right. The surgery did no damage to nerve endings; she had full sensation in her nipples. God, did she ever.

She practically climbed his body, managing to wrap both legs around his waist and hold him tightly against her sensitive cleft. His erection pulsed against her. She shifted again. Closer to the prize.

"Afraid of heights?"

"Nuh-uh." The only thing she feared right now was the *lack* of dizzying heights of sexual satisfaction. He seemed determined to drive her to the brink. She was bent over his arm as if she weighed nothing at all. The position opened her to him completely, and all she could do was tighten her legs around his waist, and hold onto his upper arms for dear life as he sucked and licked her nipples and drove her out of her mind. Her nails bit into his biceps.

"Good," he murmured against her breast as his free hand trailed a path of fire down the center of her body. Sydney felt like a too tightly wound watch as his fingers lightly brushed the damp curls at the apex of her thighs.

"Dammit, Lucas! I want you inside me. *Now.*"

His hand curved, shaping her mound and as she gasped, she could feel his lips curve into a smile against her sensitized skin.

"Why aren't I getting the big guns?" she demanded as his fingertips separated the slick feminine folds. Sydney wiggled. His wonderfully hard penis was maybe an inch from where she wanted it. And she wanted it *now.*

"This one is for you."

"I'd rather have one for *us,* right now."

He chuckled against her other breast. "Next time."

Great. She wasn't sure there ever would *be* a next time. She had to stock up on Lucas sex *now.* Except he was an extremely handy man and what he was doing to her had her body bathed in heat and then cold.

Sliding his fingers up and down the slick, swollen flesh, he found the small, hooded nub of her sensitized clitoris and rubbed insistent circles around it until she arched against him with a small cry. The tension built and built.

"Come for me, Sydney. Let go and come."

"Well, hell, I wanted . . . wanted . . ." Her spread thighs tightened around his waist, and her entire body clenched as the orgasm built. Her nails bit into the tensile flesh of his arms. The fingers inside her grew more insistent. His teeth clamped down on the side of her arched throat.

Just as she knew she couldn't stand one more stroke, one more internal caress, he slid his penis deep inside her. Her stomach muscles rippled as she came in waves of volcanic, shuddering climaxes that made her deaf and blind as her body broke apart.

It was several minutes before she came back to her body. "Holy cow," she said opening her eyes and blinking back the sweat on her lashes. "That was . . ." She turned her head, still supported on Lucas's palm. "Amazing." She finished as she looked around. "Where exactly *are* we?" There was nothing to see because they were surrounded by nothing but white—"Fog?"

Without disengaging, Lucas floated, disconcertingly, onto his back like a swimmer, his arms supporting her body. "Cloud."

"We're in the *air*?"

"And out to sea."

Her heart, which hadn't slowed yet from the mind-blowing climax, picked up speed. "How *far* out?"

"A mile or so. No one can see us. This cloud'll pass in a minute or two."

At this point she wasn't so much concerned about anyone seeing them as she was about plunging into the God-only-knew-how-deep water, filled with God-only-knew-how-many sharks.

As she didn't consider Lucas's still erect member sufficient support, she held on to the hair on his chest. His fingers tightened on her butt, which made her feel a little more secure.

The cloud did pass to reveal the harsh sunlight glinting off gently swelling, dark blue, read *deep,* ocean. There was nothing around them but miles upon miles of water, a few fluffy clouds, and air. A lot of air.

She didn't know what she felt most intensely. Sheer terror that they were up in the air with absolutely no means of support. Or flat-out euphoria that she was doing something she couldn't even have imagined a few days ago.

"Hang on, let me get sunscreen on you." He materialized a bottle of lotion and smoothed it into the parts he could reach. The rest he applied in some magical hocus-pocus Sydney didn't bother asking about.

The *hang on,* she presumed, was rhetorical.

A seagull flew beneath them.

Sydney rested her head on his chest. His hair tickled her nose, and she turned to rest her chin on her stacked hands. She didn't want to ask if he'd mind giving her a heads-up before he had a power outage, so she could brace herself for submersion.

If she closed her eyes, which she did for a few seconds, it was almost like floating on water as Lucas caught the thermals and they lazily drifted on the gentle air currents coming off the water. Holding her against him, he did a slow roll, making her long hair tangle between them like silken threads. "This is incredible." It was about a hundred exclamations beyond incredible, but she was too satiated to think of more.

"I hate to bring up something to destroy the post-coital haze, but you *are* going to fire your agent, right?"

"She's stood by me for—"

"You are going to fire your agent, aren't you? Because no one has the right to talk to you like that. I don't give a shit if she spoon-fed you broth while you were recuperating from what happened. Fire her ass."

"When I get home," she assured him, touched that he was so adamant. Of course a guy didn't have to *care* to react as he was doing. "It's too bad, but I won't be able to tell my dad and brothers about any of this. I hurt them so badly revealing our family's painful story, it's going to take a long time before they trust me again."

He combed his fingers through her hair. "It hurts."

Her heart ached. "A lot. They love me, so they forgive me. But there's still that little niggle of distrust that breaks my heart. It's too bad, because I know they'd enjoy meeting you. And you'd like all of them, too."

She'd be home in a couple of days. She'd missed her family. Missed their unconditional love. "I'll do whatever it takes to win back their respect and trust." Sydney reached out to touch a small wisp of a cloud as it drifted by. The damp coolness closed around her hand. "I've told you about my family, tell me about Doctor Knight. Is he a wizard too?"

"Yeah. A powerful one." Lucas realized how relieved he'd been when Mason had finally returned his call. He rubbed his hand along the smooth curve of Sydney's lower back to cup her firm, fine ass. "You don't need to hold on so tight. I won't let you fall." Mason had sounded distracted. Worried? God only knew he was getting older. Obviously, it had become time for Lucas to return the favor and help out where he could. He'd have to be diplomatic, of course.

Sydney peered beyond his shoulder to the gently rolling waves the distance of a couple of city blocks below them. "That's okay. I'll just use you as an air mattress. Do wizards float in water, too?"

"You bet."

She didn't loosen her hold. "You call him by his first name, but you consider him your father, don't you?"

"I—yeah. I guess I do. He's been around for as long as I can remember."

"You said your parents were struck by *lightning*?"

The anomalous event had haunted him for years. "Odds of being *struck* by a lightning bolt are one in seven hundred thousand. Odds of being killed? One in four hundred thousand. About six years ago I went to the village near Dublin where it happened. People still remembered the event years later."

"How old were you?"

"Six or seven. I was spending the month with Mason

when we heard. He was a friend of my father's, kind of an adopted uncle to me. Single, completely immersed in his scientific work. What the hell he thought he could do with a six-year-old I have no idea. He gave it a shot, but a neighbor complained that we were being neglected, and reported him to CPS."

"We?"

"He was godfather to Simon Blackthorne. Simon and I were about the same age. His parents and sister were killed in a home gas explosion."

"Wow. Both of you lost families? What are the chances? And what a terrible life change that must've been."

He shrugged. "We were young. You get over shit after a while. Both of us went into foster care, and Simon and I only saw each other once a month when we went to see Mason for visitation."

"Is Simon a wizard as well?"

"Yeah, so's Alex. Alex's parents also died. Plane crash. But he's fortunate enough to have a twin sister. Way back when, he also had a grandmother. But he never talked about her. The sister went to live with the grandmother. Alex ended up in the system and spent a lot of time on the streets."

Lucas grinned. "Mason scooped Alex up when he tried to lift his wallet. He was about thirteen at the time. Mason took him in, straightened him out somewhat, and told Simon and me to welcome him into the family. Which we did. One, because Alex was a decent enough guy who'd been through pretty much the same shit Simon and I had, and two, because when Mason told us to jump, we answered 'How high?' "

"What do the other two guys do?"

"Also work for T-FLAC. Alex was recruited first, and he pretty much dragged Simon and me into it as well. Not that we had to be strong-armed. The job sounded pretty damned exciting to three kids with more brains than prospects. And hell, Mason encouraged us.

"Now we drag his ass into the business every once in a while and use his expertise when we can. He likes being involved in what we're involved in."

Lucas shifted his gaze to meet hers. "That's the long of it. So, yeah, I guess you called it. Mason Knight is like family. So are Alex and Simon."

They slowly drifted down, then continued to float six feet over the gently rolling surf a mile offshore. He wasn't too pleased with himself. If for any reason his powers failed, he'd put Sydney in danger floating so fucking high while they'd made love. Hitting water from a hundred feet up felt like hitting cement. The hotter she made him, the less his brain engaged, and he couldn't afford that kind of inattention.

She lay on top of him as if he were a feather bed. A pretty damn hard feather bed, but he loved the feel of her sweat-dampened skin glued to his, and the way she lazily combed her fingers through the hair on his chest and had listened to him with an air of complete absorption.

"My team will be here shortly. I'm taking them with me when I go back."

"Back to the kryptonite building?" Alarm colored her response and he fought back the pleasure her concern evoked.

"I need to get inside. Find out what's in there—" He was startled by a Trace Teleport buzz. The faint vibration occurred just beneath the occipital bone on the back of his head. His team? So early? No. The TT indicated two people, not five.

"What's the matter?" Frowning, Sydney lifted her head.

"A Half just teleported in. He has someone with him, not a wizard. I'm going to follow them."

"Do you want me to—"

Lucas shook his head. It appeared his powers were fully functioning. At least for now. Teleporting them back to her bungalow, he touched her cheek as soon as they materialized and he was sure she was steady on her feet. "I'll be back."

Sydney caught his hand. "Don't you think you should at least put on a jock strap or something?"

"A *jock strap*?" Lucas looked down at his naked form and grinned. He materialized their clothes. His jeans, black T-shirt, boots, and weapons, just as he'd planned to do, then went back and tugged her into his arms for a hard brief kiss. "Stay out of trouble."

Teleporting, he followed the Trace.

He could almost have followed the *smell* of old sweat. The Half and his odiferous pal materialized on the third floor of the medical building in a room that looked more like a hotel room than a hospital room. A comfortable leather sofa, green plants, subtle artwork, and a regular bed. The equipment was discreetly hidden behind a screen in the corner.

Invisible, Lucas leaned against the wall out of the way. He didn't know the Half. He captured an ocular image and transmitted it to HQ for identification. The Half looked a lot like Alfred Hitchcock in his later years. Sixtyish, several chins, a belly that was a heart attack waiting to happen. He was wearing a cheap, dark blue suit, the white shirt unbuttoned at the collar and gaping and straining over his ample gut. His face was baby smooth, and shiny with perspiration, which he mopped repeatedly and nervously with a paper towel.

The guy with him was clearly a vagrant. Looking past the ragged, filthy clothing, matted hair, and grimy skin, Lucas guessed the man's age to be somewhere between thirty and forty.

He'd been on the streets awhile. Slumped shoulders,

and a hopeless look in his dark-circled eyes showed this guy had hit a wall. Whatever had driven him to the streets didn't hold a fire to his feet to fight back. He was resigned to being who and what he was. He'd given up.

The ragged, filthy suit he wore looked like a Brooks Brothers. Either he'd bought it himself in better days, or he'd picked it up from a charity bin; even dirty and torn, it was obviously higher quality than the Half's clothing. Instead of a shirt, he wore a sweat- and dirt-stained wife-beater T-shirt. His inexpensive tennis shoes had no laces and were so filthy they had no color.

The smell of him was so bad it made Lucas's eyes smart. He and his clothing hadn't seen water, never mind soap, in a long, long time.

Lucas had smelled worse, hell, *seen* worse, but for some reason this guy's plight affected him profoundly.

"Wait here," the Half told the other man with false cheer. He swiped the paper towel across the back of his neck, even though the air-conditioning made the room a comfortable seventy-five.

"I'll get you that meal I promised. There's a bathroom through there. Grab a nice hot shower. Take all the time you want. I'll have clean clothes brought in. Then you can eat. That work for you?"

"How many people who did this program already got their lives back together? How many went back to their families? A lot? A few?"

Lucas could tell by the guy's tone of voice that he wanted to believe, but was afraid to. "Did anyone sign up and—Did anyone sign up and fail? You can be honest with me, Gus. I can take it. Just give it to me straight, man."

The Half squeezed the guy's shoulder. "Mike, didn't I promise you your days on the street were over? Trust me, man. Clean up, eat, then you can start the program. You won't be sorry."

Program? Lucas frowned. What *program?* From what he'd observed so far there wasn't a damned thing altruistic about what was going on here. There was no *program.* "Mike" was going to be used for *parts.* Although why they'd risk harvesting someone directly off the streets puzzled him.

It was as clear as glass that Mike and people like him were an easy source of donor organs. The homeless, the disenfranchised, the forgotten. An unending resource for raw materials just there for the taking. Still, he would have expected them to use younger bodies. The only explanation for this guy was if he had a rare blood type they needed.

Mike looked the Half straight in the eye, his body so tight, so stiff, it was a wonder he didn't snap right in half. Poor bastard. A muscle jumped in his unshaven jaw and he shoved his fists deeper into his pants pockets. "I got no money. I told you that."

"Yeah. You said. Don't sweat it, bud. We got you covered."

The Halfs must have a way to test prospective donors for blood type, and disease, also for close connections. Family. Friends. Hell, acquaintances. Anyone who'd give a flying fuck when they went missing.

Although, Lucas figured it didn't matter if there *were* close family or friends who'd miss the person snatched. There was no way for them to follow a Half. The FBI or Interpol couldn't trace a wizard.

Hell, even in the wizard community, he was one of the few wizards with the power to Trace Teleport.

So the bad guys had an endless supply of raw materials.

How did they select the recipients? Other than the ability to pay?

Leonidas Karras, head of Splinter, and probably head of this operation, was richer than God, was well traveled, and moved in the highest circles of wealth and privilege. All it would take from *him* was a word here, a word there. "Need a heart transplant, but you've been refused because of age or health or lifestyle? Come to a destination spa in Brazil, I know people who can give you a new heart, no questions asked. Cost? Does it matter? You're staring down the jaws of death. X million euros, or dollars or yen. Whatever it takes, no questions asked."

Believing himself alone, Mike's shoulders slumped the second the door closed. His sigh was shaky, filled with a hundred intense emotions as he stood in the center of the room looking around.

Scared, aren't you, buddy? Anxious to get started? Hoping that you're being given a second chance? Fuck it. This pissed Lucas off. Having a face on those organs made this whole sick project intensely personal.

The guy hadn't even noticed that not only was there no window in the room, the door had locked behind the Half. He reached out to touch the strip of clean white sheet folded neatly over a fluffy blue blanket at the head of the bed. Snatching his filthy hand back before he made contact, he curled his fingers, with dirty, ragged bitten nails tightly into his palm. Bowing his head he choked back a sob.

Ah, man. Lucas knew he'd just lost the fight to stay impersonal.

You got yourself a guardian angel, buddy. Hang tough. I'll be back.

Fourteen

Sydney had black clothes aplenty, but all the outfits plunged to here, or were slit up to there. Too slinky for spy-wear. She opted for navy stretch capris and a fairly modest navy tank top trimmed in lime green; it was as spy-ish as she could get. She'd had no idea when she'd packed that she'd need a breaking-and-entering ensemble.

Not that she planned on breaking or entering anything. But if the occasion presented itself, she was going to try to get into the building behind the medical center. Lucas couldn't go near it, but she could. The wiz building had to have doors. She'd find one.

If anyone saw her, she'd just tell them she was looking for the medical building and had gotten lost. She could play dumb. If Lucas's team arrived in the meantime, maybe she'd have discovered something that might help them.

Maybe.

Hell, who was she kidding? She was dying to know what was in the building as much as Lucas was.

She stared at the closet and contemplated the toughest decision in every woman's life. Shoes. She had dozens of pairs. Not the wedges or the heels. She might have to run. The thought of why she might have to run—men wielding guns, or enraged wizards—made her heart do a little terror-induced tap dance. "Put on your big girl panties," she told herself firmly, bending to grab the natural-colored leather flip-flops with navy and green beading that went with the outfit. She wouldn't be able to run in them, but they'd be quick and easy to kick off. She preferred running barefoot anyway.

A scrunchie held back her hair. Sydney eyed herself critically in the mirror. "I'm going to interview the Kerrs." A meeting she'd set up last week before the wealthy couple had had their respective surgeries. They didn't want their names used in the book, but they were more than willing to talk. Their names would be changed to protect the vain and wealthy. The timing was terrific. She could kill two birds with one stone.

"That's all I'm doing. I've done a hundred and nineteen interviews in the past few months with no one wanting to know what I'm doing wherever I've been doing it. This afternoon is no different. I can do this."

Yeah. She could do this.

Purse? No.

Scrabbling around in a beach bag hanging over the door handle of the closet, Sydney pulled out a small notebook, a pen stuck in the spirals. She'd only used it to jot down short notes to herself, but today it would be her official interview journal. She stuffed it into a side pocket of her pants and tucked her key in the other pocket. She was ready to go.

She cast a quick look in the far corner where she knew Lucas's bags were. The bags that were loaded with guns and ammunition. Unfortunately, everything was invisible . . . Hang on a sec. Invisible didn't mean not there. Just not seen.

Sydney paused to debate the merits of taking a weapon with her. Just in case. She knew how to shoot. Her brothers had made sure she knew which end of a gun was which. And because she could never let well enough alone, after Sergio and Carlos, brothers one and two had taught her, she'd signed up at a local range for more lessons. If she was going to do something, she wanted to be proficient. Didn't mean she *liked* guns.

Hugh and José, brothers four and five, had taken her aside and cautioned her about the responsibility inherent in carrying or using a gun. They'd warned her that if her adversary was bigger and stronger than she was, and a lot more motivated, they could take the weapon away from her and use it on *her*.

For her eighteenth birthday, Ramon and Rián, six and seven, had bought her a Lady Wesson . . . which was still in her underwear drawer in her old room at her dad's house in Miami.

Sergio had been furious when he found out the others had given her a weapon, even when he'd learned their oldest brothers had given her lessons. His medieval attitude toward women ensured he'd remain single for a long, long time. He was twenty-nine going on fifty.

Seán had taken lessons with her, then bought himself a Beretta. Her twin always had to one-up her.

Sydney smiled. Thinking of her dad and brothers made her homesick. She'd been gone for five months and missed them all, especially her twin. There was going to be a family reunion of epic proportions when she got home next week.

"Gun? Or no gun?" If she shot at anybody, it would be a very bad somebody. But if they were wizards, or Half wizards, her shooting abilities wouldn't matter. Bullets versus hocus-pocus?

"No gun." If she had one more thing to carry, she'd have to break down and use a purse; totally not the look she was shooting for. So to speak. Opting to walk, Sydney set out at a brisk pace. The weather was absolutely perfect, with sunny blue skies and an occasional high fluffy white cloud. Smiling, she remembered what it felt like to float through one. Cool misty cloud, hard, hot

Lucas. Making love in a bed would seem tame after what she'd experienced.

Heading to the main hotel's lobby coffee shop, Sydney inhaled the fragrance of flowers and freshly mown grass. She'd taken the long way around, wanting to stroll past the medical building just to see what she could see. If no one was around she'd venture to get a closer look.

The sound of the surf was a pleasant backdrop to the distant buzz of a lawn mower and the muted undertone of voices and splashing from the swimming pool area.

A tennis match was in progress on the grass courts, and she paused to watch the game through the fence, which was interwoven with some kind of lacy flowering vine. The flowers were a hot pink, the leaves a lush, dark green. *Thwack, thwack, thwack.* The sound of a racket hitting a tennis ball always reminded her of summer. Her dad, a terrible but enthusiastic player, had taught her and Seán to play when they'd been pretty young. What had they been? Seven or eight? She'd been as crappy a player as her father, but Seán had taken to it like a duck to water.

She'd tried, but since her only motivation was beating her twin at a sport she hated, she didn't pursue it. What was the point of spending hours whacking a ball back and forth over a net? Now, give her a ski slope, or a good, fast, no-holds-barred soccer game, and she was more than happy to sweat.

She wondered if Lucas played tennis. He looked delectable in shorts. Worth brushing up on her game if she could see him bare-legged. On the other hand, she preferred him in nothing at all.

Continuing on her way to meet Frances Kerr and husband Hal, Sydney glanced up as a shadow floated overhead. God, was she ever going to look at a cloud and *not* think of sex? Of Lucas?

He was going to be an impossibly tough act to follow.

The thought was quite depressing. Maybe she'd join a nunnery when she got back home.

"Don't bother sitting. You're late." Nia Ledgister waved Padrick McDonald away from the chair he was about to fall into, and took a few extra minutes to reread the paperwork in front of her. He'd brought the stink of old sweat and fried food into the room with him. So much for the ocean-fresh reed diffuser on the table behind her.

She turned to the bank of monitors on the wall. Each screen showed one of the individual ORs that made up the outward spokes of the surgery wheel. The recipients would be brought into their operating rooms in the next hour. Her staff bustled about readying each room for the particular surgery scheduled. There was always an air of quiet excitement when new patients arrived.

She ran a critical eye over the way the hub OR was being set up for the organ retrieval. Her staff moved like a well-oiled machine.

The Retriever shuffled his feet, the material of his cheap suit creaked under the strain of his weight. Nia zoomed in to see what her fresh donor was doing. He wandered aimlessly around the room. McDonald had sent in a blood sample for testing and cross-matching. Most homeless people were acceptable donors. This one was a prime specimen. If a mental disorder had sent him to the streets it wouldn't affect the quality of the organs that would benefit so many worthy and wealthy people in need. He'd been retrieved before he hit rock bottom. Clean of drugs, no indication of liquor or disease. He'd tested clean for both HIV and hepatitis C.

A clean donor almost gave Nia an orgasm.

And he was AB negative.

Based on that information, five recipients had immediately been contacted, and then been teleported in as soon as McDonald indicated their ETA. The recipients were currently being prepped for surgery.

Three million, seven hundred thousand. To the penny.

Ka-chiiing.

Nia felt warm and fuzzy all over.

The Retriever shifted from foot to foot between the two visitor's chairs in front of her desk. "I was go—"

Without lifting her gaze, Nia put up a hand to stop him, then punished him by taking another five minutes to read a report she'd read twice already. Finally she looked up. "You're behind on your quota, Paddy. You still owe me five."

"Yes, ma'am." He mopped his sweaty face with a grubby paper towel. Nia shuddered with revulsion. "I'll have them to you by month's end. Swear it."

"No. I want *ten* by the end of the month. One of our Retrievers is dead. You'll need to pick up your pace if you want to stay onboard. There is no shortage of donors out there. Find them."

"Begging your pardon, ma'am, but the pickin's ain't as easy as you think. I'm bringin' *quality* donors. People that you can use all their organs. No druggies, no alkies, no diseases. That hasta count for sumpthin'."

The cold glare got even icier. "It counts for you maintaining your lucrative job. I want ten donors by month's end, or your employment here will be terminated. Am I making myself perfectly clear?"

He bobbed his head, sending droplets of sweat flying. "Yes, ma'am."

Curling her lip, Nia went back to reading the paperwork in front of her. McDonald shuffled his feet.

"The money's in your account," she said briskly, not looking up. "Go."

"I wanna see."

Nia looked up slowly. "*What* did you say?"

"I wanna see that my money is in my account."

"Have you deposited your sample?" She lifted one perfect brow.

His ears turned red. "I was jes on my way. But I don't see why anyone needs *my* sperm. What you people use it for anyways?"

She could explain it to him a hundred ways from Sunday. He *still* wouldn't get it. "Make your deposit then teleport. Now. Off the property. Don't come back without your retrievals. From now on, notify Intake before you teleport them to the receiving rooms. The money will appear in your Swiss bank account within twenty-four hours."

"I—"

Nia waved a hand and he was gone. "*Ass wipe.*" He wasn't going to retrieve any donors on the Siberian plains, but he'd be there long enough to know not to annoy her. She zoomed in on the new donor as he wandered into the bathroom, tears of gratitude making white lines down the filth on his face. "Ass wipe."

Lucas wasn't sure if the woman was repeating her epithet to McDonald, or was calling the Retriever *and* her new donor the same name in that soft, sexy Jamaican-accented voice.

A full, she was far more powerful a wizard than she let on. Here in her inner sanctum, when she didn't know she was being observed, Nia Ledgister allowed her strength free rein. Most wizards did nothing to cloak their power. It was a warning to other wizards. But this deadly, beautiful woman did a pretty damned spectacular job of allowing only a small portion of her strength to show. Like the tip of the iceberg, Ledgister hid ninety percent of her strength.

Lucas figured his ass would be toast if his own powers conked out right about now. She'd have him for lunch. She was *that* powerful. Fortunately his cloaking skills were intact, and he'd placed a strong, fifteen-minute concentrated protective spell around himself as backup. He'd only done the fifteen minutes because he'd duplicated the same protection for Sydney while he was gone, and at the time, it had been as long as he'd been able to muster.

Fuck. The second this op was over, he'd go in and see if Duncan, head of the Wizard Council, could throw some light on this power outage shit. Embarrassment over his condition be damned. Between Mason and Duncan, surely to God someone could come up with a way to fix whatever the hell was broken.

Padding around Ledgister's large desk, he stood several feet behind her chair watching the action on the monitors. She rubbed a slender, ringless hand across the back of her neck, and glanced uneasily over her shoulder as if sensing him standing there.

Time to go.

With pages of notes, and no interesting sightings, Sydney reluctantly headed back to the bungalow. The problem was, she wouldn't know if she'd seen anything that would help Lucas or not. What was she looking *for*? She wasn't sure. Taking a detour into the lobby of the medical building after the interviews, she walked, seemingly aimlessly, toward the elevators. If she was stopped now, she'd say she was heading for the bathroom. If not, she'd go up to the third floor. Maybe she could discover something new there.

Eventually, of course, they'd stop her and make her leave. But she might pick up something useful before that happened.

She had to go with the bathroom story, because two men in black suits stopped her from even calling an elevator to the ground floor. Their guns were discreet, but they weren't hiding their weapons as they politely told her she couldn't go up to the surgery floors.

Coming out of the bathroom a few minutes later, she saw a man she recognized. Politician? Famous actor? She couldn't for the life of her put a name to his face. She frowned, watching the middle-aged man greet the two men guarding the elevator bank. They clearly knew him, as one of the black-suited men pressed the call button for him.

Sydney tried to remember what movie she'd seen him in. She drew a blank. All she remembered was he usually played the bad guy.

"Sydney! *Hey!*" Waving her arms to get Sydney's attention as if they were hundreds of yards apart instead of twenty feet, Kandy teetered over to her, her platform sandals clattering on the tile floor like castanets. "Hi, baby. Oh, my God, your tits look hot."

Sydney wasn't sure of the right response. I'm having these puppies removed the second I hit Miami, and before my family sees them, didn't somehow seem supportive of Kandy's monstrous additions. "Um—so do yours."

Kandy cupped her own mammoth breasts. "Don't you just love them?"

"Very nice." Kandy's new breasts were so huge that she couldn't possibly see her feet.

Frank Langella! That was the actor she was thinking the older man looked like. He'd played Dracula.

"I'm so glad I bumped into you." Kandy's new and improved Angelina Jolie lips made her a little difficult to understand. "I'm taking the red-eye home to my honey boy tonight. I just came in so Dr. Bergen could give me a little more Restilyn before I go."

She touched the slightly red brackets beside her mouth, then flung her arms around Sydney in a cloud of Lulu Guinness, hair spray, and peppermint gum. The jangling silver bracelets pressed into her back as Kandy squeezed her tighter than Sydney thought was good for her implants. Or for Sydney.

"I'm going to miss you *so* much, baby girl. You come see me and Henry in Vegas, you hear? You're always welcome to stay with us. We got us plenty of room."

As Sydney had seen pictures of the Elvis-inspired decor of what had to be the tackiest McMansion on earth, she believed Kandy.

Ten more minutes went by as Kandy caught up on the last couple of days. Like Tony, Kandy wanted to talk about the helicopters and the lights and the armed soldiers. To Sydney, it had all happened a thousand years ago.

A woman whose name Sydney had on the tip of her tongue came and placed her hand on Sydney's arm. She shot Kandy an apologetic look from a bruised and swollen face. "Hi, I'm Solange Du Pree. Sorry to interrupt." She turned her entire body to look at Sydney. "Sydney, can we reschedule our interview tomorrow? Make it in the afternoon, instead of the morning?"

By the time they finished chatting, the sun had almost set, and the lights illuminating the grounds had been turned on. Since the women had effectively solidified her reasons for being in the building, she didn't feel like she could be ungrateful and give away her hurry to be gone.

She hugged Kandy one more time, made a date to talk to Solange at the coffee shop the next afternoon, and made her getaway.

A casual stroll around the wiz building to see what she could see was in order. But it turned out not to be quite as easy as she'd imagined. The area was crawling with people, and she didn't get far. She'd been at the resort long enough to have met dozens of people and they all seemed to be out and about. Several people she'd interviewed for the book last week paused to talk to her. They invited her to join them for cocktails, but she wanted to get back to the bungalow and hear what Lucas might have discovered.

She hadn't realized just how many guests the hotel could accommodate, but the benches around the grounds were all taken as people gathered to watch the beautiful sunset. A few couples walked along the beach as she stepped onto the shell path running in front of the bungalows. They weren't staying down here, and she knew they weren't supposed to be on this beach. People staying in the hotel had their own spectacular stretch of sand with hot and cold running waiters and all the amenities. Still, she waved, but kept walking as the sun reflected in the blackness of the ocean in a sliver of tangerine.

After fishing the key out of her pants pocket, she unlocked the door, then reached around to turn on the lights. If Lucas had been home the lights would already be on. The place was dead quiet. Sydney nibbled her lip as she kicked off sandals that hit the closet doors with a *thunk, thunk*. Was Lucas okay? Had his powers held up? Had he been caught? Was he even now lying between the two buildings? Needing her help?

The thought of him weak and helpless made her stomach knot. Should she go and look for him? "He's a counterterrorist operative, Sydney. He probably knows a thing or two." After rolling the elastic out of her hair and rubbing her scalp, she pulled the top over her head, followed by her bra, then paused to peel the stretch crop pants and tiny thong down her legs on the way to the bathroom.

A nice cool shower, fabulous-smelling lotion liberally rubbed into her skin all over, and a chilled bottle of wine would welcome Lucas back, and then they c—

She let out a wild scream as five men dressed all in black, weapons drawn, suddenly materialized in the room and surrounded her.

* * *

"Hyun Woo Lee, Ishmael Hager, Curtis Oliver, Nicolai Stepanova, Nad Amadio." Lucas introduced his team to Sydney, who was wrapped in a robe and sitting on the foot of the bed, still pink-cheeked. He was not fucking happy that his team had seen her naked. Of course, at no time had he mentioned Sydney to anyone, so their surprise at finding her in "his" bungalow was understandable.

Legs crossed, arms folded, she was apparently not thrilled with having five uninvited guests materializing while she'd been bare-assed naked either.

"I'm going to take my shower. Make yourselves at home," Sydney said dryly, getting up and making sure the front of the robe was pulled closed.

"I don't suppose there's any chance in the world that you're *not* interested in banging her?" Oliver asked hopefully as the bathroom door closed behind her and the shower turned on.

Lucas met the other man's eyes. "Remember that Burmese knife thing I showed you in the jungle?"

Oliver winced. "Loud and clear."

Lucas materialized a bigger table in the center of the room, and six chairs. Thought about it, and added one more. "Sit, ladies. Here's what we have."

Fifteen

Dressed in an aqua-colored silk dress with a thigh-skimming hem and multicolored sandals with FM heels, Sydney left the bathroom and entered what had been, half an hour before her shower, a luxurious, beachy hotel suite. Now the bed was gone.

Well, damn, she'd had plans for that bed. Honest to God, though, having wizards around was absolutely fascinating.

In her rather lengthy absence, the bungalow had been transformed into a sleek, modern command center. A long black table, flanked by seven comfortable-looking high-backed chairs, held large monitors showing . . . she had no clue what, other than a lot of indecipherable, blinking screens of information. Other unidentifiable equipment beeped softly, or flashed red and green, all of which reflected off the shiny surface of the table like Christmas lights on a black pond. The five men at the table half rose as she emerged from the bathroom. She waved them back to their seats. While the supercool spy stuff bore closer inspection, she sought out, and found, Lucas.

In a room filled with dangerous males, he was clearly the alpha dog. Her alpha dog. He wore dark pants and a closely fitted black T-shirt that showed the solid, broad expanse of his chest, and his strong, tan arms. Standing slightly apart from the others, he was talking into a headset as he watched the small, handheld monitor in his palm.

"At 0.1 ug/ml?" He sounded as though he were repeating what he was hearing for the benefit of the other men in the room. "Staphylococcal enterotoxin B, botulinum toxins A and B, and ricin. Yeah, with no interference by white-powdered materials or colored matrices—Hang on, let's get you on speaker."

He glanced up, his eyes meeting hers, although she was sure he'd been aware of her presence from the second she'd opened the bathroom door. The flare in his green eyes as he scanned her from her calculated messy updo to her tanned bare legs, toe rings, and bright red nail polish, was worth the pain in the butt it had been to fix her hair and apply makeup in a steamy bathroom with the door closed.

Apparently he didn't think the deep V of the dress exposed too much cleavage as she had, looking at herself in the foggy bathroom mirror.

A woman's voice came on in what sounded like stereo. Sydney didn't understand more than a handful of words as the woman gave a laundry list of . . . something. It didn't sound good. She wondered if anyone would notice if she took a few notes.

As the woman talked, Lucas focused on the small computer in his hand. The other men sat at the table, watching various graphics and scrolling numbers on their monitors.

Sydney concentrated on something she understood only slightly better than what was currently going on in the room.

Lucas.

As ridiculously inappropriate it was right this second, Sydney remembered the molten heat of his dark green eyes as he'd whispered for her to come. She almost felt the soft mist of the cloud around her heated body as he'd rolled her around and around in a slow, dizzying spiral to show her what it felt like to fly among the clouds.

How had this happened?

She was in love with this man. This counterterrorist operative who'd dropped into her life without fair warning. Or clothes.

Oh, God. I am in so much freaking trouble here. Lucas was not the kind of guy to settle down. And she'd never be stupid enough to ask that of him. It would be like asking a leopard to become a house cat. Not that he'd ever so much as hinted at a future together. She suspected that men like Lucas Fox never did.

But . . . he was the love of her life. The man she knew could hold his own in her riotous all-male family. He was a self-confident, masculine beauty. And she was just a passing fancy to him. Would he wipe her memory when he left? Somehow, she doubted it now.

Great, she thought, watching him input something into the device in his hand as the woman continued to give them information of the unintelligible kind. He'd leave her without a backward glance, and she'd go off and get herself twenty-five house cats. An unfortunate lifestyle choice as she was highly allergic to freaking cats. Maybe the mind-wipe wouldn't be such a bad thing. She choked back a small laugh at the irony.

The sound brought Lucas's head up. "Yeah. My conclusion, too." He looked back at the device, his voice brisk. "Shoot us those numbers." He motioned to the Asian guy with yellow-blond hair and black-rimmed glasses who immediately typed something onto a keyboard that was nothing more than a red holographic image on the table's surface.

The TV behind her crackled into life as Lucas looked up. "Right. I see it."

". . . series of nine explosions at the Nad Al Sheba

Racecourse, ten minutes outside wealthy Dubai City in the United Arab Emirates. An estimated seven hundred people are believed to be dead, thousands more injured.

"The explosions came within five minutes of each other, inciting terror and panic." The voice-over sounded somber as a camera panned the chaos and mayhem as people ran helter-skelter, trying to leave the stadium.

"Analysts are comparing these bombings with those in London yesterday, saying both acts of terror involved multiple blasts and were well coordinated, and well timed to . . ."

"Watch." The tall, skinny guy with a Russian accent and a beak of a nose, stood, bracing both hands on the table. "They'll blame Al-Qaeda."

"Turn it off," Lucas told him. "As suspected, they didn't reveal anything about the biotoxin released—" He glanced up at Sydney. "The extra chair's for you."

She quickly sat down before he changed his mind. Although she saw that he was focused one hundred percent on the business at hand and had forgotten she was even there.

"Because HQ has been monitoring the clock over there on the hotel's televisions, they knew when the next strike would hit, but not where. Obviously, the brains behind this is somewhere in that building and for some reason, every bungalow is equipped for people working for this group. Whether or not it's Splinter is yet to be seen."

Lucas tapped one of the other screens and pulled up a schematic that had the other men leaning in to see. "The attack actually happened an hour ago; the press was asked not to announce the bombing for sixty minutes to give us a head start."

"Okay, not to be obtuse," Ishmael Hager said quietly. "But I'm trying to figure out what the fuck a luxury spa—that predominantly does tit jobs—has to do with terrorist attacks and black-market organ transplants?"

"And sperm donation," Lucas added.

Sperm donations? Sydney sat forward in her seat. That was a new and icky clue to something.

The blond Asian guy's eyes widened behind his thick glasses, making him look a bit like a mad scientist, and a lot creepy. "Sperm donations? Whose?"

"Right now," Lucas told the group, "I know of one Half. I have our guys looking into it. But that's the least of the issues here. For now let's concentrate on the use of LZ17. The recent bombings have been triggered from here in Brazil, on this very property. It's not about the big bang. The bombs are vehicles for the virulent biotoxin soup that the tangos unleash with them."

"And the tangos operate from where, exactly?"

"There's a building at the north end of the grounds. Can't get within a hundred feet of it. A strong protection spell is in force, and when I say strong, I mean impossible to breach."

The group of men contemplated this for a moment. "Maybe bring in non-psi personnel?" offered the one who'd been silent until now, except for some comment he'd made after Sydney had hidden in the bathroom. While she didn't know what was said, she'd bet good money Lucas was pissed off about it. Curtis, she thought. That was his name.

"No. This is definitely a wizard op. We have to breach that security and get inside the building. It's doubtful that they would post a Do Not Disturb for wizards only. I believe that the bombings are merely smoke screens for what they're really doing."

"And that is?" asked Stepanova.

Lucas looked grim. "Selling this new biotoxin." He nodded at the curses that followed this announcement.

"Right now they're unleashing samples in significant areas around the world."

"Jesus. Those are pretty big numbers. Hundreds of thousands dead as a fucking *sales* tool?"

Lucas looked from man to man, skipping woman, in his scan around the table. "We all know what this is. Gradual annihilation."

"Gradual an—" Sydney blurted out, unable to bite her tongue any longer. "What does that *mean*?"

"The explosion process where the explosions get a little bigger each time," Lucas explained, then continued to his men without missing a beat, "I suspect they're auctioning off a biologically spliced and/or mutated version of this biological weapon to the highest bidder. See?" He pointed to the TV.

"The countdown clocks on the televisions here are counting down to the next bomb, the location of which is auctioned off to the highest bidder. It's just a small taste of what the weapon can do. I believe that the bidders are testing various cities so they can preview what they'll eventually buy. What we've seen so far is just a fraction of what will happen when the biotoxin is sold."

More curses in four different languages filled the room.

"How do we know who's bidding?" Lee asked the question this time.

"First, we need to get into that building. I suspect we'll find all the answers we need there." Lucas glanced at Sydney. "No."

She widened her eyes. "What?"

"No, you may not go. You're going to stay put."

Well, hell. She lifted her hands in surrender. "I didn't say a word."

Lucas's lips twisted into a wry smile. "You didn't have to."

* * *

The sound of steel drums, pulsing samba music, laughter, and the raised voices of the hundreds of guests at the beachside restaurant drifted on the warm evening breeze coming off the ocean. Carnival officially began the next day, but people always started partying early.

Invisible, Lucas and his men teleported into the dense shadow on the east side of the medical building. A full moon, even filtered as it was by the overhanging foliage, was enough to light their way. When necessary they'd drop down their NVGs.

The only indication of their passing, if anyone were looking, would be the movement of the foliage. However, the breeze could explain even that away. Cloaked from other wizards, invisible to the naked eye, the six men moved toward the farthest building, hidden among the trees.

Lucas used his shirt-covered arm to wipe sweat from his forehead. Heart pumping too fast, breathing too labored. God*damn* it. He was scared. Wasn't the first time. He was in a fucking scary business. An operative, no matter how well trained, no matter how vigilant, was at risk of death or worse, 24/7. He was approaching a building that had nearly killed him. Twice. That wasn't just scary, that was freaking weird.

Third time's a charm. Or a death warrant.

He knew it had to happen sooner or later, but he realized that for the first time, he'd prefer it happened *later*. Meeting Sydney had changed his shrug at the prospect of death.

Before leaving the bungalow, he'd asked all his men to place protection spells on her. They didn't ask why *his* alone wasn't good enough.

He'd explained to his team, as best he could, the ramifications of breaching the protection spell placed on the building they were going to do their damnedest to enter. He'd also told them they might have to scrape his ass off the ground once they got close. Unless, of course, what had happened to him both times he'd ventured too close had the same effect on his men. Shit. He hoped to hell not.

But then, he also hoped that what had affected him wasn't due to whatever illness was messing with his powers. He was worried enough as it was, without the added fear of having something, or someone, stripping him of his powers completely.

He suddenly realized, much to his annoyance, that he was visible. So much for that plan. Seeing him materialize, the others followed suit. They didn't question him, and he didn't explain. Visible or invisible, they were a force to be reckoned with, and their presence wasn't going to remain covert for long once bullets started flying. He left things as they were.

He glanced around the group and, to a man, they nodded. They were as ready as they were going to be.

The party several thousand yards away was getting louder and louder and judging from the shrieks of laughter that pierced the music of the band, liquor flowed freely. The revelry did a fine job of blocking out any other sounds.

Lucas paused for a nanosecond beside the large palm tree where he'd fallen unconscious. His entire body braced for passing out, for—hell, he didn't know. But he felt nothing. Nothing at all. He let out a breath he wasn't aware he'd been holding. Okay.

Years ago he'd briefly been in a foster home where the husband had been abusive. The bad-tempered son of a bitch didn't even have the excuse of liquor for his violence. If it was small and defenseless, he beat the shit out of it.

Lucas had been about eleven when he'd gone to live, temporarily as always, with the Harrises. He remembered to this day that feeling of gut-wrenching, helpless fear as "Bulldog" Harris raised his meaty fist to punch him the second time.

The first time Harris had targeted him, Lucas hadn't anticipated the blow. The second time he *knew* what it was going to feel like. Knew the explosion of white pain that would blind him as he fell to the ground. Knew utter helplessness because Harris was faster, meaner, and twice his size.

A ghost of that fear filled his senses now, even though Lucas was an adult and fully trained to deal with tangos—wizard or otherwise. Jesus. He couldn't afford the luxury of fear. *Move.* Keep moving.

He pulled out the one piece of equipment he could always count on when it was go time. His Glock, secured in a fake "fanny pack," a holster on the front of his LockOut suit. The rip and grip Velcro fastener gave, and he hefted the familiar weight in his left hand. Even though he'd checked the weapon before he left, he checked it again.

Dropping the clip into his support hand as he walked, he pressed down on the top round with his thumb. From the pressure exerted by the fully compressed magazine spring he confirmed a full clip. He felt the truncated hollow point bullet designed to expand to a large diameter on striking bone. You could never have too much reassurance.

Lucas briskly reinserted the magazine with one smooth action, seating it hard to ensure it was fully engaged. "Anything?" he quietly asked his men, speaking into his lip mic. He grasped the slide with his support hand, pressing it back just enough to confirm with his index finger that there was a round in the chamber.

Five "Negative" responses.

No security? No power grid? The hair on the back of his neck rose. He lifted the Glock, felt the comfort of its weight. The chamber check had soothed his rattled nerves. Gave him a sense of comfort knowing the weapon was fully loaded. But he was still on edge.

Fully alert to every sound, every twitch of a leaf, Lucas continued shoving aside foliage. Tick. Tick. Tick.

The shit was going to hit the fan. Experience told him that. It was the *when* that kept the game interesting.

As he visually tracked the area, blocking out the music and party noises for something a lot closer and less friendly, Lucas checked his knife. To ensure it wouldn't catch when he needed it fast, he reached up with his right hand, swiftly pulling the custom V-68 stiletto from the inverted holster strapped high on his left shoulder. Soundlessly the spring-pressed locking pin disengaged, and seven ounces of steel rested in his palm.

Not fast enough. The sheath needed tightening. He did that quickly. Tried again.

Just right.

He hefted that familiar weight in his palm, so different than the Glock. The knife had been custom-made to fit his hand. A seven-inch blade, plus a five-and-a-half-inch stacked leather handle; twelve and a half inches of hand-to-hand combat bad-ass. The blade, sharp enough to slip between ribs, had a sturdy handle with a skull-cracking butt. He bound it with a spell of accuracy, as he'd done with the Glock.

He and this knife had seen plenty of action together. Satisfied, Lucas was just about to slide it back up into the holster, when Stepanova said quietly through the earpiece, "Two. Four o'clock."

Two soldiers, carrying some serious hardware, walked fifty feet to the right of Lucas and Ishmael Hager, who'd broken off to go around a thick clump of underbrush.

"See 'em," Lucas spoke directly into the mic. He

touched his ear to connect to the rest of his team. "Hager. With me."

His heart rate leveled out at the prospect of taking out the two Half wizard guards, rather than go the next hundred meters and confront that fucking force field again.

Even without seeing him, Lucas knew Hager was right beside him. "Fox left," Lucas told the other man which guy he'd take down as he circled around to come up behind his prey.

Before the guy was even aware that he was being stalked, Lucas was on him from behind, serpentlike. He snaked his left hand over the left shoulder and clamped it onto the man's mouth, yanking his head back. As part of the same motion, he brought the long blade of the stiletto down into the soft spot near the man's collarbone. The blade slipped down to the hilt with an almost sexual ease. Two wrist moves sliced the artery. Lucas counted to ten before he released his grip and let the man drop, but he was just being careful. He knew the guy was dead by seven. Before the body hit the ground, Lucas teleported it to the garbage detail waiting just out of town to deal with disposal.

A few feet away in the darkness someone grunted in pain, a muffled sound that came just as the wedding party's band took a break. Hagar was too experienced to allow his opponent to get in a jab, especially an unaware opponent. His team member hit the ground beside Lucas's foot with a thump.

Too noisy. Damn—

"Fu—" Ishmael Hager's broken curse was blood-filled.

Lucas didn't have time to check on him. The soldier who'd gotten the drop on the highly trained and experienced T-FLAC operative dragged in a breath to yell out. Shimmering behind him, knife in his right hand, edges parallel to the ground, Lucas slapped his palm over the man's mouth to silence him. The soldier struggled, trying to reach for his holstered weapon. This one wasn't going to be textbook. Lucas wrenched his head to the left, thrust the point of the stiletto through his back into the middle part of the lung, then sliced sideways, into the heart. It was going to be a busy night for the garbage detail.

"Secure," he told the others. "Hager's down. These aren't shopping mall guards. Watch your sixes." He crouched to press two fingers under his partner's throat. Hager was dead. Fuck, shit, damn it to hell. He teleported the man directly to the designated holding room on the medical floor at T-FLAC HQ in Montana.

Adrenaline raced through his body. Who the fuck *were* these people? "Location?" he asked his men softly. Each man answered. "Let's do this," Lucas told them, his voice grim as he moved to catch up.

With a mixture of relief and curiosity, he realized that he'd already walked past both places his powers had been sucked out of him previously. Thank God. His powers were back online and as strong as ever.

Don't get cocky, he warned himself, a small part of him aware that *that* happy state could change in a heartbeat.

It was blacker than a cave in the shadow of the building. Sliding the mono eyepiece of his night-vision glasses over his left eye, Lucas joined his men. While he realized that his entire body was still braced for the debilitating sensation of his lack of power, he felt nothing other than the usual rush he got when he was on an op.

Scrutinizing the blank façade of the one-story cement building he saw no evidence of openings. No doors. No windows. Not on this side anyway. "Teleport in," he instructed.

He attempted to shimmer, but nothing happened. Through the lenses of the NVG he saw the puzzled expressions of the faces turned to him as they remained right where they were. Fucking hell.

Stepanova looked around as if he could discover the source of the block. *Take a number, buddy.* "What the hell?"

Lee muttered a curse in Mandarin. "This what happened to you?" he demanded into his lip mic.

"Stopped me cold at the big palm tree back there. Never made it this far before."

"Gotta be a way in." Curtis Oliver ran his hands over the blank face of the building as he spoke, using his gift of discernment by touch. "Ventilation if nothing else."

"Split up. Let's see what we can see." Lucas pointed west, indicating the direction he wanted Oliver and Stepanova to go. He sent Lee with them. He and Amadio would join them on the northern side of the building.

There had to be a way in. Somewhere. He checked with Oliver for a sign that he'd found a way in. The other man responded in the negative.

Motioning for Nad Amadio to keep up, Lucas crept down the length of the building. The fact that he felt none of the strong wizard power he'd felt before made him wonder if what had been protected inside was now gone.

What, and gone *where*? How did the building fit into a black-market organ transplant operation, the biochemical and bomb explosions, and the Half wizard sperm collections? Or did none of those things have anything to do with the others?

Improbable. As far as he knew, they were all controlled from this location. Right now Lucas couldn't see a damn thing tying all the elements together.

"Got a door," Oliver whispered in his earpiece. Lucas would rather Sydney was doing the whispering, but the info was welcome. "And we have company," Curtis

Oliver told him in his usual calm voice. "Big guns. You might want to time your arrival for sooner than la—"

The man cut out. Lucas instantly teleported to his position. Didn't work to get inside the building, but it worked just fine to get to Oliver, Lee, and Stepanova's location. Or former location.

In the two seconds it took him to shimmer, his men were gone.

Sixteen

In Lucas's absence, Sydney took the opportunity to catch up with her notes and make some forward progress on her contracted book. Not only had the publisher picked the title *Skin Deep,* they already had the artwork for the cover, and the back-cover copy. They were going to give themselves whiplash getting the book into stores on the anniversary of the lay-down date of *Being Michaela.*

Skin Deep was coming together nicely, not earth-shattering by any means, but a serious, sometimes humorous look at plastic surgery and destination spas. Many of the people she'd interviewed had been amazingly frank and open about the elective surgery they'd had. And a surprising number of them had not only been willing for her to use their names, they'd also been willing to allow Sydney to take before-and-after photographs.

Given a few more hours, she could probably finish the next-to-last chapter. And this time, she was making damn sure she covered her ass.

There was not one piece of information in this book that Sydney hadn't checked and rechecked. Not a single scrap of data that she hadn't confirmed with every source. With their cooperation, she'd even run background checks on the people she quoted. In every country, she'd reviewed the credentials and, when applicable, board certifications on the physicians.

At a bare minimum, Sydney had an independent secondary source to confirm every fact. In some cases, three or four. Even the translations of college transcripts had gone through not one but four translators just to verify the information. Yes, it was overkill but then, her career was on life-support. Error wasn't an option.

By ten-thirty, she was starving and called room service, ordering *Feijoada,* a stew of beans with beef and pork. The spicy national dish was delicious as long as she didn't think about some of the ingredients—salted pork trimmings like ears, feet, and tails. It was served with rice, deep-fried bananas, and peeled orange slices. The fine plating included a small pot of hot pepper sauce, so she made sure to order several bottles of water to go with her meal.

She even ordered a *Caipirinha,* a rumlike drink made from *Cachaça,* a distilled sugarcane alcohol, and lime. Since she was a cheap drunk, one drink would knock her on her ass. One of those puppies and she'd have no worries and be fast asleep when Lucas got back.

Oh, no. Fast asleep on what? The bed was gone.

Who was she kidding? Drink or no drink, there was no way she'd be able to sleep without knowing if Lucas was all right. Had he managed to get inside the building, or was he lying outside unconscious? She rubbed her bare arms even though the window was wide open and the air drifting through the slats of the plantation shutters was warm. Her stomach seized and her thoughts ran wild. If he was hurt, bleeding, or unconscious, surely his men would have brought him back. Wouldn't they?

She paced around the large table in the middle of the room, which was too large to be conducive to a good brisk gait. A sudden thought had her freezing in her tracks: Had the wizard-kryptonite zapped all of them? Were they *all* sprawled on the ground in a heap—she rubbed her arms faster. Her blood stilled. Or were they all dead? They could be dead. Was Lucas dead?

How would she know? As much as she wanted to go and check to make sure Lucas—and his team—were okay, she'd tacitly promised to stay right where she was until he got back.

It would be incredibly stupid to think she'd be of any help in a dangerous situation. She had to stay put; walk a thousand miles around this monstrous table, but stay put. Maybe she could get started on the last chapter. That would be productive and keep her mind from thinking the worst.

Productive, but not nearly as fascinating as checking out all the gadgets on the table. She bent down to get a closer look at the table's deep black surface. Beyond her own reflection was some sort of image. A map? A schematic? It was almost like looking through the water of a shallow pond to the smooth, clear bottom beneath the surface.

Even the computer monitors were models she'd never seen before. The colored lights on the huge monitors continued to blip and blink, reflecting in the surface of the table. They were sleek and as thin as a powder compact, and without the usual bulky CPU tower. Maybe the actual table was the brains of the high-tech computer system. She bent down to check out the underside. With the exception of a small silver box the size of a matchbook, it looked like the underside of any other conference table. Too bad the keyboards were no longer in evidence; her fingers itched to take one of the holographic keyboards for a spin, if for no other reason than to say she'd done it.

Even though Sydney knew she'd never write anything about Lucas or T-FLAC, she went to get her cell phone, then took pictures from every angle. Private photos. Something to document the moment for herself.

This was crazy. She was worried about a man who knew better than most how to take care of himself. "I wouldn't *be* worried, if I had any idea what was going on out there," she muttered to herself.

Fact was, he'd passed out twice doing exactly what he was doing now. She had cause to be concerned, didn't she? Her stomach growled as she paced. Contemplated a swim. Paced. Thought about another shower. Paced. Maybe a soothing bath. Paced. Watching a movie could be good.

Lucas didn't need her. And even if he did, she wouldn't always be there to cover his back. Always? Interesting thought but foolish. Lucas hadn't promised her an always. He hadn't even promised next freaking *week*.

Sydney gave a very unladylike snort. "I *know* Lucas would never need anybody. But what if—" There was a sharp rap at the door making her jump, she'd been so deep in thought.

"Room service."

She was reminded of the *SNL* skit of the land shark. Cue soundtrack from *Jaws*. "Who's there?" "Land shark." "No, really, who's there?" "Candygram."

"Stop imagining danger," she told herself firmly as her heart rate picked up speed, and her palms felt a little sweaty. Talk about overreacting. Just room service. There was no rubber shark out there to devour her. She raised her voice. "Be right there."

Grabbing her wallet, she was about to go to the door when she remembered that there was a boardroom table in the middle of the room. A little hard to explain. Detouring to the open window, she made a wider gap between the slats of the shutter with her fingers. The same young guy who'd delivered before stood outside looking bored, holding a tray.

The spicy smell of *Feijoada* made her mouth water. "Thanks, I'm kinda in the middle of something. Oh, sorry. Didn't mean to scare you." Poor kid had almost jumped out of his skin as her voice came out of seemingly nowhere. "Can you just leave the tray right there? I'll get it in a second." She pushed a few folded bills through the small opening. "Thanks."

With a genial smile the good-looking young man reached out to take the tip. Sydney saw a lined tattoo that ran along the inside of his wrist. With no fat to cushion against the scratch of the needle, that must have hurt like—

The kid reached in and grabbed her by the forearm. It happened so fast Sydney didn't have time to wonder about the how and the why. She screamed as a blur of white, accompanied by the sound of rushing air, made her close her eyes dizzily.

The son of a bitch was teleporting her.

"Amadio. On your three." Nad Amadio gave Lucas the heads-up as he came up on his right, standing to one side of the partially open door the other men had found.

Lucas's occipital bone hummed unmistakably as he picked up on the Trace left by his men and the wizard who'd taken them. Fuck. Major wizard power, nothing Half about it.

Amadio looked around. "All three?"

Lucas's adrenaline started to pump. "Taken." By whom and to where, he didn't know. And as much as he wanted to follow the Trace to retrieve them, that would have to wait. He inspected the door, which stood ajar. Steel-reinforced titanium, twelve inches thick. No handles, no obvious hinges. It was imbedded in a wall at least three feet thick, likely just as reinforced as the door. The place was a fucking fortress.

"Jesus, what's that?" the other man asked quietly through his lip mic even though they stood barely three feet apart. Lucas felt it too, the echoing slither of evil pulsed like a living thing from the icy-cold black interior.

A frigid draft washed over him through the open door, causing an involuntary shudder despite the warm night air. The hair on the back of his neck rose. The imminent danger made him feel bigger, faster, stronger as all his senses now heightened. This was exactly where he wanted to be, right on the edge with the catalyst of an adrenaline drip coursing through his veins.

He relied on a combat mind-set to prevent a full adrenaline dump that experience had taught him led to tunnel vision, auditory exclusion, and loss of fine motor control necessary to quickly press the trigger for an accurate hit.

Taking a breath he counted to four, held his breath for a four count, then slowly exhaled. All second nature. His heart rate slowed. He positioned himself on the doorknob side of the door frame, if the door had had a doorknob, so he wouldn't reach across the fatal funnel—the area where anyone in the room would likely shoot when he opened the door.

Weapon in close contact position, arm braced against his rib cage, yet slightly canted away from his body, he gave the heavy door a gentle shove with his foot. It swung wide soundlessly.

Motioning his direction to Amadio, Lucas stepped over the threshold into blackness.

It was the cool air that woke her. Had she turned up the A/C without realizing it? Dizzy and disoriented, Sydney tried to figure out why she was lying flat on her back, and why the lights were suddenly bright enough for her eyelids to glow pink as the brilliance pierced through the thin skin. Had she passed out? No, that couldn't be. Other than feeling a little lethargic and nauseated, she felt fine. Besides, she'd never fainted in her life.

Cold, she wanted to pull the covers up over her bare legs, but decided to wait until the chance of throwing up passed.

Had Lucas come back? She couldn't remember. Not remembering gave her a panicky feeling in the pit of her stomach. No. She remembered Lucas and the guys disappearing as they teleported. After they left, she'd typed away like a madwoman on her laptop until about ten-thirty, when her stomach had started growling and ruined her concentration.

Thank God. She *did* remember.

Hell yes, she remembered.

The room service guy. The same one Lucas said was a near carbon copy of a young version of his friend. It hurt her brain to think, and the thought evaporated like mist.

Dammit. Concentrate. This is important. Wasn't it? *Focus, Sydney.*

Had she fallen asleep and dreamed that he'd yanked her through a mere two-inch opening between the slats of the shutters? The how of that impossible maneuver was outweighed by the why and where.

Still dizzy, she kept motionless, waiting for the queasiness to ebb as she tried to identify a faint electrical hum and the sound of a slightly squeaky wheel being rolled over a hard surface. The faint medicinal smell of disinfectant didn't help her unsettled stomach.

Metal chinked against metal.

A frisson of terror made Sydney's heart pound hard against her breastbone.

The smell. The cold. The sounds.

OhGodohGodohGod. She wasn't in Kansas anymore. She knew *precisely* where she was. The knowledge had been there from the moment she'd regained consciousness. It was just too freaking terrifying to compute.

The rapid, panicky heartbeat echoed in her ears as she attempted to open her eyes.

She couldn't so much as blink.

Full-blown horror made her struggle to sit up.

None of her muscles worked.

She was completely, terrifyingly paralyzed.

"You've been a naughty, naughty girl, Miss McBride." The familiar female voice, with its faintly Jamaican accent, sent Sydney's dread through the roof.

The utter darkness was visceral, the evil palpable, the air so *fucking* cold, despite the LockOut, Lucas had to grit his teeth to prevent them from chattering. Whatever the force contained in this building earlier, it was now mysteriously gone. He suspected that was the only reason they'd been allowed to enter the damned building.

His Trace ability seemed to rev up, but while he felt the past presence of other wizards, he didn't sense anyone in the warehouse now. Still, he hugged the wall and walked in the blade position, with his firing-side eye and the muzzle of the Glock moving as one like the turret on a tank.

Removing the Maglite from the leg holster, he flicked it on, shining it around in an arc as he walked, the comfortable weight of the Glock gripped in his left hand as he kept his eyes moving.

The golden wedge of light revealed about sixty feet in all directions. Place was empty but for a few electrical cords, thick as his wrist, snaking across the floor here and there. The ceiling, walls, and floor were bare cement, giving no clues as to what had been housed here mere hours before.

The fact that he—they—had been able to walk right up to the building proved there'd be nothing inside. Yet he scanned ahead as he walked the inside perimeter, following the beam of light. Some hundred yards across the vast expanse, he could see Amadio mirror imaging his movements.

"Someone might've gotten sloppy and left something behind," the other man said softly through the headset.

"Yeah." Last year Lucas had tracked down a badass tango named Rodrigo Disanto by finding the quarter-inch gold cross he habitually wore on his shirt pocket. In a Dumpster. In a rat-infested ally.

He'd find something here, too.

Besides the marrow-biting chill, there was a faint smell of . . . something. He tried to ID what the hell it was. The first scent impression, and most predominant odor on entering the warehouse, was a familiar, slightly tinny, slightly acidic odor. Blood? Feces? Urine? It was definitely body fluids, but . . . something else. There was something oily mixed in it, and a metallic base note, similar to gun oil. But not.

"Anything?" Lucas asked Amadio softly, feeling again the faint occipital vibration indicating that a wizard or Half wizard had been here recently, as he disrupted their Trace.

"Negative."

Twenty feet ahead, Lucas felt yet another Trace. Jesus. Place had been crawling with wizards, a dozen or more, and recently.

Something up ahead . . . An electrical wire hanging from the ceiling. Lucas inspected it as he got closer. Ten amperes at least, the same voltage delivered by an electric chair. The end neatly severed from whatever had required the juice.

This amount of electricity indicated—What? Supercomputers? The only thing that made sense was some new sort of mainframe that required that kind of megavoltage. Possibly they'd been running the tango op out of here. Using a specialized, customized computer for the bids on the virus?

But hell, that scenario didn't compute. The bombings, the release of the virus, that entire operation, could be done from a laptop. If anyone had created a supercomputer, the techies back at HQ would have known. Forget computers, what else fit?

Given the presence of body fluids, it was more likely the cable had something to do with the black-market transplants. Had they brought donors here instead of taking them to the surgical center on the third floor in the other building?

No. That didn't make sense either. Why remove the organs here, then have to transport them several hundred yards away when they could do everything in the adjoining ORs? And even if that was the case, surely there was no need for an OR to be this massive.

Maybe it was a hangar for wizard-teleported small aircraft or helicopters bringing in patients.

Possible, but not practical. A patient could be teleported to the hospital without the use of a vehicle of any sort.

"Over here." His partner on the earpiece. "Check this out." He shone his light over two, ceiling-high, metal containers.

Lucas started across the vast empty space to take a look. "Looks like wine storage or fermenting vats."

Suddenly the place was lit up like the Fourth as arcs of plasma filaments streamed electricity in a twenty-foot electrical discharge.

The brilliant white light blinded him for a few seconds. Clearly there were no protective devices to interrupt the current in the high-power circuit, and the electrical fireworks display continued on, lighting the warehouse as bright as day.

"Hey. What's that? I'll check it o—"

"Not unless you want to be charred from the inside out. I see it." The "it" was a clear, oblong box on a stand made visible by the light of the arcing current directly overhead. The brightness of the electrical display made identifying the item next to impossible, and all they could do was wait for the electrostatic discharge to dissipate.

Blinking to regulate his vision back to darkness, Lucas met Amadio halfway to examine the piece of furniture when it occurred to him, this was no piece of furniture. "Know what this looks like?"

The other man growled low in his throat. "Yeah. They had my kid in one of these when he was born premature."

Lucas rested his hand on top of the heavy plastic dome over what was clearly an incubator. "Jesus. They're taking *babies'* organs? Why the hell am I surprised? These fuckers don't seem to give a flying shit *whose* organs they take. Or how. But, Goddamn it. *Babies*?"

"We just have an embarrassment of riches today," Nia told Sydney McBride conversationally. Other than the two of them, the OR was empty. But the doctors would be along shortly, and in the meantime Nia didn't mind a little girl talk.

Even if she was no longer a girl, and the woman on the table was incapable of speech. But her hearing was just fine. She was, in fact, a captive audience. Nia knew that because she'd been the one who'd happily administered the paralytic drug through the IV.

"I believe this is yours." She dropped the gold hoop earring onto the other woman's flat belly. "One of the nurses found it, thinking it was mine. It's not. None of my staff went into that room after it was cleaned. Ergo, it must belong to the little snoop."

Nia chuckled. "Can I confide in you, my dear?" She pulled the surgical tray a little closer, and bare-handed, started straightening the scalpels. "I've never really had close female friends, simply because there have been very few people in my life that I could trust.

"The people I work for trust *me* implicitly to run the Brazilian side of the business. After all, I do make them a considerable amount of money. Not to mention that I tidy up any messes. And, of course, I don't ask questions. Oh, you think I must have had a terrible childhood to be as heartless as I am now. Not so.

"Beatings, you ask? Betrayals?" Nia smiled down fondly at McBride's composed features. "Not at all. I had a lovely mother and a charming father."

Neither of whom had kept a promise to their only child in their lives. Well, fairly short lives, because Nia had set the house on fire just after her thirteenth birthday. She still enjoyed the sight of an open flame.

"But enough about me. Your boyfriend's three friends are already making their donations to my retirement fund. Sperm first, organs next."

The entire day and night had been productive *and* lucrative. Three extra bodies contributing organs had necessitated bringing in a dozen patients they hadn't prepared for. But Nia was nothing if not efficient. She'd managed to accommodate all the recipients with her usual efficiency.

The girl looked like Sleeping Beauty with her pretty features, closed eyes, and glossy golden brown hair spread out around her bare shoulders. "Your prince won't come, you know," she told Sydney. "They never do. And in the case of Lucas Fox, he accepted our invitation to come to *Novos Começos* when he—as I knew he would—followed the Half sent to draw him here." She chuckled fondly at the foolish man's predictability.

"We have important plans for your lover. World-shattering, life-changing plans. And you, my dear, are expendable, and totally unnecessary to his future. I'm afraid the next half hour or so will be a bit painful. But think of it this way—you'll be contributing to the long and healthy lives of so *many* people. And isn't it better to give than receive? Ah. Here's Dr. Bergen now."

Nia patted the young woman's bare arm, which she'd already strapped to the board. She'd attached the IVs; no need for a blood pressure cuff. "The first few incisions are the worst. Really. After that you pass out from the pain and shock, and we finish our work without you being aware of what we're doing. Sleep well, Miss McBride. I'll give your T-FLAC operative your love and regrets, shall I?"

Seventeen

They teleported some of the wiring and the empty incubator to Montana for analysis. A forensic team would arrive momentarily to analyze the contents of the two huge metal tanks. He and Nad Amadio had gone over every inch of the warehouse for any more clues. Twice.

In his head, a metronome ticked off the seconds. To what, he had no idea. He only knew, Goddamn it, that he had to hurry.

He met up with the other man at the north end of the building. The entire recon had been an exercise in futility, the big buildup had ended with a frustrating fizzle. "This is a wash. We'll follow the Trace and retrieve the others. Maybe we'll have more to work with once our boys in white analyze the content of the tanks."

Lucas had a bad feeling. Hell, this entire *building* gave him a bad feeling, and he trusted his instincts implicitly. They rarely failed him.

Lucas tried to teleport. Nada. Not a spark, not a waver.

"What's wrong?" his partner demanded, moving back to Lucas's side. "Jesus. You look fucking weird."

He *felt* weird. The sensation was a cross between holding a live electrical wire and spinning in a centrifuge. "Weird?" Even his voice vibrated. Fucking hell?

"You're dead white and you're *shimmering*. Not shimmering as in teleporting. Shimmering like a freaking holographic image. You don't do holographic, do you?"

"No." That was Blackthorne's power to call. "Ocular scan," he managed to get out. He had to clench his teeth to stop them chattering in time with the buzzing pulsation going through his entire body.

Amadio got some shots as Lucas stood there, helpless to prevent whatever was happening to him. The pictures would give the people back at HQ not only a visual, but body temp and heart rate. Let them figure out what the fuck this was all about.

"Get those in ASAP," his voice sounded far away to his own ears. Far away and insubstantial as though he were fading away. "Shoot a set to me as well." He'd send those to Mason on the QT.

"Will d—Hey! You're back," he said, sounding only marginally better than Lucas felt.

Unsteady, Lucas staggered before regaining his balance on the cement floor. The nearly out-of-body experience had shaken him more than he wanted to let on, even to a team member. The pictures and vitals were sure to alert someone at T-FLAC/psi. He wasn't going to be able to keep his malfunctioning powers quiet much longer.

"Okay, boss." Nad Amadio looked him over critically and nodded as Lucas regained his self-control. "Strong enough to take me with you when you Trace?"

More to the point: *Could* he Trace? Usually he could Trace Teleport from a hundred yards away from the subject, maybe more. Tonight he needed to stand where they'd stood to make the connection.

Lucas suspected he knew where his men were. He hoped to hell he wasn't too late.

Right in the middle of the media feeding frenzy, when every news source vilified her, when people, who, days before, had feted her and celebrated her success, refused to talk to her, when her family, even while they tried to support her, were "disappointed," Sydney had had a recurring nightmare about being buried alive. She hadn't needed a shrink to tell her why.

But those nightmares paled in significance as she lay, exposed and vulnerable, listening to the conversation between the woman and a male doctor who stood a few feet from where she lay, paralyzed and scared out of her mind.

Her body didn't move, but her brain was screaming. The hard, too-rapid knock of her heartbeat hurt inside her chest. Her stomach cramped painfully, and her mind was going around in frantic circles like a gerbil on a wheel.

Anticipation alone of what was to come might kill her.

"And *I'd* prefer that you take the organs now." The woman's lilting, musical voice sounded deceptively mild. But beneath the sugar, Sydney heard pure hard, cold ice.

"It's senseless to wait until the heart patient is strong enough to be teleported. We'll take the heart to her in Switzerland."

"Of course we can take her heart and teleport it to the recipient. That isn't the issue. A few days is all I'm asking." The man sounded annoyed. "She's AB negative, for Christ's sake, Nia. *AB neg!* Why waste her organs because you have a wild hair? A few days will give us a chance to bring in a dozen patients we couldn't accommodate before. Recipients, I might add, who will pay double, *triple* our normal asking price because their blood type is too hard to match and they've already given up hope of ever receiving an organ."

Exactly, Sydney thought wholeheartedly. *Let's wait.*

Lucas will see that I'm gone the second he returns to the bungalow. He'll look for me.

"She's a loose end."

"Shit, Nia! Who's going to know she's here? No one. Put her in one of the special rooms and sedate her. She's not going anywhere. We have plenty of work to keep us busy for the next seventy-two hours."

Keep fighting, Doc.

"Are you refusing to take her organs, Lewis? Because if that's the case there are seven other competent surgeons working here who will do *exactly* what I say, *when* I say it." Icebergs held more warmth than this woman's voice.

"I'm just saying that it's a waste of a golden opportunity to rush this. I'd prefe—"

But Nia cut him off. "Either call your support personnel back in, or get out. I'm sick to death of your mercurial morality. If you don't like what you do, or the fat paycheck you receive, *leave*. Doctors are a dime a dozen. And frankly, the medical staff here is just a very small cog in a very large wheel."

Sydney heard the small, surprised silence before he spoke again. "What are you talking about?"

"The transplants are a means to an end. The money we bring in is used—Never mind. That doesn't concern you. Here, take the scalpel and do your job. Do it, Dr. Bergen, or get out."

The sound of something metal bounced off the floor. One of them had thrown down—the scalpel? Since the only thing she could turn was her stomach, Sydney could only imagine the sharp metal object lying on the floor, the lights that would surely blind her if she could open her eyes. Sydney preferred the damn razor-sharp steel tool on the floor rather than in the doctor's hand.

"You might sign my checks, Nia." He sounded blusteringly furious. "But you aren't the ultimate power, now, are you?"

Keep fighting, Sydney thought again. *If you're fighting, I'm not dying. Challenge her.* Right now Nia was the ultimate power over Sydney's life or death. The woman already sounded pissed off and on edge. With every fiber of her being, Sydney prayed for Lewis to win the argument. Because right then she was more terrified of *Nia* than she was of the doctor and what he was about to do.

Something warm slid into her hairline at her temples and she realized two things. One, she was crying. Two, she could feel the course her tears took from the corner of her eyes, down her temples, and into her hair.

If she could feel *tears,* she couldn't begin to wrap her mind around how a scalpel was going to feel biting into her flesh.

The air crackled with menace as Nia said coldly, "You *dare* to challenge my authority, you fool? I *am* the ultimate authority of you and everyone in this facility, make no mistake."

"You report to *someone.* I've heard you talking to h— What in God's name are you doing with that thing in my OR?" Anger tinged with real fear sounded in the man's voice.

"My OR." There was steel beneath Nia's granite. Bile rose up the back of Sydney's throat. If she vomited now, she'd aspirate and die before they could do anything to her. The thought held a sort of morbid appeal. She knew she had a high threshold for pain—her brothers assured that some body part was always in a lock; headlock, finger lock, leg lock . . . it didn't matter. They let her fall once when they went hiking; she'd tumbled down a crevasse and skidded over a railway line in Aspen, skating for what felt like miles, pretty much on her chin.

She'd had more stitches than a quilt.

Her brothers adored her, but they'd never babied her.

Her threshold for pain was high, but these people were going to kick that up as high as it would go. Maybe higher. And she was helpless to prevent it. All she could do was lie there, the cold air wafting over her naked body, tears leaking into her hair, screaming inside.

"Are you going to take her organs or not?"

"What are you going to do if I refuse? *Shoot* me? You wouldn't do something that stupid in a building filled with people. Not to mention that any spark would ignite the stored oxygen in here."

"*There. That* takes care of the O_2 problem." Nia's laugh was light and girlish. "First of all, this OR is completely soundproof. So nobody is going to know anything for a good long while. Second, I'm a much more powerful wizard than you could possible know, Lewis."

Something clanged against the wall and the man cursed.

"I'm considerably more powerful than you could ever be. I could walk out of here looking just like you, if I wanted to. Which I don't. I could teleport your miserable dead carcass to Siberia, then produce a man who looked *exactly* like you, right down to that mole on your forehead and your shitty attitude."

The table where Sydney lay shifted, as if someone had leaned against it.

"Don't even *think* about challenging me, Doctor."

Something crackled. Electricity? Sydney felt a flash of heat across her face and chest.

Nia's laugh this time sounded triumphant. "You're going to have to do better than that, Lewis. Want to power up and see who'll win?"

"Sorry. That was stupid. But this is way beyond unreasonable, Nia. If nothing else think about the mon—"

The snick of a gun's safety being released sounded so

close to Sydney's face that she wondered if Nia was going to shoot *her* before forcing the doctor to rip out her organs. OhGodohGodohGod.

"Your blood type is B positive, isn't it, Lewis?"

"You're insane. Christ, Nia—"

The gunshot made Sydney's ears ring.

There was no getting around it. Lucas had to tell Amadio that he was incapable of teleporting as soon as they got back outside. As he filled in his team member on his glitch, the party on the beach carried on full swing in the background, the music so loud he wondered that the guests weren't holding their hands over their ears. Voices were raised to be heard. He could smell a faint whiff of booze from here, so they were putting away the liquor at a Carnival-level rate, already. Lucas bit back a smile as he thought about Sydney liberally dousing him with every miniature bottle of alcohol in the minibar to make the soldiers believe he was passed out drunk. She was really something.

"What do you think it is?" the younger guy demanded in a low voice.

Lucas started, because the question fit so well with what he'd been thinking about Sydney. "Say what?"

"How long have you had this malfunction? Who have you reported it to? And fuck, dude, I gotta ask—are you contagious?"

Lucas didn't blame him. Being a wizard was everything that he was. Take that away and—"Not that I know of. Worked with six different psi teams since this started, and everyone is fine."

"As far as you know."

"Yeah. As far as I know. You wanna take off? Be my guest, but there are four guys up there that need my help, and I'm going to make damned sure they get it."

"Four?"

"Some homeless guy, Mike, is there, too. They pulled him off the streets as a donor. They're lining them up like frigging dominos. And the longer we stand here shooting the breeze, the higher the probability of them being sliced and diced. You in or out?"

"In."

Lucas gave him one brief nod. "The best time for surgery is morning. They won't give a flying fuck about the donors, but their recipients pay shitloads of money, so they'd want the most optimum time to do the transplants." He hoped.

"They'll have to bring in the recipients. As far as I know everyone upstairs has already had their surgery. Unfortunately, since my Trace ability is once again also FUBAR, I can't tell if people have come or gone."

"Well, then why don't we go take a look-see and find out, the old-fashioned way?" Amadio asked after a moment's thought.

Yeah. For a selfish moment he wished Sydney were with him. Her presence would amp up his powers, but it was more important to know that she was safely back at the bungalow. Probably trying to break into one of the computers to satisfy her seemingly limitless curiosity and interest. That thought gave him pause.

It just wasn't possible for her to access anything. Hell, she wouldn't even be able to turn them on. They could be accessed by assigned operative voice recognition only. But he had no doubt she'd amuse herself for hours trying.

Lucas hunkered down and used his finger to sketch a floor plan on the dusty floor. "Stairwell, elevator, nurse's station."

He pointed to the rough wheel he'd drawn. He made an X. "Mike's room 319. Middle OR here for retrieval of organs; these lines are the rooms for the transplants."

"Covert or overt?"

"Let's get the men out with the minimum amount of fuss. The tangos don't know they have uninvited company, and I'd like to keep it that way until I get Sydney clear."

"Roger that." Amadio took his weapon from the shoulder holster. "I can teleport us in, and maintain invisibility for both of us, for seven point nine seconds. After that you're on your own."

"Get us here," Lucas jabbed at Mike's room. "It's the most out-of-the-way location, and quicker to go from there, to there. We'll send Mike to HQ, then retrieve our guys."

As it turned out, getting Mike to safety was the easy part. Poor bastard had fallen asleep in the tub. Since he had no clothes, Lucas teleported him to Montana as he was. Asleep and naked.

"I thought you said your powers didn't work," the other man accused softly. He turned to give Lucas an assessing look.

Lucas rubbed a hand absently across the back of his neck where a sensation close to Trace, but not, buzzed. He shook his head to clear it. Gave him a damn headache. He realized the headache had started soon after he'd entered the empty warehouse. "Comes and goes."

And he was finally ready to report this, to both the psi division, and to Duncan Edge, head of the Wizard Council.

"Trace is working now, too. They have the others in a room on the west side of the building. Alive. For now." Lucas shimmered. Satisfied that, for now, his powers worked, he gave the other man instructions, then opened the door and stepped into the brightly lit hallway.

A couple of nurses walked down the wide hallway toward them. ". . . idea. Some guest. But Belinda said

Dr. Bergen kicked everyone out of organ recovery and made them wait outside."

"He can't do the surgery alone, he has to call them back in."

"He's alone with a female patient with the doors locked? That's pretty creepy, if you ask me."

"Well, don't let Nia hear you. Is the woman a donor or a recipient?"

"No idea. It's a big secret, I guess. Must be a major celebrity." The nurse grunted disgustedly. "More important, someone ate my lunch out of the fridge again. I'm starving. Want to go to the cafeteria on our break?"

The women walked past him without knowing he was only a few feet away. Since the chances of his materializing were fifty-fifty, he wanted to teleport his men before anything else happened. Lucas's steps were soundless but he could hear his partner's whisper-soft footfalls next to him. Kid needed a little more seasoning.

Following the Trace of his men, Lucas found them in a back room. Slipping inside, he heard Amadio shut the door behind him. "Ah, crap," Lucas muttered as his nuts tried to creep up into his body. The men were alive, but unconscious. Naked, they were strapped to beds and had electrodes attached to their penises. One after the other, their bodies jerked as they were brought to orgasm by what looked like a small bull-ejaculator similar to one he'd seen used on Diablo, Derek Wright's prize Red Brangus bull sometime back.

"Jesus. How do we—disengage them?"

Extracting sperm this way was both brutal and primitive, and Lucas's balls contracted in sympathy. He went to the machine between the beds. "Like this." He pulled the plug out of the wall. "We'll send them home as is. Call it in, give Saul a heads-up." His head was killing him, to the point that his vision was blurred. Lucas tried to ignore the slicing pain.

Dispatching the operatives to Montana, Lucas turned to Nad. "Go on and head back. I want to take a look in Ledgister's office, just down the hall." And that would be quick, Lucas promised himself. Besides the headache and weakness, he was worried about Sydney. She was so headstrong and easily bored. When she couldn't crack the codes on the computers, she'd start looking for something else to amuse herself.

He wanted her to amuse herself on *him*.

The younger man shimmered and was gone. Lucas let himself out of the room, mildly entertained by thinking about how Oliver, Lee, and Stepanova were going to handle the inevitable ribbing from their fellow operatives.

He crept down the currently empty corridor, grinning. Poor bastards. This was going to take a while to live down.

So far he was maintaining invisibility. The consequences of that changing didn't bear thinking about. He glanced briefly into each of the spokes of the operating rooms. Empty. A gaggle of nurses and techs were standing around shooting the breeze, obviously the people the nurse had said had been locked out. Lucas shimmered into the last three spokes.

All the ORs reserved for recipients were dark. Satisfied that no one was receiving an organ tonight, he shimmered back into the occupied OR.

The door was now open, and the waiting staff, far fewer personnel for the donor than the recipient, filed in. They entered the brightly lit room and were moving about, adjusting equipment, readying the containers for the organs. The place was freezing. He knew it was kept cold for the benefit of the retrieved organs. After all, at this point, the donor wouldn't care.

Lot of work to do in vain. They were going to have a

collective shock when they discovered that four of their donors were gone.

And he was just about to spirit the fifth, whoever he was, from right under their noses.

Lucas saw there was no anesthesiologist. What the hell kind of operation was this? The room should have been bustling with personnel. Nurses, and a profusion of techs. The OR was barely a sterile environment. They had almost as much disdain for the organs someone had paid a king's ransom for as they had for the donor.

The nurses moved like a well-oiled machine, pointedly making a wide berth around the doctor, who had blood down the front of his blue scrubs. He sported a large, red-stained white bandage on his forehead.

He'd been shot. Lucas could smell the faint trace of weapons fire mingled with antiseptic. Also evident was the Trace of a powerful wizard, a wizard no longer in the room.

What the hell was that about? A falling-out among thieves? He'd get this donor out of there, check on Sydney, then return to see what else he could discover connecting this building to the one behind it. He moved closer and focused on the patient, not the doctor. Whoever the poor bastard was under the knife, tonight was his night. In seconds, he'd be in a comfortable hospital bed in Montana.

Even though he couldn't see who was on the table because of everyone standing so close and surrounding him/her, Lucas attempted teleporting the patient. Fucking hell. Back to powers on the blink.

"Doctor?" A nurse, standing directly in front of Lucas, said, glancing around the room with a frown. "We have no O_2."

"I checked the tanks myself, not two hours ago." The heavyset, rather unattractive blonde across the table from her sounded defensive.

"Well, there's nothing here *now,* is there?"

The doctor looked downward and gave a theatrical, weary sigh. "Betty, go get it. Go with her, Paula."

"But I—"

"Now!"

The two nurses swiftly left their posts and moved away from the table, giving Lucas a clear view of the patient just as the doctor pulled the lethally sharp tip of the scalpel back from the base of Sydney's throat.

Eighteen

It was only his years of training that allowed Lucas to remain calm and maintain his focus. Heart hammering, he attempted to teleport her again.

Once again, his fucking, *fucking* powers didn't work. He'd never prayed in his life, but he started now.

Please God . . .

Her vulnerability sliced at Lucas's heart.

If he'd walked in here a minute later—

"I'd like to get out of here before breakfast." Placing the scalpel that had nicked the base of Sydney's throat on a rolling table as he spoke, the doctor shot an impatient glance at the doors across the OR where the two nurses had passed.

"Karla. Go tell them to move faster."

Blood welled like an obscenity directly over the pulse at the base of Sydney's throat. A thin, slow-moving, wavy scarlet line trickled down the outer swell of her right breast. Beneath her naturally olive skin and golden tan, her skin was leached of color, pebbled with goose bumps from the chill. They hadn't even had the decency to cover her. Clearly unaware how closely her life hung in the balance, she lay on the table like some fairy-tale princess.

Please, God. Begging here.

He tried teleportation again.

Not even a spark.

The doctor repositioned the scalpel at the exact same

starting point as before. Out of options, Lucas knocked the knife from his hand. It clattered to the floor, causing the man to curse. "Nia," he said furiously under his breath. "Don't be a goddamned bitch. I'm doing what you told me to do. Get lost."

The remaining nurse handed him a new scalpel, without comment.

Come on, God. Lucas withdrew the Glock. He couldn't sustain being invisible much longer; any second now he was going to materialize. *What do You want in exchange for Sydney's life? Name it!* He concentrated on shimmering Sydney off the table.

The doctor shifted his arm into position, leaning forward to continue the incision. Sydney's blood seeped sluggishly, but no one bothered to wipe it off her skin.

Focus. Concentrate. Pray.

The double doors swung open with a *whoosh,* and three pairs of soft-soled shoes squeaked across the floor. Lucas didn't glance around; his eyes were locked on Sydney's still form.

The doctor looked up, scowling as the three nurses hurried back into position. "Hurry and hook that up. Let's get this over with."

Sydney's long dark lashes shadowed her cheeks. Lucas stepped in closer. Christ, sweetheart . . . Tearstains, black from her smudged makeup, tracked from the corner of her eyes into her hairline.

Wait a damn minute.

Her tears were still flowing. She had *goose bumps.* She *felt* the chill in the room. And her tears indicated that she was very much aware of what was happening. Aware of the pain.

Christ Almighty. She hadn't been anesthetized. She was conscious. Aware.

Anesthesia-awareness? Maybe some concoction dreamed up by the medical team just to torture their prey. Or a sadistic disregard for someone they considered a pantry for spare parts?

God. Are You watching this?

Lucas covered her slack hand with his. *I'm right here, love. We'll be out of here in no time. Hang in there. I—*

As soon as his fingers twined with hers he felt a small power surge. Not enough to teleport, but enough to use Empathic Perception. He reset the wall clock to read three A.M. instead of two A.M. "This donor's surgery has been successfully completed," Lucas said in a calm, even voice to the assembled surgical team. It took an eternally long second before they went into an almost hypnotic state, stopping what they were doing as if in freeze-frame.

"There have been no complications or unusual events in the past hour. All of the organs are in their correct receptacles, and this OR needs to be cleaned and prepped for tomorrow.

"The body must be removed for disposal immediately," Lucas finished as the medical team proceeded to remove their latex gloves, surgical masks, and gowns, which, if the surgery had actually happened, would be splattered and smeared with blood. Simultaneously, the OR techs began to rearrange the room, rolling instrument trays against the wall and clearing away the used scalpels, forceps, bone saws, and other assorted items before giving the shiny surface a disinfecting wipe. The doctor pulled off his gown, tossing it on the floor beside the table before he stalked out without comment.

"What's his problem?" a dark-haired nurse asked as she carefully took two of the six kidney-shaped pans that should have had Sydney's harvested organs for delivery to the recipient in an adjacent operating room. An OR tech bundled the discarded gown into a bright red biohazard bag.

"Oh, he and Nurse Ratched got into it earlier. Kicked us out while they had at it."

The blond nurse who'd gone to fetch the oxygen tanks glanced up. "What was she doing here at two in the morning?"

"The head honcho was here this afternoon. I'm guessing it was an unscheduled visit, because she was obviously stressed. Took it out on everyone after he left, not just Dr. Bergen. Shoot! Look at the time. I've got to get back to my sitter."

"Go. I'll take the body to disposal," the blonde offered.

Hoping Sydney could feel his hand around hers, Lucas walked beside the gurney as the nurse pushed it down the hallway.

Was she hallucinating? Sydney couldn't figure out if she'd slipped into some sort of terror-induced insanity. She thought she'd heard Lucas's voice. Or had she?

The surgery was over. They'd stolen her organs. She'd heard the nurses talking as they cleaned up the operating room afterward. She'd smelled the tinny smell of her own blood. They were wheeling her to "disposal."

She was dead. They'd stolen her life.

Even the bright light she'd seen through her closed lids had dimmed. A wheel squeaked, rubber-soled shoes pounded rhythmically. She tried to move. To open her eyes. If she was going into the light, she damn well wanted to see it coming.

Her lashes fluttered, letting in a sliver of light. Oh, thank God. She tried to move. Just her pinkie finger on her left hand lifted, then lowered back to the cold steel of the table beneath her. It was a start. Something tightened around her right hand.

Something. Was it a Good Thing or a Bad Thing?

The *whoosh* of doors opening, and the overpowering

smell of chemicals made her insides twist and curl with fear.

God. How could she be thinking, hearing, smelling, *feeling* if she were dead? How could she possibly have any brain function when all her organs had been taken out?

The gurney came to a stop. The acrid smells burned Sydney's nose and made her heart pump even harder. But how could that be? She didn't have a heart. She pictured what her body must look like, what she'd seen so recently done to another poor soul. Her chest cracked open wide like his, an empty body cavity exposed as though she'd been eviscerated by wild animals, like his.

LucasLucasLucas.

Sydney chanted his name over and over in her mind. It was too late. Too late for him to swoop in and save her like some storybook hero. A kiss from him and she'd be awake. Well, hell, she'd never believed in that fairy tale anyway.

Not wanting to alert the nurse of her mobility, she tilted her foot, just a little. Movement was seeping back into her paralyzed limbs. Or was it her imagination? Really, how could she move when she was dead? No heart. No lungs. No—whatever else they'd ripped out of her.

She was a shell of her former self. The macabre thought made tears sting beneath her lids.

"Crap, I hate this room," a woman said, sounding as though she were talking to herself. "Paperwork, shmaperwork. Who cares?" The scratch of a pen. "There. Signed, sealed, and delivered. The ghoul guys will dispose of you in the morning, but not before they play with what's left of you for a bit. The pervs. But hey, what do you care?"

What sounded like a clipboard being dropped onto a table, followed by the clatter and roll of a pen being tossed after it punctuated her one-sided conversation. "I'm outta here."

Me, too, Sydney thought, girding herself to *move* the second she was sure the nurse had left the room.

She could not be dead. Dead did not feel fear. Dead could not think or move their fingers. The opposite of dead was alive.

Somehow.

Despite knowing, without a doubt, that the surgery had been completed successfully, she knew, too, that she was very much alive.

Unless this was what hell was like. Thinking you were alive when you were really dead.

"Stay still," Lucas said, whisper-soft against her right ear. His breath warmed the side of her face. "She's coming back."

Before Sydney could react to Lucas's presence, the doors *whooshed* open. Shoes squeaked on the floor. "Pen? Pen? Pen? Ah." *Squeak-squeak-squeak*. The door *swooshed* closed.

Free of the paralytic, Sydney catapulted off the gurney as if jet-propelled. Her knees buckled.

Lucas materialized, sweeping her into his arms and holding her so close she could barely breathe. That was fine with her, she had her arms wrapped so tightly around his waist she was practically inside his skin. Great wracking sobs broke through her chest and up her raw throat as she buried her face against his solid chest and cried out her terror.

"I've got you, honey," he whispered into her hair, rocking her in his arms. "Shhh. I've got you. You're safe. Okay. Let's give this a shot . . ."

Air rushed around her and she knew he was teleporting them away. Away was good. Far away. Timbuktu wouldn't be far enough away.

They landed on a wood floor with a gentle *thump*. Instantly Lucas swung her off her feet in a fierce embrace. Their mouths met hungrily. Sydney fisted the back of his shirt in both hands as his tongue thrust deep into her mouth and his large hands kneaded her behind, drawing her tightly against the hard ridge of his erection.

There was no slow warm-up. She was instantly greedy for him. He didn't have to take his time to build her passion carefully, he aroused her with just a kiss. One kiss. One kiss and she was wet and on fire, her body aching and ready for him.

His mouth was a little rough on hers, hot and urgent, and Sydney reciprocated in kind. He kissed her as she clung to him, her nails digging into his back through his thin shirt.

Unable to breathe because of the tears still coursing down her checks and clogging her nose, gasping for breath, Sydney reluctantly pulled her mouth free.

Lucas stroked her hair away her face. "Tissue?"

Letting her head fall to his chest, she nodded.

His hand snaked between his chest and her face. "Blow."

"Don't l-let go," she choked out, crying and laughing at the same time as she took the wad of tissue and wiped her eyes and blew her nose unromantically, then stood there helplessly with the tissue clumped in her hand. Lucas zapped it away, still with his arms tightly around her and his hands massaging her back, soothing and exciting her.

She felt his lips on her hair. "I won't let you go. Sweetheart, besides the puncture wound on your throat—do you hurt anywhere else?"

She shook her head against his chest. Adrenaline was preventing the small wound from hurting. She imagined it would hurt like hell. Later. Right now she wanted to crawl inside him to stop the shaking. "Am I alive?"

"Yeah," he said, voice thick and rough as he tilted her

face up to his. His bleak expression twisted her heart as eyes the color of a rain forest searched her features. She could tell he blamed himself. "Prove it." She felt the rough fabric of his pants, and the smooth fabric of his shirt against her naked skin. "Make me feel alive, all the way alive."

She was naked, he was fully clothed. *No fair—Oh!* She caught her breath. Bare skin met bare skin. "I love a man who gets right to the point."

Her breasts throbbed and her nipples hardened. Sydney lifted her arms, looping them around his neck as excitement replaced the knot of fear in her tummy. Her back arched as he cupped one breast, firmly kneading the soft mound, and rasping his thumb over the sensitive nipple.

"I love a woman who starts the party naked."

Her back thumped against the paneled wall.

With a little hop, she managed to wrap her legs around his waist. "K-known many?" Hard and strong, he surged inside her wet heat, pressing her between the hardness of his body and the slick, cool wall. This coupling was primitive and raw, and God, she needed it. Just like this. Hard and fast and mindless.

Fingers digging into her butt cheeks, he made a rough sound deep in his throat as his thrusts came faster and faster. "As it happens—"

Sydney pinched his side.

"—Ouch. No." His chuckle was hot and low in her ear and his breathing quickened in pace with each plunge his body took into hers.

The desperation in him demanded a response that she was helpless to tame. She wouldn't have wanted to. The teeth-gritting pleasure he gave her wiped Sydney's mind clean of everything but the driving force of him inside her. There was nothing else but this blinding, pulsing swell of need.

They climaxed together, then remained as they were, leaning against the wall, both panting, their skin covered with a sheen of sweat.

"Let's stay like this forever," Sydney suggested after several minutes in which neither could speak.

"Let's climb into that nice big bed over there and catch our breath."

Heart still going a mile a minute, her head flopped to his damp chest. "Can't move."

He carried her to the bed, the covers swept back magically, and he laid her down on the cool, smooth cotton sheet. Following her, he pulled her into his arms.

With a cat-got-the-cream smile, she stretched luxuriously, then snuggled back against his side. Taking his arm before he could move it himself, she draped it over her shoulder, then curved his hand around her breast and held it there. "Where are we?"

He couldn't not touch her sex-warmed skin. So smooth, so silky soft. Her nipple was already hard. Her breasts were sensitive to the lightest touch. Lucas rubbed his palm over the hard bud. "On a boat, five miles out."

She couldn't really see much of the cabin from her vantage point, but she tried anyway. "A T-FLAC yacht? Very fancy." She flung her leg over his as if he were a comfy pillow instead of solid muscle and bone.

"Not one of ours." Although T-FLAC had many like it, some even more luxurious. He'd spent two weeks in the Mediterranean a couple of years ago with a Turkish terrorist and his wife. Talk about a busman's holiday.

"This one belongs to one of the legit plastic surgery patients." Lucas trailed his fingertips lightly down her thigh, feeling her damp heat against his leg.

"He and his wife are having a twofer. They won't be back on board for three days. We have the place all to ourselves." He didn't bother to mention that the wealthy couple had had one of the staterooms set up as a hospital room. If the worst had happened, and Sydney had needed anything, oxygen to sutures, they would have been available. As was an entire cabinet filled with every drug imaginable. Mr. and Mrs. Powers were prepared for any complication following their surgeries.

Lucas had a bit of experience with stitching in the field. He'd done it, and had done it to himself. Thank God she was whole. Because God help him, he wouldn't have found it easy to pierce her beautiful skin.

Sydney stopped her perusal of the cabin and looked at him closely. "You didn't know I was there in the OR. How did you know they'd hurt me and you'd need a private yacht for refuge?"

"I was searching boats the other night. Heard them mention they were going to anchor out at sea so the majority of the boat's crew was free to go to the resort for the week. I thought of it as we were leaving the OR."

"They left a gazillion-dollar boat out at sea with no one on board?" She widened her eyes.

"Couple of watchmen. They won't bother us."

"Really? Why not? You didn't kill them, did you?"

He pressed a chain of kisses to her forehead and cheek and jaw. "The dinghy is floating on our port bow on its way into the harbor. If their singing is anything to go by, they're very drunk."

"And I suppose you had something to do with their location and inebriated state?" She tried to pull back to meet his gaze but he continued his nibbling path down her neck.

His voice was muffled as he defended himself. "They wanted to go ashore."

"Hmm."

"I just sped the process up a bit."

"I can't go back there, Lucas. I'll swim back to Miami *naked,* but I am absolutely *not* going back to *Novos Começos.*"

He leaned on his elbow. "Don't worry. I'll get you home."

"Are your powers back to normal now? How did that happen?"

"I wouldn't exactly say they're back to normal."

She cupped his face with both hands. "What would you say?"

"They work some of the time."

"Great," she told him dryly. "I'll take a commercial flight, thanks."

While he wanted to tell her that he'd never let anything happen to her, the fact was she'd almost died on his watch. She could have died if he'd dicked around in the warehouse a little longer, or lingered looking for his men. Or any of a dozen things that could have delayed finding her before they'd carved her up like a Thanksgiving turkey.

His blood went cold remembering her naked body under that razor-sharp scalpel. A few minutes later . . .

Hell, a few *seconds* later and she would have been sliced open. And while he'd like to think that even that late in the game he could have saved her, he wasn't sure what the hell he would have done if Empathic Perception *hadn't* worked.

All Lucas knew was that no matter what, he'd have died for her if necessary.

She brushed her thumb across his cheekbone and the gentle, loving caress made a small part of his heart squeeze. "I'm okay. You raced in at the eleventh hour and saved the day."

"It was damned close."

"I remember."

He went back to kissing her lightly. "We should get a bandage on that cut. Maybe a shower, too, wash off the blood."

"Oh, my God." She looked up at him in horror.

"Lucas, all my stuff is at the bungalow. My notes on the black-market organs. And *Skin Deep* is almost *finished.* One more chapter and it would've been done. Dammit."

"I'll go back and retrieve all your stuff, don't worry about it."

"I do worry about it. We're—what did you say? Five freaking miles at sea? What if you teleport and drop into the ocean. Remember last time? You got a *concussion.* You were damned lucky you didn't break your neck."

"I dropped on my head. Onto the sand."

"Same song. Different tune. We'll go together."

"Not just no, but *hell* no." He threw back the covers and sat up, swinging his legs to the floor. "They didn't know who or what I was to you this afternoon. A few more hours, and they'll discover that all their donors are gone. And the organs they believe they took from you don't exist. I had to use EP to make them believe they performed the surgery."

"It worked on me, too."

Her fingers, slim and soft, curled around his arm. The diamond ring he'd practically forgotten about winked in the light. Strange how the balance of power worked. Her hands were small, delicate, his, large and strong enough to crush every bone in a full-grown man's body, yet she held him easily, her trust that he wouldn't harm her implicit in her touch. Lucas dragged in a deep breath.

Her fingers tightened, holding him in place. Ridiculous. She couldn't hold him by her side. Not with the mere touch of her hand on his arm. Yet there he was, exactly where she wanted him. Exactly where he wanted to be.

She tried tickling him a bit. "Well, just as a by the way—I bought into that whole ripping out of my precious body parts things too, you know."

"I know. Sorry, I couldn't exclude you. But the reality

is, I wouldn't have been capable of pulling off that power if I hadn't touched you and had my juice amped—" The satellite phone buzzed in the pocket of his pants, crumpled on the floor beside the bed. He stood up from the bed and reached for his vibrating phone in the pocket.

"Don't answer it." Sydney wrapped her arms around him from behind, taking a little nip on his shoulder as she ran both hands up and down his chest. He felt the soft slide as she rubbed her breasts against his back.

"Have to. Hold that thought—" He felt Sydney step away from him and bit back a protest.

"What thought?" Saul demanded. The man apparently never slept. It was six A.M in Montana. "Never mind. There's been another bombing in Montreal's *La ville souterraine*. Obliterated ten miles of the Underground City." Saul filled Lucas in on the details.

"Oh, yeah," Saul inserted just as Lucas thought he was done. "One more thing. A woman showed up here last night to see you."

"What woman?"

"Name's Christy Lee Hamilton."

"Never heard of her."

"Wouldn't take no for an answer, swore she'd camp out until you showed. Told her that could be a good long while. Sat down, took out a book, and said she'd wait."

"Who is she? What does she want?"

"I think she was looking for her baby daddy."

Nineteen

"Say what? This woman claims I'm the father of her child?" Lucas demanded.

"She didn't *say* anything. Other than ask for you, and park herself."

Lucas wasn't worried. He knew damn well he hadn't impregnated anyone. Ever. He made sure of it. Inexplicably, the image of Sydney, round with his child, made his throat close. He'd never thought of having children . . . *Forget it.*

"Lady's about twenty months pregnant from the look of her."

Lucas snorted. "What is she, an elephant? Seriously, who is she and what does she want?"

"Checking. Running DNA from her teacup as we speak. But while that's happening, better get your ass to HQ and *talk* to her. Pretty little thing. They're taking bets on the sixth floor to see if we're going to deliver our first baby at T-FLAC HQ." Saul didn't laugh as a rule, but Lucas could hear a thread of mirth running through his words.

"You left a strange woman camped out in the lobby?"

It wasn't actually a lobby. Just a huge expanse of open space at ground level with cement seating and a bunch of plants. As nondescript and innocuous and uncomfortable as possible, not hinting at the subterranean workings of the organization.

The Control let out a noncommittal grunt. "Thought

it would be best to give her a room on the nonsecure floor."

"What are we running? The T-FLAC Motel?"

"Thought you'd appreciate us putting up your girlfriend." Saul's tone was wry. "No good deed goes unpunished."

Sydney had snuggled up to him again and was now nibbling on his ear. Lucas wondered if she could hear any of the conversation. Knowing Sydney, she was probably nibbling and listening at the same time. "Jesus, Saul. Did she *say* she was my girlfriend? I haven't had a girlfriend since I was in third grade."

"Poor baby," Sydney whispered devilishly, then used the tip of her tongue to outline the shell of his ear, making him shudder.

"Hey, don't shoot the messenger. Just get to Montana ASAP. She can't have the baby here, Fox. That would just spoil the whole fucking ambience of the place."

The satellite phone beeped in Lucas's ear, indicating another call. "Gotta go."

"No. Wait. What do you want me to do—"

Lucas cut him off. "Mason?" He grabbed Sydney's hand as it snaked around his belly. "Good to hear from you."

"Son. Sorry I didn't get back to you sooner." Mason Knight's familiar voice did what it always did since Lucas had been a kid—made him feel as though someone out there gave a damn. "Okay, about this virus you had me check into. Look, I hate to say it, but my memory isn't as good as it used to be. I'm afraid I'm getting a little forgetful in my old age. Give me a bit more time, and I'll get back to you on this."

"Sure. No problem. If anyone can figure out who the manufacturer is, it would be you." Thing was, Lucas hadn't been able to wait for Mason to get back to him. The lab at HQ was already analyzing the compound for any identifiable signature. He just didn't want Mason to think he no longer had faith in the man who raised him.

"Yeah. I'm on it. Listen, Luke." Knight was the only person who called him Luke. "There's a problem you might be able to help me with. How close are you to Brazil?"

Since Lucas was five miles off the coast, he said casually, "Close enough. Why?" The little hairs on the back of his neck prickled, and it had nothing to do with Sydney's warm, damp mouth trailing across his nape, her hand wiggling like a captive bird inside the cage of his fingers right above his groin. He was doing his best to ignore her, but his penis was ready to party again.

"I'd take this as a personal favor if you could check something out for me at a beauty spa place near Rio." Mason sounded frail. And hearing his voice, realizing that the man he cared about was getting old, made him feel a little guilty. But Lucas didn't believe in coincidences. Never had.

What the hell was Knight's connection to the medi-spa? "Beauty place? You mean *Novos Começos*?"

"That's the one, son. Look, a friend of mine has gotten into a spot of bother with some electrical components he was fooling with. Says they're in a warehouse on that property. If I give you directions, would you mind teleporting into the warehouse and see just what kind of foolishness he's up to?"

Been there, done that. Curiouser and curiouser.

"I've kinda got my hands in a special project I'm working on right now," Lucas told him casually, testing the waters. Was Mason fishing, too? Did Mason know he was right there? Or did he know that Lucas had already visited the warehouse, and for whatever reason, want him to go back? Was this an innocent coincidence or a trap?

Logically he knew the answer. But when he used logic,

it sometimes meant he didn't listen to his instincts and right now, his instincts were screaming.

"Any way you can do it yourself?" he asked Mason. "Maybe we could hook up in Rio and take a couple of days off from our busy schedules in a week or so? I haven't seen you in . . . what? Six months?"

"I'd like that. I've missed the Sunday brunches with you boys. Perhaps we could contact Simon and Alex and have them meet us there?" Mason paused to sigh deeply. "About my running this little errand myself. I didn't want to bother you, but to be honest, I had a minor fall a couple of weeks ago, and I'm a little banged up. Just got out of the hospital yesterday. If you wouldn't mind . . ." His voice trailed off.

"Are you all right? What does the doctor say?"

Knight snorted in disgust. "He said a man my age shouldn't be riding a motorcycle."

Lucas shook his head. "Hell, Mason—"

"I know. I know. You told me the same damn thing. I like the wind blowing in my hair."

"All six strands of it? Get a ceiling fan."

"Watch it. I can still take you in arm wrestling."

Not since Lucas was twelve. "Don't worry about the warehouse. I'll go check it out. Anything specific you want me to look for?"

"Call me when you get inside and we'll go from there, all right?"

"Sure." After a few more minutes of pleasantries, Lucas reminded Knight to get back to him as soon as he made some sort of connection and ID on the bombings and the virus. He broke the connection and tossed the sat phone onto a nearby chair with a little more force than necessary.

"Why does he want you to go back to that warehouse that damned near gets you killed whenever you get within a hundred paces of the place?"

"So much for security on my phone," he said dryly. Twisting around, he lifted her off her knees and positioned her where he wanted her on his lap. "You heard everything?"

"I have ears like a bat," she told him with a small smile as she slid over him. For a moment the pleasure was so intense, so shocking, he couldn't move.

Sydney lifted up a little, and did all the work. She . . .

. . . moved . . .

. . . so . . . slowly, he'd have thought that she wasn't turned on. But looking at her glazed eyes, and the tension in her jaw, he realized that she was bound and determined to drive them both to the brink and beyond.

"He knows—mmm—what happened to you there, doesn't he?"

He clenched his teeth as she slid to the hilt, her internal muscles pulling at him. Lucas ground his teeth together as he braced her back with both hands. "I can't be sure of that."

"Funny—hang on a sec—Ahh. God that feels so—so—*amazing*. Don't move, let the little ones pass . . . Okay." She resumed the slow in-and-out glide, the tendons in her neck cording as she maintained the motion with difficulty.

"I admire your fortitude," he told her. "Should I just be the object you're working over, or should I participate?"

"Object," she told him firmly, her knees digging into his hips, and her arms about his neck. "I'm pretty damn sure that he knows *exactly* what's going on there, *and* in the medical building."

Lucas had the same feeling. "Why?" he managed to ask, as his brain clouded and the top of his head threatened to blow off. The woman had the sexual constitution of—Hell. He had no idea. What she was doing to him was both torture and unspeakable pleasure.

"Call it woman's i–intuit—Are you w-with me?" Her broken demand, uttered through tightly clenched teeth, was accompanied by her body convulsing around him.

"Thank God," he said with feeling, following her into the free fall.

Somehow they both ended up flat on their backs on the floor. Lucas didn't remember falling there, but that's where they were and he didn't have the energy to get them back up on the bed.

He flung one arm around Sydney, and the other over his eyes. Still throbbing from the force of his orgasm, he returned to the topic at hand. "I can't accuse someone of terrorism and stealing black-market organs without just cause. Especially the person who raised me."

She sat up. "The floor's sandy."

He couldn't feel a damn thing but the force of his blood careening through his veins. "I've known this man almost my entire life. He's been nothing but honest and straightforward with me."

Sydney tugged at his hand until he reluctantly freed his eyes and gazed up at her, flushed and rumpled and sexy as hell. "Syd, come on. I'm recovering from a heart attack here."

She shuddered. "Don't even joke about it. Come to bed with me."

He got up on rubbery legs and followed her to the bed. But instead of lying down, Lucas sat on the edge of the mattress and rested his head in his hands.

Getting up on her knees, Sydney wrapped her arms around his shoulders from behind, then lay her head beside his, her chin on his shoulder. "People change."

"No. They don't. He has principles. He's a scientist. A thinking man. An honorable man. For God's sake, he's fought terrorism alongside T-FLAC for decades."

Sydney's breath fanned his ear as she said softly, "But your gut tells you he's involved, doesn't it?"

Lucas dropped his head lower as she massaged the tense muscles in his neck with slim, strong fingers. She smelled of sex and gardenias, a combination that was becoming addictive. "God, I hope not."

"For your sake I hope not, too." Combing her fingers through his hair she let the strands fall before running her nails along his scalp again. "You are *not* going into that warehouse again."

"Not until I know the real reason why he wants me back there, no."

"What are we going to do?"

Now he sat up. "*We* aren't doing anything. I'm going to give Saul the heads-up and have him do some digging. Christ. I hate this."

He called Saul, filling him in on what details he could. His Control also warned him to not go anywhere near the warehouse again.

"Get ahold of Blackthorne and Stone. Have them contact me directly. I want to brief them on this situation with Knight myself. That said," Lucas said grimly, "I'm less than a hundred percent convinced that Mason Knight has anything to do with *any* of this."

"You know him best," Saul said reasonably. "But consider that he's capable of engineering the bombing coupled with this strain of virus."

Not what Lucas wanted to be reminded of. "But I don't see the correlation between the viruses, the bombings, and the selling of black-market organs."

"Money," Sydney inserted. "He wants a lot of money."

Lucas cocked a brow. "He's already got money. Knight was already a wealthy man. He had patents in biotech. And I'm not so sure he's as capable of this as you think," Lucas continued, directing his words to Saul again. "Maybe—and this is a stretch—maybe he could design a delivery system but Mason's never worked with toxins. Well, he's worked with some, but only in the sense of creating antitoxins. He's one of the good guys. Never even did animal testing. He wouldn't hurt a fly. If he had started exploring new theories, I'm sure he would have told me."

"But you haven't seen him in months. A lot can change in that amount of time," Sydney whispered in one ear while Saul offered practically the same sentiment in the other.

Saul cleared his throat. "Someone in the room with you?"

"Sydney McBride."

"Hi, Saul," Sydney said from over Lucas's shoulder.

There was a pause on the phone. "The lady knows my name. How novel, and how not part of our protocols."

Lucas grimaced but kept his mouth shut. The reaming on that little breach would hurt later.

Saul continued. "That countdown clock reset itself within seconds after the incident in Montreal. Fifteen hours and counting to the next explosion. Confirmed gradual annihilation. Intel tells us the military installation in Poland is the next target. Discover the point of origin, Fox, and since it's too late to nip this in the bud, rip it out by the root. The bad guys are right there under your nose. If the countdown clock is there, then the terrorists controlling this little auction have to be close by, too. Find them. Now."

Yeah. Got it. No problem. The place was overrun with bad guys. It was all in the degree. "Great." He gave a cynical laugh. "Give me the names and coordinates. I'll get right on that."

The bungalow looked exactly the same as it had the day before. Before Lucas and his guys had exchanged the bed for the table and computers.

"Place has been searched. Take only what you must," Lucas told her.

Sydney, wearing nothing but Lucas's black T-shirt, looked around. "How can you tell? It's as neat as a pin."

"I feel a slight Trace. Four Halfs did a thorough search."

A chill slithered up her spine and she grabbed an emerald green canvas beach tote and slipped her laptop inside. All her notes and chapters for the medi-spa book were on the computer for anyone to see, but all the notes she'd made about Lucas, T-FLAC, and the organ transplant business she'd hidden inside the hollow poster of the bed.

Hanging on to the ceiling-high post, she clambered up onto the bed giving Lucas a bird's-eye view of her girl parts as she shifted the mosquito netting out of the way and reached for the top decorative finial and started unscrewing it.

"What the hell are you doing?"

"I hid some notes in here." The hollow wasn't very deep. Just deep enough for the small notebook. She got it out with two fingers.

"Notes on what? The book?" He reached up, wrapping his hands around her waist to lift her down. The T-shirt—*his* T-shirt slipped up with his hands, exposing her from the belly button down.

"Cover yourself, woman. We don't have time to play." He gave her butt a light slap.

"Spoilsport. It's not like you're fully dressed." Stripping off his shirt, she handed it to him before moving out of his arms—did his hands linger for a second too long on her hips? "These are notes for a book, but not *the* book. *Another* book. Once you have the bad guys in custody, or whatever you do to your bad guys, I'm going to write a book about black-market organ trafficking."

Going to the dresser she pulled out a purple thong and matching bra. Watching him in the mirror, she pulled the thong up her legs, enjoying the attention Lucas was paying to her behind as she wriggled to get the perfect fit. She hid a smile.

In the mirror she watched him turn away and pull on his shirt. "Chicken," she mocked softly.

He turned back and tapped his watch. "Get a move on."

She waved her fingers, the lavender bra dangling like a red flag. "Yes, sir."

It was fortunate that he'd been able to teleport them to the bungalow. Even though the five-mile trip to shore had taken mere moments, she wasn't sure she wanted to risk teleporting back to Miami that way. It would be hard explaining to anyone how she happened to just drop out of thin air.

"What happened to the table and all your equipment?" Sydney asked. *More important, who is the pregnant woman demanding an audience with you?* She wiggled into her favorite faded skinny jeans, then lay on the bed to zip them. Getting up, she went to the closet.

"One of my men took care of it. If you insist on walking around bare-breasted like that we'll never get out of here."

She'd rather go back to the nice private yacht where no one could find them. But if it meant spending more time with Lucas, she was game. "I'm looking for shoes."

"Put a top on first."

Hiding her grin, she hooked on her bra, then pulled on a purple tank, followed by another in orange, tucking both into her waistband. Threading the multicolored chain and bauble belt through the loops of her jeans, she shoved her feet into flat sandals and spritzed herself with cologne. "Ready."

"I'm never going to be able to pass a flower shop without getting a hard-on."

Sydney laughed. "You silver-tongued devil. That's a lovely thing to say." She grabbed the beach bag stuffed with her computer and notes, a change of clothes, and her makeup. She was clean-faced, her hair still wet from their earlier shower. She hefted the heavy tote onto her shoulder, then reached for her favorite white dress.

"Leave it."

Raising a brow, she stuffed it into the top of the bag. "You think they'll think we didn't come back?"

"I don't give a shit what *they* think. I figure we have an hour, maybe two, before people wake up from their drunken stupors and start going into town for Carnival. I want you long gone before that happens."

She stopped in her tracks. "Aren't you coming with me?"

"I'm taking you to the airport. I'm still working." He didn't—wouldn't—look at her.

"Wow." She rested the weight of the tote on the arm of the chair. "That's a big fuck-you-and-the-horse-you-rode-in-on."

He rounded on her, his fury shooting her with every look, every word. "These sons of bitches tried to cut out your *heart*. What do you want me to do? Go with you? I don't do happily-ever-after, and I sure as shit won't let them get away with kidnapping innocent people and stealing their organs. What do you want me to do, Sydney? Turn my back and just say, 'Have at it,' as they bomb major cities around the world and infect millions of people with some mysterious virus?"

"Good point." Sydney yanked the heavy bag back onto her shoulder. "Here's a question: Can you teleport me to Miami?" She'd risk it, because the backs of her eyes were stinging, and she was not going to make a fool of herself by crying.

His jaw worked. "No."

She tipped her head back in an effort to keep the tears

from evading her tenuous hold. "You just brought us here, Lucas. You can just damn well teleport me home."

"Even if I could do that right now, I don't trust my powers to sustain it." It was killing him to send her away, especially since she had some unexplainable way of amping up his power—power he knew for sure would help him achieve his agenda. But the choice between keeping her with him and sending her to safety wasn't a choice. No way would he put her in harm's way a second time. "I'll drive you to the airport and make sure you're safely on board."

Don't cry. Do not cry. "Sounds boring."

A sound that was almost a laugh escaped him. "Nothing about you is boring, Sydney McBride. Want me to carry that thing?"

"No thank you."

"Okay. Let's go hot-wire a car."

Her chest hurt from the pressure of not flinging herself into his arms and holding on tightly. *Never let them see you cry.* "*That's* mildly interesting," she said with forced cheer. "My father will be so proud. I've never stolen a car before."

"There's a first time for everything."

Lucas hot-wired a black Cadillac Escalade from the parking lot. Sydney would have gone with the little red Maserati next to it. After all, both had full tanks of gas. But the Maserati was too exposed, and it was the kind of car people noticed. Lucas wanted metal, preferably bulletproof metal, surrounding Sydney for the duration.

If he couldn't have bulletproof, then he'd take a tank of an SUV. He settled Sydney in her seat and buckled her in. Not because she was incapable of doing so herself, but because he wanted to touch her, maybe for the last time. Inhaling the fragrance of her skin made his chest hurt.

He'd wanted to instigate a fight. But Sydney being Sydney hadn't wanted to play that game. It had been a feeble attempt to delay saying good-bye. Or worse, dragging her into his arms and—What?

That was the point, Lucas thought savagely, wanting to punch something. Slamming her door, he walked around the front and climbed in. It was barely 8 A.M. and only the gardeners and a few hardy joggers were out. Already it promised to be a scorcher of a day, and he turned up the A/C for Sydney after he drove through the arched gates of the resort.

"I don't have my passport," she said suddenly as they merged into the road going into Rio. Almost immediately they had to slow to a crawl as they hit Carnival traffic. Galeão airport was twenty kilometers on the other side of the city, and they'd have to go through the madness to get there.

Shit. He'd almost forgotten about the biggest holiday of the year in Rio. He tried to teleport over the line of vehicles, pretty much *knowing* that wasn't going to work. Which, of course, it didn't. He could have asked Sydney for a boost, but that would mean exposing his vulnerability to her. Knowing Sydney, the only way he'd ever get her to leave was kicking and screaming. Not exactly a great way to begin a covert op. Honest to God, if he didn't get his powers fixed soon he was going to . . . *What*? Ask for a fucking transfer from psi to regular T-FLAC? Shitdamnfuck.

Sydney was tapping her iPhone. He glanced over and saw her frowning and scrolling through airline schedules and prices.

"Doesn't matter. You're not going back on a commercial flight. T-FLAC has a private jet waiting for you."

She looked up from her phone. "Do you really not know who the pregnant woman is?"

"I really don't." He tapped his finger on the steering wheel.

"Maybe you forgot?"

"No."

She stared out the window. "Aren't you curious?"

"Not particularly. It's a case of mistaken identity, that's all."

"And she tracked *you*, Lucas Fox, directly to Montana and to T-FLAC headquarters? I *so* don't think so."

He shrugged. "The least of my problems right now."

"Aren't you even a *little* curious?"

"No."

"I could go and talk to her if you like. Woman-to-woman."

"That's—" *Laughable.* "A great idea."

Her head spun so fast he wouldn't be surprised if her shock had given her whiplash. "*Really?* Are you serious?"

Serious about her being somewhere safe until he knew what was going on here? Hell, yeah. They'd tried to steal her organs because she was connected to him. Until he knew the who and why, why *not* send her to HQ? "Sure. You can grill her like a cheese sandwich for me."

"You're kidding. Right?"

"Not at all. The jet will take you directly to Montana. After a few days I'll have you delivered wherever you want to go. Safe and sou—"

The sound of the back and front windshields shattering was almost simultaneous. Sydney's scream followed seconds later.

Twenty

"Down. Stay down." Lucas swerved the heavy sport utility vehicle off the road, away from traffic. The airbags exploded into the car's cabin, but in the split second before they opened, he'd pulled out his knife in anticipation and immediately started slashing at the obstruction in front of him even as they jounced down a steep grade.

For several minutes, he was literally driving blind as the heavy vehicle bounced down the grassy embankment. "Are you hit?" he shouted, fighting both the deflating airbag and the steering wheel. "Sydney? Are you hit?"

The SUV came to an abrupt stop against an immovable object, a Plymouth-sized rock. Shoving the shredded bag out of his way, he attacked the airbag on Sydney's side, while she struggled to shove it out of her way.

"Hang on, hang on, I'm working on it." He punctured the airbag, then started slicing it to aid in the deflation.

"We were smote for stealing the car," Sydney said, her voice shaking as she helped him pull the shredded airbag away from her body and out of the way. Small pieces of safety glass were sprinkled over her like uncut diamonds and as she moved, bits of glass fell from her hair and clothing. She brushed them off onto the floor.

"Does anything hurt?" he demanded, picking off the

dull shards as he scanned her for cuts. He didn't see any blood.

"What's this?" Rubbing a fine white powder between her fingers, she gave him a look of horror. "Cocaine?"

Lucas had to smile. "No drug dealers involved. Talcum powder to help the airbag deploy more easily. Is your neck okay?"

"I'm fine. Shaken, but okay. How about you?" She reached over and picked glass out of his hair.

Fucking hell. Was his goddamned job going to be the death of her? Was *he* going to be the death of her, because so far he was doing a piss-poor job of protecting the woman he—*Protecting an innocent civilian.* "Pissed."

"What happened?" She looked around, probably for another vehicle or gun-toting drug runners. "What hit us?"

The holes in the two windshields looked about the size of 9×19mm Parabellum cartridges. "Submachine gun, possibly an Uzi, fired from a car behind us."

"Occupational hazard?" she asked dryly. "So they, whoever *they* are, followed us." She glanced out of the tinted window on her side. "I don't see anyone coming, guns blazing."

"If they're good, you won't," he told her grimly, completely aware of their surroundings and alert for anything. "Won't see them, that is." Traffic continued on the freeway about fifteen feet above their position in the drainage ditch.

He twisted the ignition key off, then on again. The engine didn't turn over. Not that he'd expected the damn thing to work considering the shape the vehicle was in or the boulder he'd tried to relocate, imbedded in the front. Murphy's Law was in full effect.

"Which of the bad guys do you think shot at us?"

"Wish to hell I knew. Doesn't matter, though. First line of defense, get the hell out of Dodge."

"Isn't the first line of defense shoot back?"

"Not with you here, it isn't." He tried, even though he knew teleporting wasn't going to work worth a damn.

"What? Still can't teleport? Let's try this . . ." Sydney slipped her hand into his. He felt the jolt of their connection, but this time it wasn't strong enough to work. Not a complete surprise, he'd been wondering if or when he'd deplete the effect of her touch. Pretty fucking inconvenient that it had to be *now*.

He shook his head. "The Highway Patrol will be here soon." And/or whoever had shot at them. "We don't have time to answer official questions, and we can't sit here. Whoever tried to kill us is still out there. Even if they're stuck in traffic, an Uzi has a range of a couple of hundred yards." The thought of how easy it would be for her to be hit, by Uzi, sniper rifle, or a freaking .22, infuriated him. God *damn* these assholes!

"Here." He let go of her hand to give her the blue steel Tac-Five. He'd paused to strap the Para Ordnance 9mm to his leg before they left the bungalow. No such thing as too much firepower.

The 1911-style pistol held plenty of bullets. Even if she shot wild, it wouldn't matter. Anyone got close enough, they'd be toast. "Simple to use, just do this, this, and this." He showed her quickly, step by step, what she'd need to know to reload and fire. "Got it?"

White-knuckled, her fingers wrapped around the black plastic grip. "Yes. Who knew all those shooting lessons with my brothers would actually come in handy?"

"It's a hair trigger, so don't hold it too tight," he told her absently, focused on his psi weapons. He pushed at his powers to get them jump-started and . . . not a damn thing. He left that channel open. The stopwatch ticked in his head.

"Know what staging is?" When she shook her head, he quickly explained the method of shooting that quickly moved the trigger back to the pointer where the cylinder was rotated and locked. "So in effect, you have a two-stage trigger—Never mind—Combined, you now have seven pounds of a double-action revolver." He realized that her eyes had glazed a little.

There was a beat of silence. "The bullet comes out of this end, right?" She pointed, lips twitching.

What a remarkable woman. Her hands shook with the aftermath of the adrenaline rush, glass sparkled in her hair and on her skin, yet she maintained her composure and sense of humor.

He leaned over and captured her mouth in a quick kiss. Straightening, his hand lingered on her jaw. "If it looks suspicious, shoot it."

"Carte blanche. Cool. What are *you* going to u—Oh. Good, we're both armed and dangerous. I don't suppose I could have the pretty gun instead?" She looked from the plain, wide-bodied, no-frills black gun to his custom Glock with its rosewood grip. The Glock had been with him for ten years, it had been hand-fitted and calibrated to his exacting specs.

"Nope. This isn't about pretty. It's about accuracy and survival. The recoil on this would knock you on your ass and I want you shooting at the bad guys, not the sun." He placed the weapon close at hand on the seat beside him.

"Got it."

She looked out through the shattered windshield to the mangled and mutilated front end of their vehicle. Steam seeped through the buckled seams of the hood, drifting into the air. "Uh-oh. Houston, we have a problem."

"No kidding." They weren't going anywhere. Not in this. He couldn't even pretend that his powers might work at this point. Mentally, he had to switch gears. "If we follow this ditch for about a mile, we'll be close to downtown. Place will be insane with millions of people clogging the streets for the first official day of Carnival."

She raised her eyebrows. "We're going to Carnival?"

"No, we're going to be invisible. We'll be needles in a haystack. No one is going to follow us if we get lost in the crowd. We'll find another vehicle and get over to the airport." He leaned over and tried the passenger-side door handle. Nothing. The bent metal wouldn't budge. A sizzle, much like an electrical jolt, surged through him. He hadn't experienced anything like it since childhood, when Alex was seventeen and testing his powers. He'd accidentally sent Lucas and Simon flying into the nearby creek.

Mason had claimed *that* power surge could have, and probably *had,* fried their fool brains.

"Come out on my si—What the f—"

With a horrendous noise of unbuckling metal and the timpani of glass being restored, the Escalade became magically whole again. With a roar, the engine started on its own and the big vehicle slammed into reverse. Lucas grabbed the steering wheel, but nothing he did affected the car as it shot backward up the embankment at close to a hundred miles per hour.

Sydney screamed as she was flung against the door, banging her head on the tinted window.

"Buckle your seat belt," Lucas yelled, uselessly fighting the wheel as the powerful SUV did a wheelie in the middle of oncoming traffic, jumped the median in a screech of tires, then headed south. South. Back the way they'd come.

Away from downtown. Away from the airport. Back to *Novos Começos.*

He stood on the brakes. The action had zero impact on their speed.

Grabbing up the Glock from the seat beside him, he kept a fisted grip on the wheel with the other. No matter how hard he tried, he wasn't in control of the vehicle in any way. The 9mm was ripped out of his hand, leaving him with stinging fingers and cursing a blue streak. Someone or something was running this show.

He made a lunge for the Glock just as it tipped over the edge of Sydney's seat and fell into the footwell. She started leaning forward. He shot out his hand and grabbed her arm. "Leave it." He didn't want her putting her head down to look for it at her feet when he had no control over the speed of the vehicle. For all he knew they'd stop on a dime. She'd be thrown headfirst through the restored windshield.

"What's happening?" Sydney yelled, bracing both hands on the dashboard as the vehicle continued to pick up speed, weaving through the traffic. Lucas laid on the horn, the only defensive maneuver he was capable of right now. Despite this, the front right fender smashed into a small pickup truck, sending it spinning across three lanes of traffic.

He observed what was about to become a five-car pileup in the rearview mirror. The strong power coming from who-the-fuck-knew-where wasn't letting up. Nothing he did made any difference. Pumping the brakes, taking the Escalade out of gear, yanking up the hand brake, trying to turn the ignition key; *nothing* worked.

As he watched, the cars and truck were immobilized in freeze-frame, caught in mid-action in various stages of being airborne. It took a powerful wizard like Caleb Edge to control time like that. Time was slowing—No. He suspected time was normal for everyone but himself and Sydney. The vehicle seemed to be traveling at warp speed. The scenery blurred as the needle on the speedometer disappeared to the far right and out of sight. The entire chassis shook and metal fatigue–induced stress fractures cracked and splintered the SUV's frame.

The vibration of the steering wheel traveled up Lucas's arms until his body shook with the strength of his hold. He half expected Sydney to yell "Do something!" at any minute. But she kept silent, hanging on as they bounced and veered from one side of the three-lane highway to the other, in a series of near misses, barely avoiding other vehicles in their path. Everything seemed to be standing still as they slalomed in, out, and around cars traveling in both directions.

With one hand braced on the door, the other in a death grip on the safety harness crossing her body, Sydney was pale-faced and wide-eyed. Her lips were moving silently.

"Might as well say that prayer out loud to cover both of us," he yelled over the scream of the engine and the failing framework of the SUV.

The quiet conviction in her voice shouldn't have been audible over the cacophony of the vehicle's distress, but it was. "Hail Mary, full of grace, the Lord is with thee. Blessed art thou among women and blessed is the fruit of thy womb, Jesus. Holy Mary, Mother of God, pray for us sinners, now and at the hour of our death."

"Got anything a little less fatalistic?" Lucas asked as the car took the exit to *Novos Começos*. They'd made the return trip in a tenth of the time it had taken them when leaving. Still traveling at a breakneck speed, they swerved onto a blacktop service road running around the back of the resort. Without warning the heavy SUV shuddered to a halt in a stand of trees. Even parked at the back of the warehouse, Lucas knew exactly where they were.

A chill swept his body, and his heart started to pound

hard and fast over the sound of the engine cooling. Someone wanted his ass back in that warehouse real bad.

Mason had wanted him to return here. Christ . . . He was having a hard time trying to wrap his mind around Mason as a bad guy. Just didn't compute. Not even close.

"Okay. That was incredibly freaking creepy." Sydney's voice shook as she unhooked her seat belt and dragged in a deep, shaky breath, then huffed it out. "Did your powers go haywire?"

"Wasn't me."

"Then who's *doing* this?"

"I am, Miss McBride," an accented voice said from the backseat.

Although they'd never met, Lucas instantly recognized the Half wizard he saw in the rearview mirror. Two other men, one in the middle, the other behind Sydney, were muscle. Recognizing the Greek gave Lucas a ridiculous, almost overwhelming surge of relief.

A Splinter operation. Not Knight. He didn't have time to linger in the relief of knowing his mentor and friend wasn't involved in this clusterfuck.

Keeping his gaze locked with those of the tango Half, he said evenly, "Leonidas Karras."

"Mr. Fox." The man's smile was oily and smug. "And Miss McBride. You look remarkably healthy for a woman whose organs are, as we speak, in a refrigerated unit."

She pressed her hand on her midriff. The gasping breaths were fake as she leaned forward as if to ward off the threat of hyperventilation. From the corner of his eye, Lucas watched her discreetly retrieve his Glock from the floorboard.

"I w-wasn't done using them," she said, still faking her gasps, resuming an upright position. It was an award-winning performance as she leaned her head weakly on the back of the seat.

Only he could see the tremor, and the gun, in her hand.

Karras turned his attention from Sydney back to Lucas. Which was exactly where Lucas wanted it. He wanted Sydney to be a thousand miles away, and if not a thousand miles, then ten. Just. Fucking. *Away.*

"I believe you've been helping yourself to that which does not belong to you."

Lucas barked a disbelieving laugh. "That's rich, coming from you. What have I taken? Your donors? I get that you're a smart guy, Karras, but even you've gotta know how morally bankrupt it is to kidnap unsuspecting victims and harvest them like a corn crop for their organs."

The Half shrugged. "It is an extremely lucrative business."

"*Was* an extremely lucrative business. Be thankful that your mother-in-law got her lungs, because T-FLAC is officially closing you down." And hopefully figuring out how a Half managed a maneuver as powerful as commandeering the SUV.

Karras's laugh was robust and genuine. "You think so?"

"We have a flight to catch, so cut to the chase." Lucas gave him a cold smile as he shot a quick glance at Sydney. She was partially turned toward him in the seat, her arm supporting her body. A rapid, uneven pulse beat frantically at the base of her throat. He could almost hear her mind going a mile a minute.

He met Karras's eyes in the mirror again, at the same time feeling a nudge as Sydney slid the Glock deep inside the crease where the seat back met the seat cushion and pushed it flush against his hip.

Karras had disabled him, but he hadn't disabled Sydney. Nor, Lucas thought with satisfaction, had the Greek taken the knife strapped to his calf. "That was a showy way of getting me back here. What do you want?"

"Your impulsive stunt cost me several millions of dollars, Mr. Fox." Karras gave him an equally chilly smile in return.

"Send the bill to my accountant." Lucas twisted in his seat to look the man in the face, wondering why Karras was making no move to exit the vehicle.

The sun beat in through the window on Sydney's side of the car, heating up the inside of the vehicle like a sauna despite the tinted windows.

At first he thought it was a trick of the harsh sunlight; he blinked to focus but the picture didn't change. Karras's face melted into another shape.

Fucking hell. Not Leonidas Karras. *Nia Ledgister.*

"How gullible you are, Mr. Fox. Leo Karras is merely a businessman. He would never get his hands dirty in the day-to-day operation of a business like this. He and his associates leave that to *me.*" The softer Jamaican accent rolled over the words and the meaning of what she did and didn't say.

"What was in the warehouse?" Lucas remembered the incubator and gritted his teeth.

She shrugged elegant shoulders. "Computers. Things."

"Things I'm assuming made it possible for you and your *associates* to pull off the bombings and the release of the biotoxins?"

A small humming noise purred in her throat. "A bidding war always makes commerce more entertaining, don't you think?"

"And the purpose?"

She shook her head. "So practical. Does there have to be a purpose for acts of terror other than the enjoyment of making people run around like blue-assed flies trying to figure out who the terrorist of the week might be?"

Sydney turned to stare at her. "It's a *game*? Killing hundreds of thousands of people? Destroying businesses and homes, unleashing unspeakable horror on innocent victims is a damn *game*?"

Ledgister's dark eyes remained on Lucas as she answered, "Well, I consider business fun, so yes, Miss McBride. An elaborate, extremely lucrative *game*."

"That's sick. It's hot in here, can I turn on the A/C?" Sydney asked, leaning over to adjust the vent to her satisfaction without waiting for an answer. She put her hand on Lucas's knee to brace herself.

Two things happened almost simultaneously: Lucas gripped the Glock with his left hand, pressing the muzzle, out of sight, to his seat back at waist level. In the same second that he and Sydney shimmered, he fired through the seat, directly into Nia Ledgister's black heart.

Twenty-one

Sydney was never going to get used to this mode of transportation. The disorientation of suddenly materializing somewhere else was compounded by becoming visible smack dab in the center of the Samba Parade, with its endless stream of thousands upon thousands of dancers in elaborate costumes.

She'd lost a sandal in transit, and kicked the other one off as Lucas grabbed her and literally dragged her in his wake. She careened into a leggy, topless bottle-blonde wearing a yellow thong and a bright orange headdress that soared two feet above her head. She was an eye-popping sight to behold, made even more eye-popping because there were several hundred identically dressed women dancing in perfect synchronicity *with* her.

Since they were all dancing in perfect formations, and exactly in step, Sydney's smash-and-run upset the whole order of things. There followed lots of curses and yelling. Very colorful and specific obscenities. Sydney waved a hand over her head in apology. She doubted they even saw her.

Raucous music with a heavy samba beat blared over loudspeakers, vibrating through her entire body like a tuning fork. The beat was so seductive, so loud, so *compelling* she almost danced behind Lucas. Just imagining his face if she did so was enough to make her grin.

When she caught up to him so they were side by side,

he wasn't smiling. His sharp green eyes scanned the crowds around them in a practiced sweep. "Stay close."

He was only inches away but she barely heard him shout in the sensory overload of noise, motion, rhythm, and streams of exotic color. She nodded as he tucked their clasped hands close to his chest so they didn't get separated by the jostling crowds. Pulling her by sheer brute force toward the cordoned area reserved for spectators, Lucas waded through the tightly packed, constantly moving bodies. Stuffing his gun into the back of his waistband he pulled his shirt over it, and motioned her to do the same.

None of the revelers seemed to notice or care that they both carried guns.

The smell of freshly baking bread mingled with the musky scent of sweaty bodies, spilled beer, and citrusy lime. The sun blazed down on so many colors, Sydney couldn't begin to count them all. The crowd screamed as one of the elaborate floats passed by with its own band and very loud steel drummers. The cacophonous noise was earsplitting, compelling, and made her heart pound.

Dammit. She'd timed her stay at *Novos Começos* so that the four-day event would be the culmination of her trip. She wanted to turn around and watch the parade behind them. She'd read about Rio's annual Samba School Parade, where millions of tourists and visitors mingled with millions of locals. A four-day party of pounding rhythms, lavish self-indulgence, exhibitionist extravaganza, gender-bending anything-goes, exotic *spectacle*. And she was just passing through. Well, hell.

Lucas muscled his way through the thick crowd, forging a path to reach what might be a sidewalk near the historical buildings lining the route. There wasn't a car to steal anywhere.

Sydney was pretty much dragged willy-nilly with him, stepping on toes and bumping into assorted body parts as she did so. She did her best to keep up with his long strides even as she was yanked past the spectators who were trying to get a closer look at the approaching float.

Everyone but herself and Lucas, it seemed, was dancing, or singing, or dancing *and* singing. The pounding drums seemed to seep through her pores into her bloodstream. Or maybe it was the adrenaline rush. They'd had a busy day and it was barely noon.

She went headlong into a woman who was a man—or maybe a man who was part woman. The individual had bare, double D breasts, and a very large, *green* penis highlighted by red satin chaps. Laughter bubbled up, a little hysterically, in Sydney's throat as they bumped and parted. "Sorry."

Unlike on TV and in travel brochures, not all the women dancing were tall and beautiful. There were plenty of fat, toothless women gyrating vigorously and shaking body parts that had no business being exposed to sunlight. Sydney wondered if they'd looked in their mirrors that morning as they donned their colorful pasties and G-string and thought, *"Bonita!"*

What the hell, they all looked delighted to be there, and the crowds treated them the same as the sexy girls. Beauty was in the eye of the beer holder. A few feet behind them a woman screamed, the shrill sound pitched above the raucous revelers. Sydney glanced over her shoulder just as another woman's head seemed to explode like a watermelon. The parting crowd swallowed her whole without seeming to notice or care. Oh God. They'd been followed. How was that possible? Gun in hand, Lucas almost yanked her arm out of the socket, swinging her behind him, and backing her into the alcoved doorway of a *farmácia*.

His large body effectively blocked her view.

The stucco wall above their heads exploded in a shower of stinging bits of plaster. Once. Twice. Three times. No mistaking the sound or the result. Dammit. They were being shot at again.

"Don't these bad guys know when to quit?!" She'd been enjoying Carnival, dammit, even under the circumstances, and her delight was just sucked right out of her. Once again, she was overwhelmed and downright terrified. Whoever was shooting at them had no regard for the innocent bystanders. The sound of the bullets hitting so close made her heart thump and her palms sweat. The entire thing was surreal. This wasn't her life. Still hanging on to her arm and hand, Lucas shifted so that she was more beside him than behind him. Several more people went down, but she didn't know if they'd been shot or had fallen over as someone pushed them out of the way.

Her arm was still across his body, her hand clasped tightly by his. It was the only reality in a kaleidoscopic and crazy world. He tightened his grip on her fingers hard enough to bruise. She knew what he was trying to do, and she knew by his expression that it wasn't working.

A group of six young women passed within inches of their cover. Laughing a little drunkenly, the off-duty dancers wore fluorescent fuchsia-colored headdresses and skimpy, glitter-covered, butt-baring costumes.

Lucas put his mouth by her ear to be heard. "We're going to have to do this the old-fashioned way."

"Which is?"

"Run!" he yelled as the fourth and fifth shots pelted the inside of the alcove, much too close for comfort. He pulled Sydney with him, keeping between the dancers and the buildings, using the crowds of closely packed humanity to cover their passage. He motioned to his head, then pointed to hers and indicated that she keep low and move fast. She got it. The entire time Sydney crouched and ran she felt as though she had a freaking bull's-eye painted on her back.

The Fuchsia girls peeled off down a side street. Like Siamese twins, Lucas jogged into the parade route, dragging Sydney beside him. Weaving through the Samba dancers, they zigzagged to the opposite side of the street.

Sydney's heart was pounding faster than the beat of the music. God, she was dying to stop, put her hands on her knees, and hang her head as she gasped for a decent breath. But it wasn't going to happen, and she didn't bother to ask. She trusted Lucas implicitly and if he said run, she'd go until her heart exploded from the exertion.

She sure as hell hoped it wouldn't come to that.

Knowing Lucas, he wasn't running from whoever was shooting. He was trying to find a vehicle to get them to the airport. She knew without a shadow of doubt that if he were alone, he'd go back and hunt the shooter or shooters down like dogs.

"All these people must've parked *somewhere,*" Sydney said, out of breath. She felt like one big sweat ball, her clothes sticking to her wet skin like a shroud.

Okay. Forget shroud, she thought a little hysterically. No shrouds.

She had run at least five miles a day for a year when she'd trained for the Boston Marathon a couple of years ago. She could run. She knew how to pace herself, and what shoes and socks to wear, and all about hydration.

No shoes. No water. No freaking pacing.

"Just a few more yards," Lucas promised, not in the least bit out of breath and barely breaking a sweat. "You can do it, sweetheart."

He had a hell of a lot more faith in her than she had in herself. Unable to speak, she tugged at his hand and pointed to a five-story parking garage up ahead.

"I see it."

Her bare feet were burning from pounding the hot,

hard, uneven ground. She didn't even want to *imagine* what kind of cooties she was picking up as she ran.

They charged across a narrow, people-clogged side street, and onto the down ramp of the garage. It seemed like a mountain they had to climb; worse, the cement had ridges to provide traction for cars. Her poor abused feet weren't happy.

The smooth, curved cement wall beside them suddenly exploded in a barrage of gunshots. Sydney found herself flung facedown onto the sharp furrows on the ground as Lucas spun around and returned fire.

She felt a sharp sting over her eye. It didn't hurt, but blood poured freely from the wound. She tried to staunch the blood with her fingers as it ran into her eye.

Lucas was crouched in a low profile. He reached back and grabbed, she presumed, whatever body part he could reach, which happened to be her filthy-dirty bare foot. He tugged. Hard. "Bathroom. *Go.*"

She shot a quick glance at the rusted, green metal door under the stairs about fifty feet away. *"Homens."*

She hesitated. Safety was safety. But she wasn't leaving Lucas out here, exposed, alone.

Pounding footsteps brought a herd of suit-wearing, panting men closer. She saw them at the bottom of the ramp. Lucas got the first one right between the eyes. She was stunned at the surge of satisfaction she got seeing it. Reaching behind her, Sydney pulled out the utilitarian black gun and rolled over so she was right side up and looking down to the street. Without hesitation she shot a rotund man who was firing something that spat out bullets like gumballs out of a machine. He went down, smashing into another man beside him.

Bullets ricocheted off the walls like marbles in a pinball machine, but not nearly as musical. Beyond the garage, on the next street over, the joyous sound of extra-loud samba music was being broadcast far and wide.

Lucas got off several more shots—two more of the men fell. "Keep going," he yelled. "I'll catch up."

Silly man. "Okay," she yelled back, aiming for a guy on the far left who was gaining ground. Lucas had the same idea, and they shot the guy simultaneously right in the chest. Well, Lucas shot him squarely in the chest, Sydney's shot got him in the shoulder. Close enough.

"Good one." He didn't sound pleased.

A cadaver-thin guy with a bristly black mustache and shiny bald head swung the barrel of his gun from Lucas toward her. He looked astonished when Lucas shot him in the throat. He fell, then rolled on a diagonal halfway down the ramp.

"Didn't I tell you to go?" Lucas said furiously. Sydney was positive he was looking right at her, but he shot another man without a blink. Despite the blood blooming right in the middle of his blue shirt between the lapels of his suit, the guy kept coming like a freaking zombie. A hundred feet and closing. Lucas pulled the trigger again. This time the guy did the whole drop-and-roll thing. "You're ruining my concentration, woman."

"You're outnumbered twelve to one!" She sounded as cranky as he did as she swiped at the blood again.

"Not anymor—Shit!" He jerked as a thick red line of blood opened up on his upper arm just below the short sleeve of his black T-shirt. "Now that really pisses me off."

The last three men, not quite so gung ho now that they realized Lucas knew precisely what he was doing, came racing up the ramp anyway, guns blazing.

"Take the one on the right," Lucas told her grimly, then pumped two bullets into his two men in quick succession. "Are you going to take the shot or wait until he shoots us execution style?"

"I'm *aiming* here."

"Take the fucking shot, Sydney."

She took the shot and, suddenly, there were no bad guys left. Left standing anyway. All these dead bodies littering the parking garage were going to be hard to explain. For a moment she sat there, bare legs and filthy feet spread, both hands on the plain black gun that rested on the floor between her knees. "Your job is exhausting."

She couldn't move, she really couldn't.

Her feet were on fire, she'd scraped both knees, her eyebrow must be a big bloody mess, her makeup had sweated off hours ago, and she was shaking as if she had the DTs.

Lucas shifted so he was crouched beside her. "You did good."

She was too shaky to smile. "Yeah?"

"Yeah." He touched her cheek.

The electrical jolt on contact was hard and fast.

A blur of white and the sound of wind rushing around them brought with it an icy chill.

Sydney landed on her butt with a soft thud in something cold and wet. *Well, hell.*

Twenty-two

Lucas staggered to his feet, the chill of a harsh Montana winter biting into his tropically acclimatized skin. The icy feel of the snow and the frigid air actually felt good after their heated race through the streets of Rio.

When he offered his hand, Sydney grabbed it, scrambling to stand beside him and just a little unsteady. "A heads-up up would've been nice." One-handed, she rubbed her bare arm vigorously. "Where exactly are we? The North Po—Whoa!"

Furious, he swung her up into his arms. "What the *hell* happened to your shoes? Are you telling me you were running hell-bent for leather like that—*barefoot*?"

She looped her arms around his neck as he strode toward the single-story, glass-fronted building a hundred yards away.

They were currently walking across T-FLAC's empty, snow-blanketed parking lot. Sydney rested her head against his chest. She felt so damn good in his arms he could have carried her forever. "Montana?" she asked, lazily playing with the hair at his nape as though they were sitting in front of a fire, relaxing.

She'd been wearing sandals at some point. Of course she hadn't been able to fucking run as if her life depended on it in goddamned *sandals*. He'd dragged her all over God's creation *barefoot*. He remembered that she'd had her laptop with her at some point, and called it into lost and found for her. "You don't listen worth a damn, do you?"

She kissed his jaw. "Did you say something?"

"What the hell am I going to do with you, Sydney McBride?"

Her naughty smile made his heart twist. "Depends if where we're going has a bed or not." She pulled his head down for a mouth-to-mouth kiss that throttled up his heart rate and made him walk faster. He'd never been fond of hors d'oeuvres before Sydney, preferring to go directly to the main course, but he was learning.

The bombproof glass doors automatically swished open as he carried her over the threshold.

"Hmm," she murmured as the doors closed silently behind them, leaving them briefly in a twelve-by-twelve glass enclosure. There was nothing in the room but carpeting and four walls and ceiling of clear glass. He carried her to the middle of the room within a room.

"And we're standing here—because?"

"Backscatter X-ray. " He didn't mention that the machine was a virtual strip search, seeing beneath clothing and producing 3-D images to alert security as to what weapons or explosives were being carried into the building. "Infrared body scanner. Telling security there are two of us, what weapons we're carrying, et cetera. Ocular scanner for identification."

Even he hadn't felt the puffs of air from the ion mobility spectrometer that analyzed particles from their skin and clothing for explosive devices. The open, all-glass atrium lobby looked like a big friendly grin, until one wanted to get in or out. Then the teeth shut and you were tasted like a pork chop to ensure you were who you claimed to be.

Sydney lifted her head to look around. "Cool. How does it all work? Is it unique to T-FLAC? Is it used on wizards or everyone? What happens if you fail the spectro—*whatever*?" she demanded. God, he loved that about her, her fascination with everything, her acceptance of things she couldn't understand, her humor, her—Goddamn it. He gave her the simple version of the infrared scanners and sensors beneath the carpet. A low hum indicated that the second set of doors was about to open.

He knew Sydney was making mental notes of everything she saw. She wiggled in his arms as they crossed the atrium.

"I can walk."

They came to the glass-fronted elevator. The doors slid open, he walked inside, they closed. "I like carrying you. Six."

"Six?"

The elevator started its descent. "Floor."

"I hate to point out to you that this is a one-story building."

"We're going down. Not up."

"Hmm." She rested her head against his shoulder. "No buttons?"

"No need. Are you cold?"

She shook her head as the door slid open on the medical floor. Two orderlies waited with two wheelchairs.

"I'll take her," Lucas said firmly, walking past the pair and leaving them to follow meekly behind. "Where do you want her?" he asked, not slowing down.

"Room two-zero-eight. You report to exam room two-one-zero." The smaller of the orderlies spoke up, emphasizing the second room number, as if he expected an argument.

His strides lengthened. "I'm fine."

Out of the corner of his eye, he could see Sydney scowling up at his chin. Which he was leading with.

"Your arm—" she began.

"It's a crease." She took a deep breath to do battle

with him just as he carried her down a tastefully painted sage green corridor decorated with breathtaking black-and-white photographs of major cities around the world, matted in white, and framed in simple black metal. They could have been in a swanky boutique hotel anywhere in the world instead of six stories under the frozen tundra in Montana.

"It's not a 'crease,' " Sydney said firmly as he paused outside a handleless door. "It's a freaking *bullet* wound. Are you telling me a big superspy like you is afraid of a few *stitches*?" God bless her brothers and the lessons they'd taught her. When in doubt, cast aspersions on the guy's manliness. Gets 'em every time.

The room number was on a plaque to the left of the door that opened soundlessly.

"Put her here," the doctor told Lucas. He had a shock of white hair, bushy white brows over faded blue eyes, and a face straight out of Central Casting. He looked like Sydney's image of a lovable family doctor from a Rockwell painting, the kind that made house calls. He patted the exam table.

"Ahem, Fox? Are you going to hold her while I examine her? That'll make my job a little difficult, which means when it's your turn, I might not be as mindful of the pain as I usually am."

Lucas laughed as he gently placed her on the narrow table. He brushed her hair over her shoulders, then touched the back of his warm fingers to her upper arm. "I've always admired your bedside manner, Chris." He walked over to a nearby cabinet and returned with a blanket that he proceeded to drape around her shoulders. The thick cotton was heated, and Sydney nearly purred as the warmth touched her chilled skin.

"Sydney McBride. Doctor Christopher Kent. Take good care of her, Doc. Gotta go report in and be debriefed, I'll be back ASAP."

Lucas started walking away, then he returned and cupped her cheek. "You were hell on wheels back there. I couldn't have had a better partner."

He shot the doctor a warning look and walked out. The door eased closed behind him.

Eyes suddenly watering, Sydney glanced down. Her legs were a mess. Cuts and scratches bled sluggishly, and her legs, arms, and feet were beyond filthy. Who knew what cooties she'd brought into T-FLAC's top security building. Did they scan for that, too?

"Let's see what we have here," the doctor said genially, pulling up a stool. He started gently cleaning her scraped knees, checking below the obvious grime for significant injuries. He should have been looking at her heart.

Lucas returned two hours later to find that Sydney had been released and taken to one of the suites. He grabbed a shower and change of clothes, and reluctantly allowed a doctor to stick a couple of steri-strips over the wound on his upper arm. It, like the dozen others he'd collected, would heal.

With Lucas's intel, they'd sent a team back to *Novos Começos* in Brazil. They'd already found the computer used to auction off the bombings and biotoxins inside Nia Ledgister's safe in her private office. This discovery had averted the strike by two hours.

Karras, his entire family, and several unknown associates had been killed in an explosion on his luxury yacht as they set out to sea. More of Nia Ledgister's handiwork before she'd morphed into Karras to confront Lucas back at the spa. It was going to take awhile for them to uncover what the hell else the woman was up to and what she'd secreted in the warehouse. A geek squad had joined the forensic team on-site, investigating the remnants in the high-tech storage facility. T-FLAC was nothing if not thorough.

Lucas took a few minutes to go up to the hangar on ground level. It wasn't exactly that he was putting off seeing either of the two women waiting for him. He just wanted to see how Mike was doing. First.

A man Lucas barely recognized strode across the vast expanse of the hangar where T-FLAC kept their assorted planes, choppers, and vehicles for storage and/or repair. "Mike? Lucas Fox."

"Hey, man. I gotta thank you for what you've done." He shook Lucas's hand in a firm handshake.

"You look a hell of a lot better than last time I saw you." The guy was clean for one thing. Well, clean under the splotches of oil and grease on his coveralls. His eyes were bright, his smile goofy and wide. Lucas couldn't help smiling back. "How's it going?"

"Better." Mike studied the ground for a moment. "You know about the Boeing thing, right?"

Saul had filled Lucas in when he was being debriefed. Apparently, Mike had worked for the manufacturing giant for twenty years as an airplane mechanic. After a protracted battle with alcohol, and numerous warnings, he'd been fired. His wife had left him, taking the kids and every last dime he had. He'd ended up on the streets, but managed to get clean and sober, and just as he'd started seeing a glimmer of light at the end of the tunnel, had been kidnapped by one of Nia Ledgister's Retrievers.

Lucas clapped a hand on his shoulder. "Yeah. I heard."

"I jumped at the chance when your people offered me a job here." He shot Lucas a worried look. "That's okay with you, right?"

"Better than okay. Welcome aboard. T-FLAC is an excellent place to work. Just don't make me look bad." Lucas softened the warning with a wry twist of his lips.

Mike's eyes twinkled. "I already got the 'better watch your ass with the drinking thing' lecture from HR. Don't worry. I'm clean for good. They pointed me to the AA meeting in town. I went to my first this morning. And my hand to God, I'm going to stay sober. With this job and sobriety, I'm going to ask Julie and the kids to give me one more shot at the brass ring."

Lucas clasped his shoulder a little tighter, respect for the man's courage to face his mistakes and his future in his grip. "Only way is up. You'll make it."

Someone called for Mike, and he shook Lucas's hand once more, his shake firm and determined before he strode across the hangar to one of the Black Hawks.

Lucas walked away knowing the guy wasn't going to blow this second chance.

Now, on to the two women.

He'd deal with the pregnant one first and send her on her way. After that, for Christ's sake, he wanted to see Sydney.

His sat phone beeped in his pocket while he was crossing the hangar. "Fox."

"I'm here, where are you?"

Alexander Stone. "Here at HQ?"

"Yeah, wanna meet for a drink?"

"No time for a drink, but I *do* want to talk to you. Bar in five?"

The bar was located on the ground level, a small, utilitarian place for operatives to meet before or after an op. There wasn't even a nod at ambience. The lighting was full spectrum, the tables black metal, the chairs black plastic, and the bartender a retired operative who didn't take crap from anybody. Generally speaking, the place served more coffee than booze.

Lucas ordered two of those coffees, black, and waited for his friend in a booth facing the door.

He and Alex, along with Simon Blackthorne, had

been friends for—hell—more than twenty years? Yeah. Lucas sipped the coffee he didn't want, and checked his watch for the third time. He wished Blackthorne were there, too, so he could talk to both Alex and Simon about Mason. Did they know about the fall and hospital stay? Did they worry about his health as he got older, as Lucas did? Maybe they should try to persuade the old man to move to Montana. Knight might gripe about the weather, but having him close to the expert medical personnel at HQ would make Lucas feel a whole lot better about the long intervals between face time.

"Jesus. You're still ugly." Alex slapped Lucas on the shoulder, then folded his rangy body into the seat opposite.

They exchanged the usual insults and lies and fell briefly into comfortable silence. Lucas wondered if he should tell his friend about his power outages, or wait until he'd spoken to Knight to see what the prognosis might be. He decided to wait. "You've been casting your seed, I see. And young. What were you? Sixteen?"

Alex looked up, his dark green eyes blank. "Say what? I'm not the one with a pretty pregnant girl waiting for me downstairs. Bad Lucas, bad, bad Lucas."

Yeah. That. "I saw a kid in Brazil who's your doppelgänger. No shit, he's *you* at twenty. Has that whole swallowed-an-egg Adam's apple, the skin thing, the hair that won't stay down."

Alex frowned. "Where was this?"

"Kid's a waiter at *Novos Começos,* south of Rio. No shit. I don't mean *maybe* he looks a little like you around the eyes. I mean, photocopy of you at that age."

Alex glanced at his watch, the watch Lucas had given him for his thirtieth birthday six years ago. He pushed away from the table.

"Gotta go. I'll check it out when I get back from Paris. Unlikely he's mine, but you never know." He kept talking as he walked away. "How about hooking up in a week or so in London or Mace's place in Barcelona? We'll figure out where he is and surprise him for one of our Sunday brunches? Get together and catch up. Yeah?"

Yeah. It would be great to get together and catch up. Lucas made a mental note to carve out the time before he was assigned a new op and, as was the pattern for the past three months, it became impossible to get away.

He put in a quick call to Saul to find out where the woman was cooling her pregnant jets, then headed back to the lounge used for meetings with non–T-FLAC personnel.

He was burning to see Sydney. How the hell long would be polite enough to have a conversation with this woman before arranging to have her escorted off the premises?

He shoved open the right side of the double teak door into the spacious lounge. Again, no frills, but as utilitarian as it was, the room was still comfortable. A dozen seating groups provided ample privacy for conversation. The monochromatic room boasted its own refrigerator and cabinets filled with sodas, water, and snacks. He'd spent many a night sacked out on one of the sofas up here, too exhausted to go downstairs to a room.

A room where Sydney waited for him. He shook off the thought and the temptation as he spotted the only people in the lounge, in the back corner of the room.

A dark-haired woman pushed herself up with her arms, with difficulty, from an easy chair. But it wasn't the enormously pregnant woman who captured Lucas's eyes. It was the woman helping her to her feet. "Sydney."

She was wearing black drawstring pants and a black long-sleeved T-shirt, and red, high-top sneakers. God only knew where the damn shoes had come from. Her face was scrubbed clean of the sweat and dirt that had covered it earlier, and she'd found makeup somewhere. Her tiger eyes were smoky and sexy as hell, her lips a glossy, deep red to match the sneakers on her feet. She gave him an indecipherable look as she put a hand on the woman's back and urged her forward.

"Lucas. This is Christy Hamilton—"

He forced his gaze away from Sydney; the bruise on her forehead hadn't been covered completely by the makeup. He was responsible for hurting her, and for that, he'd never forgive himself.

The woman was attractive, in her mid to late thirties, and as Saul had mentioned, about twenty months pregnant. She was petite with pretty, shoulder-length dark hair, brown eyes, and a trembling mouth. She was about to cry. *Ah, man.* For several moments she stared at him like he was a steak dinner and she'd been starving for a month. Hungry. Yearning.

"What can I do for you, Miss Hamilton?"

"It's Mrs. I . . . You . . ." She glanced at Sydney standing beside her, then dragged in a shaky breath. "I'm Sarah, Luke."

He didn't recognize her by that name either. "I thought your name was Christy Hamilton?"

"I was adopted when I was six and a half." She waited several beats for his response.

What the hell was he supposed to say? Sorry? That's terrible? Lucky you? There was something terribly sad about her, something that tugged at a part of himself he hadn't even been aware of until he'd met Sydney.

"Before she was adopted her name was Sarah Fox, Lucas," Sydney said quietly. "Sarah is your twin sister."

He would have backed away then, if Sydney hadn't laid her hand on his arm. "Impossible. I never had a sister, twin or otherwise. I'm sorry, Sarah, or Christy, or whatever you go by now. But someone steered you in the wrong direction. I was an only child."

"We lived at one-seventy-six Kilgetty Road in Covington, Washington. Our mother's name was Sonia. She had dark hair like ours, and blue eyes and an infectious laugh. Daddy's name was Kevin. He was slight and always joked that your father was the mailman because the doctor told Mom you'd be over six feet when you gr—" Her tears spilled over. "When you grew up. And he w-was right. Daddy used to take us fishing at Lake Sawyer . . . You had a red fishing rod, and you loved digging up worms. You always baited my hook because I'd pretend to gag and you were the protective older brother . . . God, Luke. How can you have forgotten me?"

He shook his head throughout her litany of false facts. "My parents died when I was six."

"Six and a half." Her eyes swam. "They were in Ireland on vacation and were struck by lightning."

How did she know about his parents? "And where were *we* when that happened?"

"I'd been staying with the neighbors while Mom and Dad went on vacation. You were with a friend of Daddy's. When social services came to the house, you were . . . gone. Just gone. There was no sign that you'd ever lived there. They took me with them. I was adopted, and my family moved to Arizona." She let out a shuddering breath and Lucas gritted his teeth against what he wanted to say, comfort he wanted to give. This wasn't real, couldn't be real.

"Somehow—God, I've asked myself a million times in the past few weeks how this could *possibly* happen?" Tears ran down her cheeks. Sydney bent over and plucked a pack of tissues out of a purse on the edge of the coffee table. She handed several to the quietly weeping woman.

"Somehow I—*forgot* about you, Luke."

"Then we're both on the same page," he said dryly, not believing a word of it. As unwillingly sorry as he felt for the woman, not a word out of her mouth was the truth. His parents' names had been Carol and Dave. Not Sonia and Kevin. He'd lived in London, not Washington State. And he hated fishing, always had.

She swayed on her feet. "We were inseparable."

"Would you like something to drink before you leave?" Lucas asked. "When's the baby due?"

She licked a tear off her upper lip as she let Sydney help her back into the chair. "Another three weeks."

"Congratulations." He resisted looking at his watch. "Do you need a ride into town?"

"My husband's waiting for me at the motel. I'll call him in a minute." She sucked in a shuddering breath and shredded the tissue onto the inch of space that was her lap. "Mom used to make drop cookies for us. Do you remember? She put in M&Ms. Red ones for me, green ones for you because they were your favorite."

He still liked the green ones but he *still* didn't remember her or the lovely personal history she was trying to paint for him.

"Do you remember the swing in the big tree in the backyard?" she asked desperately. "Daddy only put up one and we'd fight for it all summer. Do you remember—"

"I'm sorry," he said quietly. "I really don't."

"Did you have an accident?" She swung around to Sydney. "Did he have a concussion? Some horrible illness?"

Sydney lifted her hands. "I don't think so."

"Mrs. Hamilton," Lucas said as gently as he could. "Let's try this another way. How is it that *you* showed up here after twenty-nine and a half years with this, forgive me, lunatic story?"

She rubbed between her eyebrows, as if she had a headache. "I guess it was easier to just forget the trauma of losing my parents and being separated from my twin. From you. I must have pushed the memories away because they were so painful."

His phone buzzed in his hip pocket. Still looking at her, he took it out. "Hang on a sec, Saul." He lowered the phone again. "All right, Mrs. Hamilton. What made *you* 'remember'?"

"About a week before I found out I was pregnant, I had a vivid dream. At first, I thought it was just my imagination running wild. Then the dreams got longer and more detailed. Then I started to get these flashy things when I was fully awake. I remembered you and our parents. The house and the idyllic life before their death. It was like someone opened the floodgates and I knew the memories were real. Don't get me wrong, my adoptive parents were—are—wonderful, but knowing I had a twin out there became my obsession. Especially knowing I was going to have the baby." She pressed trembling lips together and laid a protective hand over her belly. Sydney rubbed a hand down her back and looked at him. *Fix this* seemed to be written all over her face.

He remembered the damn phone in his hand. "I'm sorry. I have to take this call. It'll just take a moment." He walked across the room. "What's up?" he asked his control.

"Hold on to your hat, buddy," Saul said crisply. "The DNA test came back. PCR doesn't lie. Ran it twice as well as an RFLP. Ninety-nine-point-nine-nine percent match. The highest accuracy percentage possible in DNA testing. The woman is definitely your sibling."

Twenty-three

SEVEN WEEKS LATER

Stealing Life, Sydney's exposé of black-market organ trafficking hit every best-seller *fiction* list in the country. She'd been booked on the talk-show circuit and interviewed continuously since the book's release the week before. A year to the day earlier, she'd been swept up with her disastrous first book. That book had hit some of the same lists, and received the same accolades. Then it had all gone to hell.

She knew this book was solid, but part of her braced for the other shoe to drop. Still, she hadn't taken chances this time. Every word was true. Unfortunately, excluding herself and the people directly involved, no one would know that. The things she'd seen and heard, after all, couldn't possibly be validated. Not for a nonfiction book. Not without bringing in T-FLAC or wizards. But in her fictional account, based on certain facts, anything went. Even without mentioning T-FLAC or wizards and the amazing things she'd seen and done, the book was a candid and compelling account of the illegal harvesting of human organs.

Her publisher had wanted to fast-track the spa book, *Skin Deep,* to coincide with the anniversary of the first fiasco. But when she'd turned in *Stealing Life,* too, they'd switched gears and published the "novel" first. It was a clever marketing ploy, and one that was, so far, paying off.

The spa book came out in three weeks. She had an appointment to have her implants removed two days later. No more fake *anything* for her.

"Miss McBride! Sydney? Over here." As soon as she looked at the photographer a flashbulb went off. She wore a fitted white linen suit with a short skirt, and FM Jimmy Choo sandals. The suit hadn't required a blouse underneath, but with her larger breasts it was a little more low cut than her brothers had thought appropriate.

Sergio had tried to stick a piece of paper in the deep V between the lapels in an attempt to cover her cleavage before she left the restaurant where the family had taken her to lunch before the book signing.

Neanderthal. She felt sorry for any woman who caught *his* interest. She glanced up and caught her brother's eye. Instead of scowling at her as she expected, Sergio gave her a thumbs-up.

Sydney's eyes misted. It was an amazing thing to know that she was loved unconditionally by her family. Her father and most of her brothers and their wives or girlfriends stood nearby. Her family *was* a crowd all by themselves, but the bookstore and her publisher had done an amazing job of publicizing the event. The result was the throngs of people, milling around, reading, talking, laughing, and best of all, buying her book.

Everything was absolutely perfect. *Stealing Life* was a success, her family supported her wholeheartedly, she was vindicated, her reputation was restored. Once again she was a media darling. Life was good.

Mostly.

Lucas hadn't made any attempt to contact her, and Sydney had had her hands full finishing *Skin Deep* and writing *Stealing Life* in record time. There hadn't been a moment to focus on rejection.

Mostly.

She missed Lucas unbearably. Thought about him, longed for him, freaking wanted to know why he hadn't at least *called* her. She kept reminding herself that he wasn't in *sales*. He was a counterterrorist operative whose work would never be done. She got that he was out there saving the damned world. She got it. She didn't get why he couldn't at least have picked up a freaking phone to say hi for thirty seconds.

There was a very good chance he'd *never* call her. It stung her ego a little—okay, a lot—to think that she'd been nothing more than a means to amp up his powers when he needed the boost. To him the sex had been a pleasant bonus.

Bastard.

Damn, the sex had been *more* than good. Spectacular, in fact.

Bastard.

The only souvenirs she'd brought back from Rio were a broken heart and new boobs. She would rather have come back home with an ashtray.

"Sydney?" Molly, the bookstore clerk helping to move the line along, waved a hand in front of her. "Want to take a break?"

She'd been signing for over two hours and the line didn't look as though it were getting any shorter. Sydney shot her a smile, and flexed her fingers as another helper slid an open book in front of her with a slip of paper reading *Mary Ellen* so the book could be personalized. "No, I'm great. Thanks. Hi, Mary Ellen," she said to the young woman standing on the other side of the book-laden table in the center of the store. Sydney signed the book with a flourish. "Hope you enjoy the book."

She rubbed at the prickle on the back of her neck. The kind of sensation one got when someone was staring. Of course someone was staring. There were several hundred people crowded around her. But when the feeling persisted she glanced into the crowd.

Lucas.

The last time she'd seen him, he'd turned back after his phone call, his eyes locked on the very pregnant woman whose DNA proved she was his sister. Sydney had quietly excused herself, not wanting to intrude on what she knew was an emotionally wrenching and private discussion.

That had been forty-nine days ago.

But suddenly, there he was, leaning against a bookshelf filled with her books, arms folded across his broad chest. He wore black from head to toe. He was a little more tan, his green eyes, even from thirty feet away, clear and hot. God, he looked . . . delicious.

The crowd seemed to disappear as their eyes met, and Sydney's heart galloped with such a rush of joy at seeing him she was stunned that she remained in the chair. She wanted to vault over the table, short skirt and heels be damned, push through the crowd and fling herself into his arms.

A book was slipped in front of her and she smiled and signed her name by rote, trying to pick up speed. The sooner she finished, the sooner she could get up and go to him. When she next looked up, Lucas was gone.

Her chest ached with disappointment even though she knew he wouldn't just show up in Miami for ten seconds only to leave without talking to her.

The line was never-ending. She'd be here for *hours.*

"I've waited one thousand, three hundred and twenty-three hours to touch you again. Time's up," Lucas whispered in her ear, his warm breath caressing her skin.

Sydney looked over her shoulder to meet his eyes and saw . . .

Nothing.

She bit back a laugh. Even though she couldn't see him, the touch of his lips against her cheek made her shudder as delicious shivers raced up her spine. She wanted to shut her eyes, tilt her head, and give him better access. She wanted to be lying on a bed with a sail on it, floating on the ocean. She wanted to float among the cool clouds as he made her hot.

Another book was placed in front of her. She scribbled something that vaguely resembled her name, smiled, and said the right things.

Lucas's mouth moved in a slow caress down her neck. "You look good enough to eat. Too bad I can only taste you here in public. And here. And here."

Her heart did a triple somersault as she smiled, greeted, and signed for the woman who clutched the book to her chest like the Holy Grail.

"I love that you're such a success," Lucas said directly into her ear. "And don't want to take a second of this away from you. I'll wait it out until the last person leaves—"

"Or?" Sydney whispered under her breath, smiling at two older woman who were bubbling about the book, which they'd already read and loved—even the creepy parts, then driven two hours just to see her and get her autograph.

"Or," he began, his deep voice a seductive purr. "I can use Empathic Perception and make everyone remember having a damn good time, ensure every book is signed, that they all have a special personal memory, and drag you out of here. Your call."

Sydney covered her mouth as if to cover a cough. "Can you?"

A purring sound of agreement vibrated in her ear, like

a big cat expressing pleasure. "My power issue is good to go. Your call."

No contest. Sydney placed her hand over his on her shoulder and squeezed. "EP," she said under her breath. *"Now."*

A blur of white, and the sound of rushing wind indicated he hadn't wasted a nanosecond in whisking her away.

Sydney was laughing with pure, unadulterated joy as they materialized in her apartment. In the bedroom.

"God," he said with evident relief. "I thought I'd never get you alone."

"I'm here now. We're here now."

"You look . . ." He rested his forehead against hers as he gathered her close, his arms tight around her. "Jesus, Sydney. You're so beautiful, you take my breath away."

Circling his neck with both arms she stood on tiptoe and lifted her mouth to his. "I missed you. More than I thought possible. Wait—" she said as he slipped his hands inside the back of her jacket and stroked her bare skin. "What happened with Sarah-Christy?"

"I still don't remember her. But we're keeping in touch. Trying to piece together what happened. We're both being careful. This whole twin thing is a shocker to us both. She had her baby, by the way. I saw the little guy. I'm an uncle, I guess. That takes some getting used to, as well."

"You'll work it out. Family is good. I don't know what I'd do without all my brothers. You can skip all the baggage that comes with a shared history. Start fresh and just enjoy your relationship as adults." She ran her hands down over his chest.

"Working on it."

"Is everything resolved at *Novos Começos*?"

"To all appearances nothing has changed. The medical building is now just two floors." His lips quirked.

"And the building behind it has been replaced with a volleyball court. The storage tanks that were taken in for analysis showed what we thought they would. A rather gory cocktail of sulfuric acid and the dissolved remains of the donors."

"Ew. Sorry I asked."

"I can fix that."

Lucas peeled off the low-cut, fitted white linen suit jacket she'd spent so much time choosing. He didn't use magic, he used his hands, and his mouth and his heated gaze as he removed each item of clothing, very, very—*maddeningly*—slowly. One. At. A. Time.

The jacket fell to the floor behind her. His deep green eyes were dark with emotion as he took her in, wearing nothing but a demi bra and mile-high sandals. "You decided to keep them, I see."

She shrugged and watched his eyes follow the movement in her breasts. "Not for long. Will you mind if my breasts are smaller?"

"As long as they're your breasts I'll love them no matter what size they are." He bent to drag his lips across the valley of cleavage before brushing his fingers across the swell of her breasts before dispatching the coffee-colored satin bra.

He used magic to sweep the bed clear of the pile of clothing she'd tried on and discarded before setting out for the signing earlier, leaving just the silky cool, red, 1,500-thread-count cotton sheet.

Lucas laid her gently on the bed, following her down to lie beside her. He'd gotten rid of his clothing a whole hell of a lot faster than he'd done with hers. The wonderful shock of feeling his bare skin against hers made Sydney catch her breath. Again.

"Before we—" She pulled away from him and sucked in a calming breath, too filled with emotion to let the moment pass. "Okay . . . Hang on a second." Another breath. "Let me just say this and get it out of the way. Lucas. I love you. I think I fell in love with you that first night while I watched over you as you slept."

His eyes darkened and he clenched his jaw, then opened his mouth to speak. She touched two fingers to his mouth. "You don't have to—"

"No. This is an excellent time to clear the air. Tell it like it is. Yeah. A great time." He leaned over her, cupping her face in one, cool, broad palm, his face inches from hers, his eyes deep and intense. "Before I met you I was just going through the motions. Living day to day. No," he said, stroking her cheek with his thumb. "Not living. *Surviving*. My whole world changed when I met you. You opened my mind and my heart. Because of you, I have life, a real life. And somehow, some amazing how, *love*."

He kissed her slow and deep, as if doing so was the only thing keeping him alive. Sydney knew exactly how he felt at that moment. She felt the same way, euphoric and crazily, insanely in love.

He lifted his head. "I love you, Sydney. More than I could ever have conceived of loving anyone. I intend to spend the rest of my *life* loving you. Growing old with you, learning from you. Of all my gifts and powers, of all the magic, you're the greatest gift. The most magical part of my life. I'll never forget that, I swear to you."

"You're going to make me cry. I don't want to cry right now." She blinked back tears and touched his cheek. "God—How come I'm the writer and you're so eloquent? I feel—" *Loved. Cherished. His*. "All that and more."

He smiled. "I'll protect you with my life and my heart."

As she would protect him with hers. "You're my future," Sydney whispered, her voice thick with emotion.

"You're my purpose for being. I can't wait to live every minute of that future with you."

"It won't always be easy." His eyes flickered with emotion. "You've already seen the kind of danger being around me can put you in. That's not going to go away. I'm—"

"Magic."

Looking for more hot romantic suspense?

Turn the page to catch a sneak peek at the next thrilling book in the Night series

Night Shadow

One

MOSCOW
55 45 08 37 36 56   02 10 08
1800 HOURS

Blinking snowflakes off her lashes, T-FLAC operative Alexis Stone shot a quick glance down at the toes of her brand new, size eight combat boots as she teetered on the edge of the snow-encrusted roof. The excruciating headache which had plagued her for the last several minutes intensified. A headache was going to be the least of her damned problems if she didn't *move.*

Jump. Get it over with. Quick and painless.

What the . . . ?

Jump across, she told herself. Not down. *Across. Between* the buildings. A relatively easy jump, yet she hesitated. Terminal velocity wouldn't be in effect in such a short drop. She'd only fall about a hundred and fifty feet, not the four hundred necessary to pick up the hundred and thirty five miles an hour to achieve terminal speed.

What was she *thinking*? Mouth dry, heart pounding, Lexi shook her head to clear it.

Mathematically, a falling object—*her*—increased its velocity by thirty-two feet per second as it fell. Acceleration to gravity—

Over. Not down.

She'd be on the ground in less than two seconds—

Over. Not down.

Jump. Do it now.

Hallucinations?

Crap. She blinked white out of her eyes, her breath coming hot and fast. The training simulations hadn't aptly portrayed what it felt like to be out in the field under hostile conditions. Not the cold, not the pressure, not the frantic tattoo of her heart. Not the irrational thoughts clouding her mind. One word summed up the experience.

Terrifying.

Focus. Fortunately, she was a pragmatic woman. Flights of fancy weren't in her DNA. Or hadn't been before tonight. She'd trained with the best of the best. Now she just had to put it into action. She could do this.

Do not *imagine being shot in the back.*

Do not *picture falling.*

Do not look down.

Her mouth was too dry to even attempt swallowing. She started counting, silently, to slow the rushing thud of her pulse which made it hard to hear and caused the headache to worsen.

Her gaze climbed upward incrementally until she focused on the hotel across the alley. Only eight feet separated the two buildings.

Fifteen stories to the snowy ground below.

She'd never been afraid of heights before. Lights popped on in some of the dark windows as dusk fell like an unwelcome blanket over Moscow.

They'd followed her. She knew they had. *Jump!* her brain screamed.

Despite the bone-chilling cold, sweat beaded her face. Her entire body was damp and clammy beneath her black civilian clothing. The familiar weight of the Glock, all seven ounces of firepower, felt as heavy as a boulder in her numb fingers.

Running footsteps, crossing the roof behind her, sounded like a freaking herd of crazed wildebeests charging. Her galloping heart jumped into her throat. Too late. Her hesitation was going to cost her as the bad guys thundered across the rooftop in her wake. She glanced down at the shadowy drop just beyond the tips of her boots, then back at the dark footprints just behind her. Easy to follow her trail when her steps were clear in the couple of inches of snow blanketing the rooftop.

She'd had a five minute, eleven second head start. They'd caught up. The men following her had scaled that blasted metal fire escape in record time. And probably without being terrified the thing would pull away from the crumbling brick wall as they scrabbled for purchase.

The high pitched whine-*piiiing* and yellow sparks of a bullet ricocheting off metal just a few feet away made her flinch. Close. Too close. *Do it, Lexi. Just freaking jump.*

No. Return fire. *Then* jump.

Cautiously, but as fast as she could manage, she walked backward in her own footprints. As soon as she felt the heated metal of a four-foot wide exhaust flue against her back, she spun and dropped into a crouch behind the only cover for a hundred feet of flat white rooftop.

A dozen indistinguishable exhaust fans dotted the roof, belching unsynchronized clouds of foul-smelling steam. The steam and stink collided with the rapidly falling snow making visibility nearly impossible in the pseudo fog the mix created. If she couldn't see them, they couldn't see her. She hoped.

Crouching to below their eye level, Lexi squeezed off a half dozen textbook perfect shots. Night was falling as fast as the snow now, and the spare illumination was a thick, barely transparent charcoal. She knew exactly how to get to where she needed to be. Like a lodestone, she had id'ed the black shutters against the whitewashed walls of the safe house seven buildings southeast.

Five of the men had chased her all the way from Belorussky Railway Station on Tverskaya Zastava Ploshchad, through the alleys and up onto this rooftop half a dozen blocks away.

Piiingpiingpiing. They weren't messing around. Sparks shot out like fireworks as a hail of bullets struck metal. The men were firing blind. A waste of ammunition, but pretty much a guarantee that one of the stray bullets would hit their target. Her.

Six. There'd been *six* of them, she corrected, seeing them come out of nowhere in her mind's eye. A mathematical mistake could very well bite her in the ass. One guy was way ahead of the pack, moving fast and low, closing the gap between them.

Shifting her trigger finger off the frame of the Glock, Lexi squeezed off a shot. The impact of the bullet hitting him square in the chest knocked the guy off his feet. With a brief look of annoyance he went down soundlessly.

Went down . . . and dissipated into nothingness before his body hit the ground.

Ducking out of sight, back flat against the warmth of the pipe, Lexi sucked in a startled breath. *Shit. My first kill shot. A wizard?* Her heart beat hard enough to block out the sound of running footsteps. She felt the vibration through the soles of her boots and took a chance, angling her head so she could see them coming. And there they were. Thirty yards and closing.

Five men, dressed in black, their shadowy forms barely visible through the diaphanous curtain of rapidly falling snow and belching vapor.

Narrow eyed, she watched a second guy break from

the pack, coming at her flat out, long legs closing the gap between them. Weapon raised, he stopped, head shifting as he searched the rooftop for her.

Two other men joined him, snow veiling them where they stood, warm breath thick in the air around their heads.

"Did she jump across?" the middle guy asked the other two in his native Russian, glaring down at the gap between the buildings. Lexi followed their gazes. Her footprints teetered right on the edge. Visibility was iffy, and unless they looked closely, they wouldn't notice the faint blurring of her double steps. She hoped.

She held her breath as two more men caught up, the murmur of the voices blending. One man indicated they separate, and they spread out on the roof.

Her pulse shot into overdrive, and her mouth went dry as a metronome ticked off the seconds in her head.

They'd find her in moments. And there was no wondering what they'd do to her if they got their hands on her. She freaking knew. She'd seen too much. And she was as good as dead unless she could make that jump.

As much as Lexi wanted to plot things out to the last variable, as much as she wanted to calculate the exact trajectory necessary to leap the gap and how she should fall on the other side, she literally took a running leap of faith.

The flat-out run, followed by an ungraceful jump had her body suspended over nothing but air for what felt like an eternity. Rapid fire, followed by shouts, accompanied her leap across the abyss. Too pumped up on terror and adrenalin to feel any pain, she landed hard on the other, slightly lower, roof, and stumbled into a low run.

Go. Go. Go.

Her breath led the way as she found the extra speed necessary to leap between the next two buildings, a jump of at least twelve feet this time. Her foot skidded out from under her as she landed in wet snow on the other side. Sheer willpower pulled her upright and she kept running.

Go. Go. Go.

Chunks of cement exploded inches from her feet, sending bits of it stinging into her skin through her pants. She spun, returning fire. She knew she wasn't going to hit anyone; her aim was too wild, and she couldn't see a damn thing now that it was fully dark. Numb with cold, the snow was a soft menace as it landed soundlessly on any exposed skin. A stark black and white movie with her frantic heartbeats and sawing breath as theme music.

The whine and the hot slice of a bullet as it cut through her coat and into her shoulder made her curse under her breath. It would probably hurt like hell later. Well, no *probably* about it, but right now she didn't feel a thing. Lexi ducked behind the dubious protection of a small cement maintenance shed in the middle of the rooftop. Hat down, collar up, just her eyes visible, she scanned the area. The cold, and the vicious vice of the headache, made her eyes water and burn, forcing her to waste precious seconds blinking things back into focus.

There they were. Running, spreading out, determined to catch her. Catch her, hell. *Kill her.*

No CGI generated bad guys. No drill. This was as real as it got.

Reaching into her tac belt, she grabbed a new magazine and wiped the sweat out of her left eye onto the shoulder of her jacket. *Let the training take over.* Deep breath in. Rapid reload. Pop the empty clip, slam in a new one. Thumb the slide-stop so the slide jacks forward and fire again. And again. Chest high, level and steady. Wrist firm, firing hand pressed securely against her opposing palm. Double-tapping in controlled bursts, tiny lateral movements to avoid creating gaps in the kill-zone.

Visualize the target; see the slap of the bullet.

She squeezed the trigger. A scream indicated she'd managed to hit one, even in the dark.

She heard the thud of his body with grim satisfaction. That one wasn't a wizard. Or if he was, he was a dead wizard.

Her weapons instructor would be proud.

Two down. Four to go. And six more buildings to navigate before reaching the safe house.

She couldn't lead these yahoos there. Four more kills, or a wild goose chase across the rooftops of Moscow. In the dark. God, what a choice.

Lexi tried to come up with a plan. Heart manic, sweat stinging her eyes, she leaned against the six foot square cement housing for God only knew what.

Think.

Easier said than done when an anvil pounded behind her eyeballs, and every instinct told her to run like hell. Odds were she'd be shot within the next few minutes.

Take a deep breath. Center yourself. Think.

Somehow she had to circle around behind them.

Somehow.

Couldn't see them, but Lexi heard their voices. Whispered Russian, carried away on the light breeze, impossible to hear well enough to interpret. She prayed they'd conclude she'd managed to evade them.

For a moment a stray bit of light reflected off the snowy ground and she saw them. They'd gathered in a tight little group at the edge of the roof, a knot of dense darkness barely visible against the even bigger blackness of the night. Big mistake, boys.

Four shots. Rapid. No hesitation.

They wouldn't expect her to return the way she'd come—straight at them.

Pulling the extra fabric of her turtleneck over her mouth and nose, Lexi welcomed the few seconds of warmth. Good time for a tac-reload. Quietly, she slid the clip out of the mag well and replaced it with a fresh one, stowed the partly spent one in her belt. Then, blocking out the cold, dropped to the ground. A shallow, twelve-inch-high wall ran around the perimeter of the flat roof. On her belly, using her feet and elbows to move her forward, she crawled up against the wall, the fully loaded Glock in her right hand.

One chance to do this.

One.

She could hear them more clearly the closer she got. Confused. Undirected. They weren't sure what to do next. *Good.*

Sucking in a breath, she squeezed off a shot. Another, and another. Three down. One to go.

The remaining guy fired back, yelling in Russian as he tried to pinpoint her location from her muzzle flashes. But she'd already moved. She was practically under his feet as he fired blindly into the darkness.

Rolling to her back, Lexi aimed for the underside of his chin. She let out half a breath. The big oaf looked down just as she squeezed the trigger.

In that instant, some of those training details that seemed so hard to memorize came back effortlessly. Nine millimeter, 124-grain, plus-P rounds. For a Glock 19, that translated into a muzzle velocity in excess of thirteen hundred feet per second—

Her bullet punched into his gaping mouth and blew the back of his head off. His body instantly turned to a fine black powder.

Shuddering, she didn't pause to congratulate herself on her marksmanship or her mastery of weapon-specs. There wasn't time. All the gunplay and shouting would draw the curious, or stupid, sooner or later. Lexi hauled ass and ran as if the hounds of hell were on her heels.

Stretched out on the narrow sway-backed bed, hands stacked beneath his head, Alexander Stone dozed lightly. Since the room was on the twelfth floor, he opened one eye when he heard pounding footsteps on the rooftop just above the window.

Interesting.

Curling his fingers around the butt of the Sig Sauer lying on the mattress beside his hip, he lay still, just another shadow in the room. Seconds later, the window slammed back against the wall. A slight figure, dressed from head to toe in black, catapulted feet first through the opening as if jet propelled.

He could barely make out her slender form in the darkness. Hands on her knees, head down, Lexi struggled to catch a wheezing breath. "Shit. Shit. Shit."

Alex sat up, swinging his feet to the floor. "How was the play, Mrs. Lincoln?"

At the sound of his voice, coming as it did out of the darkness, she let out a startled yelp as she straightened. But damn if she didn't come up weapon raised.

"Turn on the light." Still out of breath, but her voice was strong.

"Hell, Lexi. I could've shot you ten times by now. Shoot first, ask questions later," Alex leaned over and switched on the light beside the bed. He immediately noticed the dark red wetness on her right shoulder. "But it looks like someone already beat me to it." Jesus. What the hell was Lexi Stone doing in Moscow? Bleeding? When the inn keep had assured him his room was ready, Alex had had a moment of confusion. *He* hadn't already checked in . . . Alex Stone. *Alexis* Stone. No relation. Not even third cousins five times removed—he'd checked.

Might be confusing for the accounting department, but he'd never expected to see her anywhere but HQ in Montana. Didn't make a damn bit of sense seeing her here.

She belonged at her desk in the research department. She was completely out of context in a shit-hole of a safe house in Russia.

Dove-soft gray eyes blinked at him, her expression a mixture of confusion and irritation. "What are you doing here?"

"Here in Moscow or here in our room?" He'd forgotten how tall she was. He was used to seeing her hunched over her computer at her desk at HQ.

"It isn't *our* room. It's *my* room. My op."

Her . . . *op*? "Do you own Moscow as well, or is that up for grabs?"

Annoyed, she pulled a black knit cap off her head and stuffed it into the pocket of her coat. Well, hell. Her hair used to be a very pretty, glossy light brown. And long. She used to wear it some sleek, complicated braid thing on the back of her head. She'd cut about a mile and a half off. Now it was chin length, fashionably choppy and a sunny blonde. "Cut your hair yourself?"

She raised a hand to her shorn, chin length bob. Narrowed eyed, she didn't bother answering the obvious. "You're supposed to be in Paris." She touched the bridge of her nose.

Damn it to hell. She used to wear *glasses* as well.

"True." He pushed back on the edge of the bed to lean against the wall, dangling his hand off his bent knee. "You wearing LockOut under that jacket?" Hip length black Thinsulate coat, black jeans, soaked to the hem of the coat, and the smallest damned combat boots he'd ever seen, carrying a Glock, and packing an attitude a mile wide.

With a fucking bullet crease in her shoulder.

Color crept into her already chill-bright cheeks. "I just went to—"

"Get shot?" he said dryly. "We'd better take care of that." He shoved himself off the bed in one lithe move, tucking his Sig in the waistband at the back of his pants. She backed up. "Did you manage to hit anyone?" Yeah. She was taller than he remembered. Her sunny hair would brush his lips if he were to hold her. Which of course he had no intention of doing. His gaze dropped to her lips. Mistake. She had the kind of soft mouth that would distract most men.

Didn't distract him. Alex concentrated on eye contact.

Up went the chin. "I was trained by Darius, what do you think?"

The best of the best. No need to ask further. "Were you followed?"

She shot a nervous glance over her shoulder at the open window and the night sky beyond. "I don't believe so."

Shit. Damn. And fucking hell. "You'd better be sure."

"I—" She wanted to tell him to go to hell, Alex could see it in the mutinous line of her lips. "I'm not sure," she admitted somewhat belligerently. Lexi. Honest to a fault.

He gave a lugubrious sigh and slid the Sig out of his waistband, not sure who else was coming through that window. "Get that coat off and go into the bathroom. Take a shower. I'll be right back."

"I'll go with you."

If he was any judge of woman, and he was, the lady was about to puke or pass out. Possibly both. "How will I explain your bloodless body to your supervisor in the—What department is it again? Accounting?" She was the girl with the glasses and great legs in the research department.

A cool look from hot gray eyes. “I’m an operative now.”

Alex cocked a brow. Recruitment had to be at an all time low if they’d made her an operative. “Strip and get in the shower. Let’s see what garbage you’ve left for me to clean up.”

“I killed five men tonight.” She sounded half proud, half repulsed.

Yeah. She was an operative all right. Not.

“Did you, now?” He shrugged into his coat, pulling the collar around his throat. The wind chill inside the damned room was below freezing. Reaching into a pocket he pulled out a cap made from LockOut, put it on and pulled the stretchy black fabric all the way down to his eyebrows. It would keep the cold out—and everything else.

“You don’t believe me?”

Fuck. Now she was getting pissy about it. Course with a first kill that was expected. The shock had to wear off, and then you either crashed or pushed through it and became a real operative. “Every word. I guess you could stand right there waiting for me to get back,” he prodded when she didn’t move. “But Muravyou is going to be pissed about all that blood dripped on his fancy carpet.”

Rurik Muravyou was the corpulent, tobacco-chewing manager of the T-FLAC safe house in Moscow. He would no sooner trust the creaky elevator up to the twelfth floor, to see a *carpet,* than he’d ever be fit enough to be an operative again. He was eighty pounds, fifteen years, and apathetically past it.

“Thank you for pointing out that I’m bleeding. Don’t you have someone to shoot?”

“Yeah, good thinking.” He motioned for her to raise her arm, which would slow the flow of blood, then swung himself up onto the shoulder high windowsill feet first. "Direction?"

"Northwest."

"Lock the window, close the drapes. Clean up. I'll be back to tuck you in and tell you a bedtime story."

Her lips tightened. "I can hardly wait."

Alex's lips twitched and he gripped the Sig tighter to focus his thoughts away from her soft, sassy mouth. "I promise, it'll be worth waiting for."